THE
PRICE
OF
EVERYTHING

THE PRICE OF EVERYTHING

JON McGORAN

SOLARIS

First published 2025 by Solaris
an imprint of Rebellion Publishing Ltd,
Riverside House, Osney Mead,
Oxford, OX2 0ES, UK

www.solarisbooks.com

ISBN: 978-1-83786-235-1

10 9 8 7 6 5 4 3 2 1

A CIP catalogue record for this book is available from the
British Library.

Designed & typeset by Rebellion Publishing

Printed in Denmark

To Kismet

Chapter One

THE FIRST SIGN of trouble was a rectangle of gray slush that appeared around Pierce's attaché outside the airport in Utqiaġvik, Alaska. He was already in a bad mood. Even non-stop on a newish ultrasonic, the flight from New York had taken over two hours. And the walk from his arrival gate to the pickup area had been like an old-fashioned mosh pit.

The BetterLates were out in force, chanting and singing like they always did, but now apparently burning incense as well, as if they weren't annoying enough. Or maybe that had always been part of their schtick in Alaska.

As extreme weather and rising sea levels had become an everyday reality, so had the BetterLates. They'd been active around the world for decades, apparently, but Pierce had never heard of them until a few years ago, when they'd changed their focus from stopping climate change to reversing it. Now they advocated ambitious geoengineering schemes: deflecting the sun's heat away from Earth with giant space mirrors, or seeding clouds around the world to make them more reflective, or fertilizing the oceans so they would absorb more carbon.

Pierce agreed with the BetterLates' cause—essentially, "Let's not kill the planet"—but he suspected they'd get more done if they didn't try so hard to irritate people. Sure enough, as Pierce was trying to squeeze past, a pair of oil workers started harassing them, but that probably had more to do with the BetterLates' stance on fossil fuels than the chanting or the incense.

Security was there in seconds, blocking off the entire terminal as they beat the hell out of the oil workers *and* the BetterLates and hauled them all away.

The commotion had made Pierce late, and he hated that. But as late as he was, his ride was later, and he hated that even more. The car was supposed to be waiting for him. That was in the contract.

His attaché case had been sitting on the ground no longer than a few minutes when Pierce spotted his ride—a massive, armored Bentley limo, clean and shiny and towering over the salt- or ice-encrusted cars jockeying around it.

Pierce smiled and shook his head. A Bentley. Somebody wanted desperately to be noticed in the crowd.

In the decades since the northern shipping lanes had thawed, Utqiaġvik had become a bustling hub of commerce and banking. It used to be called Barrow, and decades later some of the old timers still called it that. Pierce had been here half a dozen times since joining the Couriers Guild, and he'd heard those same old-timers talk about how frigid it used to be up here, how the cold today didn't compare. Still seemed cold as fuck to Pierce.

He let out a sigh that hung in the air for a moment, as if in stunned disbelief at the cold, before sailing away, intact, on the frosty breeze.

Pierce was mostly protected from the weather by his black Thintech jacket and gloves. Smart fabric was a necessity for couriers: you couldn't just take off your jacket when you had an attaché chained to a titanium alloy cuff embedded in your wrist. You needed something that could automatically adapt to any climate, and Thintech did that without fail. But it couldn't protect his ears or his face or his lungs, and while titanium wasn't supposed to conduct heat, he could feel a deeper cold slowly seeping through the cuff into the bones of his wrist, and working its way up his arm.

When he had first stepped outside the airport, the bracing chill had been a welcome change from the canned atmosphere of the long flight from New York. But that novelty had worn off in seconds.

Pierce had rested the attaché on the snow-covered ground in order to stretch his back, which had tightened up on the plane and was tightening further in the cold. He was glad his chain was long enough to let him do it. The younger couriers insisted on chains so short they couldn't rest their cases on the ground without kneeling or crouching next to them. It was a point of pride for them, a statement about their commitment to the job.

Pierce didn't need to make a statement. The surgically embedded cuff was statement enough, along with the oath he had sworn to the Guild, which stated explicitly that if he failed to protect and deliver his assignment, he would forfeit his life—and his hand, which would be given to the client as a trophy.

But while Pierce didn't need to make a statement, what he did need, more and more as he advanced through his thirties, was to be able to put his attaché down on the ground sometimes so he could stretch out his back.

He had been a courier for more than ten years now, since before there even was a Guild. He had joined in the wake of the Cyber Wars and the Upheaval, when his GI benefits had been discontinued amid all the turmoil. The *war* part of the Cyber Wars had been brief but devastating; the *cyber* part still wasn't over.

China, Russia, North Korea, they had thrown out all sorts of malware—crazy attack worms and e-bombs, self-replicating-this and Trojan-that, and all manner of AI cyber weapons. The US had too, but it was outmatched. And, as always, criminal hackers were out there too, taking advantage of all the confusion and repurposing all the new cyber tools the governments were tossing around.

The big corporations were getting hit hard, and they finally said *enough is enough*. They formed United Conglomerates—UniCon—as a sort of nongovernmental version of the United Nations. The governments of the world, rendered weak and corrupt and incompetent by the corporate interests that controlled them, failed to protect the global order. So those same corporate interests announced they would do so directly instead. As an added benefit, they would take on climate change as well.

It worked, briefly. Not the climate change stuff—that was bullshit from the get-go—but they made progress on the rest of it. North Korea collapsed first, to a momentary global sigh of relief. But then China's economy cratered, too, and took the rest of the world with it.

Things were different after that. All the malware out there couldn't just be turned off. Some of it even seemed to be evolving on its own.

Trillions of dollars in digital assets and old-fashioned

electronic banking records vanished overnight. Cryptocurrencies were unevenly affected, at first: some collapsed immediately as new generations of active AI tore through encryption like wet tissue paper, but others withstood the attacks, and even gained a competitive advantage out of it, for a little while. But without secure internet, enough of them crashed that people lost faith in the whole idea, the prices plummeted, and they became worthless. Since so much of the crypto-economy had relied on smart phone systems, those networks were attacked as well.

Out-of-control ransomware operations bricked computers in the healthcare, transportation, and energy sectors.

The internet became a wasteland, and digital communication was recognized as hopelessly insecure. The whole idea of electronic commerce of any sort suddenly seemed laughably naïve.

Ever since the first internet collapsed, UniCon had been working to create a new one—a secure, dependable, easy-to-use quantum electronic infrastructure they called U-Net. If they ever finished it, the courier work might dry up, but they'd been saying 'any day now' for a decade, and it hadn't happened yet.

Banks were still a thing, and checks. But they had lost people's trust. Cash was king, and now that the ones-and-zeroes were worthless, the feds started printing up more and more Large: hundreds, five hundreds, and even bigger denominations with four, five, even six zeroes, all of it printed on new super-high-tech, counterfeit-proof plastic paper. The US dollar had long been the standard across the globe; suddenly, it was practically the only game in every town. People complained about the feel of it, the sound. Some called it 'crinkle.' But they got used to it. They learned to love it.

Before anyone knew what happened, the world was a cash economy—cash that needed to get from A to B. Drones handled a lot of it, but you can only trust a drone with so much, especially since, without reliable digital communication, you had to rely on AI to control them.

People turned to couriers. But trusting a complete stranger with a briefcase filled with a billion dollars in $500,000 bills was tricky too. People needed assurances. That's when the Guild was formed, with its titanium cuffs, its strict rules—brutally enforced—and its absolute independence from UniCon, which was taking over pretty much everything else.

Ironically, people didn't think much of the Guild until the first member was caught trying to steal a payload. His left hand ended up taxidermized in the den of some gangster CEO. The rest of him was never found.

There'd been a big lawsuit at the time, about who got to decide what happened to the offending hand after it had been lopped off. The courts interpreted the Guild contract as saying the offended party got to keep the hand.

Pierce had already signed on at that point, and that freaked him out a bit, but he still felt lucky. The pay was pretty good, and demand was steady.

Jobs were still hard to come by, even ten years later, but back then, there was practically nothing, especially for someone like Pierce, who didn't have much in the way of connections. His once-prominent dad was already in the Otisville Correctional Facility by then, serving seventy years for thirty-seven counts of securities fraud. And while his mom was still alive, she was busy doing menial jobs and going to night school for social work. Neither of them was in a position to be of help. Couriering was one of the only jobs available—at least, one of the only jobs that required Pierce's skills, other than mercenary or muscle.

There were a few more attempted thefts in those early days, unsavory types who saw joining the Guild as a way to gain access to vast amounts of cash. They were all caught. They all lost their hands—taken by the recipient or by fellow couriers assigned to police their own—and they all lost their lives.

That had stopped any other couriers stealing their packages, and the couriers themselves stopped anyone else from trying it. Pierce had a small arsenal of weapons strapped to his body, and enough years of training that those weapons would be superfluous in all but the most extreme situations. The chain itself was a weapon, too. Opponents tended to focus on his free hand, but his chain was just long enough to wrap around a throat or an extremity, or to whip across a face.

So, yeah, he could trust himself to put his attaché on the pavement for a minute now and again. He had earned at least that much. And nothing had ever come of it. Nothing came of it this time either, other than the gray slush slowly spreading around the case.

He didn't think much of the slush, as the limo slowed to a stop with a crunchy growl of tires over salt and ice, his focus instantly elsewhere. Getting into a car with a full case was always potentially dicey.

The driver stayed in the car, staring at him through dark shades. A heavyset Inuit climbed out of the passenger side and kept the car between him and Pierce, probably fingering a weapon just out of sight. He seemed vaguely nervous, which was not unreasonable.

The rear driver's side door opened and a massive, mohawked blond unfolded himself to at least six foot six. The tip of his nose was missing, and half of one ear. Up there it was just as likely frostbite from passing out drunk walking home from a bar as from action of any kind.

"You the courier?" Mohawk asked.

Pierce held up his attaché.

"You don't dress like a courier," Mohawk said as he scanned Pierce's retinas and the microcode on his wrist cuff.

Pierce didn't reply, since it wasn't a question. There was no uniform for Guild couriers. Mohawk was referring to the round mirrored shades and ridiculous collarless sport coats that some of the couriers had started wearing, a fashion trend started by an asshole named Erno Damiani. Erno had been a courier as long as Pierce, but where Pierce had grown more cynical over the years, Damiani'd become a bit of a zealot. A lot of the younger couriers saw him as some kind of role model, a leader. Pierce saw him as more of a nut job.

Pierce scanned Mohawk's iris with the scanner embedded on the side of the attaché. The readout confirmed his identity—Henrik Schmidt.

That eliminated part of the risk, but just because these guys were who they were supposed to be, didn't mean they intended to do what they were supposed to do. Even the most loyal henchmen could be tempted when the stakes were high enough, and anytime someone sprung for a courier instead of a cash drone, the stakes were high enough. And while Utqiaġvik was now a global financial center, it had a reputation for violence that went back long before the sea ice had melted and the towers had sprung up.

Pierce got into the back of the car, hyperaware of everything around him. He enjoyed the mental exercise of calculating how he would take out the three men in the car with him if things went south. It was like a game, a thought puzzle, running through the potential scenarios in his mind, running through the steps—a dozen variations of: disable, disable, kill, kill, kill, roll into the front seat and stop the car. He had a folding knife in his jacket, another knife in his boot, three throwing spikes in his collar, and a Glock in his shoulder holster. But in such close quarters it was all about his hands. As his brain and his nerves went through the motions, his muscles remained absolutely still.

Schmidt lacked the appropriate deference that a slug like him should give a Guild courier. Pierce wasn't particularly bothered by that. Some couriers—mostly the ones with the shades and the collarless jackets—had a constant *Do you know who I am?* attitude. Not Pierce. He took note of it only as another piece of information to add to his assessment of the situation. Maybe the guy was planning on making a move, or maybe he had been in Utqiaġvik too long. Most likely, he was just an asshole.

Five minutes into the ten-minute drive to Kransky's tower, where Pierce would transfer the contents of the attaché to Kransky himself, his attention was drawn to a dull, soothing warmth coming from the attaché between his legs. He reached down slowly to touch it, drawing a sideways glance from Schmidt, sitting next to him. Sure enough, the thing was warm, even after having sat out in the cold. When he had opened the attaché in the security line to get on the plane, it hadn't felt warm at all. It had probably been resting in front of a heater vent in the airplane. The chain was still icy cold, as he'd expect it to be.

The sound of the wheels got suddenly quieter as they left the rougher roads of the outskirts and entered Utqiaġvik. It was called The City of Ice, and the name fit. The climate might have changed enough to make the seas navigable, but the land was still plenty icy.

Like virtually every other city in the world, the center of Utqiaġvik was a shock of glass-and-chrome towers. But here, they reared above streets given over to the ice and snow. This city didn't even try to keep the elements at bay; they just made sure the entrances to all the buildings opened inward and were a minimum of twenty feet tall. A thick white crust coated everything on the street. Between that and the low sun, the towers looked like pillars of ice, thrust up by some sort of glacial cataclysm.

Two blocks into the tower district, Pierce spotted Kransky Tower. Short and squat compared to the other buildings, like the man himself. But the tower gleamed like a diamond, and there was nothing shiny about Kransky. A Russian gangster-turned-supply-chain magnate, he still kept a hand in trafficking girls and drugs, even after he had bought controlling interests in several shipping concerns, a pharma company, and enough other businesses to secure a seat in UniCon.

Since the Upheaval, the line between legit and not had grown blurrier and blurrier. Organized crime had always been all about cash, so the criminal syndicates had been well-positioned to take advantage of the new economy, buying up legitimate businesses at fire-sale prices, and overnight becoming 'legitimate' themselves in the process. Some, like Kransky, got big enough to gain entry into UniCon.

As the economists liked to say, the blending of global conglomerates and criminal syndicates created 'synergies.'

The old money investors and CEOs weren't crazy about it, but there wasn't much they could do. They had created a system where advantage could be taken; it had simply never crossed their minds that one day they'd be the ones taken advantage of.

Pierce tried not to judge, or at least not much. Not judging was kind of a requirement of his job. And it was just as well, because his judgment of someone like Kransky would have been harsh.

The limousine circled around to the back of the building and turned under a massive overhang, lurching down a rough slope of ice that descended to street level, then bouncing onto the curved concrete ramp that led to the parking garage below. Three stories underground, they came to a stop so abrupt the limo was left wobbling on its chassis.

The driver still had on his shades, but he seemed to be eyeing Pierce in the rearview, as if checking to see if he was rattled.

There was a delicate and sometimes awkward balance of power between a courier and the muscle that a recipient sent as an escort. Almost invariably, whatever was in the attaché—and by extension whoever was couriering it—was more valuable than whoever had been sent to escort them.

When they got out of the car, Schmidt bumped against him. It wasn't a shove, but it was definitely contact. Pierce decided to let it go, but he raised his expectation of violence by an order of magnitude.

He was here to deliver his attaché to the recipient, Kransky himself, and that's what he was going to do. Anyone who interfered with him would regret it.

The four of them got onto a small elevator. The Inuit

looked wide-eyed into the retina scan and said, "Thirty-seven." The screen flashed the name DANIEL SILUK, and the elevator began to rise.

Pierce stood with his back to the corner, rerunning his calculations. Siluk and the driver exchanged a furtive glance.

The elevator stopped on the thirty-seventh floor, letting them out onto a gloomy hallway with dim lights, gray carpet, and dull green walls. It was darker than the parking garage had been and seemed somehow designed to mimic the effects of snow-blindness.

Schmidt walked down the hallway first. Siluk and the driver—still wearing his shades—flanked Pierce as they followed. The place seemed empty, but as they passed an expanse of cubicles on their right, a few faces peered around partitions to catch a glimpse of them.

Pierce felt increasingly uneasy as Schmidt led them into a large, windowless conference room. The walls were scuffed. One of the chairs had a broken arm.

Kransky sat at the head of the table. His face was red. Strands of hair had come loose from his ponytail, some of it framing his head like a halo, some of it plastered to his sweaty forehead.

Next to the table was a courier stanchion, the last point on the courier's delivery. The stanchions were provided by the Guild, and technically owned by them, just like the cuff on Pierce's wrist. It consisted of a small platform for the attaché and a U-shaped slot for the courier's wrist. The stanchion held the courier's wrist immobile, while the recipient checked that the delivery was all there. They were usually bolted to the floor in a vault or strong room, but they could be freestanding, too. Still, it looked out of place.

Once the delivery was accepted, the chain would detach from the cuff and from the attaché and the stanchion would release the courier's wrist. The transaction was then complete.

"Mr. Kransky," Pierce said with a tip of his head. Some couriers insisted on conducting the entire transaction without speaking, to enhance the mystique. Another of Erno's affectations. While there was arguably no *need* to speak, Pierce thought that was ridiculous, not to mention rude.

"I know you," Kransky said.

"We've done business in the past."

Kransky nodded, then pointed at the stanchion. "Well, just because we've done business in the past, doesn't mean I'm trusting you today."

Pierce briefly reconsidered his policy on speaking.

"You don't have to do this, Mr. Kransky," Siluk said. "You could just refuse the delivery."

Kransky gave him a blistering glare. "Shut up, Siluk. Another word out of you and I'll gut you."

Pierce kept his face impassive, but he was alarmed that Kransky's men would even consider refusing the delivery. Typically, the Guild would demand a triple delivery fee for refusals, on top of what had already been paid. That was serious money.

"Never mind him," Kransky told Pierce. "You just get your hand in there and let's see what you've got for me."

This moment was designed to make the courier intensely vulnerable. It spoke to the Guild's absolute confidence in the integrity and ability of its couriers to deliver, and the couriers' absolute confidence that no one would dare interfere with a Guild courier performing their duty. To do so would bring about terrible retribution. In the early days of the Guild, there were a few incidents, couriers killed in the line of duty. Those responsible suffered such spectacularly horrible deaths that it was now unheard of.

Early on, Pierce had felt misgivings about joining an institution that could deliver such suffering, but now he understood it was necessary to ensure the inviolability of the system and the safety of the couriers.

Similarly, by pledging their lives, the couriers acknowledged their commitment to delivering their payloads, and what was at stake if they failed.

Pierce placed his wrist in the slot atop the stanchion, eager to get the transaction over with. He felt the familiar click as the locking mechanism engaged with his wrist cuff, holding his arm in place and scanning his microcode.

Kransky rose from his seat and Pierce was alarmed to see a machete in his hand, already smeared with blood.

The others now stepped closer to him.

"A lot of bad shit going down in the world just lately," Kransky said, slapping the flat of the machete against his thigh, despite the blood. "That's why I'm bringing my assets closer to home. Used to be you could trust people you did business with: crooks, bankers, couriers, it didn't matter. Everyone knew they could make more money doing business together than giving the business to each other."

He looked over at Schmidt, Siluk, and the driver. "Am I right?" He paused, as if waiting for them to respond, then seemed to take their silence as an affirmation. Turning to Pierce, he shook his head. "I can't wait until they get this fucking 'U-Net' up and running, so we can stop dicking around like this. You're the fourth courier to arrive here today. The *fourth*. Let's hope you don't turn out to be a thieving piece of shit like the rest of them."

With his foot, Kransky slid a wastebasket out from behind the table and closer to the stanchion. The rim was dripping with blood.

Pierce tried not to react, but every nerve in his body was screaming. He ran his calculations. He knew his payload was intact. He had checked it when he went through airport security. He went through the possibilities before him and determined what his reactions to each should be.

Kransky tapped the scanner on the attaché and opened his eyes wide. With a faint click, the case opened. He lifted the lid higher, opening it all the way. Once he was satisfied with the delivery and closed the case, a second iris scan would release the chain from the attaché and from the cuff grafted onto Pierce's arm, ending the transaction.

With the lid in the way, Pierce couldn't see what was inside the attaché. But he could tell from the look on Kransky's face what *wasn't*.

As the Russian's face darkened with rage, Pierce thought back to the ring of gray slush on the ground at the airport, the warmth emanating from the attaché. Whatever had gone wrong with the delivery was not his doing and not his fault. No one had gained access to the attaché's contents between the airport and here, or at any point since he had taken possession.

But Kransky would assume Pierce had robbed him, as he'd apparently assumed the other three couriers had robbed him. As if it made the tiniest bit of sense for someone robbing him to show up with an empty attaché instead of disappearing into the wind. But if the payload wasn't there, Kransky had every right, if he chose to exercise it, to cut off the hand that had supposedly stolen from him, to watch the blood spray from his wrist until there was none left and he was dead. That was the agreement.

But Pierce wasn't going to let that happen.

On some level he'd always known it could come down to this. Throughout his entire career, the Guild had emphasized the number one rule of the courier: above all else, nothing was more important than the delivery. More important than the courier, more important than the wrist that the Guild owned once he joined. It was an oath, a vow, a legal contract. For some of the couriers, like Erno and his acolytes, it was almost a religion.

But Pierce had known all along it was bullshit. Being a courier was a job, nothing more. The cuff on his arm was simply hardware, and he was determined to keep the hand it was attached to.

There was no longer any conscious decision-making to be done, beyond selecting from the plans of action he had prepared. Relieved from the burden of thinking, Pierce was free to act. Ultimately, this was what he'd really been training for.

Bracing his right hand against the top of the stanchion, he flipped himself into the air and twisted his body. There was a good chance the bones in his left forearm would snap, but they would heal. There would be no healing from whatever Kransky had in mind.

The edge of the stanchion bit into the flesh of Pierce's arm. The pain was intense, but as he swung his legs through the air and clamped them around Kransky's head, he was relieved not to hear or feel the crack of bone.

Before Kransky's machete hand could twitch, Pierce's legs slammed the Russian's face against the scanner embedded in the attaché. Kransky's eyes widened in surprise and the blue light of the scanner registered his iris.

As far as the stanchion was concerned, the delivery had been accepted.

The stanchion released Pierce's arm and the chain fell to the floor, almost silent thanks to the nano-powder coating.

Pierce pushed off from the stanchion and landed on his feet behind Kransky. The Russian was still stunned, his grip on the machete loose as Pierce took it from him.

It was a quality blade, well balanced and razor sharp. It barely whispered as Pierce swept it across the backs of Kransky's legs, through his pants, his skin, and the tendons that kept him standing.

Kransky's knees buckled, but Pierce grabbed his ponytail, holding him upright as the other men drew their weapons and closed on him fast.

The driver fired. Pierce, anticipating the shot, lifted Kransky, intercepting the bullet with the Russian's shoulder. The impact seemed to remind Kransky that he had yet to make a sound about his other injuries. He made up for that now, howling at a volume and pitch that made Schmidt and Siluk slow a step. The driver was still coming, aiming his gun, and Pierce flung the machete over Kransky's shoulder. The blade spun twice before embedding with a wet *thunk* into the driver's chest.

Schmidt and Siluk stepped around him as he fell, raising their weapons, but Kransky's howling had cost them a crucial step. Pierce flung Kransky at their legs and snatched his chain from the floor. He spun his entire body, whipping every tendon and muscle and bone in his legs, abdomen, arms, and fingers, focusing all that energy into the weighted hasp at the tip of the chain itself, which cracked like a whip in the center of Schmidt's face, shredding it, turning it into a spray of flesh and blood and shards of bone that peppered Siluk's face.

As Schmidt staggered and fell, Siluk coughed and spat and clawed at his eyes. Pierce knew it was an experience that would haunt the man until he died. It would be up to him if that was in moments or decades.

By the time Siluk had cleared his eyes, he found himself staring at Pierce's gun.

"Drop your weapon," Pierce said quietly.

Siluk's eyes darted to Kransky. The Russian had been shrieking the entire time. His voice was ragged. So were Pierce's nerves.

"Drop it now," Pierce said. "And kick it over to me."

Siluk dropped the gun. It bounced once on the thick carpet. Then he kicked it over toward Pierce.

Schmidt coughed and woke up, gurgling through his ruined face. "I'm going to kill you," he mumbled, his muffled voice barely audible through the noise Kransky was making.

Pierce believed him. He seemed the type to hold a grudge.

As Schmidt pushed himself to his hands and knees, Pierce fired twice into his head. As the man pitched face-first onto the carpet, Pierce touched the hot barrel of his gun to Kransky's forehead. It sizzled for an instant, like a cigarette hitting water. The Russian went quiet as the burning metal reminded him that things could get worse. Pierce swung the gun back toward Siluk.

"Get out of here," Pierce said to Siluk.

Siluk's eyes darted from Pierce to Kransky.

"Bullshit," Kransky said, spittle spraying from his mouth. "You work for me, you cocksucker. You *both* work for me."

"I have no quarrel with you," Pierce told Siluk, ignoring

Kransky. "And you're not going to be working for him much longer."

Siluk thought for a moment, and then, without a word, he turned and ran. Pierce was relieved not to have to kill him. Kransky screamed at Siluk as he fled, calling him names, saying what awful things he was going to do to him and his family. The rage seemed to take his mind off his pain.

Pierce raised the lid to the attaché. Inside, the neat rows of bundles and bills and zeroes were gone, the empty paper bands half buried in coarse beige powder.

"You thieving bastards," Kransky spat at him.

"I didn't rob you," Pierce said, dipping his fingers into the powder, rubbing it between them. He was about to explain how he had checked the attaché, how the money had been there. He was even going to tell Kransky about the warmth he had felt coming from the attaché, how it had melted the ice on the tarmac.

But before he could say anything else, Kransky said, "That's what they all said. And they were all thieving bastards, just like you. Well, I took care of them, and I'm going to take care of you, too."

Pierce sighed as he leaned over and peered into the bloody wastebasket. Inside were three hands, severed at the wrist, right at the edge of the titanium cuff. Three couriers maimed. Three couriers dead.

Such a waste.

He checked the scanner on the attaché. Kransky's retina scan had confirmed receipt and signed off on the delivery. Pierce's work here was finished.

He brought the attaché over to where Kransky was crumpled on the floor.

"I didn't rob you," he said, looking down at Kransky.

"They didn't either."

He dumped the powder over Kransky's head.

"You filthy cocksucker!" Kransky said, sputtering and coughing. "I won't rest until I've killed you, and everyone you ever knew."

"I know," Pierce said, pointing his gun at Kransky's head.

"You guys knew what you signed up for, what you were getting paid for. You knew that if you robbed anybody—"

"I didn't rob you. Neither did they."

"Oh, fuck you, you didn't." Kransky thrust out a hand to give Pierce his middle finger. "I'll kill you, you motherfucker, I swear to God, if it's the last thing I do."

Pierce said, "It won't be." Then he pulled the trigger.

On the bullet's way to Kransky's head, it passed through his upraised finger, sending half of the digit spinning into the air, as if propelled by the jet of blood that erupted below. Then the bullet punched through Kransky's forehead and the room went silent, except for the gentle thud of the finger landing on the carpet.

Pierce took a deep breath and let it out slowly. He wiped down his attaché and chain, reprogrammed them for his iris, and reconnected them. Then he took the car keys from the driver's pocket.

As he went out into the hallway, past the room full of cubicles, even more heads peeked up at him. Turning the corner, he saw the doors to the elevator just starting to close. Siluk was standing inside.

Pierce called out. "Hold that, please."

Siluk looked him in the eye for a moment, and as the doors began to close, he stuck out his hand and they opened up again.

Chapter Two

THE LAST RED sliver of sun hovered just above the horizon. The ocean lapping at the beach seemed to reflect the sky's ambivalence, the ripples alternately striped the vivid pink of sunset and the indigo of approaching night.

It was Gloriana's favorite time of the day, and had been ever since she was a child, even though the reasons why had changed over the years. Even though it brought back sad memories as well as happy ones.

She still remembered the utter contentment she had felt as a child wrapped in her mother's arms on a different beach, thousands of miles away, as the two of them watched the sunset over the water from the sand in front of her family's tiny house.

She had known then how lucky she was to live at the water's edge, and had been glad it was her family's turn. She felt bad for the families that lived by the water before them—or even on the water, in stilt houses. They must have loved it, too, before the water took their homes and they'd had to move away.

Even as a child, she had been in awe of the natural beauty that surrounded her village. She hadn't needed to lose it in order to appreciate it. Maybe that was why its loss hit her so hard.

Her throat tightened as that memory came back to her. It had been an evening like this one when everything changed. She'd been alone on that far-off beach, her father off on some errand, her mother inside mending his shirts.

The smell had been the first thing she noticed, chemical and harsh, so out of place it bewildered her. She had wondered briefly if her father was painting or patching his boat, but she knew those smells and this wasn't them.

Then she saw something bobbing in the water, small at first, like seaweed or a jellyfish, not quite on top of the surface, not quite below. She spotted another one, and another and another. The smell grew stronger, hurting her nose. Then fish started to wash ashore, some already dead, their stench mingling with the chemical smell.

She had called for her mother, but her voice failed her, coming out quiet and scared. She called again, louder, but by then other voices were calling for parents and children up and down the beach, drowning her out. People gathered, looking and pointing, whispers merging to form a soft, urgent, ominous buzz.

Gloriana had walked into the gentle surf. Even in the fading light, she could see the ocean wasn't right. The waves were sluggish, as if time had slowed down, like in a bad dream when something terrible was happening.

Then a big wave crashed, hard and solid against her legs. It pulled back out to sea, leaving behind a large seabird at her feet, painted a thick, sticky, sickly black. The bird looked dead, killed by whatever was wrong with the water. Then its eyes opened, and it looked up at her, pleading and blaming and begging for answers, terrified but resigned, like it knew it was already dead, and so was the world it had known all its life. Gloriana's world, as well.

She could still feel the hot tears that had run down her cheeks all those years ago, as the bird tumbled back out to sea and another wave came in, rising higher up her legs. Looking down, she had seen that below her knees, she, too, was painted black. Her stomach had clenched with fear and she had begun to scream, wondering if she was already dead, too.

Chapter Three

THE BENTLEY WAS too conspicuous to drive to the airport, so Pierce ditched it a mile from the entrance and caught a SmartCab. His mind raced as he walked back through the terminal, trying to make sense of what had just happened, and what it meant—for his career, his life. As far as the Guild infrastructure was concerned, the delivery had been accepted. He had checked the tiny pager clipped onto his waistband half a dozen times and there were no messages, urgent or otherwise. But people were dead and money was missing and word was going to get back to New York, probably before he did. This was not going to be the end of it.

When he arrived at the airport, he was astonished to discover that he was right on schedule. It seemed like more time should have gone by. The BetterLates' incense still hung in the air, though he didn't hear or see any of them.

He stopped at a payphone and tried to call Jimmy Serino, the guy who had sent the disappearing payload.

Normally, he would have let the Guild handle it, but this wasn't a normal call. The receptionist answered and said Mr. Serino wasn't in the office today. Could she take a message?

Pierce declined and hung up.

As he approached security, he slowed a step. The screening line for the general public must have run to two hundred people, crowded into a zig-zagging cattle chute. As a courier, he was entitled to use the priority line, which held just a dozen people, mostly mid-level UniCon executives who didn't quite rate a private jet. But bringing up the end of the line was a pair of uniformed UniCs, UniCon's police/security force.

UniCs and couriers had an odd relationship. They both held special status, set apart from normal society. In a way, that made them kindred spirits, but they were rivals, too. As UniCon had taken over more and more of society, from corporate and criminal structures to the military and police—even entire governments, in some smaller countries—the Guild remained independent and outside of their control.

That independence was a big part of what had drawn Pierce to the Guild.

He had always liked that quote about democracy being the worst political system apart from all the others. UniCon was definitely one of the "others." And when UniCon had started expanding its reach, absorbing more and more of the things that used to be of the people, by the people, and for the people—well, the Guild might not have been any more democratic, but at least it wasn't part of UniCon.

Some cops respected that independence, maybe even envied it, but more of them resented it. Pierce was much more concerned about the Guild than UniCon, but if the local UniCs hassled him, they would not only draw attention, they would also slow him down when he needed to be moving fast.

Of course, the throng of people in the cattle chute would slow him down, too. He got in line behind the UniCs.

As the ramifications of killing Kransky buzzed in his head, he thought of Gloriana. Whenever he felt depressed or afraid or out of his depth, he felt the urge to talk to her, to reach out. But she was gone for good. Ten years had passed since they'd broken up, right before he'd joined the Guild. Now, whenever he regretted a life decision, his mind went back to the biggest regret of his life.

"Courier, huh?"

Pierce turned to see a woman in her late thirties in business attire staring at the attaché chained to his wrist. She looked up at him with a smile and cocked an eyebrow.

He turned away from her. The last thing he needed now was some fetishist causing a scene.

He felt her breath as she whispered into his ear, "My name's Suzanne, and I have half an hour before my flight."

Pierce turned his head slightly toward Suzanne and said, "No, thank you."

Anonymous sex wasn't his thing, but he'd heard horror stories, too—couriers who'd starved to death alone, their cuffs chained to radiators or basement walls.

He didn't know if he believed them, but he didn't discount them either. Couriers didn't like to talk about it, but having a titanium hasp on a cuff grafted onto your bones demanded a level of vigilance.

"Come on," she whispered, sliding her hand up his thigh. "We could have fun."

"Don't touch me," he snapped at her, his teeth clenched.

One of the UniCs turned with an appraising look, first at the woman, now walking away, then at Pierce, who earned a shake of the head for passing up the opportunity. The UniC watched the woman crossing the concourse, like he was thinking of going after her, seeing if her kink extended to UniCs, too.

But it was already their turn to go through security.

When it was Pierce's turn, he had to open the attaché. He half expected it to be somehow full of Kransky's money, but all that was inside was a faint dusting of the powder that had replaced it.

Pierce was tense, but the transportation security agent didn't bat an eye. Pierce declared his weapons, then walked through the scanner.

After they'd waved him through, Pierce wondered what he would have done if the UniCs had tried to take him in—and what he was going do when the Guild inevitably did.

He looked down at the hand with the alloy cuff, wondering how far he was willing to go to keep it, trying not to think of how much more was at stake.

He spent much of the two-hour flight planning for what he would do when the plane landed, but even with so much at stake, his thoughts were never far from Gloriana.

TEN YEARS EARLIER, Pierce's expectations for his personal life had been quaintly old-fashioned: fall in love, get married, have kids and treat them well, grow old with the wife, have fun with the grandkids, die. He accomplished the first part, falling hard for Gloriana. She was easy to love: kind, sexy, and frighteningly smart but never condescending. And she loved him too, he was sure of it. She told him so, and showed it, too.

They'd been dating for eight months and her lease was about to expire, just as she was about to go away on some two-month fellowship in Oslo. She hadn't found a new place and hated the idea of paying rent on an empty apartment for two months. Pierce suggested she move in with him, or maybe get another place together. It all seemed logical and straightforward.

Apparently, it was not.

They had never talked about marriage, and Pierce wasn't thinking about it then, but she thought he was, and it turned out their views on the institution were very different. She said marriage was a tool of oppression, of ownership, an outdated construct that had no place in progressive society.

Pierce grew defensive. So did Gloriana.

They had a huge fight, and the only thing that was clear, once it was over, was that they were over, too.

A few days later, she put her stuff into storage and left for Oslo. He never saw her again.

He was already working as a courier, but after that, he decided to join the newly established Guild.

Several years later, he heard she was working for Nolexa Petrochemicals, which made no sense at all since she was a militant environmentalist. He questioned how well he'd really known her in the first place, how much she could have changed. A year or two after that though, he read in the *New York Times* that she was in prison in Malaysia for having sabotaged an oil refinery. *That* made a lot more sense.

It hurt, the thought of her rotting away in some horrible prison—her stunning intellect, her sweetness and humor and essential decency, all of it wasting away in a Malaysian prison cell. When he thought of her, he pictured many versions: pajamas and brunch, decked out for a date, creasing her forehead in deep thought, smiling and sweaty and disheveled on their bed. He couldn't reconcile any of it with the reality of her in a prison.

He still cared for her—he always would—but they'd been apart for five or six years at that point, and he thought maybe he had gotten over her. He realized then that he never would.

Finding out she was in prison—serving a life sentence, no less—filled him with pain, and also regret. Regret that he had never gone after her, never tried again. He realized that deep inside he had hoped that someday they could try again. And now he had to acknowledge that was never going to happen.

And while he'd had a more realistic hope that she would have a long, healthy, successful life, even without him, he realized that wasn't going to happen either.

He tried to help her, talked to ambassadors and consuls, even UniCon, but it was all useless. She'd been labeled a terrorist, and that was that.

Just a few months later, Pierce's mom had died. It was a dark time.

And this was another dark time.

FOR MOST OF the flight, Pierce had been dividing his thoughts between years past and hours to come, but once the pilot announced they were beginning their descent, he banished the past and focused exclusively on the future. If he mishandled the next few hours, there might not be much of it.

He had a little bit of time. The Guild was nimble in some ways but ponderous in others, and sanctioning a courier was something they took very seriously. No one would make a move against him until the disciplinary council had approved it, and they only met first thing in the morning and at the end of the day. He had at least until 5 p.m., maybe until tomorrow morning.

He needed to get a few things from home, because it could be a while before it was safe to do so again. And he'd risk stopping into the office to talk to Diaz, get a sense of what he was up against. He had thought about calling him from Alaska, or asking him to meet somewhere neutral, but he hadn't wanted to tip his hand just yet. Diaz was a good guy, practically a friend, but this would be a tricky situation for him; no need to get him involved any sooner than necessary. Besides, this kind of conversation was best held in person, and in private.

Above all else, Pierce realized, he needed to figure out what the hell had happened to Kransky's money and find a way to prove to the Guild that it wasn't his fault. The Guild had long established that crimes committed by a courier on official business fell under the Guild's jurisdiction, for the Guild and only the Guild to deal with. The UniCs hated that—and took every opportunity to hassle couriers for infractions committed while not on official business—but UniCon officially acknowledged it. And the Guild had earned a reputation for absolute impartiality, and for delivering swift, harsh justice. But Kransky had killed three couriers—more than had been killed in the last five years—and tried to kill a fourth. If Pierce could figure out what had happened to the shipment, prove that he hadn't stolen it, then he hadn't violated his oath and his actions had been self-defense.

He spent the rest of the flight thinking about next moves, his right hand resting on his left wrist, tracing the metal with a fingertip. By the time the pilot began their final approach, Pierce had a plan.

THE AIRPORT FELT oddly tense. There were more UniCs than usual, looking edgier than usual. Pierce wondered if it was just his state of mind, but he picked it up as his car drove him through the city, too. The streets seemed oddly frenetic, even for New York.

His car passed three groups of BetterLates—apparently the incense was not limited to Alaska.

Twice he'd had to detour around groups of anti-UniCon protestors. The triannual UniConference was less than a month away, and people were getting riled up, both at the impending inconvenience and at how UniCon was ruining the world. But that didn't seem enough to explain the energy on the street.

Even the drone traffic seemed more intense than usual, all the way from street level up to the low clouds, blinking lights diffuse in the dense gray. Pierce could clearly distinguish the high-pitched whine of the standard drones, the buzz of heated or refrigerated food drones, and the throaty roar of the money drones, weighted down with armor, net cutters, and guns. There'd be countless others up there too, flying high, out of earshot.

The Fargo Courier Agency was a global outfit with twenty offices and six hundred couriers, one of the founding members of the Guild, but their flagship New York offices were on the third floor of a nondescript office building in the Financial District.

Pierce's car found a parking spot a block away. A light

rain started falling as he walked, but he slowed as he approached the building, checking his pager one last time—still nothing. It was 4:30 when he paused across the street, watching, as if he could somehow glean what was going on inside. After a few seconds, he hurried across the street.

The door swung open before he could open it, and out stepped Erno Damiani himself, looking ridiculous in his collarless jacket and mirrored shades, carrying an attaché with a very short chain.

Erno clocked him and smiled. "Hello, Pierce." He was two inches taller and a few pounds lighter than Pierce. His straight dark hair shone in the gloom, a lock of it hanging in front of his shades.

"Erno," Pierce replied, warily.

They'd known each other a long time, having joined around the same time, right at the beginning. They had both fought in the wars, and they'd bonded over that, at first. They were almost like friends for a little while. Until Pierce got to know him better.

The Cyber War hadn't been hot for very long, but for a few short months, the action had been blistering. Pierce had seen pretty much all of it, as part of a commando unit. The experience had changed him.

When they'd first joined the Guild, Erno told Pierce he'd been in counterintelligence. He later revealed that he'd been in a 'counter personnel' division. His job had been to find and take out the hackers causing all the trouble—a mission that lasted somewhat longer than the conventional fighting. Pierce understood that all was fair in war, and the hackers Erno had killed had caused immeasurable suffering, but he had a problem with how gleefully Erno talked about his exploits. He was always one of the first to volunteer whenever the Guild put out a "discipline order" on one of their own. Pierce couldn't know how the war had changed Erno, but however he'd started out, he was clearly a sociopath now.

Pierce steeled himself for a fight, studying Erno's face for any sign that he knew about Kransky.

But Erno only nodded as he passed, their attachés softly clicking against each other. Pierce didn't turn to see him go, instead watching his reflection in the window as he climbed into his gaudy bright-blue armored Chevy military SUV, with its ridiculously huge, reinforced steel bumper.

Inside, Pierce took the elevator to the third floor and let the scanner read his iris. The door beeped and he walked in.

"Hello, Wallace," he said to the receptionist.

"Pierce," Wallace replied without looking up. As if nothing was wrong.

The small seating area behind the reception desk was empty except for one of the new kids, Danny Rocha, sitting in a chair with his attaché on his lap. He was a smart kid and a hard worker, so it was especially disappointing to see him wearing a black, collarless sport coat, a pair of round shades in his hand.

Rocha looked up when Pierce walked in. The kid's eyes were dark and sunken, his skin gray. "Jesus, kid. You look like shit. What's going on?"

"I kind of fucked up."

Pierce almost laughed; there was no way Rocha's troubles were as bad as his own. "What happened?"

Rocha winced, as if talking about it caused him physical pain. "I clipped a UniC car with the small hauler. They hit *me*, actually, but, you know…"

Yeah, Pierce knew. It was never UniCon's fault. By statute. You could be sitting in a parked car and a UniC cruiser could plow into you from behind. Not their fault. And that meant it was yours. The Guild took that seriously, too. They knew it wasn't your fault, but they didn't care. They cared about friction between the Guild and UniCon.

"Sucks," Pierce said. "Assholes."

Before he could say more, Diaz opened the door to his office.

He gave Pierce an oddly inscrutable look, then held up a finger and turned to Rocha. "One more chance, kid. Pickup at 27 West Twentieth. Ask for Hector Gonzales." He lowered the finger so it was pointing. "Do *not* fuck this up."

Rocha shot to his feet, nodding frantically. "You got it, Mr. Diaz. I won't let you down."

Rocha gave Pierce a tiny nod; then he was gone.

Diaz swiveled his finger toward Pierce, then beckoned him ominously as he backed into his office.

"Close the door," Diaz said as Pierce entered the office. As soon as the door clicked, he said, "You shouldn't be here."

Pierce wasn't going to give up anything. "What do you mean?"

"Don't give me that shit. You know what I mean. What the fuck, Pierce?"

Pierce sat on the edge of Diaz's leather couch with his attaché on the floor between his knees. "Is there a grievance?"

"Well, Kransky didn't file one, but that's probably because he's fucking *dead*."

"Anything from discipline?"

Diaz shook his head and looked at the clock on the wall. "Not yet."

Pierce let out a long sigh. "What did you hear?"

Diaz shook his head. "Nuh-uh. You tell me what happened."

Pierce patted the attaché, told him how he had checked it at the airport and the money had been there, then how it was missing when he got to Kransky's. He told him about the wastebasket full of hands.

"Jesus," Diaz said. "So, what the fuck is that all about? How could someone have gotten in there and taken the money? You had it on you the whole time, right? No napping on the plane or anything?"

"You're seriously going to ask me that?"

"You got that long-ass chain, could somebody have gotten in there while you were looking away?"

Pierce gave him a look. "No."

"I've got to ask, kid, a clusterfuck like this. So, what do you think happened?"

Pierce shook his head. "I have no idea."

"So somebody fucking robbed you."

"Maybe. But I can't figure how. And there was all this, like, powder or sawdust in the attaché, where the money was supposed to be."

"Meaning what?"

"I don't know." He took a deep breath. "Meaning maybe the cash wasn't taken, maybe it was destroyed somehow."

Diaz sat back and rubbed his eyes. "In a locked attaché? How? You got mice in there? Termites? Alien space rays?"

"I don't know. The case was warm to the touch. Maybe it was microwaves."

"Jesus Christ." Diaz rubbed his eyes again. "It sounds like bullshit. Can you prove any of it?"

Pierce shook his head. "Not yet."

"If you could, that might help."

"Yeah, I know."

Diaz nodded and glanced at the clock. It was ten to five. "Okay, the sender's name was Jimmy Serino. What do you know about him?"

"Not much. I've done a few deliveries for him. He works for Frank Billings. The pickup was at Billings Tower. I called him, but they said he wasn't in. I need his home address."

Diaz closed his eyes, thinking. Then he scribbled something on a notepad, tore off a page and slid it across the desk, toward Pierce.

"Thanks," Pierce said, slipping it into a pocket inside his jacket.

"You don't tell anyone I gave you that."

Pierce nodded. "Of course."

After a long moment, Diaz shook his head. "For Christ's sake kid, you swore a fucking oath."

"I know. I do. But not for that. Not for something I didn't do, not for some whack job who'd already taken out three other couriers." Pierce leaned forward, resting his arms on his thighs. "So how bad is this?"

"Well, it's not *good*."

"The fact that Kransky was on some kind of courier-killing spree has got to count for something. Three couriers in one day? They didn't *all* rob him."

Diaz nodded thoughtfully. "You make a point. And Kransky accepted the delivery, you got that going for you. How'd that happen anyway?" Pierce opened his mouth to speak, but Diaz held up a hand. "You know what? I don't even want to know."

"You'll put in a word for me?"

Diaz grunted and closed his eyes. "Of course. But 'a word' isn't going to count much for something like this." He took a breath, thinking. "Look, the Guild doesn't want people losing faith in their couriers, but they also don't want people killing them on a whim. If you can prove that the money disappeared, and that you had nothing to do with it, then maybe they'll get behind you. Kransky accepted the shipment, and then he tried to kill you. It was self-defense. But if they think you took the money, or let someone take it from you, well. Like I said, they don't want people losing faith."

Pierce nodded, then glanced at the clock on the wall and got to his feet. "I've never been on this side of things. How long does it take, once they file the disciplinary order? How long before they start coming after me?"

Diaz shook his head. "I don't know, kid. It could be minutes, or maybe not till morning. Who knows, Kransky taking out three others might slow them down more than that."

"Right. I should be getting out of here."

"Yeah, you should." Nodding slowly. "Just figure out what happened to the money. And find a way to prove it."

PIERCE WAS IN his car and on the road by 4:57. His next stop was home, just for a minute. It was another risk, but it could be his last chance.

His apartment was near the Hudson River, in the old West Village, now called Wet Village or New Venice. The once wildly-overpriced apartments were now only moderately overpriced, and partially underwater. Pierce's apartment was on what used to be the third floor. Now it was the second.

Some buildings had been torn down and replaced, some lifted onto stilts. But others, like Pierce's, had seen their basements and first floors stripped of anything hazardous or prone to rot and given over to the water. Steel-grid roads and sidewalks had been erected on posts and new doorways punched through the walls on the second floors. Inevitably, at some point, developers would raze the entire area, fill it in and build something new—and way more expensive—but until then, Pierce enjoyed the slightly reduced rent and that fact that, for the moment at least, he didn't have to move.

To the east, farther from the river, was LoHo, one of the pricier lowland neighborhoods. Almost as expensive as the real estate itself was the mandatory membership in the Neighborhood Association, which maintained the water seals and the pumps that ran day and night.

To the south was the Highlands, or HiHo. The most expensive part of the city, it was a dense area of gleaming towers built on landfill trucked in from New Jersey and guaranteed to remain above sea level for fifty years.

As Pierce made his way up the gangplank to the entrance of his building, he could hear the water lapping below. As always, he held his keys a little bit tighter.

Inside his apartment, he detached the chain from his wrist and attaché, then dropped onto the sofa and closed his eyes, just for a moment. It had been a long day, and he wished he could just sit there for a while. But he knew he couldn't.

Heaving himself to his feet, he went to his bookshelves. With both hands, he removed his collection of first-edition Elmore Leonard Westerns to reveal an almost invisible square cut into the wall.

Everybody had hiding places in their homes. Most had more than one, and a safe, too. Pierce just had a hole.

He used his folding knife to pry the panel out, revealing several stacks of twenties and fifties, a thick brick of hundreds, a thinner brick of five-hundreds, and an emaciated handful of thousands paper-clipped to a lone ten-thousand-dollar bill.

He peeled five hundreds and ten twenties from their respective bundles and slid them into his wallet, then put the rest in his attaché.

On the shelf below the money was a thin folder: his copy of the files on the Fairview Apartments disaster, the collapse that had killed his mother. Three years of work penetrating the layers of shell corporations that obscured the identity of the owners. He slid them into the attaché, too, then closed it and set the lock.

He paused at the door and looked around, wondering if he'd ever see the place again. He thought about throwing the Elmore Leonards into the attaché as well, but decided against it. He needed to travel light. He switched off the light and pulled the door closed behind him.

Chapter Four

DUGRAY JOSEPH WAS a drug dealer. He was also Pierce's best friend and had been, off and on, since seventh grade. That was the year Pierce's folks had split up, and he and his mom had moved from a luxury apartment overlooking Central Park to the Fairview Apartments, a dilapidated high-rise overlooking an even more dilapidated low-rise in East Harlem.

It had been a tough transition, and it would have been a whole lot tougher if Dugray hadn't decided that Pierce was okay, and that they could be friends.

They were inseparable for a few years, almost like brothers. If they weren't hanging out in person, they were playing video games together online.

Those first few years, Dugray had straddled two different worlds. He was smart, a library kid who was always reading and did well in school. But he also hung out with some of the rougher kids, gangsters and wannabe gangsters.

They were in junior year when the cyber skirmishes really started heating up, and Dugray started spending less and less time in the library and more time hanging out with that rougher crowd. He and Pierce drifted apart, and by the end of that year, they barely acknowledged each other in the hallway, even as their moms became close friends.

Halfway through senior year, Dugray stopped going to school. They crossed paths at a party the summer after graduation. Pierce had been drafted and was waiting to ship out. Dugray was working a corner for Percy Townsend, who ran one of the area's bigger drug operations. They said hi, had an awkward conversation around the keg, and that was it. They didn't see each other again for seven years, not until the Fairview collapsed, killing 163 people, including both of their mothers. Pierce was on top of a rubble heap, covered in dust, digging with his bare hands, when he realized that the dust-covered guy digging next to him was his old friend Dugray. That's what brought them back together.

The collapse was criminal negligence: greedy landlords intentionally allowing the place to rot because they resented the rent control. But the official investigation had been a joke—it was quickly declared an accident and no one was ever charged, or even identified as the owner. But someone was responsible, and Pierce and Dugray had been working together ever since, spending untold hours at the library and City Hall and the Municipal Archives in Brooklyn, trying to find out who.

On some level, Pierce *knew* who was responsible: damn near everyone. It was UniCon and the whole system they had ushered into place—*forced* into place. And everyone who profited from that system.

Several other buildings collapsed that same year. It turned out the rising seawaters had undermined the reinforced concrete foundations while the constant rains weakened the structures above them. Eventually, it came out that all the fallen buildings had a few things in common: they were all strictly rent-controlled, all sitting on real estate worth astronomically more without the buildings (and tenants) than with them, and all owned by parties shielded behind countless layers of shell companies.

The UniCs quickly labeled each collapse an unfortunate accident and laid responsibility at the feet of the long-gone companies that built them, and the governmental agencies that should have been monitoring them. They wouldn't even cite climate change as a contributing factor, because UniCon had said it was going to fix that. There was a public outcry, like there always was, but within days some other terrible thing had happened and the public moved on.

Pierce and Dugray had persisted, and they had penetrated several layers of shell corporations, getting closer each time to whoever owned the Fairview and let those people die, whose negligence *caused* those people to die. Who had killed their mothers.

And who would pay.

THE RAINWATER CASCADING from a clogged gutter in the shadows curled and twisted in the wind, as if seeking Pierce out. He shuffled around trying to avoid it, but it found him wherever he moved, even under the small shelter that jutted out over the steps. The girl sitting on the top step watched him with eyes framed by thick, clumpy makeup, her eyes blank but still judging whenever the water got close to her.

He caught her tilting her head and squinting at him. There was nothing unusual about a courier showing up at a drug house, but she seemed confused by the incongruity of him waiting outside with her.

Usually, when he came to one of Dugray's drug houses, the door was answered immediately. He was starting to feel very exposed out there on the steps, under the bright light.

Pierce pulled his Thintech jacket tight and stepped out from under the roof, trying to find the source of the torrent. But all he could see was the floodlights bolted onto the second-floor bricks. The rain seemed to be falling out of them. Everything above was hidden in darkness.

He shifted his stance, trying to maintain the inscrutable demeanor that was part of the courier mystique, but after counting to ten, he charged up the steps and pounded on the door once more. "Come on, goddamn it! Open the fucking door!"

A cluster of BetterLates turned the corner onto 105th Street, chanting about the climate, oblivious to the weather. The smell of incense, woodsy and verdant, like pine or rosemary, penetrated the rain and other smells of the city.

"Jesus," the girl said, trembling like she needed a fix and hugging herself to stop it. "Don't they ever s-sleep?"

Then the heavy door behind them flung open and Pierce and the girl both turned to look up at it.

Pierce had expected to have to get past some grunt in order to get to Dugray, but standing in the door was Dugray's big boss—Percy Townsend himself. He wore a flashy raincoat, just this side of pimp, and was flanked by muscle who seemed to mimic Townsend's sneer.

Up the street, a black Escalade started, its headlights flaring in the darkness, reflecting off the rain.

The girl smiled and unfolded her arms, letting her jacket fall open to reveal a microlace tee shirt, and through it, two pierced nipples, a big diamond stud in each glinting in the harsh light from overhead.

In the old days, before carbon capture began churning out diamonds by the bucketful as a byproduct, they would each have been worth a fortune. Now they were kind of tacky.

As Townsend and his men stepped forward, Pierce saw Dugray standing in the doorway behind them, looking stressed—and even more stressed when he spotted Pierce.

Townsend ignored the girl and glared at Pierce, giving him the up and down to let him know he wasn't impressed. "You dropping off or picking up? Or you buying?"

He laughed, turning his head to the side to make sure his men knew they were supposed to be laughing too. They got the memo and started hooting and snorting, too late and too hard.

Pierce kept his head down in the shadows. "Dropping off. Dugray Joseph."

Up in the doorway, Dugray's eyes widened, then went completely flat as Townsend turned to look up at him.

"Booking your own couriers now?" Townsend asked, his eyes flashing.

Dugray forced a smile. "Just making sure I'm being careful with your money, Mr. T."

Townsend pinned him with his stare for another few moments; then his face split into a grin. "Good man. Careful with my money. I like that."

Townsend's smile slid into a sneer as he turned back

to Pierce. It became something more predatory as he turned to the girl. "What about you? You got cash?"

Her eyes widened and her mouth did, too, but all she managed to say was, "I... I... got a ten."

Townsend laughed. "Well, that's not going to be enough, is it? What else you got?"

She shook her head.

He grabbed the edges of her jacket and held them out. "You got some nice big diamonds, but you know they ain't worth shit, right?" Before she could answer, he grabbed the diamond in her left nipple and twisted it through the microlace. "This one might be, I guess."

The girl winced as he rolled the stone between his thumb and forefinger.

Pierce stepped forward, but Dugray caught his eye with a fierce stare.

The driver got out of the Escalade and opened the back door.

One of the men opened an umbrella over Townsend as he started down the steps, toward the car, pulling the girl by the nipple. His men laughed as she struggled to keep up with him.

"Ouch... Shit! ...*Ow!*" she said as they stepped down onto the sidewalk. The muscle laughed, this time right on cue.

Townsend let go of her when they got to the car. He gestured toward the open back door. "You want to get high or not?"

She stood in the rain, thinking for a moment. A small spot of blood had formed on her T-shirt, spreading as the rain soaked into the sheer fabric. Pierce wanted to tell her not to, tell her it would be okay, she could get out of the rain and get treatment, get her shit back together.

But he didn't. He just stood there watching as she looked inside the car, glanced up and down the street, then climbed in.

Townsend and his men laughed as they followed her. They slammed their doors and took off.

Pierce watched as the car drove down the block and disappeared around the corner; then he turned to look at Dugray, who shrugged and shook his head.

Pierce knew what he meant. Nothing to be done about it. Townsend was who he was. The girl was who she was. The world was what it was.

Dugray let out a weary sigh. "What the fuck do you want, man? Pounding on my door."

Pierce held up the attaché and bobbed his chin at the open door.

Dugray sighed again. "Whatever." Then he turned and motioned for Pierce to follow him inside.

This was Dugray's A-house. He had two others not far away, but this was his main spot. The place was decrepit. It smelled of old sweat, and a complex mixture of smoke, inhalables, and other chemicals, including nucaine, or 'knock,' the synthetic cocaine that was the latest scourge. In the background, a muffled din of conversations, music, and whatever else filtered through the thin walls.

They passed a couple of closed doors, and the third one opened. Two kids came out, barely twenty, their eyes wide and glazed with a nucaine high. Pierce tried not to judge them—it was a fucked-up world and he didn't blame anyone who wanted to escape it for a while. He tried not to judge Dugray either—if he wasn't selling it to them, they'd just go somewhere else.

Dugray sniffed at the open room, then wrinkled his

nose. He moved on to the next door and gave it a sharp knock. "It's Dugray," he said, loud enough to punch through the din.

The door opened and a younger man looked out. Pierce had seen the kid before; his name was Hutch. "Yo," he said to Dugray; then he looked at Pierce and sighed. Turning back to Dugray, he said, "What the fuck, man?"

Dugray glanced at Pierce, put his hand on Hutch's chest and pushed him into the room, closing the door behind him and leaving Pierce alone out in the hallway.

"The fuck do you mean, 'What the fuck'?" Dugray demanded, his voice muffled but audible through the door.

"Why's that motherfucker always hanging around here?" Hutch responded. "You know he don't buy shit."

Pierce looked around, double checking to make sure no one else was listening in.

"You best watch yourself, motherfucker," Dugray said. "Someone comes to see me, you don't need to know why. I've got my reasons, and if you have a problem with that you can get the fuck out of here."

A second later, the door swung open, and Hutch pushed past Pierce, followed by Marcus, one of Dugray's slightly friendlier lieutenants.

"'Sup," Marcus said, with a nod.

Pierce nodded back. Then Dugray grabbed him by the collar and pulled him into the room. It was small and dimly lit, with an old sofa and two wooden chairs.

"This ain't a good time," Dugray said as he sat in one of the chairs.

Pierce sat in the other one, attaché at his side. "Sorry. I didn't expect Townsend to be here."

"It's not just that. Shit's going crazy outside."

"Shit's going crazy everywhere. Any idea what's going on?"

Dugray shook his head. "The Shakes went after the Toros, that's part of it."

Pierce grunted. "What's that about? I thought they had a rock-solid distribution agreement."

In the era of corporate cooperation, the city's drug gangs had long since made peace with one another. The Shakes and the Toros, Townsend and Billings; there were still rivalries, but they all did business with each other, and they had long kept the peace. One of the few concrete benefits of UniCon taking over.

"A dozen Shakes lit up a Toro house on Amsterdam. Took out six of them. The Toros hit back, almost at the same time, like they were expecting it. Body count's up to eleven, between the two of them. Plus a few more in the hospital. These motherfuckers better chill out or they're going to send in the UniCs, big time." Dugray snorted. "Shit, I'm surprised you didn't know about it."

Pierce smiled grimly. "I've been out of town, and I've got my own problems to worry about. Any idea what sparked it?"

Dugray shook his head. "Some say the Toros knocked over the Shakes, some say it was the other way around. Nobody knows for sure. But Townsend's already expecting trouble. He told me just now there was a council meeting this morning, all the heads from across the region—Ramirez, Tyson, Maxwell, Nabov, Akado, all of them."

"Not Billings?"

"Nah, man. He got no use for the local council—he's UniCon. And as long as he is, Townsend ain't going up against him. I don't think that's a part of this."

"What did they meet about?"

"That's above my pay grade. But he told me Ramirez pulled a knife and went after Akado, right in the middle of the meeting. Said Akado was robbing him."

"No shit?"

"Crazy, right?"

"Yes, it is..." Pierce said, thinking. "Sounds like someone's starting a war."

"Looking that way," Dugray said. "Intentionally or not."

They stared at each other for a moment, considering the implications.

"So..." Dugray said. "Not the best time for chit chat. What's up with you?"

Pierce let out a tired laugh, then told him about what happened with Kransky. Dugray stopped him more than once for clarification, assuming he'd misheard.

"Jesus Christ," Dugray said when Pierce was done. He wedged a thumbnail between his front teeth, thinking. "So what happened to the shipment?"

"Well, that's the big question, right?"

"Nah, the big question is, 'Will the Guild come after you?'"

Pierce sighed. "They might be already. It's only a matter of time."

"You gonna split?"

Pierce shook his head. "I could disappear, but probably not for long. If they come after me, they'll find me."

"What are you going to do?"

"Lay low, stay ahead of them, try to figure out what the fuck happened to Kransky's Large. If I can prove it, maybe I can make things right with the Guild."

"How are you going to prove it?"

"First, I need to find the sender, see if he knows

anything about the shipment I was carrying. You know Jimmy Serino, works for Frank Billings?"

"I know who he is. I heard he just started laundering."

"For Billings?" Pierce said. "He's been doing that for years."

"No, for years he's been *dealing* with the launderers, buying the Large. Now he's *selling* it. I don't know if he's still with Billings or not, but he's supply side now."

In the old days, money laundering was a complex operation, and for some it still was, but since the return to cash, the majority of it was basically taking in people's Small and selling them Large, reducing the physical volume of the cash so it was easier to deal with. And most important, ignoring the reporting requirements.

"Huh," Pierce said. "Seems kind of small fry for Billings to be getting into."

"That's what I thought. And he's apparently underselling everyone else by twenty percent."

"That must have pissed off Nigella and Mattson," Pierce said. They were the city's biggest launderers.

"Probably so." Dugray was quiet for a moment. "Anyway, I gotta get back to it."

"Okay, sure. Can you do me a favor, though?"

"What's that?"

"I can't go back to my place right now. Can I put some cash in your safe?"

"Yeah, no problem. How much you got?"

Pierce opened the attaché and took out his cash. "Around fifty."

"That's cool," he said, taking the bundled Large from Pierce, putting it aside.

"Thanks, man." Pierce took out his files on Fairview. "You should probably take these, too."

Dugray nodded as he leafed through the pages. "Anything new in here?"

"Actually, yeah," Pierce said. He took the papers back from Dugray and leafed through them until he found the pages he was looking for. "Here you go, Infinity Investments. Turns out Infinity is owned by a company called Garnet Holdings."

Dugray whistled. "Hey, man, that's not bad. We might actually be getting somewhere."

"Yeah, maybe so," Pierce said, resisting the sad smile trying to spread across his face. There could be dozens of layers still between them and the truth. Hundreds, even.

"Come on," Dugray said, getting to his feet. "Let's put these somewhere safe."

Pierce followed him up the steps to the third floor, where Dugray opened an old wooden door to reveal another door behind it, reinforced steel with an electronic keypad. Dugray entered a code and swung it open.

The door was two-inch steel plate and the walls were reinforced concrete. Inside the strong room were a couple of chairs and a small table. A floor-to-ceiling safe faced them from the far wall.

Dugray locked the door behind them, then opened the safe to reveal a space the size of a large walk-in closet. There were several shelves, the ones on top stacked with bundles of Large, and the lower ones lined with cloth bags stamped with denominations—$1, $5, $10, $20. The bags looked full.

Dugray put Pierce's cash and his Fairview files on the top shelf, all the way to the left. He looked inside an old cigar box and pulled out a bike card.

"Here, why don't you take this."

"A bike card?" Pierce furrowed his brow. "Why?"

"Sometimes a bike's the fastest way to get around the city." He added, "You got people coming after you, a card with someone else's name on it could come in handy."

"Right," Pierce said. "Yeah, okay. Thanks." He took the card.

Pierce stuffed the card into his wallet as Dugray closed the safe. Then they went back out into the hallway and Dugray locked the door to the strongroom. He turned to Pierce and paused, looking thoughtful. But before he could say anything, he was interrupted by a thunderous bang that sounded like it was coming from the front door.

Chapter Five

"WHAT THE FUCK is that?" Dugray said under his breath, as they hurried downstairs.

They were running down the hallway when the sound of windows breaking erupted from the second floor. Doors opened all around them and confused tweakers spilled out into the hallway.

Another loud bang shook the front door, and for a moment, all eyes in the crowded hallway turned toward it. Then the door exploded in splinters and a little green ball bounced down the hallway. The tweakers watched it roll, but Pierce and Dugray dove back into the room where they'd been talking earlier, squeezing their eyes shut and covering their ears.

The universe exploded in sound and light so intense the words *flash* and *bang* didn't quite capture it.

Pierce crumpled onto the floor next to Dugray, his ears ringing and his head spinning. For a moment, he wondered if this was some kind of all-out courier assault, but out in the hallway, he saw a figure in UniC-

SWAT tactical gear pressing Hutch up against the wall, by the throat.

"You in charge here?" the UniC said, through gritted teeth.

He loosened his grip just enough for Hutch to spit, "Fuck you."

The UniC punched him hard in the stomach, caught him with a knee to the chin on the way down, and then cracked a baton across the head for good measure. Hutch gurgled on the floor, like he was going to puke.

The UniC raised his baton to hit him again, but turned when Dugray said, "I'm in charge."

Pierce slid his attaché behind him and pulled his sleeve down over his cuff, keeping his head down.

He knew the guy, Ryan Mansfield. One of the more enthusiastic UniCon adherents. He'd been involved in the Fairview investigation—the one that never charged anyone. Pierce had encountered him a few times since. He wasn't the *biggest* asshole in UniC's New York unit, but no serious list of candidates would leave him off.

Mansfield walked up to Dugray. "You run this shithole?"

Dugray looked up but didn't say anything. Mansfield swatted his collar bone with a baton.

Dugray winced and rubbed his shoulder. "That's what I said."

"Well, lucky for you, we're not shutting you down," Mansfield said. "I don't know what kind of shit you people think you're trying to pull out there, but if you're hoping to make UniCon look bad before the conference, you better fucking think again, because you will regret it. Now, where the fuck is Townsend?"

"He just left," Dugray said. "Five minutes ago."

"Yeah, it seems everywhere I go, he just left." Mansfield crouched down so his face was level with Dugray's—and barely a foot from Pierce's.

"I want you to give your boss a message," Mansfield said. "We don't know what stupid shit he's trying to pull, what kind of deal he made with anyone else, or which one of his lowlife crew ripped him off." He raised his gloved hand and poked Dugray's forehead for emphasis. "And we don't." Poke. "Fucking." Poke. "Care." Poke.

Mansfield stood and looked down at Dugray. "We know he's been buying up businesses, trying to build a portfolio that'll make him look legit, take a run at promotion. But you tell that asshole he's not UniCon yet, and if he fucks with UniCon, he never will be. Can you remember that?"

Dugray nodded and Mansfield continued. "You tell him he makes the drop tomorrow, or he's on his own."

He was turning to go when he stopped and turned back. Pierce kept his head down, but he could see Mansfield's boots, inches away, now pointing at him.

"Well, well. Do I see a little errand boy?" Mansfield said. "Hanging out in a drug house?" He turned over his shoulder and barked. "Minton. Gonzalez."

Pierce looked up but didn't say anything as the two other UniCs hustled up and trained their guns on him.

Mansfield took a cautious step back, then laughed and shook his head. "Dipping into the candy jar, huh? I guess this is where you end up, huh? Getting a fix?"

"Making a delivery," Pierce said. "And you're interfering with it." He had every right to be there, making a delivery. He would have stood his ground if he wasn't on the run, but he didn't want to raise any suspicions.

Minton and Gonzalez looked at each other and

blanched as they realized they were interfering with a Guild courier. Their guns wavered.

Mansfield sneered at them, then turned back to Pierce. "You fucking guys, with your fucking titanium cuffs. You think you're special, don't you? Better than everyone else. Exempt from the rules. Well, not for long. Soon, the U-Net will be up and running, everything will go back to normal, and you courier-types can go back to delivering pizzas." He squinted and then snapped his fingers.

"Pierce, isn't it?" He turned to the UniC with the GONZALEZ name tag. "Run his name. 'Armand Pierce.' See if anyone's looking for him, if he's run off with anyone's precious cargo." He looked at Pierce and laughed. "Who knows, maybe we can reunite you with your dad."

Pierce wasn't afraid of the UniCs, but he didn't want them handing him over to the Guild.

His mind went into planning mode: push Dugray to safety; launch off him and incapacitate Gonzalez with a blow to the throat before he could radio headquarters; keep Gonzalez in front of him as he took his taser and used it on Minton. Then run like hell.

He was tensing himself to act when the muffled sounds of gunfire and shouting arose outside. He turned to Dugray, who raised an eyebrow.

As Pierce paused, Minton came forward and grabbed them each by the shoulder, dragging them to their feet and shoving them out into the hallway.

Pierce tugged his chain, dragging the attaché a little closer.

"Hands against the wall, assholes," Minton said, oblivious to the sounds outside, which was growing louder, individual gunshots accompanied by the staccato purr of automatic weapons.

With his hands against the wall, Pierce could feel the plaster trembling. The UniCs were brutal and sloppy, but they wouldn't be out there firing machine guns.

Minton paused, looking off to the side. "What the…?"

Pierce twisted away from him and crouched low, planting his shoulder into Dugray's midsection and launching them both back into the room behind them.

"Hey! What the fuck?" Minton said, twisting to scowl at them.

He pulled out his baton and flicked it open, but a burst of automatic weapons fire hit him from the side. Most of it hit his body armor, but one bullet found his temple and another tore through his throat. He fell forward through the doorway and slapped onto the floor with a soft, deflating grunt.

Pierce grabbed Minton's rifle without taking it off his body and raised it just as Feddie Perez, a Toro enforcer, appeared in the doorway.

Perez threw himself back as Pierce squeezed off a burst, then tumbled back into view, falling across Minton's legs, shot from behind by someone else.

Pierce turned to Dugray. "What the fuck is going on?"

"Looks like the Toros are moving on Townsend, as well." Dugray shook his head. "None of this shit makes sense."

"We need to get out of here."

Dugray shook his head. "I can't leave my house under attack. Townsend would put me down if he found out. Plus… these are my guys, but you need to get the fuck out of here." He opened the closet door and pushed Pierce inside, then kept pushing, through another door hidden in the back of it, and into what appeared to be another house.

"Keep going," he said. "Side door's to the left, then to the right. Opens out onto the side street."

Pierce resisted for a moment, turning back to Dugray. "But—"

Dugray shook his head. "Don't worry about me, man. We can handle the Toros, and this UniC shit ain't going to stick to me. Townsend ain't UniCon, but he's connected. But if you got the Guild after you instead of behind you, you need to go. See if you can figure this shit out before they find your hand in a wastebasket and the rest of you in the river."

PIERCE SLIPPED OUT onto the street, tucked the attaché and chain under his Thintech jacket, and ran, the sounds of gunfire fading as he sprinted toward his car, grateful now that he hadn't been able to find a closer spot. He'd thought about stashing the case at Dugray's, but decided that, for the moment, the privileges that came with being a Courier outweighed the risks of being identified.

The rain had eased up, but the streets and sidewalks were half underwater. Pierce splashed through the shallower puddles and tried to avoid the deeper ones. His head was still ringing from the flashbang, but as the noise from Dugray's house faded behind him, he could hear sirens blaring and helicopters and drones buzzing overhead. The smell of smoke mixed with the rain, and that goddamned BetterLate incense that suddenly seemed to be everywhere.

The city was roiling. It wasn't just about a few gangs, or about a fight breaking out at a council meeting. It seemed to be everywhere.

He needed to talk to Serino, find out if there'd been

anything unusual about that Large, anything at all. He needed the Guild back on his side.

He walked past his car once to make sure no one was watching it, then doubled back, quickly got in and started it up, surging away from the curb. He drove manually for a quarter mile, then turned on Smartdrive and entered the address Diaz had given him for Jimmy Serino, in Queens. Then he sank down in his seat.

He felt vulnerable and alone. His mother was dead, his dad was in prison, and his coworkers could be coming after him at any moment. His only real friend was Dugray, and he had his own problems to deal with.

There was no law or rule that couriers couldn't be married—it wasn't like being a priest or anything—but the job was dangerous and demanding. Most of the couriers he knew with kids only saw them every other weekend.

But some of them made it work. He wondered if he could have been one of them, but then the question was irrelevant; Gloriana was gone and no one since her had come close.

Looking out the window, he realized he was just down the block from the plaza where they'd met. It had been at one of the early UniCon protests, the big ones, before they were an everyday thing.

As SOON AS he'd heard about the protest, he'd known he had to go. He'd never thought of himself as the kind of guy who went to protests, but the way UniCon was taking over everything was crazy. He didn't have a sign or anything, but when he got there, he saw a little stand set up by Free World, the organizers, with cardboard and markers and paint for people to make their own.

The woman running the stand was wearing a bright red FREE WORLD T-shirt. She invited him to grab whatever he needed to make his sign and thanked him for showing up. She was striking, Southeast Asian, and roughly his age, early twenties. She had an intensity about her, but a friendliness, too.

He thanked her for helping to organize the event. "What should I write?"

She smiled. "Whatever you want," she said. "Write whatever you feel."

Her smile made him want to keep talking to her, like he'd be comfortable talking with her, but before he could think of anything to say, she peered around him and cocked an eyebrow. He turned and saw a line of people accumulating behind him. When he turned back her smile widened—warm, familiar, slightly apologetic, with a tug of laughter at the corner.

"Sorry," he said, as he stepped off to the side to write his sign. He couldn't think of anything great, and he didn't want to be lurking over her, so he rushed to finish.

She gave him that smile again as he returned the markers. He mumbled, "Thanks," and left her alone, realizing that she was just being friendly, her job was to make him feel welcome.

But fifteen minutes later, standing in the middle of the crowd waiting for the rally to start, feeling out of place but determined to stay, he sensed someone standing next to him.

It was the woman from the sign-making stand. She looked up at him with that smile, squinting into the late-September, late-afternoon sunlight. "I like your sign!"

She was carrying a sign with neat letters in bright red paint, saying MAYBE INSTEAD OF RULING THE

WORLD, YOU COULD JUST PAY SOME FUCKING TAXES. Pierce's sign just said FUCK U! in thick green marker.

"Very succinct," she said, grinning.

"Thanks," he said. He was about to apologize, explain that he couldn't think of anything better, but then he leaned closer, looked around, and said, "But between you and me, I don't know why everyone is so upset about unicorns."

She had looked confused for a second; then she started laughing.

"I mean, don't get me wrong," he went on, "Sparkles and rainbows? *Ick!* I hate 'em as much as the next person. But people say they're taking over the world and, to be honest, I've never even seen one."

She laughed even more, a melodic sound like wind chimes or piano keys, punctuated by less melodic snorts that made her laugh harder.

"So what's with the sign, then?" she asked, playing along.

"Well..." He thought for a moment. "I guess it just bothers me that they're so disingenuous."

She tilted her head, like she was trying to determine if he was funny or just weird.

"I mean, they're not uni-*corns* at all, are they?" he said, quietly conspiratorial. "They're uni-*horns*, right?"

He gave her an exaggerated wink and nod of the head and she laughed even more, nodding with him, like that made perfect sense.

"I'm Gloriana," she said, her eyes sparkling.

"I'm Armand Pierce. My friends call me Pierce."

The PA system cut them off with an eruption of feedback followed by a voice introducing the first speaker, then the roar of the crowd, then the speaker herself.

Pierce was determined that as soon as this speaker was done, he was going to try to get Gloriana's number or ask her out, but a darker energy seemed to be descending on the gathering from the outside. The crowd surged, and the people who had been standing behind them suddenly pushed between them. Pierce looked out and saw a line of UniCs in riot gear almost encircling the crowd.

This was right after UniCon had taken over the police—that's what had sparked this particular protest. It was the first time Pierce had seen the UniCs, and he was shocked by how many of them there were, how armed and armored they were.

He started pushing his way toward where Gloriana had been standing, to warn her that things were about to get ugly, that maybe they should leave. But a wave of screams rose up from the left, and then another from the right, as the UniCs closed in on the crowd, squeezing it from opposite directions. The scene descended into panic as people ran in every direction with nowhere to go.

Pierce knew he needed to get out of there, but even more, he needed to find Gloriana. He saw a flash of her red shirt maybe thirty feet away. She was looking around frantically, her eyes stark with fear. Their eyes met, locked for an instant; then she turned to her right and plunged into the crowd. The crowd crushed around him as he went after her. He saw two UniCs chasing her, following her red T-shirt. Targeting her.

When he caught up with them, she was sprawled across the pavement and they were standing over her. Each held a hot stick behind their back, sparking ominously.

They both moved toward her, and without thinking, Pierce ran up behind them and grabbed the two hot sticks, pushing them each into the other one's thigh.

He wasn't sure it would affect them through their armor, but they both went rigid, trembling as the current coursed through them.

Gloriana looked up at him and he shouted, "Go on, get out of here!"

Her eyes stayed on him for an instant; then she scrambled away and disappeared into the crowd.

Pierce held the hot sticks in place for a few moments longer, afraid to hurt the UniCs, but afraid to let go. Then he saw another UniC charging straight for him with a gun in one hand and a truncheon in the other, swinging it indiscriminately, clearing a path through the crowd.

Pierce let go of the hot sticks and ran, pushing through the crowd as the UniC followed him, closer and closer. Fifty feet away, he could see the street, and he thought that if he could just reach it, he could lose his pursuer. But twenty feet from the sidewalk, he ran straight into a temporary fence, ten feet high, set up by the UniCs to contain them.

He turned and saw the UniC just a few feet away from him, a storm trooper in black riot gear, helmet and shiny faceplate. As the UniC raised his truncheon over his head, Pierce saw a flash of red to his right, and a woman's voice called out, "Hey, asshole!"

Pierce and the UniC both looked over, and there was Gloriana, holding a little plastic bucket. Before Pierce could figure out what it was, she'd thrown it, coating the UniC's faceplate—and much of the rest of him—with bright red paint.

She stepped to the side as the UniC lunged at her, swinging his club blindly. Pierce shoved him to the ground, and together, he and Gloriana plunged back into the crowd.

He took off the flannel shirt he was wearing over his T-shirt and gave it to her, shouting over the mayhem, "Put this on!"

She looked confused at first, but blanched when she looked down at her bright red FREE WORLD T-shirt. Pierce had intended for her to put his shirt on over hers, but she stopped and peeled her shirt off, right there in the crowd. Amid the mayhem, no one else seemed to notice, but Pierce did. He looked away, almost but not quite immediately.

Then she grabbed his hand and tugged. "This way!"

She led the way, through the violence and confusion, somehow finding a way through the UniC enclosure and out onto the street. They zigged and zagged down seemingly random streets, taking them out of harm's way.

After several blocks, they slowed to a trot, then a walk, then they stopped altogether. She turned to him with a soft smile and said, "Want to get a drink?"

Yes, he did.

They found a bar and got to know each other over IPAs and Irish whiskey.

Gloriana was a scientist, a PhD student at Princeton working on a joint project with NYU. She was from Malaysia, from a village that had been destroyed by oil spills, and she was working on a technology that she hoped would prevent that from ever happening again.

He told her about being drafted, two years in the Army, and coming home to an unrecognizable world. He told her about his parents' divorce, how his dad, the high-flying investment banker, had cut Pierce and his mother off, refusing to pay child support, forcing them to live in a dingy subsidized high-rise, before he was arrested, convicted, and sent to prison for massive fraud. It still filled him with shame and anger, but he told her about it anyway.

She told him how she had lost her parents, how they both crumbled under the challenges of life as refugees far from home, about her own challenges.

But between their sad stories, they made each other laugh, telling morbid jokes about the tragedies they had endured. The energy between them crackled with the possibility of something extraordinary.

When it was time to go, she walked him back to his car.

He insisted on driving her home, to Princeton. They had more drinks at her place and ended up in bed. She didn't want him to leave and he didn't want to go. He stayed for three days and got fired by the taxi company he'd been working for—a month before they laid off all the drivers and switched over to AI.

She called him the next night. He called her the night after that.

The following Friday, they went out for dinner and he stayed at her place until Monday. For the next nine months, they were together almost every weekend, first at her place in Princeton, but more and more at his place in the Village.

They showed each other unfamiliar parts of the city, new bands, new bars, new foods. She expanded his horizons about science and politics, sometimes pretty radical stuff. He didn't agree with her about everything, but she always made perfect sense.

Pierce had always thought of himself as pretty smart. Gloriana was in another strata entirely, but she carried her brilliance in a way that never made him feel stupid, that actually made him feel smarter when he was around her.

He'd fallen hard. He thought she had, too.

In retrospect, he recognized that she had always seemed to be holding something back. He didn't mind. He *liked* that she had mysteries, that there was always more to learn about her.

She was busy with her work, and he respected that. Maybe the fact that he couldn't see her all the time made him long for her that much more. Maybe otherwise he wouldn't have fallen so hard.

He only met her friends a couple of times, and never hung out with them. 'Work friends,' she called them. She gave him the impression that when she wasn't with him, she was at work. She always wanted to get him back home, to his place or her place. He didn't mind that either. Being at home with Gloriana was a *lot* of fun.

They'd been seeing each other for eight months when her lease ran out and the Oslo fellowship came up. Pierce proposed the obvious—or what he thought was obvious, at the time: They should get a place together.

She said no. She didn't even have to think about it. She actually kind of laughed when she said it, a derisive snort that, up until then, was the meanest thing she had ever said to him.

"Why not?" he had asked.

She'd rolled her eyes. "Look, we've got a good thing going. Why do you want to mess that up? Next thing you'll be wanting to get *married*." She'd laughed at that, but he hadn't, not quickly enough. She had laughed even harder. "Seriously? Marriage?"

"What's wrong with that?" he asked. The memory of it burned, the memory of his humiliation, of realizing how wrong he had gotten things.

"What's wrong with being *chattel*?" she'd demanded.

"What's wrong with never seeing anyone else? Being tied to one person?"

"Well, that wouldn't be any different from now, would it?"

She had gone quiet then.

"I love you," he had said. The first time he said it.

"I care about you, too," she had said.

She'd kept on talking, but he barely heard it.

She pointed out that they had never said they were monogamous or exclusive. They were having fun. And she wanted to be able to have fun with other people, too. As much as it hurt to find out about those other people, he couldn't stay mad at her. She was right; they'd never said anything like that.

He felt stupid. He felt hurt. He felt he had to take a stand. So he did.

He'd never said she had done anything *wrong*, though. Just that he couldn't go on like that.

She'd agreed, and it broke his heart.

She broke it a second time when she landed in prison.

It hurt to think of her wasting away in there, but it also made him angry. The world was so fucked up, and here was this brilliant scientist, this amazing human being who had devoted her life to fixing it, and she was being held in prison by the people most responsible for fucking it up in the first place.

Anger and sadness and pain roiled inside of him. He was trying to push it down, to pack it away, when the car announced that he was approaching his destination.

He shook his head vigorously to clear it and sat up, looking out the window to get his bearings.

Jimmy Serino's house stood out starkly in the middle of a block of indistinguishable boxy brick twins in Queens.

Serino had apparently bought both sides of the twin and combined them, then added a third floor, a driveway, and a garage, although the house still seemed dwarfed by the outsized concrete fountains and tacky statues crowding the narrow space between it and the wrought-iron fence. The fence extended all the way up to the houses on either side, as if Serino had bought their yards from them, or simply ignored the property line and dared them to do anything about it.

It was a very mob move, and a very mob remodeling job. But of course, the impunity that used to come from Serino's mob ties now came from UniCon.

Pierce parked down the block and got out. The sidewalks were damp, and a light rain started falling again as he walked toward Serino's house.

The windows were dark.

He pressed the call button on a security panel mounted on a concrete pillar next to the gate. The rain started coming down harder. He pressed it again after a minute, but there was no answer.

Of course.

He pulled the car up next to Serino's driveway, maxed out his windows' reflectivity, so no one could see in, and turned on the car's front-end proximity alert. Then he got comfortable.

Sitting in his car in front of Jimmy Serino's house, he drifted off to sleep wondering what his life could have been like if he hadn't rushed things with Gloriana, hadn't made those assumptions about their relationship, hadn't reacted so badly when they'd turned out to be wrong. He wondered how different things could be— Would Gloriana still be in prison? Would he be hiding from the Guild in his car?

Chapter Six

THE HOUSEPLANTS WERE dying. Gloriana had been neglecting them. It was understandable really. She knew she wouldn't be there forever.

It made her think about leaving, and that made her think of Matina, her cat when she was a girl. She rarely thought of Matina, because whenever she did, even all these years later, the pain of losing her came back as if it had just happened.

Relocation was supposed to be temporary, but even at the time, even as a little girl, Gloriana knew—everyone knew, even Matina—that nothing would ever be the same.

Her parents tried to reassure her, but they weren't very good at it. She could tell they were lying.

The last night in their old village, she saved part of her dinner and fed it to Matina. It was fish, but her father hadn't caught it—they didn't know it then, but he would never fish again. This was fish brought in from somewhere else, somewhere clean. But the smell of oil so permeated everything that even food brought in from afar tasted like it had come from the blackened ocean lapping on their shore.

Gloriana clearly remembered that she did not cry, but she felt sadder that night than she'd ever felt before, or probably since. Matina stayed with her, like she did most nights. But instead of curling up against Gloriana's thigh, she sat erect at the foot of the bed, alert and attentive. Neither of them slept until Gloriana finally drifted off, shortly before dawn.

When she awoke, it was to the sound of trucks approaching.

Matina had brought her a rat. It lay dead on Gloriana's chest, its legs curled up and its feet black with tar. Matina was sitting on Gloriana's tummy, staring at her intently over the rat, as if trying to tell her something. Gloriana could practically hear her saying, *This is important. You understand, don't you?*

She understood that the message was important, but she didn't know what it was. She was still puzzling over it when her father appeared and said, "It's time to go."

Matina jumped off the bed as Gloriana scrambled up and got dressed. Her father smiled sadly as she put on layer over layer, as many of her favorite clothes as she could.

When she bent to pick up Matina, he said, "The cat stays."

Gloriana looked up at him, stunned. She knew she was only to bring the clothes she'd be wearing. They had talked about that. But it never occurred to her that meant leaving Matina.

"She'll be fine," her father had said. "Cats are always fine. They find a way."

"But…"

"We'll be back soon, anyway." Such a bad liar.

The truck pulled up outside, its brakes screeching loudly. Startled by the sound, Matina jumped onto the windowsill and looked at Gloriana. Then something on the truck banged, and Matina vanished through the window.

Gloriana never saw her again.

"We'll come back soon," her father said again, too sad and weary to even try to sound convincing.

Gloriana tried to run after Matina, though she knew it was pointless. Her mother tried to comfort her as her father picked her up, screaming and flailing, and carried her to the truck.

She no longer recognized her village. The beach looked like another planet, covered in thick brown goo, scattered with brightly colored plastic—buckets and long tubes and things she didn't recognize. The people looked like they were from another planet as well, dressed in moon suits to protect them from the beach that Gloriana had walked barefoot her entire life.

Her mother got into the back of the big military transport truck and her father lifted Gloriana and passed her up. By then, the fight had gone out of her. She was limp.

Most of the village had left the day before. Gloriana was the only child remaining, the only child in the back of that truck. Everyone looked at her with pity. And she looked back at them with pity as well. They seemed sad and old, resigned to being shipped off to places they didn't know, where they would eventually die without ever feeling at home again.

The truck lurched as they started, and Gloriana looked

out the back, watching what was left of her village shrinking behind her, realizing it was gone forever.

Even after so many years, she still missed Matina, and as she finished watering the plants in the living room and moved to the dining room, she wondered, as she had so many times, what had become of her.

The jade plant in the dining room window had grown leggy and its leaves were turning yellow. The black mold had returned. She was running out of places to put the plant, and she feared the entire house was simply too humid.

It was strangely important to her that she find a place where it would be happy. She went into the kitchen and returned with a damp, soapy cloth.

Wiping the leaves soothed her, and she thought in a more detached way about why she was reacting the way she was. She hated this place, had dreamed of leaving it since she first set foot in it. But the thought saddened her now.

Leaving was always hard. Change was always frightening.

Chapter Seven

IT WAS JUST after six a.m. when the car's proximity alert sounded. Pierce woke up, momentarily disoriented, and looked out his window to see a brand new Audi squeezing past the front of his car to get through Serino's gate.

As soon as the Audi was inside, the gate slid closed again. Two women got out, one in her late forties, one in her late teens, both moving quickly and purposefully as they strode to the front door and disappeared inside.

Pierce vigorously rubbed his face to wake himself up; then he attached his chain to his cuff, got out of the car, and walked to the gate.

He pressed the button on the intercom and after a couple of seconds, the speaker crackled, and a woman's voice said, "Did you find him?"

"Um, I beg your pardon?"

"Wait, are you with the UniCs? Sorry, I mean, the UC Force?"

"Um… no, ma'am." He held up his attaché. "I'm a courier."

"Well, if you're looking for Jimmy, he ain't here."

"Do you know when he'll be home?"

She laughed, a high-pitched, unhinged kind of laugh. "No," she said. "No, I don't."

"I see. And do you know where I might find him?"

"Jesus Christ, all these questions. He's not here, okay? And don't tell me I'm a secondary recipient or any of that bullshit. His stuff is his stuff, and I am not going to get caught up in it. I don't have time for this shit, so get the fuck out of here before I call the UniCs!"

After another tiny burst of static, the speaker went quiet. Pierce heard a metal clunk, followed by the grinding screech of metal on metal. Off to the side, the daughter stepped out through the driveway gate and leaned against the pillar, hiding from the windows.

Pierce moved closer to her and smiled.

She didn't smile back. "Are you sure you're a courier?"

He held up his attaché, letting his sleeve fall back to show her his cuff. She winced and screwed up her face. "Ugh. That's so gross. I would never do that."

"I used to feel the same way," Pierce said. "Sometimes I still do."

She studied him for another second, then tilted her head at the house. "Sorry about that. She's scared. You're not the first person who's come around looking for my dad."

"Who else has been by?"

She shrugged. "Other people. Angry people."

"Angry about what?"

She paused for a moment, as if realizing that she was oversharing. Then she shrugged and said, "They're saying he robbed them. But he didn't."

"How do you know?"

She laughed, a sad and weary laugh she shouldn't have been capable of at her age. "I don't know everything my dad does. I know it's fucked up, but I also know it isn't robbing people. Especially not his own customers, people he does business with. My dad's an asshole, but he's not an idiot."

"Did he call the UniCs?"

She shook her head. "He used to think they were great. UniCon, the UniCs, the whole deal. But not anymore."

"Why not?"

She shrugged and looked away. "He's an asshole, my dad. But you know... he's my dad." She wiped her eye with a knuckle. "He's been scared lately. Really scared. I've never seen him afraid before."

"Scared of what?"

"I don't know what and I don't know who, really." She looked down. "I guess the people coming looking for him."

"Do you know where I can find him?"

She dipped her head toward his attaché. "Is that really for him?"

"Yes," Pierce lied.

She glanced at her watch. "Well, if he's not here, he's at Billings Tower. Especially lately. He works there." She laughed again, sharp and bitter. "I mean, as far as I know."

"Why do you say that?"

"He and Frank had a big fight."

"Billings?"

She nodded.

"When?" Pierce asked.

"The night before last. He was already scared, I think, but after that, he was, like, shaking."

"What did they fight about?"

"I don't know. He fought with my mom, too. He said he couldn't trust UniCon anymore. He said, like, 'I got nowhere else to go.'" She imitated her dad as she said it, a cartoonish lampoon of his New Yorker accent—an accent she didn't share. It would have been comical if not for the tears it immediately prompted.

"I called there yesterday. They said he wasn't there."

She eyed his attaché with a smirk. "Did they know you had an attaché full of money for him?"

Pierce smiled but didn't answer.

The smirk fell away from her face and she stared at him, deadly serious.

"Do you think he's dead?" she asked.

"I'm sure he's okay," Pierce said.

She sighed and folded her arms. "Well, if he's not dead yet, he probably will be soon."

"Why do you say that?"

She glanced around then leaned back, looking around the wall, up at the house, as if checking to make sure she wasn't being watched. "Are you the guy he sent to Alaska?"

"What do you know about that?"

She hugged herself and shook her head. "Just that it's part of whatever got him so scared. He said it was big. Huge... He told me he loves me." She started crying again. "He never says that."

PIERCE GOT BACK in his car, intending to head straight over to Billings Tower and talk to Serino. But then he caught a glimpse of himself in the rearview mirror— eyes crusty, hair disheveled, looking like... well, like he had spent the night in his car.

He was surprised Serino's daughter had even spoken to him. He stopped at a coffee shop and ordered coffee and a breakfast sandwich, then went into the restroom to tidy himself up.

There was a payphone out front, so while he waited for his order, he called Dugray's A-house to tell him what Serino's daughter had said.

A voice that wasn't Dugray's answered, "'Sup." It sounded like Marcus.

Pierce said who he was, and that he was looking for Dugray. Marcus said, "Dugray said if you called I should tell you he's down in Alphabet City, at a new place he's running down at Seventh and C. He'll be down there all day."

"There a phone down there?" Pierce asked.

"I got no idea." Marcus hung up.

Pierce didn't take it personally. The message had been delivered; there was nothing else to say.

He picked up his coffee and sandwich, feeling almost human as he got back into his car. But as he pulled away from the curb, he spotted a yellow Honda in his rearview, pulling out after him. The windows were tinted, but he could make out the silhouettes of the two figures in it, and as they followed him on a turn, the flash of reflections from the driver's mirrored shades.

Pierce's stomach clenched, but then an icy calm settled over him. Mirrored shades meant Erno's disciples; neither of them was tall enough to be Erno himself. Probably young, which meant he could probably take them.

But he couldn't hurt them. If it came down to them or him, he wouldn't hesitate, but they were just following orders, protecting the sanctity of the Guild. He could still get out from under the Kransky thing if he could prove whatever was happening with the Large wasn't his fault, but if he hurt or killed couriers doing Guild business, that would be the end of it. The end of him.

He spotted a big box home improvement store on his right and abruptly turned into the parking lot. The yellow Honda followed him.

He parked in the contractor pickup area, right next to the cyclone fence that enclosed it, then ran inside, leaving his attaché and chain in the car. The store was a cornucopia of potential weapons: blades and power tools, toxic and flammable substances, and all manner of blunt objects. But he already had weapons; he was looking for something else.

Less than three minutes after walking in the door, the young woman at the register had rung him up. The longest part of the errand was when he took out his wallet to pay.

"Fuck," he said, earning a raised eyebrow from the cashier.

Inside his wallet were ten twenties. The hundreds were gone.

He blew into his wallet, kicking up a small cloud of dust. "Fuck," he said again. Whatever was happening with the money, it was real. He wasn't imagining it. And he was out five hundred bucks.

The cashier cleared her throat.

"Sorry," Pierce said, distantly. He handed her a twenty and she gave him his change. He borrowed her scissors and cut open the plastic package, slipping the contents into his pockets.

He paused at the exit to collect himself, banishing the newly disappeared Large from his mind and reclaiming his earlier calm. This was no time to be distracted.

He checked the spikes in his breast pocket and the knives in his jacket and his boot, then arranged his purchases. With a deep breath, he pictured how the next minute would play out. Then he put his hands in his pockets and walked out the door.

He didn't see any sign of the other couriers until he was approaching his car. They stepped out from behind a contractor van parked next to him, one around the front, the other from the back.

They both wore shades and collarless sportscoats. They both looked young, barely twenty-one. Both carried attachés, connected to their wrists by short chains.

The one at the front of the van wore a smirk: smug and cruel and clearly copied from Erno. Pierce was pretty sure he was called Magnussen. He kept one hand behind his back.

The other one, a kid named Vance who had signed on a year earlier, looked more serious and more familiar. He cleared his throat. "Armand Pierce, the Guild has sanctioned you for disciplinary procedures. You need to come with us."

Pierce tried to look confused. "Why?" he asked. "What's this about?"

Magnussen let out a snort, and as Vance turned to scowl at him, an alarm went off inside the store. When Vance and Magnussen glanced toward the entrance, Pierce sprang.

Magnussen brought up a taser, but Pierce was quicker, slapping the weapon out of his hands, feinting to the left, then spinning to the right. He got behind Magnussen and slammed him into Vance, driving them both up against the cyclone fence. He grappled with them for a brief moment, then quickly backpedaled away.

They both launched themselves at him, then simultaneously fell to the ground, their left arms yanked awkwardly behind them, their short little chains attached to the fence by the padlocks Pierce had just purchased.

Magnussen groaned and clutched his shoulder, which looked dislocated.

Vance tried to maintain a dignified expression, even with his shades askew. "Assaulting couriers on official business? That's another infraction."

"I didn't assault you," Pierce said, leveling the taser at them as he opened his car door. "I *detained* you. I can't help it if you hurt yourselves trying to get free."

Magnussen muttered, "Fucking asshole."

Vance glared at him, then back at Pierce, getting in his car. "You really think you're going to get away? You think we're the only two couriers coming after you?" He laughed, a big fake guffaw. "You can't escape the Guild."

Pierce got in his car and drove off, tossing the taser out he window. Vance was right. The Guild had eyes and ears everywhere. As he drove back into Manhattan, he was pretty sure he picked up a black SUV on his tail. He groaned. Of course they knew his car.

He made an abrupt right turn, then another, followed by a left, zigzagging away from his pursuer. He found a tight parking spot between two vans on a side street and auto-parked into it. He connected his attaché and got out, clutching it to his midsection as he hustled down the street.

He thought about taking a Smartcab, but he couldn't risk it. Smartcabs were autonomous, self-directed AI, but they still had analog radio, just like the cabbies in the old movies, and that included a kind of fax. If the UniCs were looking for him, they'd have radioed his photo to

Smartcab dispatch, who would have forwarded it to the entire fleet.

Instead, he headed toward the subway. But as he turned a corner, he spotted a dinged-up indie cab with a human driver and waved it over. The driver lowered the window and Pierce pulled his hood down around his face. "You got a camera?"

"Is broken," the driver replied in a thick Bangladeshi accent. He leaned closer to the window as he spoke, making a point of not looking at Pierce's hooded face. He did glance at the attaché. "Where you going?"

"HiHo. New Ninth Street. Billings Tower."

The driver nodded but kept his eyes frontward. "Double fare to HiHo," the cabbie said. "You know that, right?"

Indie cabs could legally take fares into HiHo but couldn't pick them up there, so the double fare wasn't unusual: one fare for the trip in, another fare for the trip back, empty.

"Yeah, okay," Pierce said as he got in the back.

As they drove, Pierce eyed the row of photos taped to the dashboard: one of the wife, a group shot of the kids, and one of the whole family, each wearing the same forced smile as they stood in front of the house they were leaving behind, in the village they were leaving behind. In the life they were leaving behind. Visible in the background and along the edge of the photo was the emerald seawater that was chasing them away.

The sky had cleared enough that Pierce could see the gleaming towers reaching high into the air over the restructured ground of HiHo. Usually, their tops were lost in the clouds, but for the moment, they looked just like the tourist photos, springing up from the skyline like a glass-and-steel cowlick.

The break in the weather didn't last. By the time the cab was climbing the ramp into HiHo, the clouds had reassembled, obscuring the towers and washing everything else in dishwater gray.

Like much of the city, HiHo was separated from adjacent neighborhoods by sea walls and partitions, so that if one section flooded, the rest could stay dry. In HiHo's case, it probably also helped keep out the riffraff.

The ramps were like highway ramps, ascending steeply alongside each wall, then crossing over at the top and descending just as steeply on the other side—or not, in HiHo's case.

The cabbie seemed nervous as they came off the ramp into HiHo. Smartcabs zipped around them, fast and close. Any kind of collision would result in an automatic legal presumption of fault on the part of the indie.

Smartcabs were never at fault, of course. They were part of UniCon.

Pierce felt bad for the guy, and even though the rain had resumed and Billings Tower was still several blocks away, he leaned forward and said, "This is good."

The cabbie looked at him in the rearview, nodded gratefully and abruptly looked away, as if he had just remembered Pierce's concerns about the camera.

He told Pierce the fare—exactly double what was on the meter. He was grateful, but not *that* grateful.

Pierce paid the fare and tipped him. He was low on cash, but some things you don't skimp on. As soon as Pierce was out of the car, the cabbie pulled a hard U-turn that almost got him T-boned by a speeding Maserati with UniCon diplomatic plates. The cab swerved out of the way in a maneuver that must have reshaped the driver's internal organs.

The Billings Group's corporate headquarters was the least impressive behemoth in the neighborhood. It wasn't as tall or as shiny as the others, and the shine that it did have seemed garish and fake, like chromed plastic instead of metal. Like, if you looked close enough, you'd see it peeling around the edges.

Pierce found the real stuff more offensive—bastards soaking up so much wealth they trimmed their elevator buttons in platinum because they didn't know what else to do with it.

Walking along New Ninth Street, he didn't see another soul on foot. Partly this would be the weather, and maybe partly it was whatever was roiling the city. But mostly it was because the traffic in HiHo was in the air above him. He could hear a steady buzz of copters and drones, unseen in the thick gray clouds. It heightened his unease.

A pair of guards patrolled the courtyard in front of the building. They were private, their body armor and weapons top of the line. Both of their heads turned to follow Pierce as he approached, but they didn't acknowledge him in any other way.

The exterior glass was nearly opaque—fogged with condensation on the inside and pebbled with drizzle on the outside. The door slid open, and Pierce stepped into the lobby, an atrium with four low-slung sofas and tables surrounding an imposing reception desk.

Two plainclothes security types stood just inside the entrance, and another pair stood by the elevators. Their arms, chests, and shoulders bulged with muscles, and everywhere else bulged with poorly concealed weaponry. They all wore dark shades and earpieces. Their heads swiveled to track him as he walked up to the reception desk.

The woman standing there was pretty, with a professional polish that she seemed too young for. Fresh out of business school, probably marketing, hoping to work her way up in the organization. Her name tag read BRIN. She smiled and said, "Can I help you, sir?"

Piece raised his attaché. "Courier. I am here to see James Serino."

"Certainly. One moment."

She picked up the phone and turned away, speaking in a hushed voice. A moment later, she turned back. "I'm sorry, Mr. Serino is not in today. Is anyone else authorized to accept delivery?"

Pierce took a deep breath, trying to hide his disappointment as he considered his next move. The fact that his other Large had vanished from his wallet meant that maybe this wasn't about the Serino shipment after all, but Serino was still his best chance at figuring out what the hell was going on, and Frank Billings, while a distant second at best, was all he had. "Frank Billings, please."

Brin paused, one eyebrow slightly raised, her face a half-shade paler under her makeup. Then she said, "Of course," and picked up the phone again.

Pierce felt bad for her. People who worked for these quasi-legit conglomerates were always wondering where they stood in the world, wondering who was corporate and who was gangster. Bad enough worrying about pissing off a good old-fashioned douchebag boss, but knowing that douchebag might have a few dead bodies in his past must take that stress to a whole new level.

Another young woman appeared at Pierce's elbow, a couple of inches shorter than Brin and a shade less attractive, but otherwise an almost perfect understudy. Her nametag read DEENA.

Brin put down the phone and looked up at Pierce. Her smile had returned but it was smaller, harder, and colder.

"Follow me," she said as she came out from behind the desk. Deena stepped wordlessly into her spot.

Pierce followed Brin to the elevators. She waved her card over a glass panel and pressed one of the buttons that appeared. As they waited for the doors to open, one of the guards walked up behind them.

When the doors opened, all three of them got in.

When the doors opened again, Brin strode briskly out into a plush seating area. A partially frosted glass partition separated it from a large, open office with floor-to-ceiling windows that looked out at the midsections of the taller towers surrounding them. Tinted glass tempered the bright sunlight. The carpet was white, and so was the furniture, except for a heavy, dark wooden desk where Frank Billings was seated.

He was moderately handsome and fit, just a few years older than Pierce. He had a nice tan, maybe even a real one, and a veneer of corporate respectability. He looked like maybe he'd had some cosmetic work done, but his nose was defiantly pug-like. On the surface, being rich agreed with him, but his eyes told a different story. They were cold and hard, with something manic underneath, both stressed and giddy, like the pressures of his life were too much to bear, but the rewards were too great to give up.

Or maybe he was high.

The air was thick with cologne. It didn't smell cheap, but it didn't smell good either.

Standing next to the desk was an older man with the creased, hangdog face of a Russian diplomat and the dead black eyes of an assassin, now staring blankly at Pierce.

Behind them, another pair of guards bulged in the corners of the room. They held automatic weapons, and their fingers rested on the triggers.

Pierce glanced out the windows, at the narrow terrace outside. The granite was damp, but the sun beat down on it from a crystal blue sky, brilliant even through the tinted glass. Something grayish-white floated slowly past, just past the edge of the terrace, and Pierce realized it was the top of a cloud. He thought about Billings and the other UniCon types, basking in the sun up there while the rest of the city was stuck under that blanket of gray.

Billings cleared his throat and straightened some of the papers on his desk into a semi-neat pile. "Saturday morning and it's all fucking work, work, work." He turned to the older man, and said, "Ain't that right, Litchenko?"

Litchenko didn't respond in any way, but that was good enough for Billings, who turned and squinted at Pierce. "You got a delivery for me? Let's get it over with. I'm busy." He snapped his fingers at one of the guards. "Go get that courier thingy."

"Actually," Pierce said, keeping his voice absolutely level, "it's not a delivery, it's an inquiry."

Billings looked at Brin, who blanched, then at Litchenko, who didn't react. But the mood in the room changed. The goons stiffened. They seemed nervous, like maybe they didn't like their odds against a Guild courier. Pierce didn't share their assessment. They were well-armed, on edge, and far enough away from him that one of them was likely to get him before he could take down all three.

"An inquiry, huh?" Billings said, with a forced smile that bristled with hostility.

"Yes, that's right," Pierce said. "I was hoping to talk to James Serino."

"Well, he's not here today," Billings said, annoyed, maybe as much by Serino not being there as by being asked about it.

"The Fargo Courier Agency is investigating a shipment Mr. Serino sent from this location, yesterday morning. Cash, to a Mr. Kransky in Utqiaġvik, Alaska. Do you know anything about that shipment?"

Billings screwed up his face in what seemed to be a genuine rendition of confused dismissal. "Are you kidding me? A company this big? You know how many shipments we got coming in and going out every day? Jesus Christ."

"Are you aware of any irregularities with this one?"

Billings looked genuinely perplexed. "No. Should I be? What kind of irregularities?"

Pierce paused, wondering how much to tip his hand. But without Serino, Billings was all he had, and he wasn't going to get a second chance to question him.

"The cash disappeared from inside the attaché."

Billings froze. Litchenko was already frozen—that seemed to be his resting state—but Brin and the goons froze, too, picking up on Billings' body language. Even the air in the room seemed suddenly frozen in time.

"Where was this shipment to?" Billings asked, his voice tight.

"Alaska," Pierce said. "Utqiaġvik."

Billings went quiet again, as if processing.

Outside, a hot dog wrapper skittered across the terrace. Pierce glanced at it, wondering if it had fallen from one of the taller towers or blown all the way up there on an updraft. The wind pushed up a mound of cloud, like a slow-motion ocean wave breaking against the nearby towers. Tufts of it spilled up and over the low wall surrounding the rooftop terrace.

Billings barked out a laugh. "Vanished from inside the attaché, huh? Sounds like maybe one of your couriers got some sticky fingers." He laughed again and shook his head. "Jesus, isn't making sure our Large doesn't vanish exactly what we pay you people for?"

Pierce frowned. "Why do you assume it was just Large?"

Billings glanced at Litchenko with an expression Pierce couldn't quite read. It was as if he was if expecting a scolding. But Litchenko stared back with all the expressiveness of a cinderblock.

Then Billings smiled and turned back to Pierce. "Because money's like people. Nobody gives a shit about Small."

Litchenko smiled. Pierce couldn't tell if it was mirth or relief.

"Anyway," Billings went on, "seems like there's a lot of that going around, from what I hear. All sorts of half-assed organizations getting heisted. Maybe this Kransky doesn't know how to run a business."

"Kransky's UniCon."

Billings snorted and leaned forward. "Well, just because he's UniCon, doesn't mean he knows what the fuck he's doing."

Litchenko frowned. Pierce fought to keep his eyebrows in place. It was almost unheard of for anyone on the inside to say anything remotely critical of UniCon.

Billings sat back in his chair and crossed his arms. He seemed quite pleased with himself and not pleased at all with Pierce. He gave off the distinct impression that the conversation was coming to a close.

"Do you know anything about Serino laundering money?" Pierce asked.

The shock and disbelief that twisted Billings' face was so obviously fake it gave Pierce hope that he might actually be onto something. The annoyance on his face, however, seemed absolutely genuine. "Laundering?" Fake laugh. "I don't know anything about that."

Billings had been a criminal at least since his early twenties and was now a UniCon CEO—he was surely an experienced liar. But he didn't come across as the kind of skilled sociopath who could totally hide his reactions. He seemed annoyed at Serino, which made sense if they'd been arguing, and if he hadn't shown up for work without calling in.

"Really? I understand you were known to use launderers in the past."

"Yeah, well, whatever I did or didn't do in the *past* is irrelevant." He spread his hands over the papers on his desk. "As you can see, I'm a legitimate businessman."

"So I guess he was out on his own?" Pierce asked.

"If he was doing that, then yeah, he was doing it on his own," Billings replied. "This is a lot of fucking questions you got, and like I said, I'm busy as hell, so..."

"Sorry," Pierce said, looking down, trying to appear contrite. "It's just that some of the people Serino was transacting with have been complaining about getting robbed afterward."

"Well, I don't know anything about that either."

"Had Serino been doing any business with the Shakes or the Toros?" Pierce asked, trying to sound conversational.

"The Shakes or the Toros?" Billings rolled his eyes as he stood up from his desk and came around to where

Pierce was standing. The smell of the cologne grew exponentially stronger.

The clouds outside rose higher still, and the room darkened as the sunlight dissolved and the other towers faded behind a gray curtain.

"I keep telling you, and you're not listening," Billings snarled. "We got nothing to do with any of those people. This is a legitimate business. We're in carbon fuels, pharmaceuticals, engineering, transportation. We got nothing to do with fucking street gangs."

"Did you and Serino have an argument recently? Yesterday or the day before?"

Billings' face darkened. "Fuck no. Why? What the fuck is this about?"

The room seemed to mirror Billings' face, darkening further as everything outside was obscured by a dull gray wall. Before the tinted glass could lighten, two strips of fluorescent tubes came on overhead, bathing the room in a sickly light. Suddenly, it didn't seem so plush. The white carpet was worn and scuffed. The edges of the sofa were frayed.

Billings looked up at Pierce, his eyes flashing with anger. "I don't know what the fuck you want, but I don't need to put up with your courier bullshit. I'm fucking UniCon, and you're nothing." He spat—literally spat—on his own white carpet. "I got plantations in Brazil goddamnit, factories in a dozen countries. I own an energy company. A fucking *energy* company, asshole! I own processing plants in Russia, Venezuela, Angola, Canada. I got a big fucking airplane and I fly it myself. I even got my own island, with an airstrip big enough I can land that motherfucker right on it. I even give money to those pain-in-the-ass BetterLates, trying to save the fucking world. I'm that kind of legit, asshole!" He took another deep, heaving breath. "And you come in here, asking me about fucking *money laundering?*"

Part of Pierce's brain was rechecking the scenarios: How was he going to take out the three guards and get out of there? The answer was unchanged: He wasn't. Each scenario ended with him bleeding out on the white carpet.

"Didn't mean any offense," Pierce said, edging closer to the elevator. "Like I said, we're conducting an inquiry. There've been rumors of money disappearing. Vanishing Large, like you said. Crumbling or disintegrating."

Billings' eye twitched as he stared at Pierce. "I don't know nothing about any of that," he said, practically whispering even though his chest was heaving. "But it sounds like bullshit to me."

Pierce pushed the button, and was relieved when it responded to his touch, and the doors opened immediately. "Thank you for your time," he said as he stepped inside and hit the button for the lobby.

He stood there motionless for a brief, excruciating moment until the doors closed, the elevator started descending, and he started breathing again.

Drone Rustlers

As SOON AS Greg's beat-up Toyota pulled up out front, Lucas Hite kissed his wife Susan and told her he loved her. She handed him two travel mugs, one for Lucas and one for Greg, and then he headed for the door.

"Be careful out there," she called after him.

He blew her another kiss. "Baby, I'm always careful."

He was out the door before Greg even tapped the horn.

Lucas and Greg had been roommates and best friends in grad school, both working on their masters' in drone engineering at MIT. They'd finished at the same time, and both lined up good jobs starting that September—Lucas in Seattle and Greg in Atlanta. The Cyber Wars were winding down, and things were actually looking up for a change. They'd decided a couple of weeks hiking across Europe would be an appropriate way to mark that turning point in their lives.

They spent the first week eating, drinking, and partying in Strasbourg, France. Two days into the second week they boarded a train and crossed into Germany. By the time they arrived, the global economy had imploded. The ATMs were all down, the banks were all closed. They were stranded, refugees living off handouts.

When they finally made it home a month later, the jobs that should have been waiting for them had evaporated, along with tens of millions like them. The Cyber Wars hadn't lasted long, not the worst of it, but they'd changed the world forever.

Lucas and Greg did what they could to survive. Like so many other Americans, they were forced to go into business for themselves. Odd jobs at first—yard work and house cleanouts, gutters and lawns. But as the economy reached some kind of equilibrium, new industries arose, and with them, new opportunities for a pair of bright, enterprising young engineers.

The future was in drones, that much they had already realized. But while the drone manufacturers were hiring hundreds of engineers, there were tens of thousands competing for those jobs. Other niches opened up, however, and before long, Lucas and Greg had found theirs.

Lucas got into the car—it was bright blue today—and handed Greg his coffee.

"Thanks, man," Greg said, taking a sip before slipping it into his cup holder and leaning over to wave at Susan.

"Where are we setting up today?" Greg asked as they drove off.

"Old cell tower on Staten Island. I've been tracking a lot of traffic there—diverted from somewhere else, I imagine."

"Sounds good."

The job was more physical than either of them had expected, but they both enjoyed rock climbing, and there were a lot of similarities, plenty of exercise and time spent outdoors. More than once, looking out at some spectacular urban vista from on high, they'd observed that if things had gone according to plan, they would have been stuck inside some office or lab, hunched over a work bench—or, worse, a desk.

It took an hour to get to the location, and another hour to climb the tower with all their equipment and set up the rig amid the cluster of rotting cell transponders. By eleven a.m. they were scanning the drones zipping through the air around them, and waiting. Sometimes they talked, sometimes they didn't. Sometimes they basked in the sunlight; more often they huddled under a tarp.

Today they were quiet. It was cool and breezy—cloudy, of course, but not raining at the moment. The air was clear enough that they could see most of Brooklyn on the other side of the bay.

Forty minutes in, the clouds parted long enough for a ray of sunshine to cut through, like something out of the Bible or an alien invasion movie. It lit up several square blocks, slowly moving across the streets and rooftops.

As it winked back out of existence, Greg tapped Lucas on the shoulder and pointed. "Ten o'clock."

Lucas spotted it before he heard it, a tiny black dot coming from the northwest. He could identify them by sound now, but he confirmed it with the binoculars before he said anything.

"Here we go," he said. "Looks like a Takeshi Mercury Quad. Maybe a six-thousand series. That means two swivel-mounted guns and a set of Gunther Quickfire electrodes."

Guns was good. Guns meant money. It also meant UniCon. Only UniCon was allowed to use armed drones, but they pretty much controlled all the money, anyway. If you were going after money, you were going after UniCon.

"Got it." Lucas grabbed the heavy rubberized gloves and the top launcher and climbed another ten feet up the tower.

As the dot grew larger, the buzz grew louder and deeper. Unmistakably a money drone. They both pulled down their masks. Lucas felt that initial twinge of doubt and fear. The size of the things could be deceiving, even after years of doing this. The bristle of firepower could be more than a little off-putting, especially in that last moment of waiting, before switching to action mode.

Then Greg said, "On three," and any concerns were washed away in a rush of adrenaline.

Greg counted off and they fired, Lucas from the bottom and Greg from the top, two missiles dragging a composite Smartmesh net between them, spreading out to a full three-hundred square feet. If you timed it right, which by now they almost always did, you wrapped the drone in enough mesh that it was hopelessly entangled.

There were a number of different techniques, but they were partial to what was known as "The Coil." With the right gauge mesh, the drone got tangled but remained airborne. Its automatic response was to gun its motors, but if the mesh held, the drone was pulled in a circle, winding itself tighter and tighter around the tower itself.

You had to be careful you didn't get caught up in it, because the mesh could cut deep into your skin—in the time it took to unravel it, you could lose a limb. But Lucas and Greg were careful, methodical. Engineers.

The drone punched into the middle of the net and they caught a whiff of ozone as the Joltpack electrodes fired, trying to zap whoever was harassing it. The buzz of the motor kicked up a few notches and they watched as it banked into its first circle. The mesh began to wrap around the cell tower between them. Lucas climbed down a few feet to give it more space; even at full throttle, the drones tended to wind downward. They watched it swing around, then again and again, listening to the rhythmic whirr as it wrapped itself around the tower, faster and faster, until finally, with a dull *clunk*, it ran out of slack.

This was a critical moment. In a second or two, it would get its bearing and start uncoiling itself, gaining enough room and information to deploy its weapons.

They were on it immediately, working quickly and silently. Greg grabbed its frame and held it in place while Lucas slipped brackets through the mesh, immobilizing each rotor. The drone was throwing out charges, spitting like an angry cat—a *big* angry cat. The air was thick with the smell of ozone and burnt rubber and dust.

The next critical moment was disabling the guns. As soon as the rotors were still, Lucas took out his smart clips and cut through the mesh, three sides of a square, holding the frame while Greg peeled back the mesh and used a crowbar and mallet to pop off the alloy dome on the bottom. The gun was already active, the onboard computers frantically searching for a target to lock onto. Lucas held up the paddle with the facial pattern printed across it, and as the gun swiveled toward it, Greg slipped the crowbar under the bundle of wires that snaked along the gun mount and tore them out.

The gun went limp, but they kept it pointed away from them anyway, a routine safety precaution. By now, the Joltpack was depleted and the electrodes were spent. Greg pried open the casing around the gun's swivel mount, tore out the GPS tracker and used a slingshot to send it far out into the New York Bay. Then he disconnected the battery.

Lucas cut through more of the Smartmesh and extracted the drone, then lowered it to the ground on a rope. Greg reconnected the severed strands of Smartmesh and respooled it, then they both climbed down.

In less than ten minutes, the car was packed up and they were moving.

Three miles away they pulled into a multistory parking lot, found a spot between a big pickup truck and a van, and peeled off the blue plastic coating, revealing the silver paint underneath. They waited another half an hour—Lucas's least favorite part of the process. Once several other silver cars had come and gone, they exited as well, driving a circuitous route to a single garage they rented at an apartment complex five miles from either of their houses. There, they disassembled the drone, setting aside the components they could sell—guns, rotors, even the spent Joltpack—and sorting the rest into the appropriate scrap buckets.

Ultimately, they would strip it down to nothing, but for now they were focused on getting at the creamy center—the cargo module.

Lucas lifted it out and set it on the concrete floor. Greg used the diamond saw to cut through the lock.

They exchanged a look, pausing for a moment to picture what lay inside. *Schrödinger's cash*, they called it, because until they looked there could be a billion dollars—or next to nothing. They stared at each other until one of them nodded. This time it was Greg.

Lucas raised the lid and Greg said, "What the fuck is that?"

Inside, half buried in some kind of powdery dust, were thirty paper money bands, each one labeled *$10,000*, and all of them empty.

Chapter Eight

WHEN SHE HEARD the mail truck approaching, Gloriana felt a slight thrill, followed, as always, by a momentary flush of embarrassment. The mail was the highlight of her day, even though it was almost always disappointing. It was brought to her door by either Diego or Matías, the military policemen who guarded her house during the week. She'd never met the actual letter carrier.

Sometimes there was something interesting, a magazine or journal, occasionally even a letter from a person—already opened and read, of course. But usually there was nothing.

Still, the mail had always represented something powerful in her life.

When she was little, mail was such a rarity in her village that just receiving it was an event. Gloriana would receive mail once a year: a birthday present from her Aunt Zara in Kuala Lumpur.

Aunt Zara's presents were exotic and fancy, and the fact that they were delivered by the postman filled the other children in the village with envy and awe. Maybe some resentment. She wasn't close with the other children in the village. She was different from them—she spent most of her time in her own head. The others weren't mean to her, but they didn't get her. She felt the same way.

The first time Gloriana actually met her aunt was after her village was evacuated. Gloriana's parents took her to stay with her aunt in Kuala Lumpur—or 'KL,' as Zara called it.

Gloriana had seen pictures of cities before, gleaming skyscrapers rising up into the clouds. But in person, they were even more impressive. Standing on the sidewalk, looking up at them, it seemed that they should topple at any moment, that they were too tall to stay upright, too massive not to collapse in on themselves.

And then she looked down at the streets around her, at the people sleeping on the sidewalks, dirty, sick, and dying. Even then, she knew there was something terribly wrong about it. She loved the soaring towers, but couldn't understand how there could be such fancy things when so many people had nothing at all.

Zara was younger than Gloriana's father. She was beautiful and stylish and wore Western clothes. She worked in an office for an insurance company.

Once they moved in with her, Gloriana learned that her father's disapproval of Zara's career was a source of great tension between them. She couldn't tell what her mother thought of Zara. Looking back, she pictured a combination of righteous disapproval and desperate jealousy.

Gloriana had missed her village as soon as it disappeared from her sight, but after the grueling trip, the city seemed a wonderland of towers and lights.

Zara doted on Gloriana at first, but as tensions grew between the adults, Zara's impatience and irritability extended to Gloriana, as well.

In the years since then, Gloriana had developed a growing empathy for Zara's plight. Zara was young and single and had a job in the big city. She had probably worked incredibly hard to get out of the village Gloriana missed so desperately—probably had to work even harder because of the disapproval of men like her brother. And suddenly, that brother and his family were crowded in with her in her tiny apartment. What was supposed to be 'a week or two' became months, and then years.

Gloriana's parents did not adjust well to the city. Her father couldn't find work. He started to drink, despite his Muslim faith. Her mother became distracted and withdrawn. Zara grew increasingly bitter with each passing month and each new sign of permanence: the first mail addressed to Gloriana's parents, Gloriana enrolling at the local school.

Gloriana was miserable, too. She was even more different at this school, and here, she was teased for it.

If it wasn't for Miss Yahya, her science teacher, Gloriana would have shriveled up and died. Miss Yahya brought her out of her shell, recognized her aptitude, and eventually got her accepted into one of the government-run residential schools.

Gloriana still missed her village, and she missed her parents when she left KL, but as soon as she got to the residential school she realized that this was where she belonged.

It was far from Aunt Zara's apartment, and there was no money for her to travel back and forth. Six months passed before she returned to KL for the end-of-term holiday. By then, things at home had gotten even worse—her father's drinking, her mother's introversion, Zara's anger and resentment.

By the end of the two-week holiday, Gloriana couldn't wait to get back to school.

By the end of the next six-month term, her mother was nearly catatonic, barely recognizable. Her father was living on the streets, in the shadows of skyscrapers owned by the billionaires whose wealth had come from the same oil, the same greed, that had ruined their village, had ruined her father. They had taken his home, his livelihood, and his self-worth as a human being.

The last time she saw him was the night before she returned to school. She tried to get him to come home, to have dinner with his daughter and his sister and his wife, but he refused.

At the end of the next term, Gloriana didn't go home. She had won a scholarship to a national science camp in Japan and spent the following break there. Six months after that, she was recruited to the Junior Science College. She was fourteen years old.

Chapter Nine

PIERCE HUSTLED AWAY from Billings Tower, replaying the interaction with Billings in his mind and wondering what it meant. Frank Billings didn't know where Serino was, and he seemed annoyed about that. But he knew about the laundering, regardless of his denials. And he definitely knew something about the disappearing Large. Billings' reaction when Pierce asked him about money disintegrating strongly suggested he had hit a nerve. Mentioning the argument with Serino hit a nerve, too.

So what did it all mean?

Pierce kept his head down as he left HiHo on foot, walking down the ramp into LoHo.

It always felt weird descending the ramp from HiHo to LoHo, but on foot, that strangeness was even more palpable. LoHo was above sea level—just. But standing at the bottom of the ramp, in the shadows of the wall and twenty feet below the HiHo ground level, you felt like you were one breached seawall from being swept out into the ocean. During a coastal storm, that could be true. But not today.

The feeling faded as Pierce walked deeper into the vibrant, early morning bustle of LoHo. Real people walked on the street, going about their business.

As Pierce passed a bank of payphones, he felt the familiar buzz of the pager on his hip. He didn't recognize the number. It could have been a Guild disciplinary officer or a UniC, investigating Kransky's death. Or it could have been Dugray.

He went to the payphones and called the number. It rang once before a voice he vaguely recognized said, "Who's this?"

"You paged me."

"Is this the courier?"

"Wait, is this Serino?" Pierce asked, but he already knew.

"I hear you've been looking for me."

"That's right. There were some issues with that last delivery I did for you."

"Yeah, well, we can talk about that. But not on the phone."

"Is there something going on with the Large?"

Serino laughed. He sounded stoned or drunk. "Yeah, you could say that. Like I said, though, not on the phone. You remember the first place you ever picked up a delivery from me?"

It had been a prescription mill in Queens. He remembered at the time thinking it was a very strange place to pick up a shipment. "Yeah, five years ago. A dentist office, right. It was called—"

"Don't say it!" Serino cut him off. "Meet me there in half an hour. And make sure you're not being followed."

"A half hour?" Pierce said, shaking his head. Then the payphone told him Serino had hung up.

Pierce closed his eyes for a moment, thinking. The place had been called Dr. Chompers, a children's dentist in Queens, just up the block from the old Astoria Bookshop. It would take almost exactly a half hour to get there—if he had his car.

He needed a cab, and he didn't have time to find an indie with no camera.

Vendors lined the sidewalk, selling bootleg movies, fake handbags, and cheap knock-off everything. At the end of the block, he found one selling ten-dollar off-brand Holo-eye shades and bought a pair.

The vendor looked down at the attaché, then at the cheap Holo-eyes, then at Pierce, like he was wondering why a real courier would be buying cheap crap like that.

The holographic iris pattern embedded in the lenses was nowhere near the quality of the authentic ones, which could trick even a high-end iris-scanner into thinking you were someone else. But they were good enough to scramble a scan, so he wouldn't be recognizable as himself.

He put them on, hailed a Smartcab and sank a half inch into the shallow luxury of the thinly upholstered seats. It felt good to be sitting. He slid two twenties into the bill slot and said, "Astoria Bookshop."

The cab recited the destination back to him, then surged into traffic, slipping into an opening created by two other cabs.

As the cab drove across the city and into Queens, the vibe on the street was even worse than the previous night. Before he'd left Manhattan, he passed several crime scenes, including one with at least four bodies under sheets surrounded by hundreds of shell casings, and three blocks later a trio of UniC vans rounding up a dozen face-tattooed gangsters. Even the BetterLates were out thick. He passed three clusters of ten or fifteen of them, dressed in green, singing, chanting, and burning their incense.

Pierce was glad to be just another anonymous passenger in an anonymous smart cab.

The cab turned onto Thirty-First Street in Queens and pulled up in front of the bookshop.

As Pierce got out, even the drones seemed more frantic than usual, zipping back and forth in the space under the blue girders of the elevated train tracks. Pierce fought the urge to duck—he needed to stay focused on where he was heading—but when a drone smacked into a startled pigeon, sending both ricocheting off the steel trestles overhead, he couldn't help muttering, "What the fuck?"

The rain had stopped again and the shafts of sunlight poking through gaps in the train trestles looked semisolid in the thick, humid air.

Maybe the rain was to blame for the vibe on the street, people getting antsy after being holed up. But they'd been holed up longer many times, and it had never felt quite like this.

He passed a construction site, where a team of construction printers and assemblers were methodically building fluid, S-shaped walls behind a red plastic construction fence. The printers squirted concrete polymer in preprogrammed designs. The little robotic assemblers scurried around the site; some carted wet concrete for the printers, others used a Swiss-army knife of tools to cut, fasten, grind, or glue. Whenever he saw them, Pierce anthropomorphized the printers as giraffe people and the assemblers as their little dogs.

There wasn't a human worker in sight. Terrible for the economy and the dignity of human work, but Pierce found himself unable to resist slowing down a step to watch, just for a second.

There was a bench on the sidewalk; someone had cut a hole in the fence behind it, big enough for a person to squeeze through. Probably someone was sneaking in and stealing materials, but security was usually pretty tight on the automated sites. It was not unheard of for unemployed construction workers to sneak in and trash the construction bots.

It probably felt great, blowing off steam like that, but more to the point, the higher the losses incurred by the development companies going robotic, the more attractive human workers looked in comparison. Pierce didn't blame them.

The door and window holes of the semi-constructed walls were flanked by double-helix columns, and a sign on the construction fence announced that it was going to be another "Beauty Genius" clinic, charging a fortune for "enhanced genetic beauty treatments." The sign said USING SCIENCE TO MAKE YOUR WRINKLES DISAPPEAR, but some comedian had altered it to read: USING SCIENCE TO MAKE YOUR *CRINKLE* DISAPPEAR.

The clinics were everywhere in Manhattan, but this was the first one he'd seen in Queens. There were rich people all over.

Half a block away, Pierce spotted the faded sign—DR. CHOMPERS FAMILY DENTISTRY, with a cartoon tooth and toothbrush hugging, each with big toothy smiles.

The door that once led to Dr. Chompers was ajar, a

flimsy, unpainted wooden thing so swollen with rot and damp it overlapped the jamb, like it wanted to be closed but couldn't make it happen. Sandwiched between a noodle joint and a pawn shop, it was exactly the kind of door that you could walk past every day for years and never know it was there, almost magical in its invisibility.

Pierce pulled it open and started up the stairs, which creaked and groaned under him. The place stunk of mold, but so did most of the world. Pierce wondered briefly why he hadn't lost the ability to smell it.

At the top of the steps, he turned toward the small waiting area. It looked much the same as it had five years earlier, just darker and dingier. Serino was waiting for him, sitting in one of two molded plastic chairs pulled up to a rickety card table with a pad and pen lying on it.

Serino gestured to the other chair. "You're sure you weren't followed, right?"

"Yes," Pierce said quietly. "I wasn't followed."

In their previous interactions, Serino had always seemed put together, but he didn't look good today— pale skin, dark rings under bloodshot eyes. Pierce wondered if he was using, if he'd gotten messed up with one of the new synthetics. He seemed too strung out for it to just be nerves.

"Sit down," Serino said.

The place was so filthy, Pierce almost refused, but Serino seemed skittish enough to warrant special care.

Pierce sat, placing his attaché on the floor next to him.

Serino leaned forward, silhouetted against the roll blinds drawn down in the window behind him. His face was in shadows, but his eyes gleamed bright. He slid the pad and pen toward Pierce. "You're going to want to write this down," he said. "It's big. Fucking huge."

"Is this about the Large?"

Serino laughed softly. "This is about everything."

Pierce sat back. "If it's so big, why did you call me? Why not your friends in UniCon?"

Serino sat back, too, studying him. "Partly because I know you've been looking for me, and I know you're already wondering about some shit you saw that doesn't make sense. But I'll be honest with you—I got no one else to tell it to. I don't know all the details, but I know this thing is so big it has to be UniCon behind it, and for the moment at least, the only people they *don't* control are you couriers. And what I'm about to tell you is a threat to you guys in particular. Your bosses will want to know." He sat forward and smiled. "But before we get to that, I have a good faith offering. Let you know I'm for real."

Pierce cocked an eyebrow. "And what's that?"

"You and your pal are digging into what happened with the Fairview, right?"

"How do you know about that?"

"UniCon, man. They know fucking everything. And the people you're looking for are UniCon, too, so *they* know you're looking. What I wonder is, why do they give a shit? Like, what the fuck are you guys going to do about it? But I guess they hate to be embarrassed. Anyway, it all leads to the same place. It's all tied together. So, you've been breaking through the layers of shell companies, right? How high have you gotten?"

Pierce paused, then said, "Infinity Partnerships. Charter Properties owned the building. Jaxon Ventures owned Charter, Amsterdam owned Jaxon, Granite Investments owned Amsterdam, and Infinity Partnerships owned Granite."

Serino hiked his eyebrows and nodded. "That's not bad. The big guys figured you'd get through two or three layers, tops." He laughed. "You better be careful. If people knew you were that close, they'd have taken you out already."

Pierce leaned forward. "Which people?"

Serino waved him away. "I'll tell you that later. Afterwards. I'll tell you exactly which fucking people. But first, write this down, so you'll be able to prove it."

Pierce and Dugray were never going to prove it, that's not what this was about, but he wrote it down on the pad, anyway.

"Infinity is owned by a company called Garnet Holdings," Serino said, and he started counting down on his fingers. "Garnet is owned by Hudson Limited. Hudson is owned by Broadway Commercial Properties, and Broadway is owned by Crane International."

Pierce could feel himself trembling. In seconds, Serino had just revealed as many layers as Dugray had peeled back in three years. "Who owns Crane?" he asked, his voice dry and raspy.

Serino held up a finger. "Like I said, afterwards. But seriously, I gotta ask: You really think anyone out there is going to give a fuck? The UniCs? The prosecutors? The fucking *judges*?"

Pierce decided not to tell him that he and Dugray would be the prosecutors and the judges—and the executioners, too. He shrugged. "Maybe people won't be able to ignore one hundred and sixty-three cases of voluntary manslaughter, no matter how much they want to."

Serino laughed, an unhinged cackle. "'Voluntary manslaughter'? Jesus, you're so close but you're still so far off. Fairview wasn't *allowed* to happen, dumbass. They *made it* happen."

A chill passed over Pierce. "What do you mean?"

"What, you think they just waited for the rising seawater to seep into the foundation? No, no, no. Way too much money on the table and not enough time. You know how much more that land was worth without those rent-controlled towers on them? No, they drilled tiny holes into the concrete and put tanks of seawater over them with slow leaks, drip-drip-dripping." He laughed again. "Worked so well it took 'em by surprise, actually. They thought it would take six months, a year, but it barely took five weeks. That's why so many of them buildings came down right around the same time."

"Jesus…" Pierce said, his eyes drifting down the floor. "That's murder."

"Goddamn right," said Serino, leaning forward, his eyes grim. "Cold, calculated, premeditated. And it's nothing compared to what else I got to tell you."

Pierce looked up at him. "Who did it? Who's responsible?"

Serino held up his finger again. "In a minute, okay? I already gave you enough that you can figure it out. But first, you need to listen to what I got to tell you. Like I said, it's all part of the same thing."

Pierce sat up straight, trying to listen as his head swirled with what Serino had just told him. It had taken him so long to stop thinking of it as murder, to convince himself that, despite what he felt in his heart, it hadn't been done on purpose. It was greed and neglect and incompetence, yes, but it wasn't murder. Turned out he'd been right in the first place.

Serino took a deep breath. "Okay, first thing, there's people out there saying I been ripping clients off. Heisting them. But that's not what's going on. I never done any of that shit. Never would. Bad for business."

Pierce put down the pen. "I don't know why you're telling me this. I'm not going to be able to do anything—"

"Stop!" Serino slammed the table with both hands. The pen rolled off the table and onto the floor. He took a deep, shuddery breath, like he was on the verge of tears. "I told you, I got no one else to tell. You couriers are all that's left, everything else is UniCon, and this is about them."

Pierce stared at him for a moment, then nodded. "Okay."

Serino took a deep breath, calming himself. "Good. Now... Write. This. Down."

Pierce leaned over in his seat to pick up his pen. As he reached for it, his chain hit the floor next to him, sending the pen rolling farther away. As he extended his arm, leaning almost out of his chair, a long shadow appeared in the window behind Serino. Pierce glanced up, and through the grimy windows he saw the silhouette of a quad-drone hovering just outside.

The window exploded as two streams of bullets tore through it, large caliber.

Across from him, under the table, Serino's feet jerked like he was tap dancing. Everywhere else, blood fell like rain, everywhere but under the table.

Pierce felt the bullets tearing through the back of his chair. Bits of molten plastic pelted him. He dove to the side, holding his attaché in front of him as the bullets chewed through his chair, then sawed through the table.

The shooting stopped, and for an instant the only sound was the whir of the drone's rotors outside and the steady drip of blood. Then, what was left of Serino slid off the chair and onto the floor.

Chapter Ten

As soon as the sound of the drone faded away, Pierce climbed unsteadily to his feet, dazed, shaking bits of wood and plastic from his hair. He looked down at Serino's shredded body, then around at his equally shredded surroundings. Then he looked down at the pen in his hand. If he hadn't been reaching for it, he'd have shared Serino's fate.

He was rooted in place for a moment, stunned.

Then a thought came to him through the fog: *Get the fuck out of here.* He found the notepad in the debris and put it in his attaché. Then he ran to the back of the building, past bays of abandoned dental chairs, and into an office where a missing window looked out onto the rear alley. He climbed through, skin prickling. At any moment a drone could descend from the sky and start firing.

He lowered himself from the bottom, the attaché swinging from its chain, then he jumped, landing heavily on the pavement. He grabbed his attaché and took off running, pausing when he got to the street to peer around the corner. A crowd had gathered in front of the building, staring up at the jagged hole where the front windows used to be.

As Pierce turned and hurried off in the opposite direction, a pair of police cruisers sped past him, their lights flashing bright under the dark gray skies.

The sidewalk was blocked by a large cluster of BetterLates spilling out onto the road. Pierce was squeezing by behind them when another pair of UniC cruisers screeched to a halt right next to them, lights flashing.

Pierce ducked down and found himself pressed against a reinforced construction fence with a hole cut into it. Through it, he saw the double-helix columns, and realized he was back at Beauty Genius.

UniCs piled out of their cruisers, shouting confusing and contradictory orders. Pierce shoved his attaché through the hole and wriggled in after it.

The construction site was a jumbled maze of half-finished walls and utility stacks littered with bots, equipment, and supplies, all under a temporary roof that kept everything shrouded in shadows. It looked like utter chaos, but Pierce knew it was precisely arranged according to some order he didn't understand.

As soon as he entered the premises, the assemblers froze and the three printers—the giraffe people—all turned their heads in his direction. It was unnerving, and he paused for a moment, until the zap of a taser behind him on the sidewalk, followed by a throaty scream, spurred him to action. Ducking into a crouch and making sure not to scrape his attaché against anything, he made his way to a shadowy bend of the partial exterior wall one of the bots was printing. There was no room behind it, but clutching his attaché, he settled in against the concrete and pulled a bit of plastic sheeting around him.

After a few seconds, the bots seemed satisfied he wasn't a threat and got back to work.

Sitting back, Pierce could feel the wall yield, the material not yet cured. He heard a mechanical whir growing louder and closer, and he realized it was one of the printers working on the wall, coming right toward him.

A pair of powerful flashlight beams swept across the ground in front of him, dual shadow patterns of the fence sliding over everything. Pierce pulled the tarp tighter around him and pressed back, feeling his shoulders sinking into the soft, wet wall as the printer-bot pelted the tarp with a volley of soft concrete.

The two UniCs had seen the hole in the fence, and were debating whether they should search the site. Meanwhile, every twenty seconds or so, Pierce and his tarp got another layer of concrete.

Sitting there, wrapped in the tarp and increasingly encased in wet concrete polymer, he thought about what Serino had said about the Fairview collapse. That it was intentional. That his mother had been murdered.

Pierce had rushed to the site right after the collapse. He and Dugray helped the first responders clear away the rubble and search for survivors. They hadn't found any, just lots of bodies—not their mothers, but people they knew.

Memories of crushed limbs and dead faces came back to him, interspersed with images of Kransky and his men, and of Serino, reduced to a bloody pile of smoking meat. A strange guttural sound forced its way out of him and a flashlight beam lit up his tarp. He clamped a hand over his mouth, holding absolutely still until the light moved on. He realized his face was wet with tears.

He generally tried not to think about his mom. It was easier that way, less painful. But she'd been a force of nature, and when she asserted herself in your mind, you had to let her in.

The last time he'd seen her they'd argued as he tried, one more time, to convince her to move out of that place. It was no secret the building was falling apart. But Mom was adamant. She'd been penniless when she moved in there, savaged by a brutal and legally questionable prenup that she couldn't afford to fight. But in the intervening years, she had worked her ass off at a series of day jobs while earning a master's in social work.

She got a good job after that, enough that she could have lived somewhere better. But by then, she was co-head of the tenants association and part of a lawsuit against the shadowy owners and the useless management company. She was committed to the place, to the other people who lived there, and to forcing the owners to honor their legal obligations.

She'd had lots of friends in the building, including Dugray's mom.

Their faces drifted through his mind, and the fact came back to him: one hundred and sixty-three people *murdered*. He trembled with rage, fighting to breathe as every muscle strained against the horror of it.

He hadn't cried when he found out his mother was dead. Hadn't cried at her funeral, either. He wanted to, wanted to let out the pain. But he couldn't. Couldn't let himself let go. Partly, he knew, it had been because almost the only person who really cared about his pain was the person he was mourning.

He and Dugray were close now, but at that point they hadn't seen each other in years. Pierce's dad, Bradley, was a piece of shit who had left his mom and him penniless, had forced them to live in the place that killed her, and then been revealed as a criminal fraud. Bradley had only ever been about himself. Pierce would never have shared anything with him.

Gloriana was the only other person he could have talked to, leaned on, who could have told him it would be okay and made it so just by being there. But by then, they'd been split up for years and she was serving a life sentence in a UniCon prison in Malaysia.

He wondered, as he often did, how much different their lives might been if he had stayed with her, if he could have gotten over his pride, his impatience. If he could have given her the time to realize how much he loved her, to realize the kind of life they might have had together. Or if he could have opened his mind enough to see things as she saw them. If he could have stopped being so old-fashioned. Maybe she wouldn't be in a prison cell. Maybe he wouldn't be cowering under a tarp, desperately trying to stay one step ahead of his colleagues.

He understood completely why Gloriana had done what she did at the oil refinery. But he wondered how much more she could have done for the cause, how much more damage she could have caused, if she had managed to stay free.

Thinking of Gloriana and UniCon and the state of the world, his sorrow gradually receded into the background, where it usually resided. And his anger grew in its place.

He couldn't have stopped Gloriana. And he *shouldn't* have stopped her. Because what she had done was right, it was righteous. It might have been an act of aggression, but it was also, on behalf of everyone else in the world, an act of self-defense. They had forced her hand, left her no other choice. They had *made* her do what she did.

They had started it. All she did was fight back.

The flashlights winked out, bringing Pierce back to the present. Car doors slammed and the cruiser drove off.

He waited until he was sure the UniCs had left, then he tried to stand up. For one terrifying moment, he couldn't. The concrete had hardened and he was locked into place, a part of the wall.

As he fought off panic and struggled to free himself, the printer passed by overhead, giving the wall, and Pierce, another layer, as if determined to keep him in place.

He tucked his legs underneath him and pushed hard at the lip of concrete that was holding him in place. It finally gave way, with a sound that was part percussive crack and part fluid squish. He stumbled away from the wall, letting the tarp fall to the ground.

The bots all froze. The printer that had just sprayed Pierce was now at the far end of its circuit, but it pivoted to where Pierce had been, seemingly staring at him as it did.

While Pierce brushed off flakes of concrete, the printer extended itself over the wall to examine the spot where he had been ensconced. For a long moment, it seemed to be studying the damage: several layers squished out of alignment, several layers protruding from where the concrete had accumulated on the tarp.

The printer slowly swiveled to fix Pierce with what seemed uncannily like a withering stare. Its nozzle retracted, and a different tool emerged: a chisel. It could have been a trick of the meager light, but the printer seemed to give its head a tiny, exasperated shake before it started chipping away at the deformed section of wall.

Pierce said, "Sorry." Then he wriggled back through the hole in the fence out onto the street, and he hurried down the block, head down, attaché tight against his belly.

He needed to talk to Dugray, tell him what had happened, what he'd learned. But when he got to the subway stop, he used a payphone to make another call first. It was answered on the first ring. "Diaz here."

"It's Pierce."

The phone immediately went dead and Pierce's heart plummeted, but then his pager buzzed, and the display read an unfamiliar number. He punched the number into the phone and immediately heard Diaz's voice. "Who's this?"

"It's me," Pierce said.

"You shouldn't be calling, kid," Diaz told him. "Things are fucked, and getting fuckeder."

"Yeah, I know. But this is important. I spoke to Serino. He knew something was up with the Large. He said something big is going down."

Diaz let out a sharp, manic laugh. "Yeah, well, if you're going to get out of the shit you're going to have be a little more specific. Did he say what it was?"

"They killed him before he could."

"What are you talking about? *Who* killed him? He's fucking UniCon."

"It was a drone. A kill drone. I was there. It almost killed me, too."

"A kill drone? Jesus Christ, are you serious?"

"Dead serious. Any chance that was the Guild?"

"No way. UniCon keeps those things on a short leash, and they definitely don't let the Guild use them."

"That's what I figured."

"Besides, when the Guild comes after you, it'll be with other couriers."

"They already did."

"Who?"

"Vance and Magnussen."

"Jesus, did you—"

"They're fine. I left them chained to a fence in Queens. Do you know who else is coming for me?"

Diaz let out a sigh. "Sorry, kid. I'm on the outs with the Guild. Pretty sure they're going to suspend me."

"Ah, shit. Sorry this is blowing back on you."

"It's not just you. We lost two more couriers. Vanished. Chopra and Rocha. We're scrambling to figure out what the fuck is going on. Guild central is freaking the fuck out."

"Rocha?"

"Yeah, sorry kid. Maybe they just got held up in all the mayhem out there. There was riots on Staten Island. All sorts of shit going down."

"What's that about?"

"No one seems to know."

"Maybe this is all related. The money. Serino said it was big."

"Yeah, maybe." He let out a long sigh. "Look, kid. I gotta go. Keep your head down until you figure out what happened to Kransky's money, then I'll see if I can get someone to listen."

Pierce hung up the phone, but stood there for a moment with his hand on the receiver, immobilized by the realization of just how *fuckeder* he was. He still needed to figure out what was going on, but the one person in the world who could have told him was dead, cut in half by a kill drone.

Hearing the train approaching, he ran up the metal stairs to the platform. It was the W train into Manhattan. It would take him right into Alphabet City.

He found a seat and half closed his eyes, trying to rest while still maintaining some level of vigilance.

After a couple of stops, a pair of uniforms from UniC's Subway division got on and he opened his eyes a tiny bit more. They looked edgy and stressed. They made a show of glaring at him, looking him up and down.

Pierce only had a couple more stops, but he let his eyes return to slits, hoping to steal another few minutes of rest. As the train pulled out of 23rd Street Station, it lost power, coasting for several moments in relative quiet and almost total dark.

When the lights came back on after five or ten seconds, everyone on the train wore the same expression: annoyed at the minor inconvenience, but relieved that it hadn't become a major one.

As they pulled into Union Square, however, the lights died again, and this time they stayed dead. People were just starting to grumble when a transit employee yanked the doors open from the outside and yelled, "Train's down. Everybody out."

The UniCs were the first ones off. They seemed in a hurry. Pierce hung back, moving with the crowd. He was close enough to Alphabet City that he could walk.

Union Square Station was oddly crowded and buzzing with that same frenetic tension that seemed to pervade the city. When he got out onto the street, it seemed to rise in pitch.

His heart sank as he realized he had emerged into a demonstration. Thousands of protestors crowded Union Square, pushing up against a phalanx of UniCs, chanting anti-UniCon slogans. On the streets on either side of the scrum, columns of stationary Smartcabs waited patiently in place, the AIs making futile calculations on how to get out of there while the passengers locked inside made more frantic calculations about how increasingly ruined their days were becoming with each passing minute.

A cluster of BetterLates kept to themselves, ignored by the protestors and the cops alike.

Crowds protesting UniCon were common, especially in the runup to a UniConference, but the energy seemed more dangerous than usual.

Pierce pushed through the throng, but it was slow going, the crowd getting thicker instead of thinner. The lines of armored riot UniCs seemed to be growing more and more agitated.

Pierce could feel the tension building, could almost hear the clock ticking down to detonation as the chants grew louder and angrier and the UniCs stiffened, flexed, checked their equipment.

"Shit," he muttered. He was not going to get out of there before things erupted. He'd made it about a block when the crowd surged, a violent crush that Pierce only managed to escape by stepping down the concrete steps to a subway entrance.

It was the old Second Avenue Subway. The tile sign had been painted over with an image of a scuba diver exploring ancient ruins, and the words, SEE OLD NEW YORK, THE 'SUB' WAY!

One of New York's newest and deepest tunnels, the Second Avenue subway had opened twenty years earlier and run for about a decade before one of the first hurricane swarms overwhelmed its pumps. Billions had been spent on digging the tunnels, but no one had the money to replace the pumps. The newspapers called it the "Phase Three Fiasco."

Within months, someone had the idea for the "Sub Way" or "Sea Train," a tacky, dismal, tourist submarine that ran through the flooded old subway tunnels. It had become an instant institution.

Pierce didn't disapprove, in principle. The city earned desperately needed rent from the entrepreneur. The tourists got a creepy glimpse of "Old New York" (i.e., from ten years ago). And occasionally, rich New Yorkers whose quadcopters were in the shop and couldn't bear the extra five minutes of a crosstown Smartcab ride got to rub elbows with actual Midwesterners.

It was dank and smelly, and it bothered Pierce that the dozens of homeless people who had drowned when the pumps gave out were still entombed somewhere down there. It seemed crass and disrespectful.

But Pierce didn't have much choice as a roar rose up from the crowd, followed by sounds of violence and screams of horror and pain. The crowd surged again, pushing him down another step. Pierce shook his head and kept going. No one else followed, probably because it was too gross and touristy to even consider.

At the bottom of the steps, the door swung open with a waft of mildew mixed with chlorine, body odor, and cigarette smoke. The guy holding it open was about sixty, ethnically ambiguous, with an impressive belly. His head and his face were seamlessly covered with the same sparse gray stubble. He didn't glance up at the mayhem above, his face emanating the kind of baked-in boredom you get from some New Yorkers who have seen a lot of, well, New York.

"Welcome to the Sub Way," he said.

The guy eyed Pierce's attaché, but before he could say anything, he was interrupted by a squeal. They both looked up the steps to see a young woman on the top step, clutching her head, which was bleeding through her fingers. She was dressed all in black: tall boots, short skirt, torn T-shirt. The blood was vivid against her pale skin.

She stumbled down the steps, one hand grabbing the railing. She came to a stop next to Pierce, but ignored him, waving her hand in a circle at the doorman. "C'mon, c'mon…" she said.

"Welcome to the Sub Way," the guy said again, "New York's—"

"Yeah, I know," she said, cutting him off. She glanced over her shoulder as a wave of louder screams rose from the crowd up on the sidewalk. She was scared. "I need to get out of here. How much?"

"Fifteen."

"Fifteen, okay," she said, her hand falling away from the gash on her head as she pulled out a small purse and fished through it. "Crap. I only have ten."

He shrugged and turned to Pierce. "Fifteen."

"No, wait," she said, her voice rising. "I got to get out of here. They're going crazy up there."

The air was increasingly tinged with ozone and tear gas and smoke. Pierce was surprised no one else was seeking refuge down there.

The doorman ignored her and said once more to Pierce. "Fifteen."

He kept his eyes on Pierce and put out his hand. As Pierce reached for his wallet, the girl said, "But… I haven't got it."

Pierce fished a twenty out of his wallet and handed it over, nodding toward the girl.

The guy shrugged, took her ten and Pierce's twenty and stood back. "Enjoy the ride."

The girl looked at Pierce, then down at the attaché he was carrying, the chain connecting it to his wrist. "This is how *couriers* get around?"

He sighed but didn't answer. He didn't feel like explaining.

The doorman led them down a long, broken escalator illuminated by strings of Christmas lights. The steps disappeared under the water, and a splintered plywood plank led from the last above-water step to the wide hatch of a tiny, dinged-up submarine. It was the size of an old taxicab and painted yellow with black and white checks to make it look like one, a yellow submarine cheesily indifferent to the incongruity of a taxicab in a subway.

The words, *Deep C-Train* were painted on the side.

Pierce stepped back to let the girl go first, and half-heartedly put out his arm, in case she wanted to use it to steady herself. He wasn't just being chivalrous—she had a gaping head wound and the footing was treacherous. She screwed up her face at him, like he was gross.

He got on first, and she sat across from him, as far away as she could, looking out the window but maintaining her sour expression for the entire seven-minute journey.

The exterior lights of the sub were no match for the murky water, barely illuminating the old subway stop they cruised through. It was decorated with a mural of sorts, or a decal: a line of commuters waiting for the next train. It was oddly quaint, and although it seemed intended to represent a time just a few years past, Pierce found himself feeling strangely nostalgic. Emotional even.

A rat swam by and Pierce snorted, imagining it being on the payroll, like a reenactor in Colonial Williamsburg.

The end of the line was Fifth Street, just off A. The sub slowly ascended the long escalator shaft and let them out just below street level.

"Thanks for riding the Sea Train," the attendant said.

This time the girl asserted her prerogative to get off first and hurried up the broken escalator ahead of him. Pierce tried to give her some space, but he was in a hurry, too. She reached the sidewalk five steps ahead of him.

Pierce felt almost agoraphobic out on the street after the mayhem on Union Square and the confines of the sub.

The only people in sight were three teens at the top of the steps, sharing some kind of smoke. They looked at the girl and her bleeding head, then at Pierce.

They puffed themselves up, standing taller as they scowled at him. Pierce actually felt encouraged that they seemed concerned about her, even though they were probably just looking for someone to beat up and burn off some testosterone.

He gave them a look that seemed to successfully convey the sentiment: *Don't.*

The girl turned back to him, her expression of disgust almost gone. "Thanks," she said. Then she hurried off down the street.

Chapter Eleven

MATÍAS KNOCKED ON the door to deliver her mail. He was a sweet kid. Shy, maybe nineteen years old. Probably from a small village not unlike hers. As much as he seemed smitten by her, he would tell her nothing about himself. It wasn't as if she really cared, but sometimes the boredom got to her. The desperation for human interaction.

She had thought about bedding him. Diego, too. Maybe even together. But at the moment, her situation wasn't terrible, and she didn't want to risk screwing it up.

Besides, the sexual tension added a certain mild spice to her days. If she'd learned anything from old American TV shows, it was that resolving tension could be a ratings death sentence—or, in her case, a real one.

Matías handed her the mail with the same failed attempt at a sly smile that he always did, and the same tiny pause before letting go of it.

"Six years," he said, as if his words had great meaning. She leafed through the catalogues and random fundraising solicitations that somehow found their way to her, until she got to an open envelope from the Princeton University Alumni Association. It was an invitation to a fundraising event honoring one of her old professors. Scrawled across it was a handwritten note:

> *Hi Gloriana!*
> *Hope you can make it! Can't believe it's been six years already!*
> *XOXO*
> *Debbie Atcheson*

Matías was still looking at her, waiting for a response. But he didn't deserve one.

"Thank you," she said, and once she closed the door, she shook her head and smiled. She had shared one seminar with Debbie Atcheson and they had barely spoken to each other. She was now the treasurer of the alumni development committee, and she needed to do a better job of vetting the mailing list for things like house arrest, Gloriana thought. Although she did deserve credit for tracking her down in Venezuela.

Six years. So much had happened since then.

Grad school had been the happiest time of her life since she'd left the village. Coming to America was scary, yes, but incredibly exciting.

Before leaving Malaysia, she had visited her old village, the first time she'd been back since leaving, and she was both heartened and heartbroken.

The village was completely different. Modern prefab housing modules had replaced all the huts. The mature palms had been replaced with new ones. The curve of the lagoon itself had changed, in a way that was both subtle and jarring.

But the sand was clean, and the oil was gone—something she thought she would never see. She learned that the cleanup had been aided by special microbes engineered to digest and break down the oil, and she decided there and then, this would be her focus. She would focus with single-minded intensity on using her brain and her opportunities to help heal other villages faced with similar disasters.

Of course, that was before she discovered the distractions of American college life.

At Princeton, the differences that had once made her an outcast now made her a minor celebrity. She was not only an academic hotshot, she was an ecological refugee—this was back before the Bangladeshi floods, back when such refugees were still something of a rarity. She also came to realize that she was considered beautiful.

After the strictness of Malaysia's government schools, the personal freedom at Princeton was life-changing. In her first semester, Gloriana tried alcohol, several drugs, and a *lot* of sex. She told herself she was being scientific about it, methodical, as she tried each different configuration.

The dean of graduate students, Mr. Crittenden, called her into his office on several occasions to voice his concerns about her wellbeing, about her behavior. Each time, he told her the stories he had been hearing.

Gloriana never denied them, although she did sometimes correct the details.

"Well," Crittenden would say, "That sounds... interesting."

Gloriana would then assure him that regardless of what he might have heard, she had everything under control. And it was mostly true: both the stories he had heard and that she had things under control.

Later that year, she won a prestigious grant and a UNESCO Young Scientists award for "Technology Benefiting the World." After that, they pretty much left her alone.

She met Chris in her second year, in a seminar on the philosophy of environmental biology. They were sitting across from each other in a discussion group. He had watched her appraisingly as she crossed the library toward their table, not blatantly or uncomfortably, just the way guys do.

His demeanor changed over the course of that discussion. He smiled at first, with an almost playful condescension tempered by animal attraction, then a grudging respect, then an almost awed regard. When she spoke, his eyes locked onto hers with an intensity she couldn't look away from, an intensity that, at least one time, made her forget what she was saying. When he spoke, she was impressed and enthralled by his passion and intellect. Before long, the others fell silent, listening to the two of them going back and forth, pursuing each other down rabbit holes of logic, arguments and counter arguments challenging their scientific assumptions and philosophical reasoning, chasing each other deeper and deeper. By the end of the hour, she wasn't sure who was arguing what, but the argument itself was exhilarating.

She would soon learn that he didn't consider many to be his equal—which she would come to recognize as his greatest weakness.

They talked for almost two hours, and by the time they were done the others had left, one by one, or maybe all at once—neither of them had noticed.

They each had another class that day, but they blew off the afternoon to share a pitcher of beer at a nearby bar. They went back to his place, on the second floor of a huge, converted stone house just off campus, and didn't leave for three days, subsisting on pizza and beer and coffee and each other. And drugs. They were both at the height of their debauchery, and as it turned out, among the things they had in common was their dealer, a seedy guy from Trenton who nevertheless became part of their inner circle. He was a bit of a thug, but surprisingly smart in some ways. He gave Gloriana a bad vibe, but he and Chris became friends, of a sort.

Gloriana never came to see Chris as her intellectual equal, but he was close, and he had other intelligences that she found equally impressive: unshakeable self-confidence, fierce determination, creativity, natural leadership, and a personal magnetism, not to mention a rock solid—if sometimes skewed—sense of right and wrong.

They were on-again-off-again for the next six months. They were never exclusive, but he could still be strangely possessive. She began to see a side of him she didn't like. First, the possessiveness, then the entitlement, the disdain he had for those he considered his inferiors. She continued to find him compelling and attractive—she still did to this day—but the more she got to know him, the longer the gaps became, more off than on. At the end of month six, she broke things off. Neither of them got upset about it, and they remained friendly.

Two months later, she met Pierce. He was the opposite of Chris. He was kind and considerate, humble and sincere. He was hot, too—as hot as Chris, in a way, but more human and without all that smugness. The sex was great—different from Chris, but every bit as good. He was smart—not on a level with her or Chris, intellectually, but she found that didn't matter. He had other intelligences, too, and they were the opposite of Chris's. He saw everyone as his equal. His sense of right and wrong never seemed skewed. And he had none of that possessiveness—or at least he didn't seem to at first.

She fell pretty hard for him, so hard it kind of scared her. She felt herself getting pulled in, falling deeper and deeper, and even though it was great, she sometimes found herself scrambling to find some reason, anything, to hold back. To keep from losing herself.

They'd been together for eight or nine months when her landlord told her he was selling, that he was giving her a month's notice that he was breaking her lease. This was just as she was getting ready to leave town for a fellowship in Oslo—an impending separation that they had been building up to with an adolescent sense of melodrama and a frantic sexual intensity.

She told Pierce about the situation with her apartment, how she didn't know what to do about it—what to do with her stuff while she was gone, where she would live when she got back. He suggested that she and her stuff could move in with him.

She wasn't ready for that. Didn't know if she ever would be. Next thing, he'd be wanting to get married, she said, ha, ha, ha.

He didn't laugh at that, not even a little. In fact, it turned out he had assumed that's where things were heading. Over the course of a few short hours, they realized they barely knew each other at all and ultimately weren't that compatible.

The next day she had all her stuff moved into storage. The day after that, she left for Oslo.

When she got back to the States, she thought about calling him, but she didn't right away. Then she ran into

Chris. Despite her misgivings, they resumed their on-again-off-again.

She never saw Pierce again. But she thought about him a lot.

Looking at the invitation one last time, she thought about all the other people she hadn't seen in so long, and fantasized briefly about somehow showing up. But she knew it was impossible, for a multitude of reasons. She dropped the invitation into the recycling bucket, thinking that even if she'd been free to go, she probably still wouldn't.

Chapter Twelve

SEVENTH AND C was just a couple of blocks away, but Pierce realized as he walked that he didn't know the exact address. As he turned onto Seventh Street, he saw a stretch of half a dozen yellowstones, newish but already crumbling yellow brick houses, part of the city's half-assed efforts to keep New York affordable for New Yorkers. One of them had a substantial crack running diagonally across the brick facade, an incongruously upscale SUV at the curb, and a skinny tweaker on the top step, neck craned to look up at the second floor.

As Pierce approached, the kid on the steps started banging on the door. A muffled shout came from inside the house, followed by more, growing louder and closer.

Pierce paused, then backed away across the street. The tweaker kept on banging.

The front door slammed open, and the tweaker stumbled back, almost falling down the steps.

Townsend stormed out, his eyes full of rage, spittle flying from his lips as he yelled back over his shoulder,

"I don't give a shit what he said, the motherfucker stole from me and I'm going to skin him alive!"

Pierce ducked behind a truck parked across the street.

The guys flanking Townsend were different from before, more like paramilitaries than gangsters. He had traded up for better muscle.

Townsend shoved the tweaker down the steps and kicked him in the ribs, then stormed over to the SUV, looking up and down the street with a satisfied glare before one of his men opened the back door of the SUV for him and the other got behind the wheel.

Pierce hunkered lower as the car roared away. By the time he looked back around, the kid was back at the door, hugging his ribs with one arm and banging on the door with the other.

Once Townsend's car had turned the corner, Pierce headed back across the street. He was at the bottom of the steps when the door opened again.

It was Kenny, another one of Dugray's men that Pierce had met a few times. He seemed shaken from the interaction with Townsend. "You a persistent motherfucker, you know that?" he snapped at the tweaker.

"You got any?" the tweaker said, his voice tight.

Kenny ignored the tweaker and nodded at Pierce. "You making a delivery?"

Pierce shook his head. "I need to talk to Dugray."

The tweaker turned and snarled at Pierce, and Kenny snapped at him. "Quit it! I told you, we out." Then he turned to Pierce, held up a finger, and closed the door.

The tweaker turned and stumbled off, cursing and mumbling to himself.

A moment later, the door opened up again and Dugray

stepped out. "You're alive," he said, squinting at Pierce in the diffuse glare of the overcast sky.

"More or less," Pierce said. "We need to talk."

"Yes, we do. I'm headed back to the A-house." He looked up and down the block. "Where's your car?"

"Long story."

"Take a ride?"

Pierce nodded. "Sure. I need to pick up some cash from my stash, anyway."

Motioning for Pierce to follow, Dugray led him halfway up the block to a sporty but dented Toyota.

"New ride?" Pierce asked.

"Nah, had it for a while," Dugray said as they got in. "I got a few now."

"I was worried about you," Pierce began as they pulled away. "How'd that all play out, with the UniCs and the Toros?"

Dugray scoffed. "I'm fine. And yeah, I was worried about you too. Crazy days. I don't know what that was all about yesterday. The UniCs got a hard-on for Townsend for some reason. But once the Toros showed up and shot a couple uniforms, the UniCs *and* the Toros forgot all about us. I just wish they could have had it out somewhere other than my biggest-earning house."

Pierce nodded. "I saw Townsend leaving just now. Seemed happy."

"Yeah, he's a fun guy."

"What's going on?" Pierce asked.

Dugray waved a hand and shook his head, eyes closed, as if just thinking about it reminded him how tired he was. "Too much, man. So, how about you? What've you been up to since you hightailed it? You figure out what happened to that cash up in Alaska?"

"No. And the Guild *is* coming at me. I fought off two of them on my way over here."

"How'd that go?"

"I padlocked their itty-bitty chains to a fence at a Home Depot in Queens."

Dugray laughed.

Pierce almost did too. Then he said, "I talked to Serino, learned a bit from him... But now he's dead."

"No shit? Did *you* kill him?"

Pierce shook his head. "No, but I was there when it happened." He told Dugray about talking to Serino's daughter, then Billings, and how Serino paged him and they met. "He kept saying how what he was going to tell me was huge, and how he couldn't tell UniCon or the UniCs, that they were in on it and he didn't trust them. But before he could tell me, a kill drone showed up outside the window and shot the place to hell. Cut him in half, just about. If I hadn't dropped my pen, the same would have happened to me."

"A fucking *kill drone*?" Dugray said, tapping the brakes and turning to look at Pierce. "So it's got to be UniCon that did it, right?"

"Seems like. His daughter said he had a big blow-up with Billings, the night before I went to Alaska. When I asked Billings about it, he seemed pretty on edge, too... Serino also had info on the Fairview."

Dugray whipped his head around. "He did? Like what?"

"He said it wasn't negligence. It was intentional."

Dugray nodded slowly, eyes smoldering.

"UniCon's report said the rising sea level weakened the concrete foundation, and that's true, but it wasn't an accident," Pierce told him. "They drilled tiny holes

142

into the concrete and slow-dripped seawater over them. That's what caused the collapse. It was murder."

After a long moment of silence, Dugray said, "Wow." Barely a whisper. "They murdered our mothers. I mean, we suspected as much."

Pierce nodded. "Yeah, we did. And Serino had some information on who did it." He took Serino's notepad out of his attaché and handed it over. Dugray put the car in Smartdrive as he scanned it, then handed it back.

"We'd worked our way up to a company called Infinity, right?" Pierce went on. "Serino said Infinity is owned by Garnet Holdings, which is owned by Hudson Limited, which is owned by Broadway Commercial Properties, which is owned by Crane International. He said that's the top layer. He said he was going to tell me who owns Crane, but he was killed before he could."

Dugray cleared his throat and kind of pinched the tip of his nose, maybe trying to keep it together. "So, we've got one more layer of shell companies to get through. Then we'll know who's responsible for one hundred and sixty-three cases of premeditated murder."

They locked eyes for a moment, then both nodded.

"It's going to be a harsh sentence," Dugray said.

"Yes, it is."

They drove in silence after that, until Dugray pulled over in front of the A-house.

Two workers were installing a new front door, and two more were working on the windows on the upper floors, which were broken and stained with soot. Dugray stopped to give a few orders, then Pierce followed him down a narrow breezeway to the alley in back. They descended a set of concrete steps and entered through the basement door.

Dugray pulled a chain hanging from the ceiling and the place lit up. It was surprisingly clean, a production space for cutting, dividing, and packaging product.

As they climbed the stairs, the air filled with sound of hammers and drills, along with the incongruously fresh smell of newly cut lumber.

When they reached the third floor, Dugray opened the old wooden door and the steel one behind it. Then he opened the massive safe.

"*Motherfucker!*" Dugray said, walking across the dusty floor.

The cloth bags of Small on the lower shelves were right where they had been, but above them, the shelves that had been stacked with bundles of Large were now empty except for a bunch of rubber bands and a thick layer of pale dust.

"Son of a bitch," Pierce said, coming in behind him. He went over to where his cash was, what was left of it—a stack of Small and a pile of dust. He tried not to think about how much money he had just lost as he pinched the dust between his fingers, rubbing them together.

"The door was locked," Dugray said, stunned. "The safe was locked. No one else has the combination."

Pierce took a deep breath. "It happened to me again too. My wallet. That's why I needed more cash."

"Jesus Christ," Dugray said, not listening. "Townsend's going to think I stole it. Shit, he thinks I even *let* it get stolen, he's going to kill me."

Pierce grabbed him by the shoulders. "Listen to me. It wasn't stolen. It's just like Alaska. No one took the Large out of my attaché, *or* my wallet. No one stole yours, either. They destroyed it, somehow. Turned it to dust."

Dugray opened his mouth but couldn't seem to find the right words. Finally, he said, "Why would someone want to make money disappear instead of stealing it? And how the fuck'd they do it?"

"Those are the big questions, right? Why and how. Revenge, maybe? Or to take over turf?"

Dugray screwed up his face. "So what, someone's moving against all the street gangs in New York by magically destroying their Large at the same time? I don't buy it."

Pierce shook his head. "Me neither. But my money has 'vanished' twice. So has yours, now. Kransky's did four times. All these people were after Serino, thinking he somehow mysteriously heisted them. And all this business with the Shakes and the Toros, your pal Townsend, too. All of them lashing out because they all think they got robbed. Maybe they didn't. Maybe something else is going on."

Dugray shook his head. "I don't know. I can think of a lot of reasons to steal someone else's money. But to make it disappear? I don't see why. Or how."

"Me neither," said Pierce. "But I need to figure it out before the Guild finds me."

They were quiet for another moment. Then Dugray said, "Yeah, well I got my own stuff I need to figure out, like how I'm going to keep Townsend from finding out his money is gone until I can replace it. I got no interest in ending up being his next message, if you know what I mean."

"Yeah," Pierce said. "If I can get the Guild off my back, figure out what happened to the cash, maybe that'll get Townsend off your back, too."

Dugray snorted. "The man's not known for listening to reason."

Pierce shook his head. "None of it makes sense."

He was thinking once more how helpful it would be to talk to Gloriana when Dugray's mouth twisted into a half smile.

He clapped a hand on Pierce's shoulder and gave it a squeeze that was disconcertingly reassuring. "Yeah, well, if you're trying to figure out some fucked-up angle on something someone's doing with money, there's one person I can think of who could help you. And we both know who that is."

Pierce opened his mouth, impressed at how perceptive Dugray was. But before he could say, "Gloriana," Dugray said, "Your dad."

Chapter Thirteen

BRADLEY PIERCE HAD been a highly successful stockbroker, investment advisor, and currency trader up until the Cyber Wars hit and the Chinese economy tanked. Or, more accurately, he had *appeared* to be successful. As it turned out, appearing successful was his greatest skill, and with his slender good looks and stylish clothes, he was a frequent feature in glossy business magazines, which burnished his image even further. He was so good at appearing successful that people lined up to give him money to trade, money he used to pay the others a dividend and provide himself—and a steady stream of attractive young women, even before the divorce—a very comfortable lifestyle.

Armand Pierce's parents had split up when he was twelve. Over the next few years, Bradley had spent vastly more money fighting child support than paying it. Pierce used to wonder why his dad was such a dick, but then he'd just come to accept it. When the truth about Bradley came to light, it almost made sense.

It was a classic Ponzi scheme with a couple of new twists, and so successfully executed that Bradley could probably have kept it going for years if the Chinese economy hadn't been so rude as to implode. Once exposed, his scams were so remarkably obvious that, despite their best efforts, the prosecutors and regulators couldn't figure out a way *not* to prosecute him, no matter how privileged and connected he was. This was before UniCon. If it had happened now, and if Bradley'd been in UniCon, he would have gotten off with a fine. A small one. As it was, he had spent the past fourteen years living at Otisville Federal Correctional Facility.

Pierce had already been estranged from his father for years when it all fell apart. He had long since picked up on the disingenuousness and venality that would later be more broadly revealed by the Chinese collapse.

As a courier, whose most valuable and essential quality was trustworthiness, Pierce found that having the most notorious and reviled fraudster in the country for a father could make for some interesting times at work.

But Dugray was right. Bradley was sleazy, but brilliantly so. If anyone could figure out the angle, he could. In fact, his advice had been invaluable to Pierce and Dugray's efforts to peel back the layers of shell corporations hiding the owner of Fairview.

As much as Pierce was dreading the conversation he was about to have, it was a relief to get out of the city. It was also exhilarating to be driving again—really driving. Pierce knew he wouldn't be able to bring his attaché in to the prison, and the chain could be an annoyance while driving, so he had removed them both, and felt oddly unencumbered. Dugray had loaned him a car and Pierce had taken it off SmartDrive for part of the journey. His pulse quickened at the response of the accelerator and the steering wheel as he swerved into curves and shot out of them on stretches of road that, compared to the city, were remarkably free of other cars.

The novelty wore off once the rain resumed and he had to slow down when the motor began to outperform the tires. He slowed even further when he saw a sign for Munson Creek, and a nostalgic melancholy set in. When he was a kid, his grandad used to take him fishing out there. It was a happy time, a simpler time. Even though he had been a child, the world had seemed to make sense.

The last few times they had come out there, after Pierce got out of the Army, Grandad spent most of the time griping about how much it had changed, how the snakeheads and other invasives had chased away all the trout. Some had spread north as the warming climate expanded their reach. Others had shown up mysteriously around the Cyber Wars, suspected by many to be part of an ecological sabotage campaign.

Grandad was pretty cranky in general by that point. Pierce had always assumed it was his age, but he also realized how hard it must have been, seeing his son go to prison, revealed to be such an asshole. In recent years, Pierce had also begun to suspect it probably also had to do with being stuck in a world he no longer understood. Maybe that was a part of growing old in a rapidly changing world. He had already seen glimpses of the same growing disconnect in himself, the frustration and disgust at a world that made less and less sense to him. He didn't know if it said more about him or the pace of the world changing around him.

Pierce had come out there on his own after Grandad passed away, but he'd regretted it. He had caught snakehead after snakehead, but not a single trout.

Now, his melancholy gave way to a deeper funk when he found himself stuck behind a massive, oversized dump truck with *Alliance Petrochemical* in a bold font on each side.

Mercifully, after half a mile, the truck pulled off the highway onto some kind of temporary construction exit. As his car pulled around it and picked up speed, Pierce craned his neck and watched the truck entering a massive strip-mining operation. There were at least a dozen similar trucks, plus diggers and earth movers, scattered across acres of exposed dirt and rock and pools of muddy water, as far as the eye could see. Where there used to be woods. Where there used to be Munson Creek.

He turned and watched until the scene disappeared behind some still-green rolling hills. The funk turned to outright sadness as he realized the creek was no longer simply different. Now it was gone entirely.

His sadness opened the door to thoughts of his mother. He tried to picture her, tried to conjure her face, his memories of their times together. He had loved her intensely throughout his life—when he was little and things were good, through the pain of the divorce and the move to Fairview, and when he was grown up, too, as she got more and more involved in the tenants' rights movement. But as always happened when he tried to think of her anymore, the memories he tried to conjure were crowded out by pain and anger and hatred at whoever was responsible for her death.

He tried to picture Christmas mornings or day trips to the beach, rainy afternoons he knew they had spent baking cookies together. But all that came up was loss.

As he gave up trying, another memory came to him.

Drinking beers with Dugray after the big memorial service the City held for all the victims. They had talked for hours that night, mourning their mothers and catching up with each other's lives, drinking too many beers, and eventually swearing they would work together to make it right.

As THE JOURNEY to Otisville wore on, Pierce's exhaustion caught up with him, and with the car in SmartDrive, he slept the rest of the way there. It was three in the afternoon when the car woke him up with a chime to let him know he was approaching his destination. He saw that he had slept through a page from Dugray's number.

He parked in the visitors' lot and took out his notepad before stashing his attaché in the trunk. He stopped at a payphone by the entrance and called Dugray.

"What's up?" he asked when Dugray picked up.

"I couldn't wait, I ran over to the library to search Crane International. But I struck out. The company no long exists, and no other information is available."

"What about the registration? The witness?"

Pierce had done enough digging to know that the papers of incorporation were essential to penetrating each layer, often through the registration company who'd handled all the paperwork and filings to create the shell—and more specifically the witness, usually a paralegal or office assistant. They generally didn't know anything about what they were witnessing, but it was always possible they might know the names of people involved. Sometimes they were privy to all sorts of information.

"Nothing. Crane International was incorporated a year before the others. They used a different registration company, Flex Business Consultants, and a new witness, Carla Ruiz-Vargas. Flex Business Consultants was a one-man shop—Sydney Sproles, Esq. It closed three years ago and he died a year later. Congestive heart failure."

"And the witness?"

"As far as I can tell, there's no one named Carla Ruiz-Vargas in New York, New Jersey, or Connecticut."

"Fuck."

"Anyway, if you haven't talked to Bradley yet, you might want to ask him about that, too. Let me know if you learn anything useful."

"You know it."

After allowing the guards to scan his cuff, Pierce signed in without incident. He had decided not to call ahead; the Guild knew that Bradley was his only living family, so it was already a risk coming out here. He didn't want to exacerbate that risk by tipping them off that he was on his way. So he wasn't surprised it took a while for them to bring Bradley out.

The visitation room looked much the same as it had the last time Pierce had visited, three years earlier, when he had come to tell Bradley that his ex-wife had died.

The visitation windows were empty except for one all the way to the right, which was surrounded by a cluster of reporters with cameras and lights. The inmate looked familiar, but Pierce couldn't place him. Probably some minor celebrity reprobate.

As a minimum-security federal prison, Otisville saw some big names pass through. Bradley might have counted as one a long time ago, but enough time had passed that as celebrity criminals went, he was a bit of a has-been. This guy was definitely still someone: tall and broad-shouldered with long blond hair that was stylishly unkempt, like a movie star between films. He looked maybe thirty-five, the smooth skin of his youth just beginning its transition to chiseled, like a rich young man who spent a lot of time on his yacht. The orange jumpsuit actually looked good on him, like it had been tailored.

Pierce sat as far away from them as he could, at a window at the other end, but he could still hear the conversation.

"We're going to repair the climate," he was telling the reporters. "Our donors have funded hundreds of autonomous drones that will help the clouds reflect the sunlight back out into space. We can still get ourselves out of the climate hole we've gotten ourselves into, but only if we can also stop digging the hole deeper."

One of the reporters mumbled a question, and the prisoner leaned forward, listening, then replied, his voice loud and clear.

"Absolutely, I *have* said that wealth inequality is a major factor. The wealthy use far more than their share of resources and are responsible for most of the carbon in the atmosphere. Besides, it's just *wrong* to have some who are so rich while we have so many so poor. But relentless economic growth is what's really killing the planet. In biology, unchecked growth is called cancer. I don't know why people think it's a good thing for the global economy. The best thing that happened to this planet in the last fifty years was the Upheaval, because it's the only thing that caused a noticeable dip in carbon emissions. We'd probably be dead by now without it."

"Are you saying what we need is another contraction?" someone called out.

"I'm saying we can't sustain unchecked growth."

"Don't you think this is UniCon's responsibility? Or the government's?" called out another reporter.

"Yes I do, but it's a responsibility that's been shirked for decades. They've abdicated their duty."

"And you really think your geoengineering plan is going to save the climate?" the reporter asked as a follow up.

The guy in the orange jumpsuit threw back his head, making sure to give his tousled hair a slight shake as he let out a big fake laugh. "You haven't been listening to a word I've been saying! We're not trying to *save* the climate. It's too late to *save* the climate. The climate is fucked. What we're trying to do is *repair* it, to bring it back before we're all dead. But the only way even that is going to work is if we can stop trying so damn hard to kill it at the same time."

A door opened behind the celebrity and Bradley walked in, escorted by a guard. He looked the same and yet different, and enough of each that both hit Pierce with unexpected impact.

The sameness evoked memories of early childhood, before his parents split, and maybe just after, when Pierce still thought of his father as a great man who loved him. He had understood at a pretty young age that neither of these things was true, but he could still remember the blissful ignorance from before that realization. On some level, he probably still longed for it.

The differences were subtler, and maybe more striking. Three years earlier, Bradley had seemed beaten down by prison—still strikingly handsome, but weary. Now he looked younger, healthier, strangely relaxed. His hair was long and his face oddly placid. When he walked into the room, he grinned at the celebrity like a star-struck teen. Then he scanned the windows, his smile faltering into something more recognizably half-hearted when he spotted Pierce.

"Hello son," Bradley said as he sat across from him. "You're looking well."

"Hello Bradley," Pierce replied, disappointed that he didn't get the wince that using his first name used to elicit.

"Nice of you to come see me." He leaned forward and looked down, over the counter. "And nice to see you're not wearing that godawful chain."

Pierce stayed quiet, trying not to betray his annoyance.

"So," Bradley said, sitting back with a smirk. "What brings you out here?"

"Two things, actually," Pierce said.

Before he could ask about the disappearing large, Bradley said, "Well. I hope neither of them has anything to do with your obsession with the Fairview."

Pierce felt his ire rising, the way only Bradley could provoke it. "What the hell is that supposed to mean?"

Bradley rolled his eyes, then leaned forward and lowered his voice. "Still? Jesus son, are you *trying* to make enemies?"

"No," Pierce replied through clenched teeth. "I'm *trying* to find out who is responsible for my mother's murder."

Bradley shook his head. "Come on, kiddo, the investigation said it was an accident."

Pierce decided not to tell him what he now knew. "We've made some progress penetrating the layers of shell corporations, and, but we've hit a dead end. Dugray—"

"Dugray the drug-dealer?"

Pierce took a breath. "Dugray thought you might have some special insights, given your particular *criminal* background."

Bradley bristled. He might live in a state penitentiary

but he hated to be reminded that he was a criminal. He cleared his throat as though preparing for a speech. "As I told you before, these corporate entities are formed by filing papers—"

Pierce sighed. "Yeah, we know, that's how we've gotten as far as we have. But we hit a dead end at what could be the last layer." He took out his notepad and wrote the names of the companies he and Dugray had found under the ones Serino had given them. Then he slid the notepad across the table. "This is what we've got so far."

Bradley looked it over and emitted a high-pitched, and probably involuntary, grunt of approval. "Well, it seems like you've made quite a bit of progress." He put the notepad down again. "So what do you want from me?"

"That top layer, Crane International, the registration company has folded, and the principal is dead."

"What about the witness?"

Pierce shook his head. "Can't find any trace of her in New York, Connecticut, or New Jersey."

Bradley thought for a moment, then shrugged. "Well, this is a little bit outside my expertise. If you wanted to *create* one of these impenetrable shell layers, I could do that. But even I couldn't tell you how to get through them if they're done right, especially not without resources…" He shook his head. "I still can't get used to the idea that there's no more internet. Well, hopefully once the U-Net is up and running, you'll be able to get to the bottom if it."

Pierce frowned.

Bradley's mouth turned up in a half smile. "Sorry you came all the way out here for 'nothing.'"

It was a dig, Pierce knew. He considered pointing out that if Bradley wanted him to visit more, he shouldn't have been such an asshole all those years.

Before he could reply, though, Bradley said, "You could try Tony Villarica."

Pierce furrowed his brow. The name sounded familiar, but he couldn't place it.

Bradley laughed, shaking his head. "The prosecutor? The guy who put me in here?" He leaned forward. "He retired to private practice, so he's no longer under UniCon, you know?" He jabbed his finger at the papers on the table. "He knows his way around this stuff. Believe me."

Pierce was surprised. He would have thought Bradley hated the guy, but he seemed sincere enough in praising him. "Thanks, I'll look him up. There's something else, too."

Bradley smiled indulgently, as if to imply that he would help Pierce, but he'd be justified if he refused.

Pierce took a breath, wondering where to start. "There's been a wave of violent crime in the city, gangs going after each other," he said, lowering his voice. "It seems to have something to do with money disappearing."

Bradley laughed. "Doesn't most crime involve money disappearing?"

"I mean literally. It seems as though whoever is behind it isn't stealing the money but destroying it."

"What do you mean? Like, burning it?"

Pierce shook his head. "They're not burning it. It disappears. From places where there's no way someone could have gotten access to it."

Bradley laughed again. "There's always a way. Since I've been in here, I've heard tales of some absolutely ingenious heists. Look, if someone could get access to destroy it, they could get access to take it. And given the choice, taking it is infinitely preferable."

"Only the large denominations are going missing,

hundreds and up. How would anyone benefit from destroying just the larger denominations?"

He shrugged. "On what scale?"

"I don't know. Does it matter?"

"Of course it matters. If you did it on a massive scale you could theoretically induce deflation. Prices have to drop to compensate. That's what governments do when they restrict money supply. That's part of monetary policy." He leaned back in his chair and looked over at the celebrity. "I was actually just talking about that with my friend—"

"So," Pierce said, cutting him off. The last thing he wanted was to sit through one of Bradley's minor-celebrity brags as he tried to glam up the fact that he was in prison. "The less money that exists, the more the remaining money is worth."

Bradley looked hurt at being cut off like that, but he got over it. "In theory. But a government can always just start printing more. Takes a while to get it into circulation, but forget about that. Whatever you're talking about would have to be on a much smaller scale. So, why would you do it? I guess to harm your competitors or enemies or whoever's money is being destroyed. You said this was between gangs?"

"Some of it, yes." Pierce didn't want to share any more information than necessary. "Do you know a guy named Frank Billings?"

"Billings Holdings? I know of him. UniCon. Bought his way up at the last conference. A lot of people thought UniCon fudged the numbers to get him in."

"Fudged the numbers? Why would UniCon do that?"

Bradley shrugged. "Because they wanted him in. Who knows why? UniCon works in mysterious ways."

Pierce told him about Serino and the laundering and the accusations of theft. "I don't know if he was working on his own or for Billings. It doesn't seem to make sense that a successful UniCon member like Billings would bother with street-level laundering, much less ripping off his customers."

Bradley put up his hands. "Billings may have bought his way into UniCon, but by no means has he been successful. Word is he's struggling badly, taking on lots of debt." He shook his head. "There's so many advantages to being in UniCon; if he's tanking despite all that, he must be a woeful businessman indeed. They say he's a lock to get relegated out at the UniConference next month. Plenty of other quasi-legit street gangs champing at the bit to take his place. And some have UniCon backing."

"Backing? All this time I thought it was just about the numbers." As soon as he said it, Pierce realized how naïve he sounded.

Bradley laughed. "Nothing's *just* about the numbers, kiddo. Especially not when it's who you allow into your club. UniCon is always helping some up, pushing some out. From what I've heard, they haven't been happy with Billings since they let him in. They eased his way in, they can ease his way out. And he's not the only one."

"What do you mean?"

Bradley let out a sigh, dismissive and disgusted. "A lot of these organizations buy their way up, but they have no idea how to run a big conglomerate. Some adjust, most flame out." He laughed. "And a lot of the old guard that got muscled out, they're working their way back up, retaking their 'rightful place.' They're trying to restore the proper order before they unveil the new U-Net."

Pierce snorted. "U-Net? You think that's for real?"

"Absolutely. This cash-based nonsense can't last. Everyone knows it. UniCon has built a secure, quantum-encrypted global network that works, so we can be done with this cash-economy nonsense. I hear they're about to announce it any day."

"They've been about to announce it 'any day' ever since the old internet collapsed."

"Well, this time it's real. The headquarters is under construction. I'm surprised you didn't know about it, since…" Bradley's voice trailed off and his mouth settled into a flat line. He looked down at his hands.

"Since what?"

Bradley looked up, his eyes betraying sorrow and pity. "The headquarters. They're building it on the site of Fairview."

Pierce's mouth opened on its own, but he didn't know what to say. He felt a surge of rage within him, but he didn't want to process that at the moment. He didn't want to lose his shit.

"I'm sorry son," Bradley said quietly.

Pierce shook his head to clear it, then said, "Can you think of any other reason why someone would be trying to destroy money?"

"As I said, I doubt they are, but who knows? Especially if it's UniCon. They really are so many steps ahead of… everyone else. Could be they want to shake people's faith in hard cash, priming the masses to embrace the new encrypted platform when it's ready." He shrugged. "It seems a little inelegant for UniCon, but at this point, they control so much, they might figure they don't need to be elegant."

"So you think UniCon could be behind it?"

"Seems like they're behind pretty much everything these

days, so if it's a real thing, they're either behind it or they'll be putting a stop to it soon enough. But you said only the larger denominations were going missing, is that right?"

"That's right."

He shook his head with a short condescending snort of a laugh. "Well, that only makes sense if they're stealing it. The smaller denominations simply aren't worth it. Every stack of fives you take is a stack of five thousands you're leaving behind. If you're destroying the money, why not just destroy *all* of it, right?" He laughed. "Unless they just can't stand the sound of the stuff!" He rubbed his fingers together and mimicked the crinkly sound of Large. "I could get behind that. Terrible stuff, that plastic crinkle. I mean, don't get me wrong, I love big money, but I'll never get used to that new stuff."

"I wondered if that could be part of it."

"What do you mean?"

"If maybe the reason they're destroying the Large is because they can, somehow they can get at the crinkle in a way they can't get at Small."

At the other end of the room, the reporters were packing up their cameras and recording equipment.

Bradley shook his head and poked a finger at Pierce. "I'm telling you, you're barking up the wrong tree. What you've got on your hands is good old-fashioned larceny, kiddo. You just haven't figured out how they're doing it." He sat back in his chair and tilted his head toward the commotion. "My friend Topher here has quite an interest in a lot of this stuff. He's primarily an ecologist, but he's incredibly knowledgeable about many, many areas." He sat forward, his eyes sparkling. "He asks such incisive questions, like he's not just pretending to be interested in what I do, or what other people find interesting. He really cares, really gets to know things in a deep, deep, way. A fascinating man. And while you might think I'm boring and horrible, Topher thinks I'm quite fascinating. Topher!" he called out, waving the celebrity over. "Topher, come say hi."

He turned back to Pierce and whispered, "The man has an almost insatiable sense of curiosity. It's absolutely infectious."

Topher came over and stood at Bradley's side, resting a hand on his shoulder.

Bradley looked up at him. "Topher, this is my son, Armand. Armand, this is my very good friend Topher Moreland. You might know of him as the leader of the BetterLates."

Now Bradley said it, Pierce recognized him immediately. He'd seen Topher Moreland's face countless times on the news.

Pierce remembered reading about the Moreland family in some waiting-room magazine a few years back. Topher's father, Gavin, founded the company that created the carbon capture technology that turned atmospheric carbon into diamonds. They were never able to scale it to the point where it made much difference to the climate, but the technology had made them billions anyway, and the resulting diamonds made even more before the diamond market cratered.

The company was hit hard in the Upheaval though, and when Topher took it over, he gave it a veneer of social justice, using some of his money to fund the BetterLates, to proselytize about the need for environmental remediation or geoengineering, crazy-sounding but apparently legitimate schemes to reflect sunlight into space or absorb carbon into the ocean.

Moreland had been in the news a few months earlier, after he and a bunch of BetterLates chained themselves to a shale refinery. The plant had been offline for a day, and Moreland was given a nominal fine, but he refused to pay it. He said it was a matter of principle. Apparently, he was still in jail as a result. Maybe it was a matter of principle after all.

Moreland smiled. "Very nice to meet you, Armand." His teeth were perfect. His eyes locked onto Pierce's with focus and intensity.

"You too," Pierce replied.

"Armand was just asking me about monetary policy," Bradley said, his voice tinged with something oddly like pride. He turned back to look at Pierce. "Moreland and I actually met over a conversation about monetary policy. We talked for hours and hours. Go figure, right?"

Moreland grinned. "It was a fascinating conversation." He turned to Pierce. "I understand you're in the Courier's Guild, is that right?"

Pierce smiled politely and pulled back his sleeve.

Moreland grinned. "Fascinating, I bet you've got some crazy stories to tell."

Before Pierce could reply, Bradley said, "Armand is looking into some mysteriously vanishing money."

Moreland smiled again. "Disappearing money? Well, I think we've all experienced that at some point or another, right?"

Bradley laughed more than the joke warranted. "No," he said. "He thinks they're *intentionally* destroying it."

"Oh, no!" Moreland said, putting up his hands in mock horror. "We work so hard to raise money! It kills me to think of people out there destroying it when they could give it to a good cause instead." He gave Pierce a warm, fake smile. "If you find these guys, tell them to send the money to the BetterLates. They could at least get a tax deduction."

Pierce was determined not to buy it. "I heard you earlier, saying the world needs a major financial contraction. Aren't you worried about the people that would hurt?"

Moreland's eyes seemed to crystalize as he stared back at Pierce. "I absolutely am. But I worry more about the people already being hurt. And the people not even born yet who are going to be hurt if things keep on the way they are going."

"I thought you were going to fix the climate."

"Well, we're trying. But it's not going to do much good if we don't stop breaking it at the same time. If you're stuck in a hole, you've got to stop digging, right?"

There was a passion in his voice, a barely contained intensity. Then it went away, and the smile came back.

Bradley's face was set in a familiar, disappointed frown that reached across the decades from Pierce's youth. He seemed mortified that Pierce was challenging his friend.

"Anyway," Moreland said brightly. "It was a pleasure meeting you."

As he turned to leave, Pierce said, "What's with the singing?"

Moreland turned back. "I beg your pardon?"

"The singing or chanting or whatever. And burning the incense. What's up with that?"

Moreland gave him a cold smile. "We don't burn incense, we *diffuse* it. The BetterLates don't burn anything, that's part of not digging the hole any deeper. As for the other stuff, well, people used to look to God for salvation, until they realized they had to save themselves. But they still like the trappings of religion. It's a comfort."

Pierce thought of Erno and his followers, the jackets and shades and fetishization of the chain and the attaché. He wondered if Erno had made a similar calculation.

"I know it's important, trying to fix the climate," Pierce said, for some reason determined to get under Moreland's skin, and Bradley's, too. "But do they have to be so annoying about it?"

Moreland shook his head, then looked down at Bradley, who was staring at Pierce, mortified. "See you inside."

"No, wait," Bradley said, putting a hand over Moreland's, which was still on his shoulder. He stood up and flashed a glare at Pierce, shaking his head in anger and disappointment. Then he turned to Moreland. "I'll come with you."

Chapter Fourteen

GLORIANA HADN'T WANTED to be an academic, but she knew that was the only way she would get to do the research she wanted to do. She studied what she did because she wanted to make a difference *herself*, not to teach students how *they* could make a difference years down the road. And she did make a difference. As an associate professor at Nanyang University, she had created fertilizers, plant-safe antifungals, and increasingly powerful and targeted strains of *Neptunomonas Petrophilos*, the oil-eating microbe. She saw the difference her work made, helping to clean up terrible spills, and sparing other villages and wildlife areas the type of scouring that used to be necessary, that left them clean on the surface but sterile as well.

The thing that gnawed at her, though, that kept her awake at night, was that all of her funding came from Nolexa Petro Fuels, the same people whose carelessness and avarice had destroyed her village. And it was not an arm's length relationship.

They loved her. She wasn't just one of their top researchers—and they retained a substantial financial interest in her discoveries—she was also their poster child, a public relations powerhouse. Instead of hiding the spill that destroyed Gloriana's village, they made it part of her narrative, how this beautiful young scientist had been inspired by tragedy as a young girl to make the world a better place. And how Nolexa Fuels had made it possible through their commitment to the environment.

Speaking engagements and interviews became a bigger and bigger part of her job. Her hatred of it was mitigated by the fact that it took the place of teaching. And even as she was absorbed deeper and deeper into the Nolexa Fuels apparatus, she was still able to do her research. And that was the most important thing.

One of the limitations of the earlier versions of *Neptunomonas Petrophilos* was its inability to remain active below the surface of a mass of oil. It needed oxygen and nitrogen from the air or the water to remain active, so the oil had to be broken up, by time or chemical dispersants, in order for the microbes to work. Gloriana helped overcome that limitation, creating strains that needed much less nitrogen and oxygen, but could also penetrate large, thick spills, tunneling in and aggressively breaking down the oil while frantically churning out more and more microbes with such gusto that the oil became emulsified with oxygen- and nitrogen-rich water and air.

She won awards for her work, and Nolexa exploited them every chance it got.

In fact, it was during one of those appearances, three years ago, during the last UniConference in New York, that things had begun to change permanently between Gloriana and her employer.

The company had brought out their star microbiologist to be the bright, shiny, young, non-white face of the company—and by extension, some would say, the face of UniCon.

Gloriana had delivered her address to a standing ovation, and afterward Nolexa CEO Carlton Davies invited her to accompany him to a shareholder banquet. She wouldn't have to speak, she just needed to be there. And although phrased as an invitation, it was clearly not optional.

The expensive Scotch and scallops seared on slabs of Himalayan salt were enough to keep her pleasantly occupied during the tedious financial reports. But something Davies said caught her attention.

In addition to researching and creating new and improved versions of *Neptunomonas Petrophilos*, Gloriana was also responsible for overseeing production of the existing strains. And, as Davies boasted, they were producing a *lot*. At first, she thought it commendable that Nolexa was creating such a massive reserve, that they were committed to keeping enough of the stuff on hand to deal with any situation that might arise. Maybe even enough to share with their competitors. But Davies made it clear that was not what they were doing. They didn't have enough.

With the amount they were producing, there should have been a huge quantities on hand. That left only one explanation: Nolexa wasn't stockpiling vast quantities of *Neptunomonas Petrophilos*, they were *using* it. A lot. And that meant they were spilling, a lot.

The realization hit her just as the meeting broke up.

Gloriana walked out and kept walking, losing herself in the crowd outside the hotel.

That's when she spotted Chris, out on the sidewalk with the protestors.

She hadn't seen him in a couple years at that point. They'd broken up, as far as that went. But this seemed like fate, like he had been sent there to be with her at that moment.

He disappeared into the throng of protestors, and as Gloriana went after him, the crowd grew tighter and tighter, half of them dressed in green. Most carrying signs accusing UniCon of all manner of dastardly deeds, and all of them true. She hated herself for being a part of it, regardless of her motives.

As she wandered through the crowd, everybody seemed to be pressing closer to a stage setup on the outskirts of a park. That's when she heard Chris's voice, amplified, and she turned and saw him up on the stage.

"I don't know about you people," he said, his voice booing over the PA. "But I am sick to death of UniCon."

The crowd roared.

He smiled at them, that roguish smile that had charmed her back at Princeton. "I'm sick of their corruption, their malfeasance, and *all* their other bullshit."

The crowd roared even louder, and Gloriana roared along with them. Before long, he spotted her in the crowd. His smile broadened. His eyes twinkled and he waved. She waved back. Several in the crowd tracked his eyes and saw that he was waving at her. They looked at her differently after that.

She listened to the whole speech, and while she didn't agree with everything he said—there was an odd tone of bravado that she didn't like—his words left her with an energy that swirled into the anger that had been churning inside her since Davies' unintentional revelation back at the UniConference. By the time he finished, she had come to a decision.

When Chris came down off the stage, he kissed her, before either of them said a word. They went out for a drink, then back to his hotel, and they stayed up all night, drinking and fucking and talking science and politics and philosophy. It was just like back in college, except that she was distracted in a way she had never been with him before.

He fell asleep at five, but she stayed awake, her thoughts coalescing into something big.

At breakfast, as she told him what she was thinking, his eyes began to gleam. By the time they went their separate ways, they had the beginnings of a plan.

It only took a little bit of digging once she got back to Nanyang University to discover that with this new tool in their toolbox—the tool she had given them—Nolexa was cutting more corners than ever before. Instead of minor incidents a couple of times a year, spills were happening every few weeks. It was only a matter of time before there was a spill of devastating proportions.

She was outraged. Her microbes were powerful tools, but they were no magic bullet.

Even as she was coming to these realizations, her worst nightmare was realized. There was a spill, a big one, at a facility with a history of such spills—the very facility whose spill had devastated her village when she was a child. This one was ten times worse. And the sea currents were pulling the spill in the same direction they had twenty years earlier. Right toward what was left of her village.

Nolexa put out booms to contain the spill and sprayed it from the air with Gloriana's *Neptunomonas*

Petrophilos, but it wasn't enough. There was simply too much oil.

The village—the sterile, artificial remnant of the place of her youth—was destroyed completely this time.

Gloriana had been working on *Neptunomonas Petrophilos-5*, a new generation that was more voracious, more aggressive, and more capable of thriving deep in petroleum-only environments.

But with this latest spill, she realized that if she wanted to protect the world, she was going at it the wrong way, treating the symptom instead of attacking the underlying problem.

That's what she told herself. But deep down, she knew she also wanted to hurt Nolexa Fuels.

She booked a company helicopter, saying she needed to see the refinery where the spill originated, Nolexa's largest facility in Southeast Asia. She brought with her several gallons of *Neptunomonas Petrophilos-5*, and she poured it into the primary feed from the crude tanks into the refinery itself.

She got back on the helicopter and directed the pilot to return to Nanyang University, but ten feet off the ground, they stopped rising. The pilot tilted his head, listening to someone speaking into his ear as they hovered just off the ground. He turned and looked at her, his expression unreadable behind large dark sunglasses. Then they slowly descended back down to the pad.

She'd been a prisoner in one form or another ever since.

Bank Run

"HE DON'T LOOK so good, does he," the Latino kid said to Henshaw, tipping his head in the direction of the guy in the blue porkpie hat five spots ahead of them in line. The guy wasn't much older than Henshaw, but he had white hair and a bright red neck. His face was blotchy and he had stopped sweating, despite the intense heat.

"No, he doesn't, does he," Henshaw replied.

The kid's name was Munoz. He was in his mid-thirties, had a wife and three kids. He worked for a plumbing contractor and planned on going out on his own once he'd saved up enough, specializing in installing condensation rigs.

Henshaw had been in line in front of Tempe Savings and Loan for close to six hours now. He'd arrived at six a.m. with a money belt under his shirt and a gun in his pocket, just in case. He'd felt nervous at first, probably more about the gun than the money. He didn't show it, didn't tell anyone he had it. It was just for protection. Just to be safe.

Munoz had arrived a couple of minutes after he did, got in line right behind him.

They were there for the same reason, although neither of them would say it out loud. No one in line would. And no one asked, either.

For the first hour or so, no one had said anything at all. Practically the only sound was the steady buzz of drones overhead and, in the distance, some of those crazy BetterLates that seemed to have taken over the city, with their singing and chanting and incense.

The bank's drone port was closed, though, so the drones hovered in the sky above them. One by one they got tired of waiting—or their batteries ran down—and they zipped off back the way they had come. After a while they stopped showing up and it was quiet again, except for the singing, which seemed to be getting closer.

Everyone standing there in the heat was clutching a bag or a box or an envelope, or else telling themselves no one could see the money belts bulging around their midsections or the thick wallets in their pockets. As the line got steadily longer, a pair of UniCs showed up, Financial Crimes Division, and began patrolling the length of it, just in case. That's why they were *all* there: just in case.

Half a dozen hooligans were hanging out in the parking lot of the Taco Bell across the street. The cops kept a pretty good eye on them.

The BetterLates rounded the corner and came down the street, chanting and singing about fixing the environment while they smelled up the street with their goddamned incense. They'd been around a lot lately and it was getting on everyone's nerves. Henshaw knew they had a point, the BetterLates—it was kind of hard to argue with that when it was a hundred and fifteen degrees outside.

But the chanting and the incense made it feel twice as bad. They were like human humidity. Maybe that was the point.

Somebody threw a soda bottle at them, then someone else did. Suddenly everyone was throwing trash at them. Henshaw, too. He felt guilty, but they brought it on themselves, being such weirdoes. There were two pairs of cops now, but they didn't do anything to stop it.

The BetterLates pretended not to notice, but Henshaw was pretty sure they started parading just a little bit faster.

When they disappeared around the corner, everyone in line cheered. Even the cops were laughing. That kind of broke the ice. People started talking after that, but even then, there seemed to be an understanding: you didn't talk about why you were there. It was like they were all afraid they would jinx something. But they talked about everything else—their lives and their loved ones, their dreams and their fears.

Henshaw and Munoz agreed they didn't believe in banks all that much, especially not since the Upheaval.

Henshaw remembered the stories his grandparents had told him when he was a little child, about banks failing during the Great Depression. Growing up, the Depression had seemed impossibly long ago, but seventy years later, he realized it was the blink of an eye. So much about the world had changed so drastically since he was a child, and even more since his grandparents were children, but people were the same. Having lived through enough of it, he had seen that history really does repeat.

But as much as he didn't trust the banks, Henshaw

always kept an account open, and now he was glad he did. If more people had, maybe the line would be moving a lot faster. Some of the younger people didn't have accounts at all. That was part of what was taking so long—half the people in front of them weren't just making deposits, they were opening new accounts. Mostly, though, he suspected the bank was just stalling. The scoundrels.

Munoz was one of the ones who didn't have an account, having lived his entire adult life in the post-Upheaval world. He kept his money at the Safety Vault store around the corner, or at least he used to.

Munoz smiled condescendingly and said even as a kid he'd never trusted all that e-commerce stuff. Said he could never understand how Henshaw's generation fell for it the way they had, that they must have known everybody was getting ripped off, way before the Cyber Wars and the Upheaval, but they'd gone along with it anyway.

Henshaw almost called bullshit on that—if Munoz had been a teenager before the Cyber War, he probably did more online than Henshaw did, and trusted it without a second thought. But he seemed like a nice enough kid, and it was a tricky situation. Henshaw didn't want him taking offense and then being stuck next to him for however many hours they still had to wait.

Instead, he just smiled politely and said, "That's just how things were." That's what people his age generally said when younger folk asked them what they could possibly have been thinking. There wasn't any better answer.

As the line at the bank got longer, some people went down the block instead, to the car dealership or the electronics store. Not a bad idea, Henshaw thought. Tie up your cash in something concrete. Most car dealers let you bring the car back within seven days for a refund. The line at the bank was barely moving, and Henshaw was seriously thinking that maybe he should cross the street and get a car instead, but by the time he got to that point, there were almost as many people lined up there. He figured it was best to stay where he was. He didn't want to have to explain to Loretta why he'd come home with a new car instead of a certificate of deposit.

A few spots in front of them, a sweaty, sunburnt woman in a bright yellow cotton dress was telling the guy with the blotchy face he needed to get somewhere indoors, get something cool to drink. He called her a cunt and accused her of trying to take his place in line.

Munoz and Henshaw laughed, but tried to hide it. The old boy was an ornery cuss, but he might have been right about her.

They were still laughing when a sleek black Audi pulled up to the curb. The license plate said DR NOSE. The driver got halfway out, putting one foot on the baking street but keeping as much of his body in the air-conditioned car as he could.

He looked up and down the block, his tanned face contorted in disgust and disbelief. "This is the line for the bank?"

The thugs across the street were staring hard at the back of his head. There were ten of them now.

"Yes, it is," said the woman in the yellow dress. "And it starts way down there." She seemed to take great delight in pointing at the back of the line, past Henshaw and Munoz. There were about thirty people in front of them, and there must have been at least fifty behind them now.

He called out to the people near the front of the line. "I'll pay you a thousand dollars for your spot in line."

An old woman about six spots from the front turned to look at him, but then she frowned and turned away. The white-haired guy snarled, "Fuck you," getting a laugh from the crowd that he didn't seem to appreciate.

"Okay, two thousand, then."

"You pay me in twenties, I'll take it," Munoz called out, earning a much bigger laugh.

Dr. Nose glowered at him.

Eventually, a college kid in the middle of the line sold his spot for five grand. The kid got his money, gave up his spot and started walking toward the back of the line.

Forty minutes later, the line hadn't moved, but the sun had, creating a small strip of shade along the storefronts that everyone pressed themselves into.

It was too late for blotchy-face, though. He toppled like a tree and hit the sidewalk with a thud.

"Heat stroke," Henshaw said, trying to banish the thought that if more people dropped, he'd get into the bank a little sooner.

"No doubt," Munoz replied, probably facing a similar ethical struggle.

The cops ran over. As one of them took vital signs and loosened the guys' shirt, his partner ran to their squad car and backed it up right next to the man on the pavement.

As they carried him toward the back seat, he regained consciousness, at least enough to grab a No Parking sign and start flailing and kicking, calling them every name in the book. The cops tried to tell him he could die if they didn't get him to a hospital, but he was howling with rage.

The line bowed ever so slightly, the front and the back curving out into the sunlight so everyone could see what was going on.

Finally, the police got the old guy's hands off the signpost. They stuffed him into the back seat of the squad car and sped off with a squeal of tires.

"Should have taken the two grand," someone called out from behind them.

Henshaw and everyone around him turned and saw Dr. Nose standing there with a smirk on his sweaty face. He had an expensive-looking leather satchel in his arms.

Two of the troublemakers from across the street were approaching him from behind, their faces stony and their stride determined.

Henshaw didn't care about the guy, but he shouted a warning anyway. It was already too late.

One of the thugs stepped right up to the doctor, putting all of his weight behind a fist that hooked across the doctor's face. The doctor's nose kind of exploded, jetting blood across his face. The second thug landed a savage kick to his right kidney.

As the doctor dropped to his knees, the first kid tore the leather bag from his grasp. Before he hit the sidewalk, the thieves were sprinting back down the street.

Their friends at the Taco Bell were laughing and hollering, cheering the two on as the remaining pair of cops set off after them, chasing them past the Denny's at the end of the block. As soon as they disappeared around the corner, the laughter from across the street stopped.

Henshaw said, "Oh, no."

Munoz said something worse.

The thugs were all crossing the street toward the bank line. Their eyes were hard, burning black, like their pupils were dilated with the thrill of the hunt, or with something pharmaceutical. But instead of running, the prey stayed right where they were. Maybe there was nowhere for them to go, but Henshaw made a conscious decision not to make a run for it, and he figured everybody else made the same calculation. It wasn't bravery. It was desperation.

He had his entire life's savings with him, or more accurately, the savings he'd managed to rebuild since the Upheaval. He'd heard enough of the rumors to believe they were true. He wasn't giving up his chance to protect what was his.

The thugs started trotting, gathering momentum as they approached.

Henshaw and Munoz exchanged a glance. Henshaw reached back and wrapped a sweaty hand around his gun.

The closest kid was just stepping onto the curb when a voice at the end of the line let out a strangled cry, a garbled sound of confusion, frustration, fear, and surprise. It was the college kid who had sold his spot in line. "My money!" he called out. "Oh, no!"

Everyone paused and looked at him. He was standing on the sidewalk holding out his hands as dust and bits of disintegrating paper spilled between his fingers.

Henshaw knew what he had to do. Everyone else did, too. The entire line surged forward, stampeding toward the entrance to the bank. When he got to the knot of people wedged into the bank's corner entrance, Henshaw threw himself against their backs, trying to claw his way between them and get inside. He'd spent too long waiting in that hot sun to give up now, and too long building a life for himself and his Loretta to see it all crumble into dust. He pushed aside the woman in front of him, his desperation outweighing the shame he felt at his behavior.

Then a hand grabbed him from behind and he was thrown to the ground.

He found himself looking up into the barrel of a gun and the hard eyes of one of the thugs. He didn't even reach for his gun. He knew he was slow. He'd fumble it. He'd get shot.

"Where's it at? The money?"

Not ten feet away, one of the other lowlifes smacked the glasses off a bald guy with a mustache. He grabbed the plastic bag out of the guy's hands and reached inside it, then growled and dumped it onto the sidewalk. It was that same coarse sawdust.

"No!" cried the bald guy. "My money... My savings. That's everything!"

Up and down the line, people were checking their bags and boxes and money belts. A chorus of gasps and shouts filled the air. Munoz was kneeling in the street and weeping.

Henshaw ignored his robber. He unzipped his money belt and pulled out a handful of scraps of paper mixed in with dust that stuck to his sweaty fingers as it sifted between them and onto the pavement. Little scraps of paper fluttered in the air as they settled to the ground as well, but within seconds they were gone, too, turned to dust like the rest of it.

A soft breeze picked up. The first breeze all day.

The gangsters cursed and ran, disappearing through the parking lot of the Taco Bell.

Henshaw stared at the sidewalk. A lifetime of hard work and saving and planning, all of it gone. He couldn't bear the thought of facing Loretta, of telling her, of seeing the look on her face.

But maybe he wouldn't have to. He still had his gun.

Chapter Fifteen

Pierce let the car do the driving back toward the city. He wanted to sleep but he also needed to think. His conversation with Bradley had left him even more confused about what was going on with the Large. It did seem crazy that the money was disappearing, but he'd seen it himself. When he was younger, he'd felt like he understood how the world worked. But he'd seen the collapse of too many things that once seemed immutable to have much faith in the permanence of anything. Still, even as the world had been torn apart and reshaped in ways he could never have imagined, he could at least trust his own senses.

Now he wasn't so sure.

Why just the Large? Obviously, you could hurt someone more by destroying their Large instead of their Small, but if that's what you're after, why not destroy all of it?

He thought about Bradley's theory, that if the Large really was disappearing, maybe it was UniCon, undermining confidence in cash. Seemed crazy, but it was the best explanation so far. Of course, they'd have to make sure their own Large was safe, but presumably, they would have figured that out. But where did that leave him? It wasn't like he could just ask UniCon if they were remotely destroying Large for whatever purpose, maybe get them to write him a note that he could show the Guild.

Pierce was stumped as to what his next step should be.

The clock was ticking on trying to figure out what was going on with the money, and it was ticking loud. He was only going to stay ahead of his fellow couriers—or manage to fight them off—for so long.

Whatever was going on was spreading, growing. Maybe if he could just stay alive long enough, the phenomenon, regardless of the cause, would become so widespread, so apparent, that the Guild would be forced to acknowledge that the disappearance of Kransky's Large was part of it, that Pierce wasn't to blame and he had acted out of self-defense.

But the chances of that seemed slim—and more like none if he wasn't hunkered down hiding out somewhere instead of out trying to figure out what the fuck was going on.

And in the back of his mind, another clock was ticking too. Because if his time on Earth was running out, so was his time to figure out who was responsible for Fairview. To make them pay.

And he did have a lead on that.

He spotted a payphone along the side of the road and, with a sigh, told the car to pull over. He typed ANTONIO VILLARICA into the info screen and got a hit, an address in Queens. But no phone number.

He stared at it for a few seconds, trying to think of where else he should be going, what else he could be doing to forestall what seemed like his increasingly inevitable demise.

Then he got back in the car and redirected it to Villarica's address.

It was a neat brick single with a patch of grass out front and a garage in the back. The lawn was tidy, but the strip of garden next to the front door was just a patch of mulch with a couple of scraggly marigolds.

Pierce retrieved his attaché and chain from the trunk, then rang the doorbell and stepped back. After a few seconds, he heard a scratching, fumbling sound and the door opened to reveal a gaunt man in his eighties. His shirt hung on him, the collar gaping away from his sagging neck. Behind him in the gloomy, darkened house, the television was tuned to a news channel.

"Can I help you?" he said, eying Pierce's attaché with mild curiosity and the rest of him with the level of suspicion you might expect from a retired prosecutor. He kept one hand behind the door, and Pierce wondered if he was holding a gun.

"Antonio Villarica?"

"A courier, hm? Do you have a package for me?" He seemed appropriately suspicious, but also a little excited.

"No, actually. I was hoping to ask you a few questions."

Villarica's face soured. "I'm retired."

"I'm Bradley Pierce's son. He thought you might be able to help me with an investigation."

Villarica raised an eyebrow that somehow managed to convey first suspicion at the mention of Bradley, then surprise at the off-the-books investigation, then a dawning recognition. "Armand Pierce."

"Yes, that's right. My mother died in the Fairview collapse. I'm looking for answers."

Villarica leaned through the doorway and looked both ways. "You don't accept that it was an accident?"

"Accident or not, someone's responsible and I want to know who."

Villarica stepped back and opened the door wider. "Come on in."

As he entered the house, Pierce heard a heavy metallic *clunk* and when Villarica closed the door, he saw an old .38 sitting in a bowl along with a set of keys and some rubber bands on a small table.

The place had the look and smell of *old*. The furniture was traditional, quality but worn. The air was stuffy, just this side of musty.

The cable news was going through a national weather round-up: droughts and floods, wildfires, plagues of insects, and the latest on Tropical Storms Wilson and Xavier, churning toward the Carolinas and the Texas panhandle.

Villarica gestured toward a faded brown wingback armchair as he lowered himself into a depression on the righthand side of the matching sofa. A smaller depression to his left remained empty.

Looking around the place, Pierce wondered if this was where he was headed, if he survived his current predicaments. Old and alone. He already felt like he was losing his place in the world, like it was passing him by. He glanced at the empty indentation on the sofa next to Villarica. He didn't even have that.

Pierce sat and Villarica said, "He's many things, your father, but one of them is very smart. A terrible waste, really. I don't know if I can help you if he couldn't, but I'll try."

"Thanks. I don't know how closely you followed it,

but the UniCs closed the case without ever uncovering or revealing who the owner was. I'm investigating on my own, trying to penetrate the layers of shell companies. I've hit a wall and my father thought you could help me."

Villarica let out a long, sad sigh. "You know that if UniCon closed the case, they want it closed. There's no way you're going to get them to open it again, no matter what you find."

"I know."

He stared at Pierce, studying, appraising. "So then what are you going to do with the information?"

Pierce kept his face blank. "I just want to know."

Villarica stared at him another moment, as the news shifted to an update on U-Net. The correspondent quoted experts who were cautiously optimistic, like they had been for over a decade.

"Okay," Villarica said, shrugging almost imperceptibly, like maybe he realized he didn't much care if Pierce was after more than edification. "How can I help?"

Pierce pulled out his notepad, vaguely embarrassed at how ratty it was starting to look. As he handed it to Villarica, he tapped the top page. "Crane International. I was hoping you might have some insights."

On the news, a young woman was reporting on the explosion of gang violence in New York, as well as several other places, including some sunbaked suburb in Arizona, which was under an intense heat alert.

Villarica looked over at the television and shook his head, then back to Pierce. "Have you looked into the registration company?

"Yes, Flex Business Consultants, but—"

"But they went out of business and Sydney Sproles is dead, right?"

Pierce couldn't hide his surprise. "How did you know?"

Villarica smiled sadly. "I've been out of it for a while, but I was in it for a long, long time."

"The witness was a Carla Ruiz-Vargas, but she doesn't seem to exist."

Villarica smiled. "Sweet lady, Carla, even if she worked for a crook. I interviewed her a number of times over the years. Ruiz-Vargas is her maiden name. She used it whenever Sproles asked her to do something that could come back on her, which happened a lot." He took Pierce's notepad and started scribbling in it. "Carla Jackson, her name is," he said, pausing to stare off into the distance for a moment thinking.

Pierce kept perfectly still, not wanting to disrupt Villarica's train of thought. He was dismayed at the thought of how many Carla Jacksons there could be in the city of New York.

On the television, an overhead drone shot showed a dusty, sun-baked commercial district, with store windows smashed and cars overturned. Black scorch marks streaked the storefronts and splotched the street where cars had been set fire. Business-owners stood around looking defeated as they assessed the damage.

The drone rose into the air and the shot widened out. A band of BetterLates came into view, marching down the street. Pierce shook his head, thinking how bad it had to suck having your business trashed and looted in the middle of an ungodly heat wave, and then to have the BetterLates show up to serenade you.

Villarica made a clicking sound with his mouth, then he started writing again. "Can't remember to take my damn pills, but I remember stuff like this." He handed the notepad back to Pierce.

Pierce looked at it. An address in Queens. "This is Jackson's address?"

Villarica nodded and stood, letting Pierce know the visit was ending. "At least it was a couple years ago. Not too far from here, as I recall. Right off Vernon Boulevard."

"That's great. Thanks." As Villarica herded him toward the door, Pierce stopped. "One more question, though. I've been hearing about instances of money disappearing, mysteriously vanishing, Large turning into powder or disintegrating. Ever come across anything like that? Any idea what might be causing it?"

Villarica screwed up his face as he opened the front door. "Money disappearing, huh?"

"That's right."

No," he said, shaking his head. "Never heard of anything like that."

PIERCE PUT THE address into his nav; it turned out Carla Jackson lived less than two miles away. As Vernon Boulevard swung close to the East River, Manhattan came into view on the other side of it. Pierce tapped the brakes and slowed to a stop. Across the river, in the distance, smoke rose from several fires, but in front of that, directly across, was the future home of U-Net, rising on the site where the Fairview Apartments once stood. The skeletal structure bristled with cranes and buzzed with construction bots. A huge concrete printer, massive compared to the ones in Queens, was perched on the top floor. Brightly colored cement bots curved around the outside of the structure, on a track, like a roller coaster.

If Bradley was right, if UniCon was somehow making Large disappear to undermine faith in cash and generate interest in U-Net, this could be where it all came together.

He thought about Kransky, the hands in the wastebasket, about Diaz's other missing couriers, about the Shakes and the Toros going at each other, and people missing from Townsend's operation. He thought about Serino's murder, all the other deaths caused by whatever was going on with the disappearing money, and the idea that it was all to pave the way for U-Net. And one hundred and sixty-three people had been murdered to free up the real estate for its fancy new headquarters.

If UniCon was behind it all, behind the Fairview and the disappearing cash, all the related death and mayhem, there would be no one to hold them accountable, except maybe Dugray and him. But if he could prove it to the Guild, he could still keep his hand, and his life. Maybe even his job, if he still wanted it after all this.

The Guild was after him. And he couldn't keep evading them for long. He was close to finding out who was responsible for Fairview, but running out of time to do it. And Carla Jackson's house was less than two miles away.

IT HAD SIDING instead of brick and there was no driveway or garage, but otherwise Carla Jackson's house was a lot like Villarica's. It had the same vaguely depressing feel.

The windows were dark, with no signs of life, but Pierce rang the bell anyway and a few seconds later a curtain was pulled back behind one of the small panes of glass set in the door. A face appeared in the shadows, a gaunt man in his forties with pale brown skin and rings under his eyes as dark as the gloom he emerged from.

"What do you want?" he said, hoarse and resentful, sad and angry.

"Are you Mr. Jackson?"

He looked down at Pierce's attaché, and for a moment there was light in his eyes, as if he was considering that maybe Pierce was bringing him money. Then the light faded. "I'm not expecting any deliveries. What do you want?"

"Is Carla Jackson home? Just need to ask a few questions."

The man's eye twitched and his face trembled. "No, she's not fucking home. She's dead!" he shouted, flecking the glass with spittle.

Pierce was stunned, and also devastated. "I'm so sorry, Mr. Jackson. I didn't know."

The door ripped open, and the man stood there, his face blotchy and his chest heaving. "Wait a second," he said, looking down at the attaché. "Was that for Carla?"

Pierce was at a loss. "I'm sorry, no, it's not. I'm not here on Guild business. I was hoping to ask a few questions about the Fairview Apartments. My mother died in the collapse."

Jackson stared at him for a moment. "Sorry about your mother," he said quietly. Then his shoulders slumped, and he stood back from the door, shaking his head. "All right, whatever. Sure, come on inside and ask your goddamn questions."

The similarities to Villarica's house extended to the television in the corner, playing the same news channel. The smell was different—more dirty laundry than stale and musty—but it felt just as sad, just as lonely.

The television news cut to a commercial, one of those UniCon public-service-type feel-good ads, with families smiling in ecstasy for no reason other than that life was good, thanks to UniCon.

Jackson glanced at the television and shook his head, then turned to Pierce and folded his arms, waiting.

Pierce cleared his throat. "Do you mind if I ask... how your wife died?"

"How do I know I can trust you?"

"I don't know." Pierce held up his attaché, his cuff. "I'm a Guild courier, so you know I'm not UniCon. But it's okay if you don't want talk about it. I understand."

Jackson sighed again and waved a hand. "Fuck it. I don't care. Every morning, I wake up without Carla... If you're here to kill me, it wouldn't be the worst thing to happen to me today." He rubbed his eyes, then pulled his hands down across his cheeks before letting them fell back to his sides. "She was gunned down. Walking home from the grocery story two blocks from here."

"Do you have any thoughts about who might have done it? Any suspects?"

He laughed bitterly. "Well, yeah. It was UniCon."

"You think someone in UniCon did it?"

"Did it, knew about it, signed off on it, let it happen, whatever. Whoever did it used a drone."

"A drone?" Pierce felt a chill.

"Yeah, a drone," Jackson said, accusingly. "So who else could it be, right? As far as I'm concerned, everyone at UniCon was in on it, including the goddamn UniCs." He fumed silently for a moment, struggling with his emotions. "So, what did you want to know about Fairview?"

"I'm trying to figure out who actually owned it, who was responsible. The forms for one of the shell companies were witnessed by a Carla Ruiz-Vargas."

"Yeah, that's my Carla. She did a lot of that stuff for that sleazebag boss of hers. He made her do it. She used her maiden name because it all seemed so goddamned shady."

"I am trying to determine who owned a company called Crane International."

He nodded. "Yeah, I remember that. Not when she signed it or witnessed it or whatever, but a year or two later, right before the last UniConference. She wouldn't say why she was so scared, just that something terrible had happened involving Crane International, one of the shells she had witnessed. She wouldn't say what happened—to protect me, she said—but she was terrified it was going to come back on her, either from the cops or the people she worked for, or maybe people working against the people she was working for. But she was sad, too. Really sad."

"This was right before the last UniConference?"

Jackson nodded distantly, then looked over at Pierce. "Come to think of it, that was right around the Fairview collapse. Do you think they're connected?"

"Yeah," Pierce said quietly. "I think they are."

Jackson nodded and went over to the built-in bookshelves. He started rummaging around in the cabinet underneath.

On the television, a reporter was shoving his over-sized microphone into the face of a guy who looked to be in his early thirties, except for his crushed and defeated eyes, which looked decades older. He had a nasty abrasion on his forehead. The chyron under his face said, EDUARDO MUNOZ – BANK PATRON.

"We were all lined up when it happened," Munoz was saying. "Those bastards in the bank left us out there intentionally, for hours, in this heat. People were dropping like flies…"

"Here it is," Jackson said, pulling a small notebook out of the cabinet. He shuffled toward Pierce. "She wrote it all down, in… in case anything happened to her." He shook his head. "I decided not to give it to the UniCs, partly because I didn't trust them to do anything with it, partly because I didn't trust them not to kill me on the spot."

He held it out to Pierce, a small faux leather address book, like his grandmother used to have.

Pierce took it from him. "Thanks. Thank you for trusting me."

Jackson laughed, a harsh and bitter bark. "Don't be ridiculous. I don't trust you. I don't trust anyone. I just don't care if they come and kill me."

The book opened to the Gs. Among the three companies on the page were Garnet Holdings, and instead of an address or phone number, it said, *Hudson Limited*. Dugray had spent three months connecting those two.

He quickly flicked to the Cs and found Crane International. But next to it, there was nothing, no address or a phone number, no parent company, no name. It was blank.

"Shit," Pierce said under his breath. He put out a hand and steadied himself against the back of the sofa, suddenly fighting back tears of anger and frustration and disappointment.

"Find what you were looking for?" Jackson asked.

"No," he whispered.

Jackson softened, as if he had picked up on Pierce's distress. "It doesn't really matter, though, does it?"

Pierce looked up at him, confusion turning to anger.

Jackson put up his hands defensively. "I'm not saying it doesn't matter that it happened, but ask yourself, who bought the land? Who benefited from it being cleared? UniCon, right? If one of them did it, they were all in on it. I'm just saying, as far as I'm concerned, they're all responsible."

In the sudden quiet, the reporter on TV spoke. "Wait a second. You were all waiting in line to get your money out of the bank?"

"Hell, no!" the guy he was interviewing—Eduardo Munoz, bank patron—said, scowling at the reporter like he was an idiot. "We were trying to get our money *into* the bank, before it disappeared. But they wouldn't let us in, and now it's too goddamned late." He started to cry, wiping his nose with the back of his hand. "The money's all gone. Everything's gone. Now I got nothing."

The TV cut back to the studio, and the news anchor said, "Reports of a similar phenomenon in Barrow, Alaska have not been confirmed. Tempe Savings and Loan issued a statement that all deposits received would be credited to their customers' accounts, but that they had found nothing to substantiate rumors of 'disappearing money.' UniCon has also labeled the supposed phenomena a hoax."

"Son of a bitch…" Pierce mumbled.

"Jesus." Jackson shook his head, distracted for a moment from his personal misery. "The whole world has gone crazy."

WHEN HE GOT back to Dugray's A-house, Pierce was shocked to find that the car was not in SmartDrive. Somehow, he had driven there on his own, utterly distracted as he was. His head was spinning. Money was disappearing, and not just from his attaché or his wallet, not just in New York and Alaska. If it was happening in Arizona as well, it could be happening everywhere.

There was only one worker left, up on a ladder fixing one of the third-floor windows. He looked down when Pierce banged on the door. Some kid Pierce didn't know answered the door, looking Pierce up and down. "The fuck you want?"

Pierce held up his attaché. "Courier delivery for Dugray Joseph."

The kid slammed the door shut.

A minute later, Dugray opened the door. He glanced up and down the street with nervous eyes and quietly said, "I'll meet you around back." Then he shut the door.

Pierce went around back. Before he could knock, Dugray opened the basement door and pulled him inside.

"What's going on?" Pierce asked, keeping his voice low.

"Shit's nuts out here. My guy Rennie's gone missing. Mirwani was coming after me hard, but his Large is gone too, and Townsend doesn't want to hear about it. He took Mirwani out himself. Shot him in the face. I told him I'd already delivered my Large to Mirwani, saved my ass for the moment, but shit is bad out here. Townsend's losing his shit because he's vulnerable. He's hoping to get into UniCon next month, and he's been going nuts with the mergers and acquisitions, buying up whatever he can get his hands on to pad his portfolio, totally overextending himself. Now this shit's going down while he's still being assessed. He's freaking out and I got to figure out what's what before he starts looking hard at me, you know what I'm saying?"

"I hear you. Look, we need to talk—" Pierce began, but Dugray held up a hand to stop him.

"Nigella's dead," Dugray said. "So's Mattson."

Pierce paused, absorbing that. "Any idea who did it?"

"Who knows? Probably UniCon, whoever killed Serino."

Pierce told him about Bradley and Villarica and Carla Ruiz-Vargas, her murder-by-drone.

"A drone, huh?" Dugray said. "So you think that's UniCon too?"

Pierce nodded. "Either UniCon or someone acting with UniCon's blessing."

Dugray replied with a grunt. "What else did your dad say about all this? About Billings?"

"He had a hard time believing that anyone would destroy money instead of taking it, but he also said that if it was really happening, maybe UniCon's aim is to make people distrust cash, to make them more enthusiastic about the U-Net, to think that hard cash is no better than all the ones and zeroes that caused so much trouble before. The worse cash looks, the better U-Net will look in comparison."

Dugray scoffed. "New quantum network my ass. The shit just don't work. They proved that."

Pierce shrugged. "A lot of people are thinking this time it could be for real." He paused. "They're building the U-Net headquarters where Fairview used to be."

Dugray's eyes smoldered. "I knew something was going up there…" Before he could say anything else, the front door banged open upstairs, and a chorus of heavy foot falls passed over their heads. Then a voice shouted, "Yo, Dugray! You in here?"

Dugray got to his feet. "That's Marcus. I sent him out looking for Rennie." He gestured for Pierce to follow and said, "Don't speak."

Pierce nodded and followed him upstairs to the kitchen.

Marcus had three guys with him now. One guy was skinny, like he was using, but he still had a little muscle left, so he couldn't have been using more than a couple months. He had a Marine Corps tattoo on his shoulder—globe, eagle, and anchor.

The guy next to him was massive, with a big, bushy afro, a matching beard, and a pair of dull eyes taking up most of the space in between.

A third guy was sitting upright in a kitchen chair, his dark skin beaded with sweat. He wasn't tied or handcuffed, but he looked like he might as well have been. Pierce assumed this was Rennie.

"I swear, Dugray," the guy in the chair started. "I didn't take nothing, and I wasn't trying to hide or run away or anything. I was trying to get that shit back myself."

Dugray grabbed the other kitchen chair, set it down across from the kid and sat in it. "Back from who?"

"I don't know, man, that's what I was trying to figure out. I don't know who took it, and I don't know how. I had that shit locked up tight. I thought maybe it was Mattson, 'cause I changed some of it with him, and I heard someone say they got heisted after buying Large off him, but he was already dead. Nigella, too."

"So whoever heisted you," Dugray said. "Did they take everything?"

"They took all the Large. Left me with the shitty Small they couldn't bother with."

Dugray looked at Pierce over his shoulder.

"Did they leave anything behind?" Pierce asked. "Any like, sawdust or anything?"

Rennie's eyes went wide. "Yeah! Yeah, they did! Whatever they used to take the money, it left behind some, like, sand or something."

The marine standing behind him started to fidget.

Dugray looked up at him. "What is it?"

Marcus glared at the guy.

"What?" Dugray said again.

"I seen this shit before," said the marine.

Dugray stood. "What's your name?"

"Cairo."

"Seen what shit?"

"This money stuff. With the Large disappearing and all. The sawdust."

"Where?"

"Angola."

"*Angola?* What the fuck are you talking about?"

"I was there last year. My unit was attached to a UniC operation, protecting UniCon oil fields from one of these Congolese-financed guerilla groups."

"I thought UniCon and the Democratic Republic of the Congo made nice," Pierce said.

"This was right before that," Cairo said. "In July. Shit was tense. Every day, mortars and sabotage and all this stuff. Kidnapping employees. And UniCon don't play that, so they brought us in. But the Congolese were embedded with the locals, who they were funding out the ass, paying them to go in there and cause trouble. We're fighting them off, but there's only so much you can do against money like that. Then UniCon brings in this, like science unit, and they got this scientist with them. I don't know what that was all about, but the next day, these villagers start offering to switch sides, first a couple, then like half the village. They said the Congolese were going nuts, fighting among themselves, like they went crazy or something. The Congolese stopped paying the locals and started torturing them, saying they were stealing from them. A buddy of mine who went in with the mop-up team, he said the village was a mess, blood and bodies everywhere, both villagers and insurgents. There were only a few insurgents left. The rest were either dead or deserted, disappeared into the hills."

Dugray looked at Pierce, then back at Cairo. "So what happened?"

"The one the UniCs interrogated said their money disappeared. They didn't know who took it, but it was gone. And they said there was some kind of dust left behind. And it wasn't sand."

"You said it was UniCon. Do you know which company owned the oil facility?"

"Hell, yeah. It was plastered over everything." He laughed and held up his hands, slowly spreading them to suggest a large sign. "Nolexa Petro Fuels."

Chapter Sixteen

PIERCE WAS STILL staring at Cairo when Dugray turned around in his seat and met his eye. They needed to talk in private.

Dugray turned to Marcus. "Get these guys something to eat and some drinks if they want. Then set them up on the third floor." He looked at Cairo and at Rennie. "I'm not done with either of you."

Pierce followed him back down into the basement. At the bottom of the steps, Dugray said, "What the fuck is going on?"

"Nolexa is where Gloriana used to work," Pierce said.

"Gloriana, your ex-girlfriend terrorist who's now in prison?"

"My *microbiologist* ex-girlfriend terrorist, who used to worked for Nolexa, and who is in prison, yeah."

Dugray bobbed his head, like he was doing mental math. "Yeah, okay. I see where this is going."

"Is there a library around here?"

"A library?" He laughed. "Dude, the world's going

crazy. You got a book report to write?"

"I need to find out more about this Angola thing, see if it's the same thing we got here." And also see if there's any news about Gloriana.

THE NEAREST LIBRARY was five blocks away. It was rundown and smelly, but it was also one of the only places around that had the kind of security software and processing power necessary for electronic data communications. People thought of the internet as a thing of the past, but parts of it still hobbled along, including the datanet, a basic newsfeed and database system. It could only be accessed through powerful terminals with massive security layers. Pierce had read somewhere that ninety percent of the terminals' computing power was engaged solely with fending off malware.

The library was also one of the places you could go when you didn't have anywhere else to go. Pierce tried not to think of it like that.

He found a datanet terminal toward the back, semi-hidden behind a column but with a view of the entrance.

As soon as he activated the browser and clicked through the performance warnings to open the connection to the datanet, the cursor got laggy and the screen flickered with flashes of Arabic, Cyrillic, Chinese, and Korean. It took several minutes for the search window to load, and another minute for the words he typed to show up in the search field: NOLEXA ANGOLA CONGOLESE REBELS.

The search itself was probably completed in a nanosecond, but it took several minutes for the query to make its way through the filters to the server and several more for the results to make their way back.

The top four hits were all from the previous June, short news stories about the abrupt and unexpected end to a standoff between Congolese rebels and the energy company Nolexa. All four pieces included brief speculation of what could have caused the end of the siege, as well as long, verbatim statements from Nolexa and UniCon, praising the end of hostilities.

Next he searched GLORIANA LEONG. The top hits were a few years old, stories about her arrest and conviction. Then he came across a tiny mention in the *New York Times*, an article about another "eco-terrorist" that also mentioned Gloriana Leong, saying she "had been convicted of eco-terrorism and sentenced to life in prison, but had been transferred to house arrest."

"Holy shit," Pierce whispered. Less than a week after the events in Angola.

The only other hit was an interview in something called *Microbe Monthly*—the definitive journal of microscopic life. There she was, a little older, but otherwise looking just like she had ten years ago, standing in front of a quaint, two-story yellow stucco house, with an ornate iron fence. You could see straight through the front windows to the ocean.

Pierce's breath caught in his throat as he studied her slender face and long black hair. Her eyes, both dark and bright, penetrating and yet relaxed, burning with intelligence and curiosity and sparkling with humor. Her mouth was bent into a wry half smile, both playful and wise.

He sent the article to the printer as he did a quick search for Billings Holdings.

The first half-dozen stories were three years old, mostly stories about Billings' rapid growth just prior to the company's admission into UniCon, with lists of the different companies and industries it had acquired or invested in and the countries of origin of those investments. There were also a couple of recent stories focusing on how, even after joining UniCon, the company had been faltering, sinking into debt.

A few of the journalists cast vague suspicions about the circumstances surrounding Billings' entry into UniCon. The wording was extremely judicious, but even so, casting such aspersions on both a UniCon member and UniCon as whole could be dangerous. The fact that the editors ran with it meant there was almost certainly plenty to back it up.

He skimmed the article from *Microbe Monthly*. It was excruciatingly boring, mostly diving deep into Gloriana's scientific work, but the introduction included the interviewer's impressions of her house arrest in a beachfront house at the end of the main road at the easternmost tip of a small town called Corlinas, in Monagas, Venezuela, two hundred miles east of Caracas.

The writer used words like "idyllic," "scenic," and "comfortable," and described the Venezuelan security contingent as, "relaxed and surprisingly congenial."

Pierce put the printouts into his attaché and left. Hurrying back to Dugray's house, still in a daze, he saw another courier across the street. Pierce turned his attaché sideways, so it would be blocked from sight by his body, but the man kept his head down, walking fast. He seemed equally dazed, and Pierce wondered if he'd just had a shipment disappear.

"How was the library?" Dugray asked when he let Pierce in the back door.

Pierce told him what he'd learned.

"So, you think she was in on whatever happened in Angola?"

Pierce shrugged. "She's a world expert on microbes that can break down petroleum, as well as plastics—which Large is printed on. Right after Angola, she got moved from maximum security in Malaysia to what sounds like a pretty cushy house arrest in Venezuela. Maybe UniCon got her to do that thing in Angola, like what's happening here. Maybe she made a deal."

"Venezuela, huh? What's that about?"

"Nolexa, I guess. They have heavy a presence in both Angola and Venezuela."

Dugray thought for a second. "So you think this ex-girlfriend of yours halfway around the world is using microbes to destroy our Large?"

"I don't know. I have a hard time picturing her doing UniCon's dirty work, but who knows what could have happened to her in that prison? And even if she has nothing to do with it, she might have some insights into who *is* doing it and why."

"So what are you going to do?"

"I don't know. I've been thinking maybe I should get out of town until shit cools down."

"If it ever does. But yeah, I've been thinking you should, too."

"I might need to borrow some money."

"You know this ain't the best time, right?" Dugray said. "How much do you think you need?"

"Enough to get to Venezuela."

* * *

DUGRAY STILL HAD lots of cash in twenties and fifties, and even more in dirty, wrinkled-up tens, fives, and ones. There seemed to be a direct correlation between the value of the denomination and its condition, and probably also to the desperation of the person who had used it to buy drugs. Singles were by far the worst, reeking of the misery of those who had scraped them together for a hit. Pierce was struck by the contrast to the immaculate stacks of freshly printed Large he was used to working with.

Dugray hadn't been crazy about parting with the fifties and twenties, but he conceded that if Pierce showed up at JFK with a pillowcase full of filthy ones and fives, it might draw suspicion.

He lent Pierce a car, too, a beat-up orange Nissan. It had a clean title, registration in the glove box, and no other issues, but wouldn't be missed if it sat in long-term parking for the rest of its days.

Money and a car weren't Pierce's only worries, though. Visiting his father at Otisville might have seemed like a bold move with the Guild looking for him, but overseas travel was something else entirely; airports were *teeming* with couriers. Boarding an international flight out of JFK airport was borderline suicidal.

He parked in the long-term parking, stashing his gun under the driver's seat. The rest of his weapons he put in his attaché, and stowed it and his chain in the trunk, briefly wondering if he would ever see them again.

Just walking through the concourse, he spotted three different couriers. They all wore the same serious expression, as if they were focused on their own problems rather than looking for Pierce. The Guild was global, so there was no real escape, but he was glad to be headed somewhere they wouldn't be actively looking for him.

The woman behind the Avianca Airlines counter gave him a nice smile. "Good afternoon, sir. How can I help you?" she said in faintly accented English. Her name tag said MARITZA.

"I'd like a ticket on the next flight to Anzoategui Airport in Venezuela." He pulled up his sleeve and placed his cuffed wrist on the counter. "Courier rate. I'm doing a pickup."

"Certainly, sir." She scanned his cuff, then tapped at her keyboard and looked at her screen. "Next flight leaves in four hours, with a layover in Bogota. There are also a few leaving after that. They have two stops, but they cost slightly less."

"I'll take the one stop."

"Absolutely. Any weapons to declare?"

Couriers could bring weapons on to flights, but they had to file a lot of paperwork to do it. "No, I'll be picking that up there, too."

"Certainly. I'll just need your passport and face print." Pierce knew the camera embedded in the counter had already taken his picture and run it through the database. He slid the passport he always carried across the counter to her. No turning back now. If he was on the no-fly list, the mood in the room was about to change drastically.

Maritza stopped typing and looked up at him, then back down at her screen. "Of course, Mr. Pierce," she said. "And now I'll just need your travel voucher."

"I'll be paying cash, I'm afraid." This was by no means unheard of, but it suggested a certain half-assedness.

She looked at him appraisingly, then smiled again, this time awkwardly, as though embarrassed for him. "Certainly," she said. "That will be three thousand and thirty-seven dollars."

Dugray had given him forty-five hundred, on top of the Small Pierce already had. It wasn't a pillowcase full of damp fives and tens, but it was a crumpled manila envelope with a rubber-banded bundle of fifties and three bundles of twenties, all of them bulky and uneven.

Pierce handed her two of the bundles of twenties, a grand each. As he started counting out fifties, she let out a loud sigh and stacked the twenties into a bill counter.

Pierce put the fifties on the counter. As Maritza started counting them, he risked a look behind him. The line was substantially longer than when he had gotten in it, and toward the back was a young courier, in shades and a collarless jacket.

Pierce pulled the sleeve of his jacket, to make sure his cuff was covered.

Mercifully, Maritza finished the fifties. Then she started counting out his change. Pierce almost told her to keep it, but that would have raised even more suspicion.

As he put the change in his pocket and Maritza held out the ticket, a woman two lines to his right let out a shrieking, high-pitched wail. "My money!" she cried. "It's gone."

The woman was frantically rifling through a cloth handbag. Then she held it up and dumped the contents onto the counter. In addition to a compact, lipstick, keys, and a dozen other things was a cascade of beige dust that hit the counter and rolled out into a cloud.

The ticket agent let out an even louder squeal. Two UniCon guards snapped their rifles into position at the two screaming women, eliciting a chorus of more screams from the line.

As Pierce took his ticket, he looked at Maritza and for an instant their eyes met, an acknowledgement of the bizarreness of the situation, and maybe even the world in which it was taking place. A smile tugged at her lips, an honest, off-the-clock type of smile, and Pierce smiled back at her. Then she let go and he hurried off, anxious to be done with the transaction.

"Thanks for flying Avianca Airlines!" she called after him. "Have a nice trip!"

Chapter Seventeen

GLORIANA WAS SPENDING more and more time on her little beach just lately. She was going to miss it, miss her little house and even the simplicity of the life she had led there. She was a woman of intense intellectual curiosity, she knew that about herself, but she was tired, more tired than someone her age should be. After two years in a Malaysian prison cell, she was grateful for the small luxuries she now enjoyed.

She'd never regretted what she did to Nolexa, but she had paid a steep price.

Nolexa had put out the story that the damage from Gloriana's sabotage was minimal, but during the secret trial and the sentencing, she learned it was far worse than the public knew. The refinery had only been shut down for a couple of days, but the microbes proved remarkably difficult to eradicate from the system, and many millions of dollars, maybe even billions, had been spent cleaning, recleaning, and eventually replacing huge portions of the refinery, some more than once, as the microbes recolonized the new equipment.

Sitting in the courtroom, Gloriana had listened to all of that with a mixture of horror and glee. They were not going to pull their punches when it came to sentencing. They were powerful and vindictive, and apart from what they would do to her, they made it clear that her aunt would face a lifetime of bureaucratic harassment, or worse. But she also knew she had hurt Nolexa. She had punched them back. And they had felt it.

A year later, she learned from one of her guards that Nolexa was a tattered remnant of what it had once been. The entire leadership had been sacked, and once they were relegated out of UniCon, a few of those deemed responsible for the spills were even prosecuted.

That victory kept her going—it may have even preserved her sanity. With Nolexa out of UniCon, her official persecution eased off considerably. No longer an enemy of the super-state, she was now just another prisoner. But they were still dark days.

Not long after that, though, a man from UniCon came to talk to her, a man named Litchenko.

Things had changed, he said. Nolexa had been purchased by another company, another member of UniCon, and renamed Petrolinus. The new owners understood why she had done what she did, and there were no hard feelings as far as Petrolinus was concerned. Or UniCon.

They thought it was terrible that her aunt was under such constant threat, and that conditions in the prison were so bad. And they were frankly relieved that Nolexa's previous owners were no longer part of United Conglomerates.

Litchenko offered her a way, maybe not to make things

right, but to make things much, much better. For herself and her family. And for UniCon.

The threat was plain—do what we ask, or stay there and maybe find herself back in UniCon's sights—but the benefits were attractive. Her aunt would be left alone, and they would move Gloriana from her prison cell to house arrest, not in Malaysia or anywhere near it, but somewhere nice, somewhere right on the water, like where she'd grown up.

And all she had to do was a minor tweak to some of her pre-existing research and implement it. She had published research along similar lines, and they told her that was why they had approached her. As it turned out, what they asked of her was pretty much identical to research she had already done, but never published. She wondered if they had known about it, and if so, how.

It was a strange couple of weeks. They set up a cot in her old lab at Nanyang University during the break between semesters, put a couple of guards in the hallway and set her to work.

In a week, she had tweaked her *Neptunomonas* to do what they wanted. It actually only took her three days, but she milked it a little longer, afraid they were going to send her back to prison or kill her when she was done. Plus, she was so happy to be back in her lab she didn't want to leave it. But she also wanted to see if it worked in the field, and after a week she was restless.

She bred a large batch of *Neptunomonas plastiphilos-1* and they flew her to a UniCon military camp in Angola, next to an oil field owned by Petrolinus Corporation.

She was the chief science officer on the operation, caring for the microbes, making sure the transport and distribution medium was just right, and loading them into the drones.

The drones flew over the nearby settlement and diffused their payload. A few days later, they misted the village and surrounding area with an anti-microbial, to kill the *Neptunomonas plastiphilos-1* and make sure it didn't spread. The Petrolinus people told her the plan had worked like a charm. Gloriana told them that charms don't work. Science does.

As a special surprise, they told her, they had flown in her boyfriend.

She started to tell them she didn't have a boyfriend; then the helicopter landed and there was Chris, in the flesh, right in front of her.

She hadn't seen him in two years. He'd changed, but she was so excited to see him—to see any friendly face, really—she could barely contain herself. He brought her a few things from her old apartment, to bring with her where she was going next—a couple of wood carvings and some photos of her family and her childhood village, with a couple of photos of her and Chris he'd had printed.

They didn't have much time together, and only a few minutes in private. He told her that he had approached Billings, had told him about her secret biotechnology. He had given Billings the idea that it could be helpful with Petrolinus's problems in Angola. She was angry at first, about using her ideas for another big oil company, another *UniCon* company, but Chris saw the project as both a proof of concept and a way to get her moved to a better place. She had to admit, he was right.

In those few minutes together, they planned a future.

After that, they put her on a plane. She didn't know where she was going. Even after she arrived at her little house on the beach, she had no idea where she was.

It was Diego who told her she was in Venezuela. He thought it was hilarious that she didn't know.

That was a year ago.

Soon, she'd be getting ready to leave. She wouldn't have said it out loud, but she was going to miss it.

She was excited about seeing Chris again, but ambivalent too. Life with Chris was exciting and challenging—important, even—but it was never easy or simple or comfortable, not like it had been with Pierce. You couldn't just "be" with Chris. He was never easy that way.

Someday, maybe they'd have quiet time together, just the two of them. Maybe they could get to know each other again. Maybe they could even get to the level of intimacy and affection she'd had with Pierce. Maybe. But even if it was possible, a lot of other things would have to happen first.

Thinking of those other things filled her with trepidation and more than a little bit of fear, enough to spoil the moment. She got to her feet, brushing the sand from her pants, and turned to go back inside.

Then she froze, her fear and trepidation obliterated under a wave of other emotions at the sound of a voice she hadn't heard in years.

Chapter Eighteen

PIERCE WOKE UP as the plane circled General Jose Antonio Anzoátegui International Airport. It had not been a nice trip. His mind had swirled with anxieties—disappearing cash, sabotaged apartment towers, and threats that seemed to come from all sides—all that on top of wondering how it would be to see Gloriana again. Would her eyes sparkle? Would she be glad to see him? Would she even *agree* to see him? How would she react to his questions? What was her involvement in all this? What answers would he get, what would he learn, what would it mean?

He'd slept, but it was fitful and haunted and he woke up more tired than he'd been beforehand.

In a daze, he made his way through customs and immigration. The woman checking him in scanned his cuff and asked the purpose of his visit. When he told her he was picking up a delivery, she stamped a seven-day travel permit and waved him through.

He followed the current of travelers toward the exit, and finally found himself outside.

It was just past noon, local time.

The exterior of the airport was like any other, but behind the smell of bus exhaust and jet fuel was the subtle fragrance of a thousand exotic flowers and foods and unknown brands of detergents and body care products, none of it individually detectable, but all of it combining to tell Pierce's lizard brain that he was far from home.

He was also struck by the heat, a wall of it.

A line of Smartcabs waited patiently at the curb, but other cars, dented and dirty, drove slowly past them, each with the top half of the driver extending out the window and over the roof as they shouted to the travelers leaving the airport.

A driver in a beat-up Kia SUV singled Pierce out, calling to him in English, "Driver! You need a driver?" He patted the door. "Best rates!"

Pierce nodded and walked over to him, past the Smartcabs.

"Where you go?" the driver asked, his eyes darting around, looking for Pierce's luggage.

"Corlinas," Pierce said.

The driver tilted his head. "Corlinas? In Monagas?"

Pierce nodded. "Si."

"Two hundred miles?"

Pierce nodded again. "Si."

The driver looked dubious, then thoughtful. "Two thousand Bolivar," he said, almost apologetic. Roughly a hundred and fifty dollars.

Pierce held up four fifties. "Two hundred dollars."

The driver nodded and smiled. "Mi nombre es Pablo."

Pierce got in, and as they pulled away he said, "Mi nombre es Pierce."

* * *

THE HUM OF the tires over asphalt turned to the crunch of gravel as they left the highway, and Pierce sat up in the back of the car, blinking his eyes and looking around. Even after sleeping on the planes, and despite the blare of stress in the back of his mind, the monotony of the four-hour drive had lulled him to sleep. They were driving down a narrow, rutted dirt road encroached on either side by dense green. The road rose, and a gap in the brush revealed a flash of blue ocean behind it. He caught another glimpse, then another. The glimpses became more and more frequent, the sea closer and closer.

As they passed a couple of small, white stucco houses, Pablo glanced at him in the rearview and said, "Good thing you're awake. This is Corlinas. Where to now?"

"It's at the eastern edge of town. The last house on the main road."

They drove past a barbecue stand and a little cantina where two old men played dominoes in the shade of a sagging awning. The road they were on would hardly have qualified as a main street, but the ones leading off it were barely even streets at all. As the road curved gently around, the end came into view, and with it, the house from the picture: the same yellow stucco, the same iron fence with the gate wide open, the same bench and planter on the porch.

Pierce felt a mixture of giddiness and trepidation at the sight of it.

When they were fifty yards away, a pair of Venezuelan UniCs came around the side of the house. They looked too young, holding their rifles as if they were children playing at soldiers.

At the sight of them, though, Pablo tensed and tapped the brakes. He looked at Pierce apologetically, letting him know this was as far as he was going.

Pierce nodded. "And you said I can catch the bus back to the airport back on the highway, right?"

"Si," Pablo said. "Every two hours or so."

"When does it stop running?"

He shrugged. "Eight? Maybe nine?"

Pierce said, "Gracias," and handed him the four fifties. Then he grabbed his Thintech jacket and got out of the car.

The sun was headed toward the Western horizon, and the late-afternoon heat felt heavy and thick.

The UniCs had disappeared again as Pablo turned the car around and sped off. Suddenly, Pierce was alone on the dusty road.

As he approached her house, he felt vertigo, not thinking about vanishing Large or microbes or the Guild coming after him, he was thinking about *her*, about seeing her face, looking into her eyes. He was excited and nervous; would there be a hug, or even a kiss? A smile? Or would she slam the door in his face, leave him to turn around and head back to New York?

Maybe he should have asked Pablo to wait.

As he neared the house, he spotted the UniCs again, sitting on the porch. One of them was smoking, which somehow made him look even younger.

They didn't get up, even as Pierce walked up to the gate. They just looked at him with eyes half closed against the heat.

"I'm here to see Dr. Leong," Pierce said.

They looked at each other, then shrugged at him.

"Is she here?" he asked.

That set them off laughing. The one who wasn't smoking said, "Well, she not going to be anywhere else."

Then the front door opened, and there she was. Less flawless than in his memory, than in her twenties. Her face had lines that hadn't been there before—not surprising given what she'd been through. They gave her an air of seriousness that suited her, a maturity that somehow made her even more compelling.

"Buenos días, Dr. Leong," the guards said together, grinning.

"Buenos días, chicos," she said without looking at them, her face frozen, her eyes fixed on Pierce's, curious but wary.

"Hi," he said.

She stepped slowly out onto the porch, her eyes never leaving his. "Hi," she said. "What are you doing here?"

"I'm here from *Microbe Monthly* magazine. It seems your subscription is about to expire on the..." He paused, trying to remember the exact phrase. "'The definitive journal of microscopic life.'"

She snorted, and a flicker of a half-smile transformed her face, transporting him back in time. He wondered if it was going to bloom into the smile he remembered. A thousand iterations of it flashed before his eyes. She bit her lip, resisting the smile, and cocked an eyebrow at him. "Well, I'm sorry you came all this way for nothing, but my subscription to *Microbe Monthly* is prepaid for the next two years."

Pierce glanced over at the guards, who were looking back and forth between him and Gloriana, vaguely confused.

"I need to talk to you," he said. "I need your help. But also... I just found out you were here. I thought you were still in Malaysia."

She took his hand and held it up so his sleeve slid out

of the way, revealing his titanium cuff. A barely audible gasp escaped her lips. She looked up at him with new sadness in her eyes. "Jesus, you really did it."

The touch of her hand lit up every nerve in his body. "Ten years ago," he said, his voice hoarse. "Not a lot of options, you know? This or UniCon."

She lowered his hand but didn't release it as she stepped back through the doorway, tugging him with her. "Come on in." Pierce glanced again at the guards, but she shook her head. "They don't care."

It seemed they didn't.

He followed her inside, barely able to see as his eyes adjusted to the gloom. She closed the door behind him, then pushed him up against it, pulling his head toward her and crushing her lips against his.

If the touch of her hand had lit up his nerves, the touch of her lips *detonated* them, from his toes and his fingertips to his frontal lobe. His brain was too stunned to know what to do, what to think, but his hands and his lips moved with purpose, roaming her, remembering her. He felt like, after way too long, he was finally home.

She stepped back, looking up at him, almost as surprised as he was. She opened her mouth, like she was about to apologize, but gave him a little more of that smile instead. "I guess I missed you," she said quietly.

"I missed you, too."

She pulled him over to a small sofa. As they sat, she let go of him and scooched slightly away, putting a safe distance between them. His hand felt cold and empty.

She cleared her throat, tucking her hands between her thighs. "You said you need help. What kind?"

He laughed at the ridiculousness of the situation. She grinned and shrugged, as if to point out that *he* was the one who had come all this way. She was just sitting at home under house arrest.

He shook his head. "How are you doing?"

"Surely you didn't come all this way to ask me that."

"Partly, yeah."

She nodded slowly, thinking for a moment. "I'm... okay. I guess." She looked around her, at the ocean through the kitchen door behind her. "This is a lot nicer than where I was before."

The place was small, but not cramped, and nicely done up, its plaster walls draped in Mayan prints. It smelled faintly of sandalwood. There was a small living room with a sofa and a couple of chairs, and beyond that a rudimentary kitchen with a breakfast area. Glass doors opened out onto a tiny, pristine beach, and, beyond it, the ocean.

Pierce wondered for a moment if he had misinterpreted the situation, if *Microbe Monthly* had been wrong and she wasn't under house arrest at all. Then he noticed the ankle bracelet peeking out between the bottom of her thin cotton pants and the strap of her sandals.

"It killed me," he said, "knowing you were in that Malaysian prison."

"It killed me being there. Almost literally. But it's better now. What about you?" She reached over and pushed up his sleeve with one finger, delicately running another one across the titanium so that all he could feel was a slight vibration. "A courier, huh? Jesus. What's that like?"

He looked away, for some reason not wanting to meet her eyes. "It was weird at first." He laughed. "Okay, it's still weird, to be honest, but it's been okay. I travel a lot, which is good and bad. I get to not be part of UniCon. *That's* good."

She nodded. "It is. That seems to get harder and harder every day. But the Guild...? Are you really ready to let them cut off your hand if you get robbed? Let them kill you? I mean, that's the deal, isn't it?"

"That is the deal, yes. But as it turns out, no, apparently I'm not ready to let them do that."

"Good." Then she stiffened and her hand tightened on his. "Wait, did something happen? Are they after you? Is that why you're here?"

"Something did happen," he said. "And yes, the Guild is after me. That's the other part of why I'm here. I wanted to see you, but I also need your help, your expertise. To help me figure out what the hell is going on."

She sat back. "Okay, so tell me... What the hell is going on?"

"Strange stuff. In New York. Maybe other places, too. Cash seems to be... disappearing. Large. I heard you might have been involved in something similar in Angola last year. I wanted to ask you about that, and about your work on the *Neptunomonas* microbes, if maybe they're related."

She bit her lip, thinking for a moment. "Do you have any money?"

"Do I have any money?" he replied, confused.

Her eyes flashed with mischief. "Yes. Do you have any money?"

"Um... sure," he said. "No Large, though. Whatever's going on seems to affect only Large. But, yeah, I have some money."

She nodded. "There's a cantina up the road. They have decent whiskey in the back. Tell them you want their best. Scotch, if they have it. Whatever they have won't be worth more than forty dollars, so don't pay more than fifty. Bring it back here. Then we'll talk."

* * *

THE GUARDS WERE playing cards when Pierce stepped out onto the porch. They looked up with blank faces, then returned to their game. He stepped off the porch and started up the road. The breeze had died away, and a small cloud of flies found him in the heat. He could hear waves breaking beyond the dense foliage to his left. The road curved, and when he reached the spot where Pablo had dropped him off, he saw the cantina up ahead. He turned and looked back at Gloriana's house, almost hidden by the bend in the road. He paused, unable to fight the feeling that if he let it disappear from his sight, he might never see it or her again. But he turned and continued walking.

The two old guys who had been playing dominoes were gone from in front of the cantina. One of them was now behind the counter inside.

"Buenos días," Pierce said.

"Good afternoon," the old man replied, with a thick accent and a friendly smile. "Cerveza?"

"Whiskey."

The bartender reached for a shot glass from the shelf behind him.

"I'd like a bottle," Pierce said. "Your best. Scotch, if you have it."

The bartender raised an eyebrow and smiled. He ducked behind a curtain and returned a moment later with a bottle of Ballantine's, blended. "Seven hundred fifty Bolivars," he said as he put it on the bar.

Pierce wasn't a big Scotch drinker, but Gloriana seemed to know the deal. "Fifty dollars US," he said, holding up a fifty.

The bartender shook his head and Pierce shrugged and turned, as if to leave.

"Si, si, si," the bartender said quickly, holding up the bottle and beckoning.

Pierce handed over the fifty and with the bottle in hand, walked a little bit faster on his way back. He felt a moment of irrational relief when the house came back into view. The guards were right where they'd been, although they had abandoned their cards in favor of staring at him. One of them eyed the bottle in his hand with a mixture of disgust and longing. The other one seemed amused by his partner's reaction.

As Pierce opened the door, they both looked away.

When his eyes adjusted, he saw Gloriana sitting at the table in the breakfast area. Her hair was damp and she had changed into a thin, summer dress, some kind of short wrap or toga with a clasp over one shoulder.

Two glasses sat on the table next to a ceramic bowl with a handful of ice cubes.

"I wasn't expecting company, you know," she said, motioning him to the chair across from her.

He put the bottle on the table and sat. She picked it up and looked at it for a moment, then twisted off the top.

She put two cubes in each glass and poured them each two fingers.

"To the craftsmanship and dedication of the Scottish people," she said, raising her glass and waiting for him to clink it.

He did and they both sipped. She closed her eyes and took a moment to savor it, then gave him a shy, gentle smile, and quietly said, "Thank you."

He raised his glass and smiled back at her. As he sipped his drink, that sense of vertigo returned and he felt for an instant like he'd been transported back in time, back before so much that had happened, that had changed the world, changed him and his life. Then the feeling was gone. He was back in the present.

Swirling the booze and the ice, Gloriana took another sip, then rested one edge of the glass on the table. "Now, where were we?"

"I had questions," Pierce said.

"No, I meant before that." She gave him a look that he couldn't read. "Where were we before you broke up with me."

"I...? I didn't break up with you. I just... I mean, it seemed to me that in *your* mind, we were never really together."

"Really? I seem to remember being together a *lot*."

"You know what I mean." He hadn't wanted to go down this road, but this was where they'd left off. Arguing. He softened his voice. "Sorry. I didn't come here to fight."

"Good," she said, softening her voice as well. "And I know what you mean. I get it. I just... That's just not where I was, back then."

Pierce almost pulled a muscle resisting the urge to say, *And what about now?* Instead, he said, "I know. And I wish I'd been able to give you the space you wanted." He raised his glass, and just before taking a sip, said, "I think about you a lot, you know."

"That's nice," she said. "I think about you, too."

He did not ask how much. "Good," he said. "I'm glad." He laughed and she did, too, her eyes staying on his, looking deep inside him, just like the night they met.

She let out an exaggerated sigh. "Okay, well, I guess we'll put a pin in that and get back to it later." She put down her drink and sat upright with exaggerated seriousness. "You said you had questions. What do you want to know?"

Chapter Nineteen

PIERCE PUT HIS drink down and leaned forward. "What happened in Angola?"

Gloriana thought for a moment, "How much do you know about what I've been up to, since we were together?"

He shrugged. "I know you went to work for Nolexa, which was a bit of a shock. Then a few years later, you sabotaged one of their plants—less of a shock—and they threw you in prison. Last year, something went down in Angola, and they transferred you here, where a writer for *Microbe Monthly* tracked you down and interviewed you."

"Is that how you found me?" she asked. "*Microbe Monthly*?"

He nodded and sipped his drink, enjoying the burn as it went down.

She raised her glass. "Very clever."

He raised his back.

"Nolexa was a means to an end, you know? Something I *had* to do so I could do what I *wanted* to do." She nodded slowly to herself, as if once more rechecking the calculus that had led her to that decision. "I was happy enough, in a way, working for Nolexa. But I knew I was living a lie."

"How do you mean?"

"I got to do good science. Important science. And I got to do it in a *really* nice lab. I mean, they got me anything I asked for. State of the art. The government labs? The university labs? They were all so broke. I honestly don't know if I could have done what I did without Nolexa's funding. But I was working for the enemy. From day one, I knew it. I told myself it was a bargain I had to make, a bargain with the devil that would allow me to do what I needed to do to make the world a better place."

"Now you don't think so?"

She shrugged. "I don't know. I mean, definitely not *now*, knowing what I know. But absolutely, sometimes you have to work with people you don't agree with, even people you hate. Such arrangements are often necessary for the greater good. But in this case, I guess I was deluding myself. Do you remember what I was working on in grad school?"

"A microbe that could help break up oil spills."

"*Neptunomonas Petrophilos*. Very good." She gave him a wink and he felt himself blushing. She didn't seem to notice. "Well, at Nolexa, I perfected it and started producing it at scale. They told me they were using my work as part of a broader effort to prevent environmental damage, preventing spills as well as doing everything they could to remediate them. They also claimed they were doing all sorts of other stuff to minimize carbon emissions and particulates, that sort of thing."

She shook her head, like she was still mad at herself for having ever believed them. "Three years ago, they brought me to the UniConference, to show me off. Their young, female scientist of color—an environmental refugee, no less—who was working for them because they were doing such great things for the environment. But then I figured out they had been lying to me. The whole fucking time. They weren't using *Neptunomonas Petrophilos* as a last-ditch measure to clean up the spills that slipped through all their other safeguards. No, they saw it as a get out-of-jail-free card, so they didn't have to spend so much on other safeguards. I thought they were stockpiling it, but they were using it up as fast as I could produce it."

She took a breath and let it out. "After I found out, I started digging into Nolexa's operations and learned that since I'd come up with my *Neptunomonas Petrophilos*, their rate of spills had increased five-fold. Five hundred percent. They weren't reporting most of the spills, they just doused them with *Neptunomonas* and moved on. And they weren't involving me in the process—I guess because they knew what I'd think. But that meant the people applying it didn't really know what they were doing. Plus, since UniCon had done away with mandatory environmental impact studies, Nolexa had no idea what impact widespread usage would have. I had done my own research, and I was satisfied it was reasonably safe—I mean, in a big spill, in a dire situation, it would undoubtedly be a net positive—but they didn't know that. As far as they were concerned it was still possible the microbe itself could have had devastating environmental impacts."

She looked out the window, her chest slightly heaving as she thought about it. "I was livid. I was going to just quit, but I knew that wasn't enough. So I decided to expose what they were doing, copy their secret files and release them to the press—the alternative press, who would still cover it. Who weren't controlled or cowed by UniCon. But then they had another spill. A bad one."

She wiped her eye. "It hit my village, or what was left of it."

"*Again?* A second spill?"

She nodded, her face like stone. "The place was never the same after the first spill, the one that forced our relocation. It was unrecognizable as the place where I'd grown up. But at least it was still there, you know? This time, it was obliterated. Gone. Bulldozed under."

"I'm so sorry," he said, now resting his hand on her knee.

"That's when I decided to spike the whole refinery." She looked up at him. "Do you understand?" It was a real question. A challenge.

"Absolutely."

"It hurts," she said. "Seeing the things you believe in twisted and perverted and used for all the wrong purposes. Seeing science, *my* science, *my* work, being used to promote the very behaviors I'd been fighting against all my life. And I miss the science. It hurts, as a scientist, not to be doing science. To be forced out of the habit of doing science. To be wasting my education, my talent."

They sipped their drinks in silence for a moment; then she continued.

"They put me on trial, then they put me in prison, for life. It was bad. Really, really bad." She closed her eyes and took a deep breath, like she was powering through the memory. "So, when they came and asked for my help, they said they would get me out of there. They also threatened my Aunt Zara, the only family I had left. But they didn't need to make any threats. I had to get out of there."

"Who's *they*?"

She let out a sad laugh. "There's only one *they* anymore: UniCon. In this case, in the form of a company called Petrolinus that had bought what was left of Nolexa."

Billings! Pierce thought. "What did they want you to do?"

"Someone there had read something I'd written, some cocky article bragging that I could create microbes that wouldn't just break down petroleum, but could target specific petroleum-based products." She shrugged. "That's what they wanted me to do, and that's what I did. That's what saved my aunt from a life of bureaucratic persecution—or worse—and got me moved from a maximum-security prison in Malaysia to a cute little beach house in Venezuela."

He leaned forward. "Which 'specific petroleum-based products'?"

She took a breath. "SDP nanocrystalline polyethylene."

"Crinkle," he said. "Large."

She nodded and finished her Scotch. He finished his, too.

"Who did you work with?" he asked.

"At UniCon? A guy named Delroy and a guy named Simms. Plus some other guys. All men. Some in suits, some in uniforms."

"What about Frank Billings?"

She shook her head as she carefully poured them each some more scotch. "No, I don't think so. He owns Petrolinus, right?"

"That's right."

She slid a couple more ice cubes into her drink, then plopped two cubes into his glass, splashing some whiskey onto the table. She wiped up the spill with her finger, then licked it.

He opened his mouth to ask another question, but she put the just-licked finger to her lips. "My turn." She used the finger to stir her drink then sucked the liquor off it again.

"Okay."

"How did you end up in the Couriers Guild?"

He shrugged. "There wasn't anything else to do, really. You remember what it was like: there were no opportunities, especially if you didn't want to work for UniCon, or some company trying to join UniCon. I had already been doing some courier work, here and there. After we split up, I got a job driving for a different cab company, then it got bought up by a bigger cab company, part of UniCon. They were all going AI at that point, so it was only a matter of time anyway. I quit. With my military background, I got a job with an armored car company—they were expanding pretty quickly back then too. But then that got bought up too. UniCon, again. The Guild was just starting, but they had made very clear—I mean, it's written into their charter—that they were to remain independent." He shrugged. "I was a soldier. I was trained."

He held up his wrist and looked at the cuff encircling it. "The surgery wasn't too bad, and the cuff isn't too bad, either." The first few years he had nightmares about it, but he didn't mention that. He hardly ever got them now. "You get used to it."

She nodded slowly, studying him. "I'm not crazy about it, intellectually. I can't approve of the idea of surgically altering people with no other prospects so they can tote around rich people's money. It's just wrong on so many levels."

He opened his mouth to protest, but she silenced him with an upraised hand.

"But... there is something about it that's kind of hot."

He closed his mouth and she smiled, almost shyly.

"Okay," she said. "Next question."

He realized he was suddenly discombobulated, and in the back of his mind, he wondered if that was the intention of that remark. He cleared his throat and took a deep breath, collecting himself. "When Billings' people came and asked for your help, that was for Angola?"

"That's right."

"How did that come about?"

She shrugged. "They didn't include me in the planning. From what I gathered, a facility they were building was being attacked on a daily basis. A Congolese competitor was funding the operation, paying the locals to damage pipelines, kidnap workers, that kind of thing. These UniCon people, Petrolinus, they were confident there was no real local resistance to their presence, but they couldn't seem to stem the flow of money coming in, so they asked me—or told me—to create a microbe that would."

"Who's they? Delroy and Simms?"

She shrugged. "And some other guys. UniCon, I imagine. Petrolinus."

"Whose idea was it?"

"At Petrolinus? I don't know."

"How much work was it to create the microbe?"

She stretched and sat forward. "To be honest, not much. I had pretty much already created it, although I didn't know for sure if it would work in that climate. I had been working on a microbe that could be used to break down plastic in the ocean, for the big Pacific garbage patches. One of the challenges of getting the petrophilic microbes to work on big spills—or in refineries, for that matter—is that they need oxygen and nitrogen. If they're completely covered in oil, they shut down. So I'd been working on targeting different types of petroleum-based plastics, years ago, before I got arrested. It was pretty much done, but I got locked up before I could field test it."

"Field test it?"

"Yeah, you know. With something like that you need to test it in different..." She stopped and looked up at him, then waved her hands. "It's technical. Just... it was before we finished testing it."

"Okay. So, how did they release the microbe?"

"They used drones and released it as an aerosol. I didn't know if it would work, to be honest, if the microbes would live long enough to do what they wanted. But it worked perfectly. They actually had to spray the area with an antimicrobial agent a few days later. They must have been pleased with the results, otherwise I'd still be in a Malaysian prison."

He waited a respectful moment. "What about New York?"

She looked up at him. "What about it?"

"Are you involved in anything similar in New York, or anywhere else?"

She furrowed her brow. "No."

"Do you know anything about it?"

"No. Why, what's going on? What makes you think it's the same thing?"

"Well, you tell me. We've got money disappearing from all different types of places, some of it from places where no one could get to it. Hell, some of it disappeared from my pocket. What's left behind is a kind of pulp or sawdust. And it's only affecting the big bills, the Large."

"Hundreds and above?"

He nodded.

"Because of the plastic substrate," she said.

"Presumably."

"That does sound like *Neptunomonas Plastiphilos*." She said it with a vaguely proud smile. "They could have reproduced what I did for them in Angola. I tried to hide my tracks, research-wise, but they could have saved some. They could have regrown the stock, if they knew what they were doing."

"You said they used drones to release it. Any reason why they couldn't do that in New York?"

"I don't know. They'd have to test it and tweak it. It's not that easy, but maybe."

"Any reason why they would?"

She shrugged. "I'm not so up on what's happening in New York these days, but if they're doing the same kind of thing, maybe it's for the same kind of reason: Making their enemies poor, weakening the competition, whatever." She looked right at him as she said it, and he got the strong feeling that for the first time she was lying to him. Then she smiled. "Or maybe God is doing it. Too much money is the root of all evil, right?"

"Some people think it might be UniCon, undermining confidence in paper money to pave the way for their new internet, U-Net."

She grinned, her eyes bright. "That's a fascinating theory... If they do manage to get U-Net up and running, I'm sure the porn industry will be grateful, but I'm not so sure about the rest of us. I have no doubt that if they ever do come up with something workable and secure, it will be structured to give UniCon a permanent power advantage. Frankly, it wouldn't surprise me if figuring out how to ensure that advantage is the thing that's been holding them up all these years. But that would be the end of it, you know. The end of history. All the inequities will be baked in, written in stone, in perpetuity."

"So you're saying we're all fucked?"

She laughed. "As a species? Maybe not. We've got some difficult times ahead of us, but I imagine humanity will come through it all somehow. As a society though, yeah, I think so. And as individuals, definitely, yes, each of us, fucked. From the moment we're born."

She flashed him a big fake happy grin to counter the direness of her words before continuing. "People think UniCon is this revolutionary development, but it's really just a dropping of pretense, an incremental step along a path we've been following for hundreds of years. The same people are in control now as have always been. They've just stopped pretending they aren't. That in itself isn't getting any worse than it's ever been, it's just that the evil it causes has been compounding all this time." She shrugged. "Now, things are coming to a head."

"You mean the climate?"

"I mean all of it: the climate, the water, pandemics, nanoplastics, wealth stratification, oppressive police, an unfair and unworkable financial system. We're going backward, not forward." She paused. "Okay, my turn again. You're a courier, not a cop. If money is being stolen or destroyed, how come you're here investigating, and not the UniCs?"

Pierce swirled his drink. "Well, I don't know what the UniCs are or aren't doing, but I have a personal interest in figuring out what's going on."

"How so?"

"Well, like I said, something did happen." He told her about Alaska, about the Large disappearing from his attaché.

"Wait," she said, a cryptic smile tugging at her lips. "It was locked in a courier attaché, and it just disappeared?"

He nodded. "The wrappers were there, but no Large, just dust. And earlier I noticed that the attaché was warm to the touch."

"Right," she said distantly, then her eyes looked alarmed. "So, wait, your payload disappeared, does that mean...?"

"The Guild is after me, yeah. Do you know what was happening?"

She stared at him for a moment, then shook her head. "No... What happened next?"

He told her the rest.

She blanched, whispering, "You killed them..."

He nodded. "It was them or me. The one who stopped trying to kill me, I let him go."

"Whoa." She looked away from him, her eyes seemingly focused on nothing.

"There's been a lot of killing," he said. "I mean, not by me. I hadn't killed anyone since the war. But in New York, a lot of violence. A lot of people thinking they've been robbed, lashing out at the most likely suspects. Gangs going after one another, thinking they've been robbed. Launderers killed by people thinking they've double crossed them. The Guild going after couriers. I know of several people who've been killed by UniCon, one right in front of me."

She sniffed and looked away. "Sorry," she said as she wiped away a tear.

He stared at her a moment, surprised at the intensity of her emotions. "So," he went on, "that's the boat I'm in. The money disappeared on my watch, so the Guild is coming after me. I need to figure out what happened and prove it, so they don't… you know." He wiggled his hand in the air and snorted a brief laugh.

She didn't laugh with him, instead staring at him and nodding slowly. "That's a lot to be dealing with, Mondo."

He froze. No one else called him that. It had been a long time since he'd heard it.

Her face was unreadable, but he got the sense that behind it, her amazing brain was working feverishly.

He shrugged. "You've been dealing with a lot too."

She smiled. "Yes, I have. How have you been apart from all that? How're your mom and dad?"

He let out a short, bitter laugh. "Bradley's the same, of course. Mom died."

"Oh, no," she said, resting a hand on his thigh. "I'm so sorry. Your mom was great. How did she die?"

He told her what happened, about the Fairview.

She put her other hand over her mouth. "I didn't know. Mondo, I'm so sorry."

He told her about Dugray, too. About their investigation, about Serino, about the kill drone.

"Jesus, Mondo," she said. "No wonder you wanted to get out of town."

He nodded and looked down at her hand on his thigh, feeling the warmth of it. Feeling the warmth of the whiskey, too.

They were quiet for a moment, then she straightened up, as if a thought had just occurred to her. "How do you feel about short walks on the beach?"

He smiled. "One of my favorite things."

THE BEACH BEHIND the house was maybe thirty yards wide, naturally curved and utterly private, flanked by jetties of piled rock extending far out into the water and so high Pierce couldn't see over them. The lowering sun washed the clouds above them in pink and gold, but on the horizon, over the water, the sky was a deep, dark blue.

They walked along the water to one of the jetties, holding hands. He was reminded of a day they'd spent at the beach together when they were dating. He remembered how happy he was—how fucked up the world was, how fucked up his life was, but how happy *he* was, nonetheless.

He cleared his throat, shaking himself out of it, and gestured toward the rocks. "Are you allowed to climb up there?"

She nodded. "Yeah, but I don't like to. There's a fence. It ruins the illusion."

She swung his hand as they turned and walked back to the other jetty.

"There used to be more of it, from what I gather," she said. "More beach. Sad to think that someday it will probably be gone altogether." She took a deep breath as she looked around. "It's lonely, but not a bad place to be imprisoned, I guess."

"No," he said. "I've definitely seen worse."

They turned back once again and stopped near the middle of the beach. Next to a blanket already on the sand, not far from the edge of the water. The waves lapped gently, just a few feet away.

"A short walk on the beach, right?" she said, swinging his hand once before letting it go.

"That was lovely."

The sun was sinking low, casting a surreally beautiful orange light.

"I'm hungry," she said. "Are you hungry?"

"Haven't eaten since two airports and a four-hour drive ago."

She glanced at the sky with something like trepidation. "Let's go inside. I'll ask Matías to get us some arepas. Come on." She looked back and beckoned him. "Come on."

Her demeanor was still playful, but there was an edge to it, an impatience. Pierce glanced back at the beach, at the golden light.

"We can come back out at sunset," she said, standing at the door, waiting for him.

The house was dark inside, but she didn't turn on any lights. Pierce asked to use the bathroom and she directed him up the steps. As he climbed the stairs, she opened the front door and called out, "Matías!"

Then she spoke with him in Spanish.

Unframed photos lined the wall along the stairs, but the light was too dim to make out any details except for where a shaft of light shone on one of Gloriana as a child, smiling wide, standing in front of a small hut in a village. It made him smile.

There were two rooms at the top of the stairs. One of them exuded the feel of tile and mirror and water, and the faint scent of a woman's fragrances. Pierce pulled the chain on the bare bub hanging overhead, illuminating a simple tile bathroom with open shelves and wicker baskets.

His face in the mirror looked dirty and haggard, but relaxed in a way that he hardly recognized on himself.

When he got back downstairs, the kitchen light was on, spilling pale light through the darkening house.

Gloriana was sitting at the kitchen table with two tall glasses of water. "Matías is getting us arepas from the place down the road." She slid one of the glasses of water toward him. "You should drink. It's easy to get dehydrated this close to the equator."

They both downed their waters, then there was a light tap at the door.

"Arepas!" she said, beaming, and hurried over to the front door. She spoke in hushed Spanish for a moment, then exclaimed, "Ooh! And mail!"

She returned wearing a shy grin and carrying a grease-stained paper bag, two bottles of bright red soda, and a slim sheaf of mail, mostly magazines. Gloriana seemed almost embarrassed at how excited she was.

"Very possibly the most humiliating aspect of house arrest is how excited I get for the mail," she said as she tossed it onto the kitchen counter with a dismissive shake of the head. "It's not like I ever get anything interesting."

Pierce glanced at the pile. "I don't know, is that *Microbe Monthly* I see?"

She pointed a rigid index finger at him, struggling to keep a straight face. "In this house, we do not make light of *Microbe Monthly*!"

Pierce put up his hands defensively. "Wouldn't dream of it!" He laughed. "But seriously, if you're that excited, aren't you going to see what you got?"

She shook her head again. "Whatever is in there cannot hope to compete with a real live person from the outside world."

Her smile told him he wasn't just *any* real live person from the outside world. He grinned back at her.

Then she said, "I'll save *Microbe Monthly* and take my time with it when I'm alone." Both their smiles faded and they shared a sad, knowing look. No matter how long he stayed, the clock was already ticking towards his departure.

"Should we eat outside?" he asked, stepping toward the door.

"Not yet," she said, looking past him, then groaning.

"What is it?" he asked, following her eyes. That's when he saw it, sixty feet out, stretched between the ends of the two jetties: a lattice of wire lit up with reflected sunlight, flashing a fiery gold as it flexed back and forth in the tide.

"It's okay." She sighed again. "It's nothing. I just... There's a moment, when the sun is setting and the light catches the fence out there. I don't like to be out there then." Her voice was sad and quiet. Even as they looked, the light started to fade. "It only lasts a minute, but it ruins the illusion. Reminds me that I'm a prisoner."

In seconds, the sun had sunk lower, the angle had changed, and the wire fence was once again invisible.

"Sorry," he said.

"It's okay," she said. "It's stupid anyway. I know why I'm here. I know what I am. I should be grateful for the reminder. Come on," she said, handing him the bag and a bottle, changing the topic and the mood. "Let's eat outside."

They went out to the blanket. The sun had disappeared behind the house, but the sky was still orange and red.

Pierce was hungrier than he realized, and he plowed into his arepa. He had eaten half of it when he stopped to drink some soda.

It was a strange cross between cola and cream soda. He held up the bottle, trying to look at it.

Gloriana laughed and took a gulp. "Frescolita," she said. "I couldn't let you leave Venezuela without trying one."

They ate in silence for a moment. Then Pierce said,

"Interesting relationship you have with your jailers. They seem pretty friendly."

"They are," she said, washing down some arepa with a sip of Frescolita. "They're good kids, in their way." Then she added, "But they're still my jailers."

He nodded and they ate in silence for another moment.

"So, what's your plan?" she asked. "After dinner, that is?"

He took a bite, giving himself time to consider that. "I wanted to see you, talk to you. Get your insights into what is going on, who might be behind it. I guess I kind of hoped you might have some more info about that."

"Sorry," she said, glancing at his hand before locking eyes with him, momentarily looking hard enough to cut glass.

He waved away her apology. "No worries. You've been here, out of the loop. I get it." He drank some Frescolita. "But I should get back, straighten things out. There's a bus up on the highway. I can take it back to the airport."

"They say it's not very dependable after sunset. You can stay here, if you like. Crash on the sofa." The hardness in her eyes had been replaced by a sparkle, but he couldn't be sure it wasn't a reflection of the rising moon.

It was seven p.m. and getting dark. He had no idea how long it would take to get back to the highway. He might wait for hours before being sure the bus was done for the night. Besides, he didn't *want* to leave. He felt happier than he had in a decade.

He thought about the world he'd left behind, steeped in corruption and inequality, roiling with strife and violence, looming with several kinds of dread. He didn't want to go back to it. Especially not if this was the alternative.

"Thanks," he said. "That would be great."

They finished eating without speaking, feeling the breeze, listening to the lapping of the waves, watching the stars come out. The wind picked up and light flickered on the horizon, illuminating a bank of clouds.

"Storm coming," she said. "I love sitting here, watching the storms. There's a place in Western Venezuela, Lake Maracaibo. They call it 'The River of Fire.' It's the lightning capital of the world. Every night, huge spectacular lightning storms. Apparently, it's quite famous, but I'd never heard of it until I came here. Sad to think I'll probably never see it."

A bright flash showed the clouds, already closer and bigger.

"Nice," Gloriana said. The rumble of thunder reached them a few seconds later.

A moment after that, there was an even bigger, closer flash. Pierce laughed without realizing it, like a child.

Gloriana grinned at him in the semidarkness. "It's pretty great, isn't it?"

"Spectacular."

The breeze picked up again, and she moved his plate out of the way and scooted closer, pulling his arm around her. It was an oddly familiar gesture after a decade apart, but it felt right, perfectly natural.

"It's beautiful here, but it's lonely," she said softly, leaning against him. "It's nice to have company." She turned to look up at him. "I'm really glad to see you."

He looked down at her face and found himself suddenly unable to speak, unable to look away. She didn't look away, either. Their faces were just inches apart. The moment stretched out and their gaze gathered meaning.

She reached up and touched his cheek and he thought they were going to kiss, but they both whipped their heads around as a brilliant flash lit up the clouds, now towering almost directly above them. They pointed and *oohed* in unison; then they both laughed.

She kept her gaze out over the water. He pulled her warm body even closer, realizing how much he had missed this casual intimacy with her. He was suddenly overcome. He was just thinking how glad he was that she was looking out over the water, when she turned and looked up at him, her brow furrowed.

"Hey," she said, her whisper caressing his cheek. "Are you okay?"

"Yeah," he whispered back. "I'm great."

A scattering of fat raindrops pelted them and stopped.

"We should get inside," Gloriana said, standing.

A gust of wind pulled at her dress, whipping it tight against her body. Then the downpour started in earnest. The back door was barely fifteen yards away, but by the time they got inside, they were drenched.

Gloriana slid the door closed behind them and as the rain pelted the glass she started to laugh. He laughed, too—both of them standing there, dripping onto the kitchen floor.

"Oh my god, we're soaked!" she said.

Her dress was plastered to her body and water dripped from her hair. He could feel his eyes glued to her, the curves of her body, the playfulness in her smile, the joy and intensity in her eyes. He stared at her with a longing that felt sudden and intense, but that he knew had been there since the moment he had left her. Since the moment he had met her.

Her laughter trailed off and she turned serious, as if she recognized the look in his eyes. As if she felt the same way.

"I've missed you, Armand Pierce," Gloriana said quietly.

"I've missed you, too," he replied, hoarse, his voice not quite working right, as if all his blood and brain power and everything else was done with speaking for the moment.

"You know I'm not in a position for any kind of relationship, right? Not like before. It's impossible now, even if I wanted it."

"I know."

"Good." Her right hand reached for the clasp on her left shoulder, and with a flick of her finger, the dress slowly fell to the floor, the damp fabric peeling away from her damp skin, unveiling her body, naked except for the device around her ankle.

She stepped closer to him and started unbuttoning his shirt, her eyes on his the whole time. She tugged the shirt off him and hung it on a hook, while he took off everything else. They held each other and kissed, soft and gentle, aching with restraint, hands roaming each other, reacquainting themselves with the skin, the flesh they'd been missing for so long.

Together, they made their way into the living area, and fell back onto the sofa.

A moment later, they gasped in unison. For an instant, she froze, eyes tightly closed. For that moment, he sensed that she was gone, alone, lost inside herself. Then she opened her eyes, looked deeply into his, and smiled, running her hands once more through his hair as they started moving.

PIERCE WOKE UP on the sofa to see Gloriana walking in from the kitchen area carrying two glasses of water, gloriously naked.

She gave him a wink and perched on the sofa beside him, offering one of the glasses of water. "Thirsty?"

He nodded and sat up. "Thanks," he said, then he drank the whole thing down.

She looked at him sideways and ran the fingertips of one hand from his hip up to his ribs and then back down to his thigh. He got the feeling maybe she was drinking him in as well.

"Let's go to bed," she said, holding back a yawn.

He nodded and they stood. He noticed she'd hung the rest of his clothes over the kitchen chairs to dry. She took him by the hand and led him up the stairs, the muscles in her back and her behind rolling hypnotically in the bars of moonlight slanting through the windows.

At the top of the steps, she waved a hand at the bathroom. "You can use my toothbrush if you like," she said, her voice hushed and intimate.

He thanked her and did, then slipped into the bedroom.

It was a tiny room, with a bed, a nightstand and a small chest of drawers, all illuminated by the soft, warm glow of a small backlit night light, an impressionist painting of a beach, deserted and pristine. She was sitting on the bed, fiddling with a small metal box on the bedside table. As he came around to the far side of the bed, Pierce almost tripped over a knapsack on the floor.

"Careful," she whispered, as the air filled with the scent of incense.

"I smelled that when I came in," he said, lying down next to her. "Is that sandalwood?"

She nodded. "It reminds me of my childhood. My parents used to burn it. Before things went wrong. But it's not burning, actually. It's a nanosonic diffuser, so you don't have to burn anything. It was a gift."

"From whom?"

He felt her tense up, too. "Just… a guy I used to kind of date."

Pierce didn't push it, instead trying to get the conversation back on track. "Is that like the diffusers the BetterLates use?"

She was fidgeting with something in the shadows beside the bed, but she paused without looking at him. "The who?"

"The BetterLates. You know, the environmental group? They dress in green and chant and march and clog the sidewalk, generally make pains in the ass of themselves?"

She shook her head. "Don't know them."

He laughed. "The BetterLates are everywhere these days. They do all this stuff to fight against climate change. They take a vow not to burn anything, so no matches or candles or cigarettes, or regular incense. They're kind of crazy. Like a cult, in ways, really."

"That doesn't sound so crazy."

"No, I guess it's not. And definitely, good for them in a way, for sure. But the chanting and marching and burning incense? Or not burning it, actually, because—"

She put a finger over his lips. "Goodnight, Mondo Pierce." Then she kissed him.

"Goodnight," he said, strangely emotional at the unexpected tenderness.

She rolled over away from him, then scooted back, grabbed his right wrist and pulled his arm around her. "So when *do* you have to get back?" she asked in the darkness.

"I don't know," he said quietly. "I wasn't planning on staying this long."

She laughed. "How long *were* you planning on staying?"

"I don't know. I didn't know if you'd even let me in the door." It was true, and he felt a warmth inside as he thought about how things had gone since he arrived. Better than he'd dared to hope.

She squeezed his hand. "Yeah, I guess it could have gone either way."

"I can't believe I'm actually here with you," he said, barely a whisper. "I know I've said it before, but I think about you a lot. Never stopped."

"Me, too," she said quietly. "I often wonder, what would my life be like if we could have just... made it work? Your way or mine. I'm sorry I couldn't be what you wanted me to be."

He held her tight. "You've always been everything I wanted. I'm sorry I couldn't see that at the time." They were quiet for a moment, then Pierce said, "I could come back, you know. I mean, if you wanted me to."

He felt her nodding. "That sounds nice."

He drifted off to sleep, for the first time in a long time looking forward to tomorrow.

Chapter Twenty

HE WAS A beautiful man, Gloriana thought, watching Pierce as he slept. Seeing him, feeling him, being with him, had brought back the intensity of her attraction to him, the depth of her feelings. She felt a wistful pang as she pondered once again the road not taken, how different her life would be if she could have been happy settling down with him, or if he could have given her enough time to come around.

But she'd never know.

She got up and went to the bathroom. Then she went downstairs and poured herself a glass of water from the pitcher in the refrigerator. As she stood there drinking it, she scanned the cover of *Microbe Monthly* in the glow of the nightlight over the sink.

Her old graduate advisor had a piece on an interesting new development in biofuels. She'd save that to read when she was alone again. Something to look forward to. As she tossed the magazine aside, something else in the mail caught her eye: a semi-crumpled and slightly torn postcard of the Eiffel Tower.

She gasped when she saw it, and she took it over to the light to study the back.

HAVING FUN IN PARIS. BEEN HERE FOR TEN DAYS. WILL BE LEAVING IN EIGHT DAYS AT ONE A.M. ALL FOR NOW. LOVE, MORRIS.

She read it three times, muttering, "Shit, shit, shit," under her breath. It had priority postage, but the postmark was illegible. It looked like it had gotten jammed in a postal machine somewhere along the way.

She grabbed the World Wildlife Fund calendar from the fridge and checked the date. "You have got to be fucking kidding me."

Ten eight. October 8. That was tomorrow, at one a.m. No, that was tonight! They were coming tonight. She looked at the clock. Eleven-fifty-five. She had just over an hour.

"Fuck, fuck, fuck, fuck, fuck," she muttered, telling herself not to panic as she scrambled around the kitchen.

It was insanity that they would be coming to get her so soon after field tests. She figured she'd have at least a month. Something unexpected must have happened to cause them to move things up.

Forcing herself to calm down, she opened the cabinet under the sink and took out the plastic bin with the cleaning rags. She reached through the rags and pulled out a small bag of white powder.

She filled another glass with water and tapped a third of the powder into it, then swished it around until the powder was gone. She cut a slice of lime, then cut it in uneven halves. The bigger piece went in the glass with the powder, the other piece went in her glass.

She hurried back upstairs and stopped at the door, watching Pierce for another moment, almost nauseous with regret. For a moment, her resolve faltered, but she had come too far. There was too much at stake. She had to stick to the plan.

When she sat on the bed, he stirred.

"Hey," she said, her voice just above a whisper.

He opened his eyes and looked up at her. He smiled and it broke her heart.

"Here." She handed him the glass. "It's important to stay hydrated."

He sat up a bit, still partly asleep. "What?"

"Drink that down or you'll regret it in the morning."

She drank hers and waited for him to do the same. When he was done, she took his glass and put them both on a shelf.

She got back into bed and gave him a slow, lingering kiss. Then she lay next to him, clutching his hand between her breasts. He fell back to sleep almost immediately, but she waited another five minutes, partly to be safe, partly to soak in the moment. Then, she got up and quietly opened her drawers and fished out a sheer satin camisole set. She stepped into the bathroom to dress, then went downstairs.

With the front window open, she could hear Diego and Matías quietly talking outside, could smell their cigarette smoke.

She poured an inch of scotch into her water glass, then took two glasses from the top cabinet and poured some in them, as well. She divided the remaining white powder into the two fresh glasses, then gathered all three and headed for the front door.

"Hello, chicos," she said softly as she stepped outside.

They were sitting on the wooden bench with their feet up on the porch railing. Their rifles were leaning against the house. When they saw her, they quickly took their feet down and sat up straight. Then they stared.

The cool breeze caressed her skin. She could feel her nipples hardening under the satin, casting shadows under the same porch light that would be rendering her sheer clothes almost transparent.

"Toman una copa conmigo," she said, holding out the two glasses. *Have a drink with me.*

"¿Que hay de tu amigo?" Diego replied warily, glancing up toward the bedroom window. *What about your friend?*

"Él está durmiendo. Él es aburrido," she said with a pout. *He's asleep. He's boring.* "Y quiero divertirme," she added. *And I want to have fun.*

Matías' eyes were practically bruising her flesh. Another time she might have found it comedic. But she was out there for a reason.

"No me hagas beber solo," she said with a pout. *Don't make me drink alone.* She held out the glasses again, and this time they each took a glass without hesitating.

"Salud," she said, gulping down half the whiskey.

Diego and Matías each drank a little bit less than that. She sighed and moved over to the railing between them.

She said something about how good it was, then took another sip, coaxing them to do the same.

They did, both grimacing at the taste. She forgot sometimes that not everybody liked scotch. Maybe she should have mixed it with Frescolita.

She remarked that it was chillier than she had expected and asked if she could sit. Before they could answer, or get up, she squeezed in between them on the bench.

She told them to drink up, and she finished her whiskey.

They did, grimacing even more, maybe getting the bulk of the drug in that last gulp.

She put one hand on each of their thighs, feeling their muscles tense, feeling the warmth through their fatigues.

"Pienso en ustedes dos como amigos," she told them. *I think of you two as friends.* She kept her hands perfectly still, and in moments, she could hear their breathing slow, almost in unison.

She waited another few minutes, silent and still despite the adrenalin coursing through her. When she finally stood up, they slumped sideways into the space she left behind, Matías' head resting on Diego's shoulder.

She smiled at them one last time. Then she went inside to pack and get ready.

Chapter Twenty-One

PIERCE AWOKE WITH a smile and the hint of a headache, squinting into the bright morning sunlight streaming through the window. It had been a longer, deeper sleep than he'd had in years.

Gloriana was already up. He went into the bathroom and peed, brushed his teeth, and washed his face. As he headed downstairs, still naked, something caught his eye, made him pause. Most of the photos that had been taped to the wall were gone, including the one of Gloriana in her village.

But one of the remaining photos caught his attention. Gloriana, all grown up, sitting in an outdoor café. It looked like Paris. With her, holding her hand on the table, was Topher Moreland.

"Son of a bitch," Pierce mumbled to himself as the bitter and cynical side of him elbowed aside the smitten schoolboy.

The photo next to it was older, with an even younger Gloriana and Moreland. Pierce wondered if this was before or after Gloriana and he had been together. A bunch of other college kids were in the picture with them, including one who stood out from the others. Everybody else, Gloriana and Moreland included, had a kind of goofy earnestness about them, but this kid had a cold, hard look in his eyes, a look Pierce recognized. A *face* he recognized.

A young Frank Billings.

Maybe Gloriana hadn't known who the kid in the photo was, Pierce told himself, his mind racing chaotically as he adjusted to this new information. Maybe he was just another kid at the party, a coincidence. And maybe she didn't know Christopher Moreland had created the BetterLates, which she said she had never heard of.

Maybe.

He hurried downstairs.

She wasn't in the living room.

He grabbed his clothes from where they had been hanging to dry and pulled them on; then he went barefoot out onto the beach.

The soda bottles from the night before were on the sand where they'd left them. He scanned the jetties, then stared out onto the water for a long minute, thinking she could be out there swimming, about to surface at any moment. But there was no sign of her.

He felt a growing unease as he went back inside and checked the entire first floor.

He called out her name, quietly, mindful of the guards outside. "Gloriana?" The sound of it was absorbed into the small house, dull and flat and weak. He ran upstairs and searched the bedroom and the bathroom, the closet and under the bed. The knapsack he had tripped over the night before was gone.

Back downstairs, he quickly put on his shoes, then took a deep breath before opening the front door.

Instantly, he saw two clusters of dark red spots on the wooden floor of the porch. He leaned out the door, his eyes following two trails of blood droplets, past the edge of the porch, around to the side of the house. Diego and Matías lay dead in the garden, already attracting flies. Their heads were touching, a bullet hole in each. A tiny puddle of blood had collected beneath their heads.

Pierce was terrified for Gloriana, but he knew the missing knapsack meant she hadn't been abducted. She was part of this.

He ran inside to get his jacket and saw a note on the coffee table, folded like a tent.

On the outside was written, *Mondo*. He snatched it and opened it. Inside, it said, *Sorry. I didn't know.*

Then he saw what had been under it: Gloriana's ankle bracelet, neatly severed, its LED light blinking red. That's when he heard the trucks approaching.

He grabbed his jacket and dashed out the front door, diving into the prickly bushes across the road. Thorns raked his skin and snagged his clothing as he wriggled his way deeper, as the trucks drew closer and closer. He stopped when he heard the brakes squeal, as the trucks skidded to a stop in front of Gloriana's house. He watched through the foliage as a dozen UniCs streamed out of the caravan of military vehicles, then he turned and plunged deeper into the thick brush.

THE BUS STOP consisted of a bench and a plywood roof mounted on two half-rotted posts. But by the time he got there, Pierce was glad to have the shelter. After half an hour of fighting his way through the dense brush and ten minutes jogging up the road, he was hot and sweaty, covered with cuts and scratches and dirt. He had paused in the bushes to put on his jacket, but his shirt was already streaked and speckled with blood.

Two older women were already waiting when he got there. Deep in conversation, they didn't stop talking as he approached, but they both gave him a quick appraising glance.

"Buenos dias," he said.

"Buenos dias," they both replied, watching as he lowered himself onto the bench.

When a military-style UniC SUV roared past, he pushed himself to the edge of the bench, behind them. He watched as it turned down the side road that led toward Corlinas, toward Gloriana's house.

When another one came by, the two women wordlessly moved in front of him, blocking him from view.

When it passed, one of the women smiled down at him. "¿Estás bien?" *Are you okay?*

"Si," Pierce replied. "Gracias." He used the sleeve of his jacket to wipe the sweat off his face. It came away faintly streaked with blood.

In ones and twos, more people showed up to wait. By the time the bus arrived fifteen minutes later, a dozen people were standing there, chatting with one another and ignoring Pierce.

One of the two women who had hidden him from the UniCs turned to him and said, "Anzoategui Aeroperto?"

He nodded and she waved her hand, motioning for him to get on ahead of them. Usually, Pierce would have declined on the grounds of old-fashioned chivalry. Instead he mumbled, "Gracias," and got on the bus.

The fare was thirty Bolivars—about three dollars. He paid with a ten, saying it was for him and the two women behind him who had been so kind.

He found a seat by a window and closed his eyes.

He felt incredibly foolish, naive, believing that Gloriana would miss him the way he missed her, would feel the same affection, attraction. Maybe even love.

Images of the past day came back to him, a slideshow of smiles and confidences and sex, each image undermining the notion that it had all been a ruse. For a moment, he allowed himself to believe that maybe her affection, her passion, had been real. That whatever else had happened was apart from that, outside of it.

Then he cursed himself again.

She had shown a fondness for Diego and Matías, and now they were dead. He had a hard time picturing her killing them, but he barely knew her anymore. People killed for freedom. He pictured her, watching him sleep, having just killed or just about to kill Diego and Matías. A chill went through him. But the image wouldn't hold together. He couldn't picture her as a killer. Not like that.

The important thing, he told himself, was that he had gone there for information, and while he hadn't figured out *everything*, he had learned plenty, so much he was still processing it. He'd learned from what she had told him and what she hadn't, what she'd lied about, and what he'd seen.

The bus lurched over a hill, and the landscape outside abruptly changed from brush and grassland to a tangle of pipes and ducts behind a tall cyclone fence. In front of it was a massive white storage tank labeled, with bold red letters, PETROLINUS.

Frank Billings.

He'd been behind Angola, and he had a presence in Venezuela. He'd had Gloriana moved there. His fingerprints were all over this. But why?

Gloriana had worked for him in Angola. She had apparently partied with him in college. Why would she lie about knowing him?

It was possible that, house arrest notwithstanding, she *was* behind what was going on in New York, whatever that was. It wasn't like it had been difficult to get in to see her.

Billings' operations in New York were not unaffected by the money microbe, but he certainly wasn't bearing the brunt of it, not like the Shakes and the Toros and Townsend. According to Gloriana, she'd been coerced when she'd worked for Billings in Angola, but she'd certainly come out ahead because of it.

On the other hand, if Billings had used his UniCon connections to put her there, couldn't he have simply used them to have her released from house arrest, as well, instead of killing the guards and spiriting her away?

More compelling was her claim that she'd never heard of the BetterLates. That had been hard to believe on the face of it; Pierce had seen them in every country he'd delivered to. Yes, she'd been locked up, but given that she knew—intimately, it seemed—the founder and leader of the BetterLates, the idea that she'd never heard of them was preposterous.

Why had she lied about that? Pierce smiled, thinking maybe she was embarrassed about having gone out with such a smug prick. But the smile faded as he realized what the most obvious explanation was.

Gloriana and Moreland were working together. And they might have been working with Billings, too. Maybe the local UniCs weren't in on it. Maybe, Petrolinus notwithstanding, Billings' influence didn't extend down here anymore. But for the moment at least, Billings *was* part of UniCon. That meant that UniCon was almost certainly behind it, too.

Or maybe whatever Billings was up to was a last ditch effort to avoid relegation. Or maybe it was his exit strategy, maybe he knew he was on his way out and he was softening up New York, taking out his once-and-future competition.

But the simpler explanation was that Frank Billings and Gloriana Leong and Topher Moreland were all playing for UniCon. Part of Pierce resisted the idea, but he knew that was naïve. *Everyone* played for UniCon, one way or another. Everyone but the Guild.

A few more pieces came together in his mind: Gloriana's aerosol microbes, the nanosonic diffuser, and the non-burning incense the BetterLates had begun using right before the money started disappearing. That's how they were spreading the microbe.

He took the note out of his pocket and looked at it again. *Sorry. I didn't know.*

What didn't she know? That she was going to kill those two boys? No, he still couldn't accept she had killed them. That she was going to leave him in the lurch like that? Maybe.

His thoughts churned, but as he slipped the note back into his pocket, it occurred to him that maybe "sorry" wasn't for what she had done already. Maybe it was for whatever she was about to do next.

Chapter Twenty-Two

AFTER A YEAR spent in the little beach house and its grounds and two years in a prison cell, Gloriana felt overwhelmed by her freedom, by the open spaces, even within the cramped confines of the helicopter. Beneath them, the Caribbean Sea extended uninterrupted in every direction. Above them, the cloudless sky did the same.

She pulled herself closer to Chris, just to hold on to something. He turned to look at her, his face inscrutable behind his dark shades, starkly reminding her just how little she knew him anymore.

The events of the night before kept playing through her mind. She'd been sitting in the living room, waiting, when she'd heard feet crunching on the gravel outside, then the soft pops of a gun with a silencer on it, one right after the other. She ran to the door and there was Chris, with two men she didn't know.

She was intensely relieved to see him—thrilled in a way, but horrified as well. She knew what had happened before she even looked. But she looked anyway. Diego and Matías, slumped in their chairs, eyes still closed from sleep, blood trickling down each of their foreheads.

"There was no need to do that," she said, her voice catching as she spoke. That had been the first thing either of them said to the other.

Chris strode up to her and put his arms around her, holding her until she did the same. It seemed to be a test, but she put her arms around him and felt his around her, and for a moment, all the intervening years and all the changes disappeared. They were back in grad school, young and idealistic and hot for each other.

"We have to be extra careful," he said into her hair, his voice soft but cold. "We can't afford loose ends. Not now." He had taken her by the shoulders and stared into her eyes. "People are going to die," he said. "In order for things to get better for the world as a whole. Innocent people are going to suffer. We knew that going in."

Looking over his shoulder, she had watched as his men grabbed Diego and Matías under the arms and dragged them to the side of the house, where they wouldn't be visible from the street.

Meanwhile, Chris was looking over her shoulder, too. He pulled back from her and said, "Is someone else here?"

She looked back over her shoulder and saw Mondo's clothes hanging in the kitchen. "You told me no one was going to get hurt," she said. "That was the whole reason for the drugs. Diego and Matías, they were out cold. You didn't need to kill them."

"Is someone upstairs?"

She didn't say yes. She almost said no. But before she could say anything, Chris moved around her, through the living room and up the stairs, two at a time.

Gloriana had run after him, half whispering, half shouting, "No! *No!*"

He stopped halfway up the stairs and looked at the photos taped to the wall. Half of them she had already packed up, the ones from her childhood. She was leaving behind the ones he'd printed for her. The photos of them. He seemed to consider that for an instant, glancing back at her before bounding the rest of the way up the stairs.

She caught up with him in her bedroom, standing over her bed, looking down at Pierce sleeping. She realized how ready Chris was to kill, how willing. This was not theoretical or abstract. This was pulling the trigger and taking a human life.

Maybe she'd been naïve.

"No," she whispered again, fiercely.

"Really?" He laughed and tilted his head, studying her. "You knew I was coming."

She felt her face go hot. It had been a long time since she and Chris had been together, and even then, they'd never been exclusive, but you couldn't always tell where he stood with that. "No, I didn't. I didn't get the postcard until tonight. Didn't see it until barely an hour ago. And what are you doing here now, anyway? You just did the field tests, right? New York? Alaska? You shouldn't be here for another month at least."

"Heard about that, did you?" He gave her a look she couldn't read. "Billings is getting jumpy about the UniConference. Your little miracle bug worked better than we could have imagined. It's already causing quite a stir. We need to act fast before UniCon figures it out."

He raised his gun once again, aiming at Pierce's head. She grabbed his arm and pushed it down.

"I said no." She glared at him.

"Look, I know this isn't easy," he said. "Nobody likes this part. But now is not the time to turn soft."

"If you shoot him, I'm out."

He sighed and then smirked. "Well, I hope you didn't fall in love with him."

She couldn't tell if that would have made things better or worse. "Just don't."

Pierce shifted in bed, revealing the cuff on his wrist.

"Wait a second," Chris said, leaning over the bed to get a better look. "I know this guy. That's Armand Pierce, isn't it? The courier?"

"Yes."

"Jesus Christ. I knew his dad back at Otisville. You know him?"

She studied his face, wondering if this was a test, too, wondering if he knew the answer, if telling the truth would make him more or less likely to pull the trigger. But that truth was that she had loved him once, more than she had ever loved Chris. Maybe she still did. "I knew him. A long time ago."

"Uh huh." He frowned at her, like he knew what that meant. "What the hell is he doing here? What does he know?"

"Just what he's read in magazines."

"He came to Otisville asking his dad about 'disappearing money.' He came all the way down here to talk to you, for God's sake. He must know something."

"He had questions, but I didn't answer them."

"Questions about what?"

"About your field-testing in New York. He knows something's up, but it sounds like by now, a lot of people do."

"He knows about *you*."

"A lot of people know about me."

He snorted, staring at her, annoyed. Then his face softened a bit. "Look babe, this is *all* about you. You're the key. I just want to make sure you're safe, that there are no loose ends to come back at you."

"If you do it, I'm out," she said again, her voice steely.

Chris's face twitched, like he was holding back a snarl. "You don't tell me what to do."

"Leave him here for the UniCs to find. He doesn't know anything and by the time he explains his way out... things will be different."

Chris shook his head and laughed, but it was devoid of humor. "Whatever," he said, his eyes smoldering. As he shoved the gun into his waistband he added, "But the way things are about to go down, you might not be doing him a favor."

Chapter Twenty-Three

As THE PLANE circled JFK, the clouds broke, revealing a dozen plumes of smoke rising over Brooklyn and a few more over LoHo. A squadron of police helicopters hovered over HiHo, their flashing lights reflecting off the glass-and-chrome towers. Pierce wondered if Gloriana's microbes were spreading across the city, bringing confusion and mayhem. He wondered how much damage they would cause, how many trillions of dollars they would erase. And, as he had since fleeing her house, he wondered why she was doing it.

The clouds closed in again as the plane descended, and Pierce felt a familiar gray mood close over him as well. It replaced the ache he'd felt since finding Gloriana gone, somehow muddled the memory of the joy he'd felt the day before. Depressing as it was, dangerous as it was, he was relieved to be back.

As he made his way through JFK, banks of televisions teased stories about the upcoming UniConference, the approach of Tropical Storms Wilson and Xavier, and an update on climate-remediation efforts, including controversy over an ambitious high-altitude cloud-seeding program.

But the big story was breathless coverage of the wave of riots, gang violence, and mysterious robberies spreading through Brooklyn, Queens, and Manhattan. Pierce had almost pushed his way through the knot of travelers when the newscaster mentioned similar clusters of disturbances popping up in Alaska in addition to the ones in New York and Arizona.

The police were blaming copycats, but Pierce stopped and stared at the screens, thinking back to what Gloriana had said about testing the microbes in different conditions.

New York, Arizona, Alaska, Angola. Temperate, desert, arctic, tropical.

UniCon was global. If these were field tests, this was just the start.

As the crowds began to drift away, Pierce started running. He'd been thinking of the mayhem spreading through New York, but whatever was going on was starting to look much, much bigger.

He hurried to long-term parking and found Dugray's orange Nissan. As he was retrieving his attaché from the trunk, he heard footsteps behind him, soft and light. He didn't turn around, but angled the attaché so he could see the reflection in the glass-covered control panel. It showed a tall man with blond hair and a long beard wearing mirrored shades and a collarless jacket, coming at him fast. Derek Lindy was part of Erno's inner clique. He wasn't carrying an attaché.

Jesus, Pierce thought. *That didn't take long.*

His gun was still under the passenger seat. The rest of his weapons were in his attaché. He grasped his chain, leaving it unconnected from his attaché. He didn't turn around, but shifted his feet into position while he waited for Lindy to take two more steps.

"Pierce," Lindy called out, and Pierce turned to look at him, keeping his left hand in the trunk of the car.

In addition to the requisite jacket and shades, Lindy wore a sneer. It was kind of a trademark for Lindy, but in that moment, it also reflected a misguided confidence that he was outside the range of Pierce's chain.

Lindy shook his head. "You might think I'm enjoying this, Pierce; that Erno is, too. But we're both disappointed. Erno was shocked. He thought you'd be the last guy to interfere with a shipment, to take a taste of the Large. But I knew it was coming, been waiting for it all along. And I don't judge, either, these fat fucks in their towers, soaking the rest of us for every penny." He shook his head, then took out his gun. "But none of that matters, really. You violated your oath, so my job is to bring you in. Or bring you down."

Lindy was an asshole, but he was good. Pierce would have to play this just right.

While Lindy was talking, Pierce had been running through the plan in his mind. As Lindy's sneer turned into a cruel smile, Pierce slowed his breathing, slowed everything around him, and silently counted to three.

Then he looked over Lindy's shoulder and widened his eyes, like he'd just seen Godzilla. Or God.

Lindy didn't buy it for a second, but Pierce didn't need a whole second. Lindy didn't turn to look over his shoulder, but his head moved the tiniest bit. He didn't blink, but his eyes flickered away from Pierce.

And in that instant, Pierce threw himself to the side and snapped around, twisting his entire body, putting as much force as he could into his legs, his hips, his core, his arms, and, ultimately, the chain at the end of it.

Lindy's gun went off, aimed halfway between where Pierce had been and where he was now.

The bullet pinged off the concrete wall and Lindy's sneer faltered as Pierce's chain closed in on his face, maybe as he remembered how long it was. He ducked, just a bit, and the chain cracked against the side of his head, splitting his scalp, sending his shades flying in three directions.

The chain clattered to the concrete floor, then scraped across it as Pierce jerked it back.

Lindy stood for a moment with blood streaming down the side of his head. Then his eyes rolled up and he fell backward.

Pierce checked to make sure he was still breathing, then dragged him out of the way, propping him up against a concrete pillar. He brisky closed the trunk and returned to the car, checking to make sure his gun was still under the passenger seat. Then he got out of there as fast as he could, pulling Gs as he spiraled down to ground level.

He paid at the booth—surprised he'd been gone barely two days. Then he merged onto the highway and sped off.

Lindy had been waiting for him at the airport. The clock was ticking faster and louder. He couldn't get close to Billings. Gloriana was in the wind. But he knew where to find Topher Moreland.

He headed upstate, to Otisville.

HE WAS APPROACHING the Hutchinson River Expressway when a pair of unmarked black SUVs came up behind him fast, lights flashing and sirens wailing. His heart sank as soon as he saw them. This was it.

Then, before he could fully experience the fear, before he could even ease up on the accelerator, they swerved around him and sped off.

His heart was still racing when his pager went off. It was Diaz. As Pierce looked at the display, another half a dozen pages came in, all from Diaz, buffered from when Pierce had been on the plane.

Pierce pulled off the highway at a charging station and found a payphone.

Diaz answered immediately, his voice flat and suspicious. "Who's this?"

Pierce looked around before he answered, Diaz's paranoia exacerbating his own. "It's me. You paged me."

"Jesus Christ, where the fuck've you been?"

"I left town. Seemed like the smart thing to do. I just got back."

"Well, you were smart to get out of town. Coming back, not so much."

"What's going on?"

"It's a fucking mess, kid. Chopra's dead."

"Fuck. Who killed him?"

"I don't know. It could've been the client, could've been one of us. I heard a couple got picked up by the UniCs."

"The UniCs?" Pierce repeated. "And the Guild allowed that?"

"I don't know what they did or didn't allow. Communications are a mess. But I do know they're coming after you. Erno and his pals. Superseding orders."

"From Fargo? How high up?"

"No, from the fucking Guild itself. From the top. And not just you, they're going after all the Couriers under

268

suspicion. Maybe they brought the UniCs in for backup. Never thought I'd see it happen."

"Me neither," said Pierce said. "I just had a run-in with Lindy."

"Lindy? Fuck. You okay?"

"I am. He's not."

Diaz let out a sigh. "So now they'll be after you for resisting procedure."

"Procedure?" Pierce said with a bitter laugh. "Bullshit is what it was."

"You don't have to tell me, kid. I'm just saying, now they've got something else to throw at you, even if you straighten out the Kransky thing. I'm just the messenger."

Pierce exhaled, calmed himself down. "I know. I hear you. And I appreciate the heads up, I do."

"I know, kid. And I know this is all bullshit, but that don't mean it's not for real. The Guild trustees are taking this shit serious. Deadly serious. Speaking of Kransky, though, you made any progress on that disappearing money thing?"

Pierce took a breath, about to speak, but then he stopped. Yes, Diaz was a friend and an ally. A good man. But if the Guild's trustees were terrified, then so was Diaz, and it probably wasn't smart to trust someone that scared. "No," he said. "Nothing yet."

Diaz laughed, a soft, weary rasp, like he knew Pierce was holding out on him, but he also knew that was the smart thing to do. "Right."

"Do you think that's what all this other stuff is about?" Pierce said. "All these couriers going missing, do you think their shipments disappeared?"

"No idea. I don't know what the fuck is going on."

It crossed Pierce's mind that maybe the Guild was what this was all about, UniCon trying to take out the one piece of the pie they didn't control yet. Or if it was about U-Net, undermining confidence in the Guild was part of that. "Okay," he said. "Well look, I got to keep moving."

"Yeah, you do. Stay safe and keep in touch, okay?"

"Yeah, you too."

"One last thing."

"Yeah?"

"When I said they were going after all of them, the guys under suspicion? That includes Rocha. He took a shipment and disappeared."

Pierce cursed under his breath. "Did you call him?"

"Of course I fucking called. No answer. I'd go check on him, but I've got too many fires to put out here."

"Yeah, there's fires all over."

"I hear you. Just thought you'd want to know."

Pierce sighed. "Is he still on Third Avenue?"

"Yeah, that's right. Across from the old Fairview site."

Of course. "I'll try to check in on him if I can."

"Thanks, kid. Good luck out there."

TRAFFIC WAS SO heavy even the SmartDrive-restricted roads were bogged down with volume leaving the city. Pierce hit delays as he turned onto the Cross Bronx Expressway, and again getting off it.

When traffic slowed to five miles an hour, Pierce opened the window. He'd spent so much time in airports and on planes that he relished the fresh air, even with the haze of smoke and the slight tang of pepper gas.

There was another fragrance though, one he couldn't place at first; then he heard chanting and immediately recognized it as the BetterLates' incense. Both the smell and the sound seemed wildly out of place on the highway. Looking around, he spotted a dozen of them parading down a wide avenue parallel to the expressway. As he looked on, a mob materialized around them, an odd mix of street toughs and middle-aged store-owners, even a few old-fashioned Bronx mafia types. Some carried bats or other crude weapons. They converged on the BetterLates with sudden and terrible violence, surrounding them, overwhelming them.

From the middle of the scrum, an incense diffuser flew straight up, the vapor tracing a curlicue as it spun through the air. Even as vivid splashes of red appeared on the BetterLates' green shirts, Pierce felt his eyes drawn to the device.

He wondered if the crowd had figured out the BetterLates were causing all this through that incense of theirs, if that's why they were attacking. He wondered if the BetterLates themselves even knew the part they were playing. Probably not. He felt bad for them.

Pierce turned to watch through the back window as a pair of UniC vehicles arrived, but the scene disappeared behind him as the cars surged forward and the highway took him underground.

When he re-emerged, he saw a haze over the Bronx, lit up by flashing lights, various colors indicating the different types of emergencies. Even as he left the city and headed into the Hudson Valley, the sky was filled with police copters and drones.

It seemed like things were coming apart.

When he got to Otisville, he parked in the lot and tried Dugray from the payphone out front. There was no answer.

The same woman was at the visitation check-in. "Bradley Pierce again?"

Pierce shook his head. "Topher Moreland."

She tilted her head at him, then tapped at her computer. "You just missed him, I'm afraid."

"What do you mean?"

"Well, not 'just.' Released three days ago. Right after you were here last time, I think."

"Are you fucking kidding me?"

She gave him a look that made it very clear: no, she was not kidding, and she did not appreciate his tone.

"Sorry," he said.

"Mmm-hm. He paid his fine and they let him go."

Pierce growled in anger and frustration

She raised an eyebrow. "Is there anything else I can help you with?"

Pierce ground his teeth for a moment, then let out a sigh. "Yes. Bradley Pierce, please."

THE VISITATION ROOM was empty this time. Bradley came through the same door he had three days earlier, looking like he'd aged ten years. His hair was greasy and unkempt. His face looked gray and washed out. He scowled when he saw Pierce.

He seemed more like himself.

Bradley lowered himself into the chair across from Pierce, slowly, like he was achy and old. "Two visits in three years, huh? What do you want from me this time?" He seemed like a wounded animal, ready to lash out.

"So," Pierce said, which was the extent of what he had scripted out. "Moreland got out?"

Bradley bit his lip and looked down. "Yes, he did," he said quietly.

"I thought he was in here as a matter of principle."

"I don't know why you dislike him so," Bradley said. "He's a great man, who's trying hard to save the world from itself. If you took the time to understand him, I think you'd really like him."

"Do you know of any connection between Moreland and Frank Billings?"

Bradley snorted in derision. "Don't be ridiculous. They're from two completely different worlds."

"He would have told you?"

Bradley sat up straighter. "I would have *known*."

"Have you been following the news? The riots?"

He nodded. "Yes. It feels safer in here sometimes."

"It's all tied to the disappearing Large, what I was asking you about last time."

Pierce expected Bradley to dismiss it outright, to explain why that was a ludicrous notion and why Pierce, by extension, was stupid for having said it. Instead, he just nodded.

"Did Moreland seem to know anything about it?" Pierce asked.

Bradley smiled wistfully. "He knew a lot about everything."

"You said he asked a lot of questions about money and finance."

Bradley mustered a brave smile. "He was just being nice. He knew more about macroeconomics than I'll ever know. Do you know how his father made his money?"

"Carbon capture technology."

"Nope. He made *millions* on that; he made *hundreds* of millions from the diamonds it produced. But the real money, the *billions*, he made from shorting the diamond cartels, betting against them because he knew once his technology got out, the cartels would implode. And they did. That's how the Morelands made their fortune."

"Then they lost it in the Upheaval."

Bradley nodded. "A lot of it, yes. A lot of people did. But he's still very rich."

"So... did he seem interested in what was going on with the Large?"

"No more than you were."

Pierce laughed. "Well, I was pretty interested in it."

Bradley just shrugged.

"So, he paid his fine and left, huh?"

"Yes. He did."

"You miss him?"

"Of course I do. Look at this place. Topher was a breath of fresh air around here. And now it's just back to..." He waved his hands at the gray walls surrounding them.

"Did you know he was leaving?" Pierce asked.

Bradley looked down again. "No."

Pierce felt bad for him, and that made him dislike Moreland even more: not because he'd hurt Bradley, but because he'd made Pierce—after all these years—feel sorry for him.

"So, did you talk to Villarica?" Bradley asked, audibly pulling himself together.

"I did. He was helpful, but I'm back where I started." He explained how Villarica had identified Carla Jackson, and how he had gone to visit her. "I missed her by a week and a half. She's dead."

"That's a tough break, kiddo."

"Gunned down on the street. By a drone."

"A drone?" Bradley said, lowering his voice and looking around. "I heard about that. Townsend's people were behind it then?"

"What are you talking about?"

274

Bradley shrugged and sat back, as if taking a moment to savor knowing something Pierce didn't. "They're saying Townsend has been using drones to take out his enemies. He's got some sort of 'special dispensation' from UniCon." He leaned forward again. "Which says to me he's a lock to be promoted at the UniConference. They'll probably give him Billings' spot when they kick him out."

"Son of a bitch," Pierce said, slumping back in his seat. "So, if Townsend's out there tying up the loose ends from Fairview, then they're probably *his* loose ends. Townsend was behind Fairview."

"That would make sense," Bradley said. "If UniCon is about to let him in, they'd want to make sure the Fairview accident wasn't going to come out and embarrass them."

"It was murder, you know," Pierce said quietly. "The Fairview. It wasn't neglect. It wasn't an accident. The building was intentionally brought down."

Bradley went still. "You know this?"

Pierce nodded.

"Well," Bradley said, his eyes drifted off into the distance, maybe moistening. He opened his mouth as if to speak, but just shook his head instead. After a few seconds, he said, "I'm sorry, son. I really am."

They sat in a silence for a moment. Then Bradley cleared his throat. "I've been hearing talk about your money thing too. The disappearing cash you were talking about."

"Heard what?"

He laughed, wiping his eyes. "I still think it's bullshit, but a lot of the guys in here are talking about it. Some are even saying they've lost money. Thought you'd want to know."

Pierce grunted and stood up to go, still dazed by the revelations about Townsend. "Thanks, Dad."

Bradley laughed. "'Dad'? I haven't heard *that* in a long time."

Pierce turned to go, still distracted. Then he stopped and turned back. "One more question. Why did Moreland leave now?"

Bradley let out a sigh. "He didn't say, but I imagine he thought it important to be there for the BetterLates' big launch. He probably wanted to meet with his sponsors and prepare."

"The big launch?"

He nodded. "His high-altitude drone fleet."

"His what?"

"The drones, the drones." He leaned forward, snapping his fingers, shaking his head at Pierce like he was an idiot. "You know Topher didn't create the BetterLates so do-gooders would have an excuse to dress up in green and annoy people, right? It's about saving the planet." He said it with a forced nobility, as if he'd had some part of it. "They're sending up drones to seed the clouds with atmospheric aerosols as part of his Solar Radiation Management program, to reverse global warming."

"Aerosols... When?"

"Tonight, I believe."

Pierce stared at him as more pieces fell into place. "Where?"

"Everywhere. All over the world. This is big." His voice cracked as he said it. "This is the moment people will look back on and say that Topher Moreland saved the fucking world." He said it with pride, but with sorrow as well. While Topher Moreland was out there saving the world, Bradley Pierce was going to be right here in

Otisville Correctional Facility, old and forgotten.

Pierce felt a wholly unfamiliar fondness for his father, an empathy that he had never felt before. He wanted to tell Bradley everything was going to be okay. But as more and more pieces came together in his head, he was increasingly certain that was far from the truth.

He thought back again to what Gloriana had said about testing in different conditions.

"How do they know this stuff is going to work all around the world?"

Bradley rolled his eyes. "Well, they've been testing it, of course, in different climates. They're dispersing the aerosol with a gadget Topher invented. He called it a nanosonic diffuser."

Chapter Twenty-Four

THE ADDRESS OTISVILLE Corrections had on file for Topher Moreland was on Oneida Drive, in Greenwich, Connecticut. Pierce had pictured a massive stone mansion on the beach—based on a slew of assumptions, including Moreland being the kind of spoiled rich kid and pampered adult who'd had so much handed to him that he felt entitled to everything else as well. He'd scolded himself for making assumptions, but when he found the place, he said out loud, "Son of a bitch. I nailed it."

The grounds were small, but the house was glorious, a stone mansion right on the water with a circular driveway and a cobblestone courtyard, separated from its neighbors by a tall fence on either side.

Only two things detracted from the grandeur. One was the cars and bikes, a dozen of them at least—cheap, beat-up, and rundown—taking up half the courtyard, with a few more parked or discarded on the street out front. The other was the handful of BetterLates drinking beer in the grassy circle in the center of the courtyard.

Next door, a neighbor was on a ladder, putting up storm shutters. He looked tanned and well-fed, with salt-and-pepper hair. He glanced over as Pierce parked on the street and got out of his car.

"Excuse me," Pierce called out to him, pointing. "Is that Topher Moreland's house?"

The guy looked across the tall fence, over at the other house, then turned back to Pierce, pausing a moment, as if he couldn't decide whether he should bother to answer. "Not for long," he finally said. "Thank God."

"Is he selling it?"

"It's in foreclosure. I might just buy the damn place myself to make sure some other freakshow doesn't buy it."

"Do you know if Moreland's in there?"

"Last I heard, he was in jail," the guy said, then made a point of returning to the task at hand, letting Pierce know the conversation was over.

As Pierce walked through the gate, the BetterLates went inside through the front door, but Pierce got the sense that didn't have anything to do with him. As he crossed the courtyard, he looked past the green lawn and hedges and glimpsed the ocean lapping at Topher Moreland's private beach.

It made him think of Gloriana's place, of Gloriana, and he paused at the bottom of the wide granite steps, almost felled by the stab of pain and longing, the sense of betrayal. He took a deep breath, then climbed the steps toward the heavy wood-and-brass doors flanked by massive planters overflowing with flowers and vines.

The doors were ajar, and as he approached them, he heard voices inside, soft and conversational, absolutely unthreatening.

He opened the door and entered an entry hall with a vaulted ceiling and a Persian rug over a black-and-white marble floor. A huge crystal vase stood on a mahogany table.

To his right and down a step was a large living area; much less formal, with a brown suede sectional sofa wrapped around a coffee table made of a granite boulder, sheared level and polished to a mirror finish.

A dozen BetterLates were sprawled on the sofa, their green-clad limbs overlapping and interlaced. Pierce couldn't tell if any of them were the ones from outside.

The air was heavy with the smells of sex and sweat and beer and cannabis inhalables. A handful of vape sticks were scattered on the coffee table, along with a dozen spoons and several empty ice cream cartons. In the background, he recognized the smell of the BetterLate's incense, and something else familiar, faint but oppressive, sickly floral yet oddly chemical and fake, like room freshener.

"Where's Moreland?" he asked, urgent but hopefully non-threatening.

Two of the girls popped their heads up and looked at him, one with long black hair and one with a reddish bob and freckles. No one else seemed to have heard.

"Moreland," Pierce said. "Where is he?"

The girls looked at each other. The one with the dark hair shook her head and the one with the freckles turned back to him and pointed tentatively toward the kitchen. "Maybe in there?"

The kitchen was cluttered but unoccupied. It was sleek and elegant and high-end, but the sink and the countertops were littered with dirty plates and glasses. The recycling container was overflowing with beer bottles.

The window over the sink looked out onto a green lawn and then the harbor.

Pierce ran upstairs and checked the second floor, then the third. He disturbed two couples on the third floor and one threesome on the second, all in various forms of entanglement. He asked them if they'd seen Moreland, but the most he got was distracted head-shakes.

In the master bedroom, a painting sat on the floor, leaning against the wall. Above it, a large wall safe stood open and empty.

On the dresser across from it stood a photo of Moreland and Gloriana. He'd taken whatever was in the safe, but he'd left that behind.

Chris, Christopher, Topher. Gloriana's college sweetheart, who had developed the smokeless incense diffuser. Pierce had known it since she disappeared, since he saw the other photo of them in her house in Corlinas. He hadn't needed any other confirmation, but now he had it anyway.

Topher Moreland and Gloriana weren't just college sweethearts, they were still together in some way. Had they killed Matías and Diego together, and set Pierce up to take the fall? And what were they were up to now? Helping UniCon's continuing plan of world domination? With *Frank Billings*, of all people? It still didn't make sense, still didn't feel right.

Apart from anything else, UniCon was built on Large. They couldn't replace all their Large with Small—there probably wasn't enough Small in existence. Unless they had some sort of inoculation or microbe-proofing.

But if it didn't make sense, Pierce had to acknowledge it was probably a failure of imagination on his part, a lack of understanding of how the economy worked anymore, or what the world had become.

As he came back downstairs, he could see out onto the back patio, where a BetterLate with a beard and no shirt was grilling steaks on a solar grill.

He looked up when Pierce came out the back door.

"'Sup," the kid said, with a friendly nod. He was nineteen years old at most, and high on more than life. He had the slouch of a stoner but the build of a swimmer.

"Smells good," Pierce said.

"Yeah, if you dig the meat thing." He poked himself in the chest with the handle of the barbecue fork. "Which I very much do."

He raised an eyebrow at Pierce.

Pierce nodded, although it had been so long since he had eaten meat he found himself slightly repulsed at the thought of it.

"All right," the kid said. "Topher has the good stuff, too, man. This shit would have cost a fortune even in the old days, you know what I'm saying? I'm Cody, by the way."

"Pierce. So Moreland was here?"

"Yeah, man. In the flesh. With his lady."

Pierce felt an irrational twist in his belly. "Gloriana?"

"Yeah, that sounds right. Man, she was smokin' hot. And smart as shit, too, apparently, some sort of scientist or something. Makes sense, I guess, if she's with the big guy." He laughed at that. "She's probably got, like, superpowers and shit."

"When did they leave?"

"Hour ago. Maybe an hour and a half."

"Do you know where they went?"

"Not for sure. He said something about Teterboro. He invited us to the house to eat whatever we wanted, you know? Empty out his cryo-freezer and everything. That's why I'm cooking these bad boys."

"When was this?"

He shrugged. "He put the word out this morning. I showed up a few hours ago and there was already some people here. I guess it's like, a party to celebrate the launch tonight, you know? That we're finally doing something to fix the climate and save the world."

As he spoke, a girl even younger than him came out from the kitchen carrying a beer. Her green BetterLate shirt was tied up tight under her breasts, and her green sweats were rolled down low on her hips. She eyed Pierce suspiciously.

"Right on," Pierce said, wincing as soon as he did. "And where is that again?"

"The launch? All over the world, all at the same time. But the main one is local, in Teterboro. At the Quadport. I imagine that's where they were headed."

The girl gave Cody a beer; he said, "Thanks, boo," and kissed her on her nose. "This is Pierce," he said, pointing the fork at him. "This is Gretch."

She snuggled up to Cody and squinted at Pierce.

"Hi," Pierce said, but she didn't respond. He turned back to Cody. "Yeah, I want to watch that. What time is it again?"

"Sunset. Like, six-thirty."

"Just in time for the evening news."

"Nah, man. Moreland said he's not even having the media there. People think he's all about getting press for himself, but he's about the cause, end of story, man. He does all that media and publicity stuff for the cause, not for him. Now that we're moving forward, he said we don't even need the press. They'd just get in the way."

"Makes sense," Pierce said. "So was anyone else here with him?"

"What are you, a cop?" the girl asked, stepping away from Cody.

Cody cocked his head at her. "Boo, don't be like that."

Pierce raised his hand to reveal his cuff. "Courier, actually."

Cody laughed. "No way! That's sick."

Gretch was unimpressed.

"But I'm here because Topher's a family friend," Pierce said. Technically true. "I heard he got out and I wanted to say hi. Give him my dad's regards."

"That's cool," Cody said. "Topher's got all sorts of friends. Got them everywhere."

Gretch wasn't buying it, but she didn't seem to care other than being annoyed at Cody for ignoring her suspicions.

"Whatever," she said, and went back inside.

"So was anyone else here with him?" Pierce repeated

"Oh, yeah!" Cody laughed, then leaned closer and lowered his voice. "He was with this total asshole in a suit. I mean, I don't know what that was about. But like I said, friends of all sorts."

"Do you know who it was?"

"No. One of his 'generous funders,' he said."

Pierce looked out over the water one last time. An empty skiff was out in the water, circles rippling away from it. The setup felt oddly similar to Gloriana's house in Venezuela, like with enough sunlight and water and proper care, that could grow into this. He felt that stab of sadness and hurt again, but he also felt like he was getting past it. Like, if their houses were so similar in ways, maybe they were similar too. More so than he had thought.

He told Cody to take care, then turned to go.

Cody seemed disappointed. "Dude, are you sure? Gonna be meat soon. More than I can eat."

"Sorry, I gotta go. Maybe next time."

Rather than go back through the house, Pierce headed toward the front via the narrow side yard.

"Won't be no next time, dude. Topher's getting rid of the house and everything." As Pierce glanced back, Cody's face turned solemn. "Too much money is the root of all evil."

"What did you say?"

"That's something Topher likes to say. He said his girlfriend taught him. 'Too much money is the root of all evil.'" He paused and looked around, his eyes misting up. "And Topher walks the walk. So he's giving all this up."

Before Pierce could say anything else, he heard a chorus of high-powered motors approaching fast, followed by screeching tires. He peered over the hedges and saw UniC SWAT vehicles, at least four of them. They were coming in fast and quiet, and that meant they were coming in hot. Diaz's comment came back to him, about UniCs arresting couriers, and it crossed his mind that maybe they had followed him here. He doubted it, but he also didn't want to get caught up in a UniC sweep, or have to fight his way out and add another batch of problems to the pile he was already dealing with.

The hedges in front of him shook violently; they were coming straight toward him. He knew they'd be coming around both sides. And the fences on either side of the house were too high to get over without being caught.

He sprinted back into the rear yard.

Cody looked up at him, confused.

"UniCs," Pierce said without slowing down. "Bad guys."

Cody dropped the barbecue fork and ran without hesitation toward the water.

Pierce vaulted up the back steps and in through the kitchen door. From the bottom of the back stairway, he saw Cody through the window, taking three splashy strides through the tiny waves before diving into the water.

The front door crashed open and screams rose from the living room, the death knell of countless buzzes.

Pierce continued up the back steps even as several sets of boots thumped up the front stairway. He ducked into the master bedroom, where the trio he'd interrupted earlier had now gained a fourth. The new participant might have been Gretch, her green clothes added to the crumpled garments on the floor circling the bed like a ritualistic wreath.

They seemed oblivious to Pierce, and to the approaching footsteps.

"The cops are here," he said as he scanned the room, quickly finding and ruling out the closet, the hamper, and under the bed. "Bad guys."

He couldn't tell if they'd heard him or not, but none of them looked up. They seemed pretty engrossed in what they were doing. He noticed the open window, lifted the screen and climbed through, lowering himself out of sight just as the UniCs stomped into the bedroom.

Just below his feet was the narrow, sloped roof of the dining room bay window. It would barely be a two-foot drop if he fully extended himself, but the roof was sloped at such an angle that even from that height, it would be impossible to keep his balance on it.

He pulled himself back up, just enough to peek through the window. The quartet in bed were still oblivious. One of the cops raised his arm and Pierce recognized the object in his hand as, with a loud snap, it loosed two darts into the scrum.

The darts somehow found the guy in the middle of the pile. He arched his back so violently that his companions—all women, as it turned out—were flung off the bed and onto the floor.

Glancing toward the front of the house, Pierce could see the back half of a UniC SWAT van parked on the sidewalk, empty, its lights flashing and its doors open. Beyond it, out on the street, was Dugray's car.

Pierce's arms were starting to ache as he tried to calculate the angles. If he hit the roof below him just right, maybe he could he spring off it, over the fence, and into the neighbor's yard. He was about to try his luck with it when he heard a familiar voice say, "Where's Billings?"

Pierce raised himself up again to see Ryan Mansfield, the UniC who'd beat down Dugray's guy Hutch a few days before. The cop's face was red and sweaty with worry, or fear. He had a taser in one hand and a baton in the other.

Two of the women on the floor said in unison, "Who's Billings?"

"Don't fuck with me. I don't have time for this," Mansfield said. "We tracked him here. We know he was here." He put away his taser and pulled out his gun, then stepped forward and put the barrel against the tazed kid's kneecap. "One knee, then the other knee, then I shoot him in the balls," he said, turning to the girls on the floor. "You get three tries. After that I kill you all. Where did Billings go?"

The kid on the bed rolled onto his side and puked.

One of the girls dashed for the door, and Mansfield flicked out his wrist and cracked the side of her knee with his baton. She squealed and crumpled to the carpet. He laid it across her four more times in the space of two seconds, painting bright red welts across her back, arms and buttocks.

She rolled into a ball, moaning and sobbing and quivering.

Mansfield turned back to the others, and one of the women—it *was* Gretch—said, "There was an asshole here earlier with Moreland. He had on a lot of bad cologne, and he had kind of a nubby nose—"

Billings' cologne! Pierce thought. That's what he'd smelled in the living room.

Mansfield held up a small photo of Billings.

"Yeah, that's him," said Gretch. "He left with Moreland like an hour and a half ago."

"Where were they going?"

"Moreland's big drone launch is tonight. That's what we're celebrating."

"Tonight?"

"At sunset."

Mansfield turned to one of the other cops. "Fucking Billings. What is that asshole up to now?"

PIERCE RELEASED THE window and hit the sloping roof below him, using his momentum to springboard himself over the neighbor's fence. He almost made it, but his foot clipped the fence and he tumbled over, hitting the ground awkwardly and harder than he would have liked. He rolled into it best he could and came up running.

The guy who had been working on his storm shutters

was still up on his ladder, watching the police activity at Moreland's house. He looked down and saw Pierce running across his yard and called out, "Hey!"

Pierce didn't reply and didn't slow down. He got into his car and got the hell out of there.

He needed to get to Teterboro Quadport; that's where things were coming to a head.

He'd been wrong about a lot. Billings, Moreland, Gloriana, they weren't doing UniCon's bidding. And Billings wasn't simply clearing the decks in New York so he could pick up on the street right where he left off. He was thinking much bigger than that.

Billings had bragged about funding the BetterLates, and Moreland had talked about his sponsors. All kind of friends, Cody had said. Billings was funding Moreland's big project, and maybe they *were* going to seed the clouds and restore the climate by reflecting more sunlight. But they were also planning on using the drone swarm to release Gloriana's microbe. Everywhere around the world. All at once. They weren't cementing UniCon's position, they were taking it down, taking the whole system down.

For a moment, Pierce tried to think of how he could prove all this, how he could use this knowledge to get out of his predicament with the Guild. But he realized that was never going to happen, not after his scuffle with Lindy. Not with Erno after him.

And more to the point, soon it wouldn't matter. If Gloriana and Moreland's plan was for real, if this was actually going down, his personal mess would be nothing compared to the maelstrom about to reshape the world.

He let out a nervous, manic laugh at the thought of it, but then he thought about the carnage he had already seen caused by the microbes from the BetterLates' diffusers—the test cases. He tried to picture what it would look like extended across the planet and a shudder ran through him.

Moreland and Gloriana would get the redistribution of wealth they saw as so necessary to restore balance. More important, the blow to global economic growth—the economic contraction Moreland talked about at Otisville—would reduce carbon output, more than any global agreement could ever hope to achieve. It might be enough—combined with the geo-engineering—to reverse at least some of the damage that humanity couldn't seem to stop inflicting.

It was crazy, Pierce knew, but he saw the logic. The scope of it was breathtaking.

He had a hard time picturing Billings as part of such a scheme. He tried to revise his idea of who the man was to make it fit. Then he realized Billings wasn't in it for any grand purpose. He was in it for himself.

He was in it to say a big fuck you to UniCon, before they had a chance to kick him out. He hadn't been laundering money to earn a percentage or capture market share; he was stockpiling Small, as quickly as he could. Because once all the Large was destroyed—ninety-nine-point-nine percent of the money supply—all that smelly old chump change would skyrocket in value, just like Bradley had said, a thousand times, ten thousand times. Billings would be a very big fish—the biggest fish—in a massively shrunken pond. He'd be the richest and most powerful man in a drastically transformed world.

TETERBORO QUADPORT WAS adjacent to the old Teterboro Airport, a busy commuter hub built over reclaimed wetland. There had been a big ruckus over the expansion at the time, but as the water tables rose, wetlands protection became a non-issue. Wetlands were everywhere now—including most of Teterboro—and even the most ardent environmentalists were busy with more pressing matters, like preserving the *dry* lands.

Security appeared tight, but Pierce chained up his attaché, and when he told the guys at the gate he had a delivery for Frank Billings, they conferred for a moment, then let him in. People usually let you in if they thought you were bringing cash.

The flight area was surrounded by another fence. Big, temporary signs hanging on it announced that the Quadport would be closed to commuter traffic for the day. Instead of the usual rows of commuter quadcopters, the entire area was taken up with hundreds of small, solar-powered high-altitude drones, their glassy, gossamer photovoltaic wings spread wide, looking both delicate and awkward at the same time. From a distance, it was hard to gauge their size, but they appeared to be just a foot or two across, with the solar sails maybe three times that.

Pierce drove along the perimeter of the fence, curving around the quad field toward a low, hangar-like building. A cluster of private security vehicles was parked out front, but there was no sign of Billings or Moreland. Or, he realized with a visceral disappointment, Gloriana.

As he approached, a pair of security contractors in tactical gear strolled toward him. One hung back a couple of steps, assault rifle in hand, pointed at the ground but ready to come up.

Pierce lowered his window and held up his wrist, then patted the attaché. "Courier," he said. "Delivery for Frank Billings."

"You shouldn't be here," said the one in front. His name tag said SGT. NELSON.

Pierce frowned. "I beg your pardon? Are you telling me you are willfully and intentionally interfering with a courier delivery?"

They both shifted their stance and exchanged a quick glance. The one in the back looked scared.

"He's not here," Nelson said flatly.

"Is he coming?"

Nelson let out an impatient sigh. "Look, all I know is, this entire area is being cordoned off for a special project today. All quad traffic is being diverted elsewhere. Even with a delivery, they shouldn't have let you in. If you have official Guild business, you need to go through Quadport Security. Now I'm going to have to ask you to leave."

The guy behind him fingered the trigger on his rifle.

"Okay," Pierce said. "I'll note that the delivery was refused."

The guy with the shifty trigger finger opened his mouth to protest, but Nelson silenced him with a raised hand, then smiled at Pierce to let him know he wasn't troubled by that.

Pierce nodded, then turned the car around and left.

Cody had thought Moreland meant the Teterboro Quadport, but that could have been an assumption if Moreland had said he was going to Teterboro. Billings had a place in Teterboro too.

Pierce had picked up a delivery there a few years back. He remembered exactly where it was, but he still had trouble finding it. The area had changed so much, he had to detour several times, including once around several square blocks that had been abandoned to the rising water, semi-submerged and transformed by swamp grass. A few small structures around the edge of it were covered in thick mats of vines.

When he finally found the warehouse, he almost drove right past it. What had once been an oversized wooden shed covered with peeling, dark green paint was now a large metal warehouse, at least sixty feet tall, painted powder-gray with a tasteful red *Billings Corporation* logo on one corner.

A tall fence surrounded the property, attached to the front of the warehouse on either side. There didn't seem to be a gate; the only way to get onto the property was through the warehouse. It had a steel door with a security panel beside it and an omnidirectional camera hanging above it.

Pierce parked out front, and as he assessed the situation, a large box truck drove slowly past. Fifty yards down the road, a section of fence slid open and the truck drove through it, curving across the asphalt toward the back of the warehouse. By the time the truck disappeared behind the warehouse, the fence had slid back into place.

Pierce grabbed his gun from under the seat and slid it into his waistband as he got out. Walking up to the door, he made sure his attaché was clearly visible and his gun less so. He was about to use the buzzer, but tried the knob and found the door unlocked.

Inside was a small, unoccupied office area. A pair of swinging doors with small windows led to the main warehouse area. Pierce stepped through them with his gun in one hand and his attaché in the other.

The warehouse was big. Two box trucks were parked at one end, with room for half a dozen more. A couple of workers were unloading plastic-wrapped pallets from one of the trucks with a pallet jack, adding them to a massive cube of similarly wrapped pallets, four or five layers tall. Two pairs of guards with assault rifles were watching over the workers—or maybe two of them were watching the workers and the other two were watching the first two. Another four stood in the open bay door. Pierce wondered if they were keeping an eye on the others, or if they were focused on external threats. He also wondered whose responsibility it was to lock the front door.

But he stopped wondering about all that when they turned their attention—and their guns—toward him. At the same moment, he realized what it was they were guarding.

Cash. A mountain of it. Presumably all the small-denomination notes Frank Billings had been accumulating, that Serino had been acquiring for him. The denominations might have been small, but the pile was big enough to give Pierce pause—to force him into an involuntary thumbnail calculation of its worth—at a moment when he couldn't afford to pause.

Snapping himself out of it, he held his attaché higher. "Delivery for Frank Billings. Is he here?"

He held his gun down at his side, almost behind him. If the conversation included gunfire, he'd be on the losing end of it.

"Who the fuck are you?" said the guy closest to him. He seemed to be in charge.

They all wore the same uniforms as the guys at the quadport.

"Courier," Pierce said, raising the attaché even higher. "I'm looking for Frank Billings."

"He's not here." The guy turned to one of the other guards and motioned for him to come forward, then turned back to Pierce. "You shouldn't be here, either. I'm going to have to ask you to leave."

The underling came up beside Pierce with his gun not quite pointed at the floor. It was clear he was there to escort him out, but Pierce ignored him.

"Do you know where I can find him?"

"Billings Tower, I imagine. In HiHo. Maybe you can make an appointment."

The guard behind him gave him a gentle nudge with his rifle. A bold move, with a courier.

Pierce half turned to go with him, but then stopped. "What about the drone launch tonight?" he asked. "Is Billings going to be there?"

All of them, including the workers, turned to look at the guy in charge.

"I don't know anything about that," he said. "Now get the fuck out of here."

By the time Pierce was climbing into his car under the watchful gaze of his paramilitary escort, he had finished the rough calculations he had started earlier. If they were all singles, that mountain of cash was worth roughly a hundred and seventy million dollars. If they were twenties, it was more than three billion. And if they were fifties, it was seven or eight. Most likely it was a combination of all the Small—singles, fives, tens, twenties and fifties—and still well over a billion dollars.

It was a lot of money, and it would be worth a hell of a lot more if Moreland and Gloriana were able to execute their plan.

Pierce drove off, his head spinning from the sight of all that money, and all those guns.

He still had several hours before the launch. He wanted to see Gloriana again. To ask her if she was doing this voluntarily, to make sure she was with Moreland because she wanted to be. And to find out if she had killed Matías and Diego, to hear it from her lips that she hadn't.

He needed to tell Dugray what he'd learned, warn him.

He couldn't stop Moreland and Billings. Billings' men were heavily armed paramilitaries. Pierce wouldn't succeed on his own, armed only with his pistol and his chain, a couple of knives and some throwing spikes.

He could go to UniCon. *They* had the firepower. Hell, if he tipped them off about an existential threat like this, they'd probably find a way to make all his other problems go away. For an instant, he glimpsed an ideal world where all his troubles disappeared. Would it be so wrong, if he was doing it to save the world?

But Gloriana and Moreland thought the end of the world was exactly what they were trying to prevent. Going to UniCon for help, helping them cement their control over everything, he wouldn't be saving *the* world, he'd be saving *UniCon's* world.

That's when it really hit him: apart from anything else, if he'd found himself on the same side as UniCon, maybe he was on the wrong side.

Chapter Twenty-Five

DRIVING BACK THROUGH the city, Pierce could see that even in the time he'd been gone, the chaos had worsened. Smoke hung over the Bronx and Queens. Through the haze, the sky looked like a reverse image of a starry night: speckled black with police and media copters and drones, most hovering in place. Things were bad, and they were almost certainly going to get worse. If Moreland and Gloriana's plan succeeded, things were going to blow up in a fundamental and far-reaching way, a second Upheaval, even more disruptive than the first. But even if it didn't, the effects of what had already happened would be causing devastation for months, or even years. He wondered if it was even possible to put the genie back in the bottle, spray the planet with Lysol or something, or if the microbes already released would just slowly spread until they covered the world anyway.

Pierce's head had been swimming as he drove—a swirl of anger and sorrow and anguish and regret. But by the time he pulled up in front of Dugray's A-house, he had achieved a kind of steely calm. Maybe he was in shock, stunned by the magnitude of what was happening.

The damage from the Toros' attack had been fully repaired, even painted over. Like it had never happened. Pierce knew that part of what Dugray was selling was safety and dependability for his customers, and brass-balled invincibility to any rivals looking for signs of weakness, especially now.

Hutch was standing at the top of the steps, arms folded, legs braced wide.

Pierce stood at the bottom of the steps and said, "Delivery for Dugray."

"Bullshit," Hutch said quietly out of the corner of his mouth. "Get the fuck out of here."

"It's important."

"Fuck off, man. Shit's hot right now, he don't have time to be talking to no fugitive courier."

"He needs to hear what I have to tell him. Now."

"Get the fuck out of here."

"Look, if you don't call him, I'm going to have to walk past you, and either you're going to look bad because I took you down, or you're going to look worse, because you took me down and kept important information from getting to Dugray. Either way, he's going to be pissed at you. Or you could just lean back through the door and shout, 'Tell Dugray his boy Pierce is here.' Then he gets to decide if he comes out or not. Seems like an easy choice to me."

Hutch huffed. Then he leaned back without taking his eyes off Pierce and shouted over his shoulder through the partly opened door, "Yo, tell Dugray his boy Pierce is here." Then he said to Pierce, "If *he* decides he ain't coming out here, *I'm* going to decide to kick your ass."

Pierce nodded. "Fair enough."

Dugray looked different when he appeared at the top of the steps: bigger, more solid. Much, much older.

"It's cool," Dugray said quietly to Hutch. He looked around for a moment. The streets were empty. It was still early for the rush, but there should have been some kind of traffic. He glanced down at Pierce and said, "Around back." Then he turned and went back inside.

Hutch cocked an eyebrow at Pierce. "Around back," he repeated, as if he'd been partly vindicated.

Pierce walked down to the end of the block, then around and up the alley. There were two guys stationed at either end of the alley. That was new.

They watched him pass, like they knew he was coming.

The back door was open. Another guy Pierce didn't know stood outside it with an assault rifle. He watched, not saying a word, as Pierce approached, walked past him, and entered.

Dugray was waiting inside, along with close to twenty people, some working money-counters, most measuring out pills or powders, using an assortment of scales, counters, and packaging devices.

Pierce had never seen them in action, another side of what the organization was really about, and what Dugray was a part of.

"So you went to Venezuela?" Dugray said, stooping to pick up a burlap money bag. He gestured for Pierce to follow him upstairs.

"Got back a couple hours ago," Pierce said as they ascended.

"Good to see you're alive," he said.

"You, too."

"Not something to take for granted these days."

He stopped in the kitchen and grabbed two beers, then led Pierce up to the strong room.

A machine pistol with an extended cartridge lay on the table. Dugray opened the door to the safe and put the money bag inside, on the floor. He didn't mention the gun, so neither did Pierce.

They sat in the two chairs, facing each other over the table, over the machine pistol; then they tapped the necks of their beers together and each took a sip.

"Look, I need—" Pierce started, but Dugray held up a hand.

"You can't keep coming around here," Dugray said. "Townsend don't like you. He don't trust you. Thinks you're up to something. Plus, a lot of shit's been going down, even more since last I saw you. I can't have no distractions. I need my wits about me, you know what I'm saying?"

Pierce nodded. "Yeah, okay."

"This organization is shaking itself up like a motherfucker," Dugray said. "I need to keep my people alive, keep *myself* alive. Townsend's been on a tear."

"What's going on?"

"Guy's paranoid as shit. Understandably, I guess. But he's taken out most of the guys above me, and I don't want to end up like them." He let out a weary laugh. "It's crazy, man. All these vacancies, I been moving up and up and up. If I'm not careful, I'm going to end up the man in charge, and nobody wants that. Already, I'm suddenly like, Townsend's right-hand man, and there's people in the organization who feel like I jumped over them, that by rights it should be them and not me." He laughed. "They got a point, too. But it's not like I can move backwards, you know? I got to watch my back."

He drank again. "Good to see you, though, man. A friendly face."

"You, too," Pierce said with a nod.

"So. How was Venezuela?" He grinned. "Did you see your girl?"

Pierce grinned and nodded. Embarrassed. "Yeah, I did."

"How was that?"

Pierce shook his head again. "I'm still trying to figure that out. Great and terrible. But I also figured some other stuff out. This thing with the money—it's big."

"No shit."

"No, I mean really big. Global. She's in on it. Gloriana. All this mayhem we've seen around here? It's all from a microbe she developed—*Neptunomonas Plastiphilos*. It breaks down the plastic paper the Large is printed on, same as in Angola."

"Why? And why here? And how did she manage that if she's in prison?"

Pierce took a deep breath. "It's a field test, a proof of concept. Same thing in Alaska, and Arizona. And she's not doing it alone. She's working with Topher Moreland—"

"The BetterLates guy?"

Pierce nodded. "And Frank Billings."

Dugray screwed up his face. "Billings and Moreland? What the fuck are you talking about?"

"Crime of the century, as far as I can tell." Pierce took a deep breath. "Billings and Serino weren't selling Large, they were buying *Small*, stockpiling it. Billings has got hundreds of millions. Billions maybe. I've seen it. Mountains of it. Moreland and Gloriana, they're about to launch their drones, all around the world, seeding the clouds to make them more reflective, to reverse warming, for the climate, right?"

"I heard something about that."

"Well, they also want to shut down the global economy, to cut emissions, prevent climate collapse and buy time for other stuff to work."

Dugray shook his head. "What are you talking about?"

"I know. It's a lot. But the microbe that's been obliterating all the Large around here? They're going to release it with the cloud seeding. Globally. Everywhere, all at once."

Dugray went still for a moment, thinking. Then he whistled.

Pierce nodded in agreement. "I know, right?"

"Wait, and UniCon is on board with this?"

"No." Pierce laughed nervously. "I really don't think they are."

"Jesus. Frank Billings is taking on UniCon? I wouldn't have thought he had it in him."

"I don't think Serino knew what it was all about, at first. Then he figured it out and wanted to stop it."

Dugray snorted. "So why'd he turn to you?"

"I don't know, I think he couldn't imagine Billings doing something like this without UniCon approval, so he needed to tell someone who wasn't UniCon. He knew I was looking for him. I guess he heard what happened in Alaska. Figured I'd seen it first-hand. And as a Guild courier, I wasn't under UniCon's thumb. He wanted me to tell the Guild whatever he was about to tell me, and then he was going to take his family and try to disappear."

"Hide from UniCon? I don't think that's a thing."

"The man was terrified. Turns out he was right to be. They killed him before he could tell me what he knew."

"Damn. So the geoengineering thing, is that all bullshit?"

"No, I think that's for real, but I guess Moreland and Gloriana think the only way the cloud seeding will work is if we slam the brakes on emissions, as well. Their takeaway from the Upheaval is that the only way to cut emissions is by shutting down the global economy. They figure, take out all the Large, the economy goes into freefall. And Small is suddenly worth more. A lot more. The rich get poor and the poor get richer. Except Billings. He comes out on top."

"Jesus," Dugray said. Then he shrugged. "Frank Billings is an asshole, but he's not as bad as Townsend, or those shadowy motherfuckers controlling UniCon."

"People are going to get hurt."

"People are already getting hurt, man. People are *always* getting hurt. Maybe it's time to give someone else a turn at the bottom of the pile, you know what I'm saying?"

Pierce looked over at the sacks of Small in the safe.

Dugray followed his gaze and smiled. "I'm not saying I'll be unprepared if it goes down like you say. But it's not about that."

Before Pierce could respond, Hutch called upstairs in a hoarse whisper. "Yo, Dugray! Townsend's here. He's running up."

Dugray bolted upright and his eyes flickered with fear. "Fuck," he said, hurrying over to the safe and locking it. "He don't know about my Large disappearing. *His* Large. He finds out now, he's going to think I robbed him, just like the motherfuckers he killed."

Heavy feet were already pounding up the steps.

"Dugray!" Townsend's voice boomed from the stairway.

"Up here, Mr. Townsend," Dugray called back. He slid the machine pistol off the table and leaned it against the wall behind him just as Townsend appeared, coming up the steps, followed by two bodyguards.

Townsend took up the entire doorway, even before the bodyguards stepped up behind him. He squinted at Pierce for a second, and said, "This motherfucker again?"

"Yes, Mr. Townsend," Dugray said. "Taking care of business."

"Right..." he said suspiciously, keeping an eye on Pierce. "Wish these other assholes were as careful as you, Dugray. Be careful with these motherfuckers, though. Been hearing a lot of shit about couriers lately. Not quite as dependable as they used to be. Anyway," he motioned to the safe. "I'm here for my money."

Dugray looked confused, almost enough to hide his panic. "Your money?" he laughed. "I—I ain't got it all yet. It's only Tuesday."

"I know, I know," Townsend said, waving a hand. "I just need what you got so far. These other motherfuckers messing with my cash flow." He shook his head. "Can't trust nobody these days." He hooked a thumb at Pierce. "Not even these motherfuckers." He turned back to Dugray, his face darkening as he twirled his hand in the air. "Come on, motherfucker, I ain't got all fucking day. I said get me my goddamn money."

Then he pulled a gun and the two bodyguards stiffened. "Unless you pulling the same shit as these other motherfuckers."

Dugray's eyes darted at Pierce. Then he turned and started fumbling with the dial on the safe as Townsend stepped up behind him.

Pierce ran the scenarios, and he knew that none of

them would end well once Townsend saw there was no Large in the safe. He had some questions he wanted to ask before that happened. He cleared his throat and said, "I know you killed Carla Ruiz-Vargas. Were you behind Fairview, too?"

Everybody froze, then Townsend turned slowly around. He was grinning but his eyes were furious. "Fairview, huh? So, you the courier they said been poking around, huh? I thought that was bullshit, but you were there, weren't you? In the room with Serino that night."

He pointed his gun in Pierce's face and laughed. "Well, let me tell you a bedtime story then. Before you say goodnight forever."

Townsend laughed again, and so did his men. "Fairview was Frank Billings, your pal Serino's double-crossing piece of shit boss. We had a good thing going, me and Frank. I brought in the girls for his operation, he brought in the drugs for mine. Business was good for both of us. We both wanted into UniCon, so one day he tells me they've got a job for us. If we do it, we're in. They want us to clear some real estate for them, to make room for their new tower. He owned the buildings, I controlled the territory. He already had a few layers of shell corporations to insulate him, but for something like this he wanted more. So, he took care of that while I took care of the dirty work. My men drilled the holes, brought in the seawater. It was easy. Worked like a charm. But when those towers came down, the motherfucker double-crossed me. UniCon invites him in, and when I say, 'What about me?' They say, 'Who the fuck are you?'"

He turned to look at Dugray over his shoulder. "Believe that shit? After I did all that work, he made a deal with them, never mentioned me. But by then, the motherfucker was UniCon. Didn't matter who was right, I couldn't touch him, not if I ever hoped to get in there."

Dugray's face was blank, but he was trembling.

"Motherfucker was sloppy, though," Townsend continued, turning back around to look at Pierce. "Loose ends all over the place. And he don't know how to run a business, not a legit one. Motherfucker's debt ratio is for shit. He couldn't get through the background check to rent a room in one of my buildings, much less hold on to his place in UniCon. So, UniCon comes to me, they say, 'Looks like the motherfucker double-crossed you after all. But tell you what. He's on his way out. So you clean up the mess he left behind, make sure none of this stuff comes back on UniCon, you can have his seat at the next Conference.' Better late than never, right? So I'm tying up all the loose ends, nice and neat. Soon I'll be in and he'll be out, and when he's no longer untouchable, you can bet your ass I'll be touching the *shit* out of him."

"Loose ends like Carla Ruiz-Vargas?"

He laughed. "Oh, you mean Carla Jackson? Yeah, she was one of them. Serino, too. I thought he was the last one." He glanced over at Dugray, like he was sharing wisdom. "That's the thing with loose ends, you see? The longer you leave 'em loose, they more loose ends they make. Here I am, thinking I'm done, that Serino is the last one. Then I find out he told some courier some shit he shouldn't have, and the courier goes to the widower Jackson. I don't know what the widower told you, but he wasn't supposed to tell you nothing. Motherfucker took the settlement and signed the agreement." He looked over his shoulder at Dugray again. "You can't be nice with these people. It just never works. You can pay them off, nice big settlement and a nondisclosure, but people don't respect that shit." He turned back to look at Pierce. "Well, call it a lesson learned. He's tied off for good now. Nice and proper."

"You killed him?"

Townsend shrugged. "Motherfucker shouldn't have taken the money if he couldn't keep his mouth shut. He signed a contract." He gestured toward Pierce's wrist. "You know, like an oath. But shit, if you'd have left things alone, I wouldn't have had to, so you look at it one way, this shit's on you. But UniCon don't tolerate loose ends. I guess that's how they ended up running the world. And now there's just one last loose end left."

He pulled back the hammer on his gun, and Dugray said, "Two."

Townsend looked confused as he turned to look at Dugray. Pierce snatched Townsend's gun away from him as Dugray shot him in the head. Then Pierce shot the two bodyguards.

In the relative quiet following the gunshots, Pierce met Dugray's eyes and said, "I guess this means you're the man in charge."

As Dugray's slack-jawed men filled the doorway, Pierce's words seemed to sink in. "There's been a change at the top," Dugray said loudly. "Anybody who wants out of here, should go. Now. If you ain't believing, you best be leaving, you hear me? But if you go, you don't come back. Ever. We're running Townsend's operation from now on, so if you go, you need to keep going until you're no longer on our territory, or anywhere near it."

He waited two seconds. No one flinched.

"Good," he said, like he fully expected everyone to stay with him. He turned to Marcus and put his hand on the back of his neck. "You good?"

Marcus nodded. "Yeah, I'm good."

"Then put two more men out front and out back. Have somebody get rid of this fat fuck and his renta-cocksuckers and dispose of them *properly*."

As his men snapped into action, Dugray turned to Pierce. "You. This way."

Then he turned and walked off.

Pierce followed, shouldering his way through the cluster of gang members. He caught up with Dugray down the hallway, as his men strategized over how to carry the three massive bodies down the stairs.

"Look, man," Dugray said, leaning in close. "Things are changing, and they're never changing back. Even if UniCon rebuilds the global network, like in the old days, it ain't going to be like the old days. No one's bringing back your mom or mine, no one's undoing all that's been done. Things never go back. You know that, right?"

Pierce nodded. He did know that. He also knew Dugray was saying more than what he was saying.

"Billings was Fairview," Pierce whispered.

"Yeah, he said that, didn't he?"

"We need to go after him. Now. Or never."

Dugray shook his head. "I can't. I got my hands full here. But..." He fished a set of keys out of his pockets and motioned for Pierce to follow him farther down the hallway. He unlocked another reinforced steel door and opened it, revealing a small room packed with an astonishing array of weaponry: a dozen shotguns, scores of handguns, a row of machine pistols, even a couple of single-use, mini-grenade launchers. "I can help out in other ways."

Pierce whistled. "You been expecting trouble?"

"Hell yeah. And I believe it's here. I got a lot more than this, so you take whatever you need." He reached over, smiling, and slid a chrome-plated Kimber nine millimeter off to the side. "Except for that one. That's mine." He slapped Pierce on the back. "Do what you need to do, do what you think is right. Any luck, I'll see you on the other side."

The View From Above

THE BREEZE WAS crisp and fresh, steady out of the west, and the sun was bright, like it pretty much always was this high in the crystal-blue sky. Osmand loved taking coffee out on the terrace. The weather was always perfect, and the view was otherworldly in its gorgeousness. All the helicopters and drones coming and going could be a pain in the ass, but it was a small price to pay. All in all, it was a lot like heaven.

Osmand's tower was not the tallest, but it was among them. He actually didn't want it to be the tallest. A skyline, in order to be properly appreciated, was something to be looked up at, not down on.

He had the best of both worlds. And a lovely terrace with trees and flowers, even a pond. Combined with a nice cup of coffee, it made for a damn fine start to the day.

He looked at his watch, then made his way to the southeast edge of the terrace. Even at seventy-three years of age, the little boy in him still had the urge to spit from that height. He smiled at the thought, like he always did.

The clouds below looked like a white ocean, surging past the towers. Every now and then, they would part, and the world below would come into view. That was pretty spectacular as well, especially at night. New York wasn't what it used to be, but it was still truly something.

In fact, the *world* wasn't what it used to be, but his little corner of it was just fine. He'd managed to ride this crazy tiger of a world and come out on top.

He checked his watch again. His drone was due to arrive any minute. He sipped his coffee as he waited, and something caught his eye atop one of the nearby towers.

Simon Dorner, of North American Agro Science. His tower was a block southwest, across New Eighth Street. It was a few stories shorter than Osmand's.

Dorner was a decent enough fellow and a shrewd businessman, but a little sanctimonious at times. Osmand didn't much like him, but he was always friendly to him. You made enough legitimate enemies in business, he figured. It didn't make sense to rack up any more just because you didn't like them.

Osmand waved, but Dorner didn't wave back. He seemed oblivious. Well, to hell with him anyway, Osmand thought. He turned back, scanning the open air for some sign of the drone, but Dorner caught his eye again. He was moving oddly. His robe was flapping in the breeze, and he was walking with a shuffling gait. As Osmand watched, Dorner stepped up onto the small barrier wall that surrounded the roof terrace.

"What is that crazy bastard doing?" Osmand mumbled to himself.

Then Dorner jumped.

Osmand dropped his coffee. "Holy shit!" He ran to

the southwest edge of the roof, but Dorner had already disappeared into the clouds.

Osmand knew the man was still falling, even though he couldn't see him. It would take another fifteen or twenty seconds to hit the ground from that height. He stood there, staring down at the clouds, trying not to think about what would happen to Dorner's body on impact. When enough seconds had passed that he knew the man was dead, he took a step back.

Before he could think of what to do next, Osmand heard a familiar throaty whine, and he looked over to see a black dot in the sky, growing quickly as it approached. He moved quickly back to the designated drone landing spot at the southeast wall.

He recognized the drone as his, with the red Honda logo on the side. It approached fast, maybe a little unsteadily, then it hovered, canting a bit to the left. He'd have to order a tune-up.

The drone slowly moved forward and Osmand stuck out his face and opened his eyes wide, although he knew he didn't have to.

A light on the drone blinked green and it settled down onto the roof. Osmand grabbed the handle on the top and pulled it out to a comfortable length, then he turned and wheeled the drone inside.

Many men in his position would have someone else do this for them, but not Osmand. He hadn't gotten where he was by trusting people with his money. As he approached the open sliding doors of his penthouse apartment, he looked over at Dorner's tower and shook his head.

Crazy goddamned times.

The vault was in the living room, behind the center section of the floor-to-ceiling mirrors, just beyond the curve of the wall and out of sight of the sliding doors leading to the terrace. Osmand put his palm against the smudge-proof mirror, right where he knew the scanner was. A faint glow appeared beneath his hand, and he opened his eyes wide as his iris was scanned once again.

The mirror slid a couple inches out from the wall, then moved silently to the side. The heavy steel door behind it glided out of the way as well, and Osmand wheeled the drone into the vault.

He always felt unpleasantly like Scrooge McDuck when he did this, but it was hard not to marvel at all that money. It was easier not to get caught up in it, back in the old days, when wealth was just numbers on a computer. But here, when you saw it, the stacks and stacks of it, the zeroes after zeroes, it was quite a thing. On a practical level, he looked forward to UniCon finally unveiling the quantum encrypted U-Net; but he was going to miss coming in here and just looking at it.

He wheeled the drone onto a black circle in the middle of the room and pressed a button on the wall. The circle began to rise, a pedestal that lifted the drone to a comfortable height. Osmand punched in his code and let the scanner read his thumbprint.

The top of the drone unsealed with a hiss, slightly louder than usual, and released a small cloud of dust as well.

Staring at the drone as the lid slowly opened, Osmand knew right away what he was seeing, or wasn't, but he waited until the thing stopped moving before he said, "What the hell is this?"

The drone was empty, or rather empty of cash. Instead of seven million dollars in five-thousand-dollar bills, there was a pile of dust and twenty-eight uninhabited paper bands labeled *$250K*.

For a few seconds he just stood there, bewildered. Then he felt the anger coming over him. He stormed out of the vault, not even bothering to close the door behind him. Grabbing his phone, he punched in a number and started pacing back and forth as he waited for security to clear so the damn thing would start ringing.

Once it did, it was answered almost immediately.

"Hello, Osmand. Guess you had a pretty good week, huh?" Brett Pullinger was his banker, his racquetball partner, and some sort of distant cousin that the two of them could never keep straight. He sounded tired and somewhat on edge.

"Cut the shit, Brett. Where the hell is my money?"

"Sorry if the drone's late, Osmand. We're having a hell of a crazy morning here." In the background, phones were beeping and there was a strange buzz, like many, many hushed conversations, all at once.

"The drone's not late, Brett. It's empty. And I want to know where the hell my money is, and why it isn't here."

"Empty?" Pullinger's voice sounded ninety-nine percent shocked, but with a hint of resignation that turned Osmand's blood cold.

"That's right. All that's in there is a bunch of empty bill wrappers, like some kind of *fuck you*. And I don't think it's even the tiniest bit funny."

"Was there some kind of powder or dust in there, too?"

"Yes! So you better tell me what the hell is going on here."

"I don't know, Osmand. Just—"

"Just what?"

"We've been getting a bunch of calls like this. I don't know what's going on."

"Well, you better—"

"Look, I've got to go. I let you know if I learn anything. Otherwise, I'll have Carter from Fulfillment follow up to get a claim filed."

"Bullshit you've 'got to go,' you're going to… Brett? You better not hang up on me… Brett?"

Osmand trembled with rage, his fingers purple and white as they gripped the phone. He could feel the fury building inside him, the pressure in his head, sharp needles of it, like it was trying to break through.

He flung the phone across the room as hard as he could. It hit the far wall and exploded, spraying glass, plastic, and metal.

He paused and took a deep breath. He knew he shouldn't be letting himself get upset like this. Sure, seven million was a lot to go missing, but Carter from fulfillment would straighten it out. He reminded himself to look at the big picture. He still had nine billion in his vault.

He'd find whoever took his money, or whoever lost it. He'd get it back and he'd make sure whoever was responsible paid a steep price for what they did. In the meantime, everything was going to be fine.

He took another deep cleansing breath, counting it in and out, just like Janice, his second wife, used to tell him to do.

When his lungs were completely empty, he paused. Just as he was about to start breathing in again, he heard a faint sound that he couldn't identify. It sounded vaguely familiar, like something from long ago. It sounded sort of like a mouse gnawing at something in the walls. But there were no mice in that building, and certainly not that high. But that wasn't quite it anyway. Then it came to him, from his childhood, the faint clicking, scratching noise that used to come from the woodpile sometimes when he was a kid. It used to creep him out sometimes. His dad would tell him they were wood borers, and there was nothing to be afraid of, but it used to scare the devil out of him, especially when he had to bring in logs for the fire.

For a moment, he was transported, remembering it. He could practically smell the wood, smell the smoke from the fire.

Then he smelled something else, something totally unfamiliar, and it brought him back to the present.

It was a faint, yeasty, earthy smell. Combined with the strange sound, it left him feeling uneasy. He started stalking around the apartment, looking for it, listening and smelling. Like a hunting dog, he thought.

The unease he felt intensified as he began to close in on it, and realized he was drawing closer and closer to the vault.

There couldn't be a mouse in there, he thought; the thing was airtight and watertight. Of course, that was only if you didn't leave the door open, which he had. He hurried over to it, wondering what could have gotten in there so quickly.

He stepped into the vault and froze. The sound was undeniable, the smell overpowering, but his brain couldn't process what it was he was seeing. It was like the walls were melting, spilling onto the floor, like he was hallucinating. He wondered if he was having a stroke.

But when he approached the shelves, he realized it was dust, cascading off them. He put his hand under it and realized it was the same stuff from the drone. It was covering all his money. He pushed some of the dust out of the way with his hand, reached in and picked up a bundle of five-thousands with a band that said *$500K*.

He held it up on front of him, reassured for a moment by the solidity of it, the reality of it. Cold hard cash.

But it wasn't cold, it was warm. The whole room was strangely warm. And it wasn't hard either, it was softening in his hand. As he looked closely, the print started to blur, and then the whole bundle just collapsed, like a clod of dirt. One second it was a tightly wrapped brick of crisp five-thousand dollar bills, straight from the treasury, the next it was a handful of dust.

"No," he said, his voice cracking, his throat dry from the dust that filled the air.

He spun around slowly, watching as the fortune he had spent his life accumulating—*earning*—dissolved into dust.

"No," he said, "*No!*" again, and again, as his entire life turned to dust.

A cloud of it followed him as he stumbled out of the vault, out onto the terrace. The breeze blew it away from him, helped clear his head, but he kept walking, unable to make sense of what was happening.

He found himself at the edge of the terrace, where he had stood waiting for the drone just a short while ago. Where he had watched Simon Dorner fall to his death. *Jump* to his death.

Straight ahead of him was the Alliance Petrochemical Building, and the penthouse where Doug Bartle lived. Osmand looked up to see Bartle standing on the edge of his building. Almost as soon as Osmand looked at him, Bartle jumped too. Just like Dorner.

Osmand spun around in circle, and by the time he was back where he started, he'd seen half a dozen of his peers standing on the edges of their terraces. Two more jumped while he was watching.

Whatever seemed to be happening was happening for real. It wasn't a hallucination. It wasn't a stroke. His money was gone. *Everything* was gone.

He looked over the edge, at the clouds below him. They looked soft.

He told himself it would be quick, painless. It would be like flying.

At first, as he pushed off from the edge of the terrace, it was. The side of the building slid past him at such speed it felt like he was soaring, skimming the ground instead of plunging toward it.

As Osmand fell, he realized that Jordan Bates, who lived next door in the Eurasian Chemical tower penthouse, had jumped at the same time he had.

Now, they were locked together in this same moment, falling at the same rate, a block away from each other, as the rest of the world flew past them.

Their eyes met, Osmand was sure of it. He wondered if he should acknowledge the man, wave or something. It was as ridiculous to do it as it was not to. But Osmand had never liked Jordan Bates. And if now wasn't the time to snub someone you disliked, when was?

Then they entered the top layer of clouds and Jordan Bates vanished. Osmand was quickly soaked. He felt disoriented, like he couldn't tell up from down. Then he came out the bottom of the clouds, low, and it was suddenly *very* obvious which way was down. He was moving impossibly fast, already impossibly close to the wet concrete below.

Directly beneath him, a young woman was getting out of a Smartcab. Osmand wasn't aware of any sound coming out of his mouth, but there might have been, or it could have been the air whistling through his clothes.

Whatever it was, for some reason the young woman looked up.

She opened her mouth to scream, but she never got a chance.

Chapter Twenty-Six

PIERCE HEADED BACK to Teterboro in Dugray's car. It was hours before the drone launch, but with the city in chaos, there was no time to delay. The UniCs had shut down FDR Drive, and he soon found himself in bumper-to-bumper traffic. In a sick joke of fate, Smartdrive was detouring him past Fairview.

Pierce crept past a billboard with a rendering of the future headquarters of U-Net—a gaudy behemoth totally out of scale with anything around it—over the slogan UNICON: BUILDING TOMORROW TODAY.

A concrete bot swung by on a track, curving around the skeleton and ascending steeply into the sky. The cement-filled bot was the size of a large laundry cart and bright green, color-coded so the humans could keep track of it. On another track, a yellow bot zipped by going the other direction, coming back down empty. Pierce was reminded of a roller coaster he'd ridden when he was little.

A pair of workers in hard hats stood just outside the

construction fencing, watching the bots doing the jobs they used to do.

The partially constructed tower that now stood there took up the entire block. The street around it was pocked and warped into a lunar landscape—covered in concrete dust. Pierce flashed back to clearing the rubble after the collapse of the Fairview Apartments, him and Dugray and hundreds of others, trying to find survivors. Trying to find their mothers.

The memory threatened to overwhelm him, and he involuntarily shook his head and tapped the brakes, taking the car out of Smartdrive. An instant later, a no-parking sign just to his right rang like a gong and began wobbling violently back and forth. A round silver dent had appeared in its middle.

The two construction workers stepped back and frowned at the sign, as if wondering what had happened.

But Pierce realized immediately. He raised his foot over the accelerator as he whipped his head around to scan his surroundings. Sure enough, there was Erno in his big blue armored Chevy SUV. The reinforced steel bumper suddenly looked less ridiculous than usual. He was two cars back and one lane over, turning off a side street and trying to change lanes to get closer while leaning out the driver's side window and aiming an automatic pistol. His hand and sleeve for some reason spattered with blood.

Pierce stomped on the accelerator and cut the steering wheel hard to the right, lurching up onto the sidewalk and flattening the dented sign. The construction workers went running as a bullet pinged off the frame of Pierce's windshield, sending a web of cracks across the glass.

Erno forced his massive Chevy through the space Pierce had just vacated, using his bumper to push aside the cars on either side of him. Pierce drove down the narrow sidewalk, the side of his car scraping along the chain-link fence as he bumped and bounced over the construction debris that littered the concrete.

The space between the parked cars and the construction fence was way too tight for Erno's Chevy, so Pierce stayed the course, driving along the sidewalk to the end of the block. He thought for a moment that he had gotten away, but when he skidded around the corner, he saw a flash of blue and then Erno's grille coming at him.

The impact set off the airbags and pushed Pierce's car sideways, halfway through the construction fence. Pierce reached under his seat for his gun, but it was gone, sent tumbling by the impact. He was dazed, but he scrambled though the passenger side window and tumbled out onto the ground, pulling his chain and his attaché with him.

He scrambled away, searching for cover, but as he looked back, he saw Erno, his shirt streaked with blood, climbing over Pierce's wrecked car with an assault rifle and a katana sword slung across his back. In one hand he had his pistol extended in front of him. In the other, he was carrying a small cooler bag. Pierce knew what that was for.

The fierce arsenal Dugray had given him was in the trunk of the car. All Pierce had on him were his knives and his throwing spikes. And his chain and his attaché. As he ducked behind a wall, a printer buzzed past, squirting cement onto a curved wall that looked like it was going to be part of an atrium.

With a throwing spike in each hand, Pierce shot to his feet and threw one of the spikes, aiming at Erno's midsection. Erno twisted to his right and dove as he squeezed off a shot that pinged several times off exposed metal beams. Pierce tried to ignore the danger that the bullet could ricochet into the back of his head as he threw the second spike, just in front of where Erno was diving.

He didn't wait to see where it landed, but he was gratified by a stifled grunt of pain behind him as he ran deeper into the construction site.

He ducked behind a storage locker to get his bearings. The concrete floor stretched out in front of him, punctuated by a grid of steel beams, row after row of them, interrupted only by a handful of cinderblock structures, probably elevator shafts or utility conduits. All around him, welding bots were working on the steel structure and printer bots were building walls. Tracks wound up the outside of the structure, bringing the concrete carts up to the printers on the higher levels.

Pierce needed to make his way through the skeleton of the building, avoiding all the moving parts, and find another way out. Either that or he needed to kill Erno before Erno could kill him.

He zigged and zagged and circled around, hoping to put some distance between them, but his heart sank when Erno called out, distressingly close, "Pierce! Have some class and don't make this harder than it has to be. You swore an oath, man. Does your word mean nothing to you?" He laughed bitterly. "If not, what else is there? People look up to us, Pierce. They look to the Guild for stability and security—for equity, even. But without rules and tradition, without *enforcement*, there is no Guild. And then where are we?"

Erno had a point, Pierce knew, but he no longer cared. The Guild did all those things, but it was also cruel and barbaric. And so was this fanatic psycho.

At the far end of the building, Pierce could see the construction fencing, and through it a bright blue smudge: Erno's car.

He took a deep breath and started running down one of the rows of steel beams. Almost immediately, the air was filled with the racket of automatic weapons fire. Bullets sparked and pinged off the steel beams. He could hear them zipping past, could feel their breeze.

Pierce dove to the side, and ran down the next row of beams, before changing lanes again. But the bullets followed him.

He ducked behind one of the cinderblock structures, hoping to use it for cover as he kept running, but found himself trapped in a cul de sac, hemmed in between two cinderblock structures, and stretching between the two, a wall of cart tracks and a massive cement-pumping unit.

As he ducked in a corner to reassess, the track next to him began to tremble, then shake. A bright red cart rattled down the track and stopped under the pump. In seconds, the cart was filled with cement, almost to the top, with such precision that not a drop of it fell outside the cart. As soon as the pump stopped, the cart took off.

"Pierce!" Erno called, again, his voice echoing off the concrete and steel. He sounded close. "Stop fighting now, and I'll just take off the hand. I'll give you a nice clean cut. Give you a fighting chance." He laughed. "Since we're such old friends."

Pierce was in the corner where the wall of track met the cinderblock structure. He tucked his attaché against his midsection and hid behind a fifty-gallon drum. The track began to shake again and then a purple cart pulled up under the pumper, leaving seconds later brimming with wet concrete.

Beneath the racket of the carts and the pumper, Pierce could hear shoes on the gritty concrete, getting closer and closer. Erno stepped out from around a cinderblock wall less than twelve feet away, his back to Pierce. The handgun was gone and the cooler bag was tucked in his belt. Now he was just carrying his rifle.

Pierce had to move. Now. He pulled his last spike and launched himself.

Erno turned almost immediately and swung his rifle around, his left arm glistening with blood. Pierce threw his spike and Erno screamed as it struck his trigger hand, lodging between two of his metacarpals. He staggered backward, firing wildly, filling the air with bullets and noise. His scream was still fading a few seconds later when his gun clicked empty and the last bullets finished ricocheting off the steel beams.

Pierce was astonished to realize he hadn't been hit. He pulled his folding knife as Erno tossed his rifle aside and drew his katana, snarling in pain as his damaged hand wrapped around the hilt.

They stared at each other for a moment, then Erno came at him. Pierce ducked as the blade hissed through the air over his head. It was already smeared with blood.

Pierce lunged forward, extended himself fully to slash Erno across the thigh, then pulled back. It was a deep cut, but it hadn't hit an artery. Erno was a trained killer, and it wasn't the type of wound that would slow him down. Erno stifled a grunt of pain and swung his sword once more, passing within inches of Pierce's head. He seemed off his game, like the wounds had gotten to him, but Pierce knew he couldn't fight Erno off for long, not with a knife.

There was nowhere to turn, nowhere to hide. As Erno

closed in on him with a vicious grin, the tracks behind him began to shake. Erno brought his sword up over his shoulder, winding up for a blow that would surely split Pierce's skull. The tracks began to rattle louder. Pierce held up his knife. It looked almost comically tiny in comparison with the katana, but Pierce hoped it would be just enough.

Erno roared as he swung the katana, and Pierce ducked to the side and brought his knife up to intercept it. The sword snapped the blade from the hilt, sending a violent jolt up Pierce's arm. But it was enough to deflect the blow, and as a bright yellow cement cart appeared behind Erno, Pierce swung his attaché, looping the chain around Erno, pinning his arms to his sides. Then he drove his shoulder into Erno's midsection and forced him back against the cart, flipping him up and into it just as the pump began dropping its load of cement. Erno dropped his sword, his legs thrashing as he tried to free himself from the chain and the concrete.

Pierce tried to extricate his chain, but Erno had hold of it now, and even as the cement continued to rain down on his head, filling the cart, he pulled Pierce closer. His other hand emerged once again, holding the sword. Cement sloshed over the rim of the cart and as the flow of it trickled to a stop, Pierce knew he only had seconds to free himself before the cart dragged them both up the side of the building and dropped them into some pumper feed up on the twentieth floor.

The attaché bobbed to the surface. Pierce pushed Erno's sword hand out of the way with one hand while he grabbed the attaché and dragged it closer with the other.

Erno pulled the chain taut and a smug grin spread across his cement-covered face.

Pierce wiped off the attaché's control screen, activating it. He opened his eyes wide and heard two clicks as the chain disconnected itself from the attaché and from Pierce's cuff.

Erno's grin faltered as Pierce stumbled back. The cart trembled for a moment as Erno tried to vault himself out of it, but it jolted forward and he lost his footing, slipping back under the concrete as the cart disappeared up the track and around the building.

The sound of the cart quickly faded, and for a moment Pierce found himself alone, in a stunned quiet. He felt a sense of emptiness at the loss of his chain and his attaché, the loss of his identity, but a sense of lightness as well. As he walked back toward the two vehicles, the tracks behind him started to rattle, and another cart arrived for its load of concrete.

Pierce brushed wet concrete from his sleeves, and thought about the blood already spattering Erno, already smeared on his sword. Diaz had said couriers had gone missing. Pierce wondered how many of them had been killed by Erno already, and how many more Pierce had saved by dispatching him. He also wondered about the Guild, about what kind of future it could possibly have.

Part of the reason people—including Pierce—had been willing to swear the courier oath was because they knew they'd never intentionally violate it. The consequences were an abstraction. In exchange for an oath they would never break, they got protection, stability, and identity in an unpredictable world and a place in that world that wasn't beholden to UniCon. If the Guild was ready to kill so many of its own, giving them so little chance to prove their innocence or loyalty, who would stay? And who would be crazy enough to replace the fallen? If the

Guild killed its own as readily as Townsend or UniCon did, with so little regard for the sacrifices they had made, how was it any better?

Dugray's car was halfway embedded in the construction fence. It was clearly totaled.

Erno's Chevy, partially on top of it, was unscathed apart from a jaunty new angle to its steel bumper. The motor was even running.

Pierce climbed over Dugray's car, over the fence, and back down to the street. He brushed himself off.

The trunk of the car was open, and Pierce tugged out the duffel bag Dugray had given him. The rear door wouldn't open, but there was no sign of his own gun. For all he knew, it had flown out the window when Erno slammed into him.

It was a shame, he thought. He liked that gun.

He tossed the duffel into the back seat of Erno's massive Chevy and climbed in behind the wheel, which was sticky with blood. Probably the same blood that had been on Erno's sleeve, on his katana. The blood of some other courier.

He looked up at the street sign.

Third Avenue.

He was just down the block from Rocha's apartment.

He wondered if the blood on the steering wheel was Rocha's, wondered if that was why Erno was in the area.

Fuck.

Pierce backed the Chevy off his wrecked car and drove slowly down Third Avenue, rolling to a stop in front of a high-density rental block. It was one of the newer ones, but it was already falling apart. The gray vinyl cladding was warping and pulling away. Some of the cheap windows had already been replaced with even cheaper ones, different sizes and shapes, most of them not sitting quite straight. It gave the place a sort cockeyed, crooked-teeth look.

He felt an emotional numbness setting in as he fished a handgun out of Dugray's duffel and checked the magazine. He got out and walked up to the entrance. There was no directory, just a screen, a keypad, and a perforated microphone. Pierce pressed the ? button, and enunciated into the microphone, "Danny Rocha." The screen flashed, CALL DANNY ROCHA, 753?

Pierce hit the enter button, but there was no reply. He tried again. Nothing.

A guy in his early twenties walked up, unlocked the front door, and went in, walking across the tiny lobby without looking back at the door slowly closing behind him.

Pierce grabbed the door before it closed and held it for a few seconds to give the kid time to get wherever he was going. Then he slipped inside.

He took the elevator to the seventh floor, and when he got to 753, he stopped.

The door was ajar.

He slowly pushed it open.

The apartment was tiny, maybe six by eight, with a single window at the far end. It was completely empty, but the walls on either side were covered with panels of varying sizes and shapes.

He pressed one panel on the right and a partition slid up to reveal a tiny, almost two-dimensional galley kitchen. He pressed a smaller one on the left and a toilet and sink slid out of the wall. He pressed the next one and the toilet disappeared, to be replaced by a small table with a phone on it. Pierce stared at the phone for a moment; then he picked it up and punched in the number for Rocha's pager.

A few seconds later, a muffled buzz arose from somewhere in the apartment. He lowered the phone and looked around, telling himself that it made sense: if Rocha was on the run, he wouldn't take his pager with him. That's what Pierce told himself, again and again, as he tried each one of the panels.

In rapid succession, a sofa slid out of the wall, then a coffee table, a television, and finally, folding down out of the wall like something from an old movie, a bed.

The rumpled sheets were drenched in blood. Lying on top of them, arms crossed over his chest, was Danny Rocha. His throat had been slit. His left hand was missing.

He looked small. And young, like a child. Next to him, at the foot of the bed, was his attaché, wide open and empty apart from a thick dusting of powder.

Pierce was disgusted.

He had always thought of UniCon as the big bad, and it was. It was responsible for so much evil in the world, so much damage. And he had always thought of the Guild as a bulwark against that, and it was. But it was this, too.

Somehow, when it was Pierce's hand on the line, his life, the perversity of it all hadn't been so clear to him: He had sworn an oath, he had made a commitment, and violating that commitment was on him. But seeing Rocha dead, seeing the kid mutilated, it brought home to him how truly twisted the whole thing was, both the Guild itself and the world that would tolerate it. And he was, too, for going along with it. What the hell had he been thinking? What kind of world was it, when becoming a courier had seemed like his best option?

Pierce stood motionless, staring at the kid as rage and sorrow welled up within him in equal measure.

A pager buzzed, and Pierce flinched, thinking it was Rocha's before realizing it was his own. Diaz.

He picked up the phone again and entered the number from the pager.

Diaz answered right way. "Rocha? You're alright? Jesus Christ, kid, I thought—"

Pierce cut him off. "He's dead. They killed him."

"Pierce? You're calling from the kid's place?"

"They killed him. They cut off his hand."

"Fucking savages," Diaz said, his voice strangled with frustration and pain. They were both quiet for a moment, then Diaz said, "Look, you should get the fuck out of there. They shitcanned me and put Erno in charge, told him to clean house."

"Pretty sure he's dead, too."

"Erno? You killed him?"

"I'm pretty sure. I wish I'd done it slower."

"Good. Fucking prick..." Diaz said. "Look, there's something else. The Guild is... I don't know. It's UniCon now. They took it over."

"The Guild? They can't fucking do that."

"It's a done deal, kid. It's over. They bought a majority of the member agencies, had a legitimate vote on a new charter. But they didn't even need to. They're too big. Too powerful. They said it, and thus it was so."

Pierce closed his eyes. "Bastards," he said, but he didn't even feel it. What he felt more than anything else was that things were coming to a head. One way or another.

"I know, kid," Diaz said. "I guess it was inevitable. Look, I'm getting the fuck out of Dodge. I've got a little saved up and I'm getting out. I don't know where things are going to stand with you and the Guild now that Erno's gone, but you might want to think about getting away for a little while, too."

A picture flashed through Pierce's mind, of him and Gloriana, lying naked on a beach, a different beach, one that UniCon didn't own. He shook his head to banish the image. "Yeah, maybe. I have a couple things to do first."

"You were right about the money disappearing," Diaz said.

"I know." Pierce thought about telling him what he thought was going down, but it all sounded too crazy. Diaz didn't seem like he had it in him to hear it.

"I don't know what the hell is going on, but maybe when things cool down, you could make a case, explain what happened."

Pierce laughed. "Yeah, maybe."

Diaz laughed too, a sad, weary rasp. "Yeah, I guess not. Well, you take care of yourself out there. Been a pleasure working with you, kid."

"You too, Diaz. You said you got a little saved up?"

"Not much, but some, yeah. Why?"

"If you've got Large, see if you can trade it for Small."

PIERCE ROLLED UP to the quadport in Erno's big Chevy. The world felt like it was somehow shifting on multiple axes, movements too complex and erratic for him to get his bearings, to plant his feet under him.

A roadblock had been setup in front of the quadport, and as Pierce pulled up to it, a pair of paramilitaries came toward him, fingering their weapons and telling him he needed to go back the way he had come.

Pierce turned the car around, but before he could drive off, two other contractors stepped out into the road in front of him and waved him to pull over. Some kind of motorcade rounded the corner toward them, four motorcycles in the front, followed by two massive tractor trailers with the Billings logo on the side. Next was an armored van, then three plush-looking Armalux armored SUVs with tinted windows. Another pair of motorcycles guarded the rear.

Frank Billings' convoy, probably carrying the cash from his warehouse. As they rumbled by, Pierce got out of his car to watch.

The idea had seemed insane from his first inkling of it, but even as he had become increasingly convinced this was where things were headed, he still hadn't quite believed that it could happen. It was too crazy, too outrageous. Too *big*.

Seeing it all coming together, though—Billing's mountains of money, Moreland's house that he would never return to, Gloriana's squadron of drones—made the whole thing real.

Billings was taking his money and getting out. When the dust settled, he'd end up the man on top. He was a thug and a lout, a mass murderer with the blood of a hundred and sixty-three innocents on his hands—including Pierce's mom, and Dugray's too.

Maybe whoever was currently on top, the shadowy figures pulling UniCon's levers, maybe they were even worse. But there would always be something fundamentally wrong with any world where Frank Billings was at the top.

The guards waved the convoy through the gate, which started to close as soon as the last vehicles went through. Once inside, the convoy turned and doubled back past him. As Pierce watched, the rearmost SUV peeled away from the others and came toward him, pulling up just inside the fence.

The back door opened, and Gloriana stepped out.

A white hot freezing cold electric jolt of emotion ran through him, blasting away everything else. He wanted to say something smart and cutting or honest and vulnerable. He wanted to ask what the hell she was doing and why. He wanted to tell her what he felt about her, lay himself bare and see if she felt anything in return. But at the sight of her, his throat clenched so tightly he could barely breathe.

She came up close and hooked her fingers in the fence. She smiled, like she was glad to see him, but it faded into sadness. "I'm sorry about what happened," she said softly. "How I left. I didn't know."

"What are you doing?" he asked, glancing over her shoulder as the SUVs slowed to a stop and the trucks continued speeding toward the hangar.

She shook her head. "I thought you'd have figured it out by now."

"*Neptunomonas*. You're going to spray it into the atmosphere. You're going to destroy all the money."

"Just the Large."

"I'm surprised UniCon didn't figure it out."

"They will. They may have already. But not in time. They're big and slow and rigid in their thinking. They transformed the world in their image. They can't imagine someone else would transform it again."

"Look, I agree that UniCon is—"

"It's bigger than UniCon. Older than UniCon. It's a global kleptocracy that's killing us all. The corporate-controlled police and military, brutalizing their own people. The billionaires in those towers." She glanced around at the Manhattan skyline visible behind her. "They won. They came out on top. Fine, whatever, every system has winners and losers. Maybe they won fairly, or maybe everything was rigged from the start, but that doesn't even matter anymore, because now they're just running up the score. They can't stop themselves, trying to win more and more, leaving less and less for everyone else. And killing the planet doing it. Killing everyone on it. Today, they're killing everyone *else*, but in the long run, they're killing themselves, too. Maybe more slowly, but just as surely. They even know it. But they can't stop. So we have to stop them."

"So, is this about wealth disparity or the climate?"

She shook her head. "They go hand in hand, don't you see? The rich use the resources and create the pollution, they burn the oil and coal and methane and pump out the carbon; and the poor deal with the floods and the droughts, the heatwaves and wildfires. That inequality is part of what's killing us. Look, we're not sending everyone back to the stone age. Most people, the vast majority, will be better off in the long run, since the money they have will be worth so much more. But the people in these towers, the ones wringing all the wealth out of the system, using up all the resources, they'll have to live like normal people, at least for a generation or two. It will be good for them."

A second SUV was now curving around to where Pierce and Gloriana stood talking.

"So, the cloud seeding?" Pierce said. "Is that even for real?"

"Of course it's for real. And it will help stave off disaster. But it will never be enough, not unless we stop making the problem worse. We need to get out of the hole we're in, and this will help, but we also need to stop digging. *Neptunomonas* will make us stop digging. For a while at least."

"By wrecking the global economy?"

She gave him a wry smile. "We tried asking nicely. The time for politeness is past. The climate's already at a tipping point. Soon UniCon will announce their new global data network, electronic commerce and everything else, all under UniCon's firm control. And then it will be too late. Large will be a thing of the past and UniCon will control the future. The time to let *Neptunomonas* out is now."

"Why Billings?"

She shrugged. "A necessary evil. Someone had to pay for it. Someone with UniCon-level resources who didn't have UniCon loyalty. Someone who knew they were getting relegated, who wasn't invested in maintaining the status quo, and might want to invest in whatever came next. And with Chris and me both imprisoned, we needed someone outside, on the ground."

"The collapse that killed my mother, the one that killed a hundred and sixty-three innocent people? Billings was behind it. And it wasn't an accident, it wasn't neglect. It was intentional. It was murder."

She put a hand over her mouth. "Are you sure?"

"One of his accomplices told me."

Pain filled her eyes, then anger. "That bastard. I didn't know." She took a deep, steadying breath and set her jaw, resolute. "I'm sorry about that. I hope you believe me that I didn't know. Once this is done, I'll... I'll do whatever I can, whatever it takes, I'll make sure he pays."

Pierce was quiet for a moment, wondering if she meant

it. Wondering what that payment would look like. "What about Moreland?"

She tilted her head, studying his face. "He was necessary, too."

He wanted to ask if she was in love with him, how long they'd been together. Instead, he just nodded, and she smiled again, soft and sad.

"I really am sorry about how I left," she said. "About leaving you like that. I knew this was coming, but I had no idea it was happening now. I wish we'd had more time together."

He believed her. He knew that was probably naïve, but he did. "I do too."

"When I left… That wasn't how it was supposed to happen."

"Did you kill Diego and Matías?"

She shook her head and looked at the ground. "No. That wasn't supposed to happen, either."

The second SUV pulled up behind hers.

"Who killed them?" he asked.

She shook her head and wiped her eye. "That's not important," she said, as if trying to convince herself.

One of the doors to the second SUV opened and Topher Moreland stepped out.

"Gloriana," Pierce said, his voice quiet but urgent. She looked up and stared intently into his eyes. "I love you."

Her eyes brightened, even as they filled with tears once again. She gave him a crooked, knowing smile and said, "I know."

She looked down and mumbled something. It might have been, "Me too," but Pierce couldn't tell for sure. At the same moment, Moreland called out, "Very impressive, Mr. Pierce! I thought you'd still be in Venezuela."

He walked up behind Gloriana and put his hand on her shoulder. It was intimate and familiar, but also controlling and possessive. "Come on, let's go," he told her.

"I have to go," she said to Pierce, as Moreland, gently but firmly, pulled her away. Pierce tried to read her eyes, but there was too much going on in them.

"Where?" he said.

"Not far," she told him. She slowed a step and her eyes hardened for a moment. "Don't try to stop us, Mondo. This is our last chance. All of us. The planet. There is no other way."

Moreland turned her around and she lowered her head as he guided her back to her SUV. Gloriana opened her door but paused before she got in. She looked back at him with a half-smile. "Maybe we'll see each other again... afterward."

Pierce nodded but didn't say anything. She got in and closed the door, disappearing behind the black metal and smoked glass.

Moreland walked around to the other SUV and shook his head as he opened the door. "Probably not," he called out in a stage whisper, then with a smirk, "Give my best to your dad."

Then he got in and both vehicles pulled away, toward the convoy still making its way across the tarmac.

One of the guards who had waved Pierce to the side of the road came closer. "Okay," he said, waving his gun. "On your way."

For a moment, Pierce just stood there, watching the convoy curve across the tarmac. He thought about the arsenal in the trunk.

"Now," the guard said. "Get going."

On some level Pierce hoped the guard would instigate

the violence, give him an excuse to do something stupid. If he kept waiting, the guy almost surely would. But as the convoy disappeared behind a hangar, the turmoil in his chest faded just enough, sinking down into his belly, into long-term storage.

Pierce smiled at the guard. Then he got in the car and drove away. He turned onto the commercial boulevard that ran alongside the quadport. On his right was a string of fast-food joints and big box stores, and just past them, the highway. On his left was the tall chain link fence surrounding the quadport.

He drove a hundred yards down but slowed when he caught sight of the convoy separating out on the tarmac, each vehicle going its separate way. He pulled over in the tiny parking lot of a cargo services company overlooking the quadport.

A lone BetterLate was already there, sitting in a lawn chair, watching, waiting, getting high. He bobbed his head in greeting but didn't offer Pierce the joint.

The clouds had parted, and the sun was low, painting the airport with stripes of golden light and long blue-black shadows. The solar wings of the dozens of drones glinted. In the distance, the towers of New York glinted, too, looking both grand and insignificant from so far away.

Billings' trucks continued across the tarmac, toward a large cargo plane with the Billings logo. The plane's ramp was down, and a small cluster of workers waited next to it. Billings and his money and his plane were going to ride out the storm on his own private island.

Pierce wasn't going to stop Gloriana and Moreland. He couldn't have if he wanted to, not if there were dozens of other launch sites around the world. But he wasn't going to try.

He didn't have much confidence that what they were trying would work, but the world was definitely broken, and no one else was fixing it. Maybe they'd do better the next time.

Dugray's words echoed in his mind. Pierce had been trying to save a world that was already gone. The last thing he wanted was to perpetuate a new world that should never have existed in the first place.

As he looked on, Gloriana stepped out of her SUV and walked up and down the rows of drones, occasionally kneeling down to make small adjustments and double-check things. Even from a distance her movements seemed gentle, delicate, loving even; like a shepherd tending her flock, or a master gardener with her flowers.

She had lied to him, right to his face. She had perhaps set him up for murder. But he still trusted her. He trusted that she was smarter than he was. He trusted that her intentions were pure. He trusted that she had lied to him because she felt she had to. Lives would be lost because of this, but others would be saved. And she hadn't killed Matías and Diego.

Pierce no longer had any idea what was best for the world. But if Gloriana saw a way to fix it, who was he to stop her?

She turned and gazed in his direction, but she couldn't know it was him from that distance.

Moreland walked up behind her. He put his arm around her and pulled her tight, but she shrugged him off.

Pierce smiled.

Beyond them, across the tarmac, pallets were being unloaded from Billings' trucks and loaded onto his plane. So much money.

As Gloriana and Moreland stood to the side of the drones, the third Armalux SUV pulled up next to them and Frank Billings stepped out.

Pierce's breath caught in his throat and his muscles tensed. It was the first time he'd seen the man since finding out he was responsible for Fairview. At that moment, he didn't care about anything other than making Billings pay for what he had done.

Moreland leaned his head toward Billings, as if trying to hear him better. As they spoke, Billings kept looking away, back toward his money.

After a few seconds, they both nodded. Gloriana checked her watch. Then all three of them stepped back, away from the drones.

A shiver ran across the formation, the drones' solar wings trembling in the late-day sun. Then all at once, they rose, a vast diaphanous veil ascending into the air, sparkling in the sunlight.

Billings slapped Moreland and Gloriana each on the back. Then he got back into his SUV and headed across the tarmac toward his cargo plane.

Moreland and Gloriana watched for several more seconds. He put his arm around her again, and this time she let it stay there. He waved to a passenger quadcopter parked nearby and its blades began to turn.

Gloriana continued to watch the drones as they spread out, separating, like dandelion seeds on a gentle breeze. Then the clouds closed back in, darker now, more threatening, and the drones faded away, absorbed into the graying sky.

Moreland pulled her toward the copter, and she let him. They disappeared around the far side of it, and a few moments later, she reappeared in the open hatch.

She looked out, maybe toward where she and Pierce had been talking earlier. For a sick moment, he imagined that she was looking for him, that she would see him, that she would come to him, *be* with him.

More likely she was taking one last look at the world she was about to transform.

Pierce realized he was crying. He felt more pain than he thought possible. Moreland and Gloriana were going off together, somewhere impervious to the turmoil about to descend on the rest of the world. But he wished them well. Or he wished *her* well, anyway. If that meant wishing him well, too, so be it.

"Beautiful, isn't it?" said the kid in the lawn chair. He was crying too.

Looking back at the tarmac, Pierce saw Billings approaching his plane.

It occurred to Pierce that Gloriana and Moreland might have signed a deal with the devil to make their plan happen. But that plan was now off the ground.

And Pierce had made no such deal.

Chapter Twenty-Seven

GLORIANA WATCHED THE drones lift into the sky. It was as perfect a moment as there would ever be. As wildly unlikely as it seemed, she had succeeded up to this point. That was undeniable, unequivocal. She could bask in that success. And at the same time, for this moment, she could feel optimistic about the rest of the plan. The sun was even out.

She was still trying to figure out how she felt about Chris, but he had inarguably done exceptional work. He'd handled the logistics flawlessly—especially impressive since he'd done most of it from prison, even though he'd been there entirely by choice. He said he needed an alibi, but Gloriana suspected he just wanted to be a martyr, and to prove his genius, orchestrating everything from inside. And he had. He'd even run the climate tests from there.

They had known from Angola that the tropics would be fine. Now they knew about the temperate zone of New York, the Arizona desert, and Utqiaġvik, north of the Arctic Circle. None of them slowed or impeded *Neptunomonas Plastiphilos* the slightest bit.

Not everything would go according to plan. Nothing ever did, especially not anything so grand and ambitious as this. There were too many variables, too many moving parts. But for the moment, it was still possible that it might.

And even if it did, people were going to get hurt. It was a certainty. It was baked into the math. Some people would have to suffer more in order for many, many more to suffer so much less. In order to save humanity from itself, and for the species to continue on the planet, for future generations to be given the chance to suffer or not, depending on their own choices and their own dumb luck.

But she hadn't hurt anyone yet—Matías and Diego notwithstanding. She felt sick with guilt about them, but she didn't accept the blame, not really. She was an accessory, but she hadn't agreed to that part of the plan, wouldn't have if she'd known, and hadn't personally done anything to harm them. And at that moment it was still possible, however remotely, that few others would be hurt. Still possible that people would simply adjust to the new reality and move on with their lives, try their best to get along, to take care of the one planet they had to live on. Someday, they might even be grateful to her and Chris for saving their planet despite them, for giving them one more chance to be responsible stewards.

But she also knew that was unlikely. There would be violence and war and people taking from each other as they scraped to get the most of the remaining resources.

That was why, standing there watching those glimmering golden dots of light rising higher and higher into the sky, she didn't want the moment to end. The drones were so tiny, she wasn't sure if she could still see them, or if her brain was conjuring them for her. But she knew that if she looked away, she'd never find them again. If she looked away they'd be gone, and with them, this moment. And that could only, inevitably, open the door for the next one.

Chris reached out and took her hand once more, something that once would have been enough to set her body on fire, would have electrified her mind with possibilities. Now it was just a hand. And Chris was just a man. Brilliant and beautiful and visionary—but damaged and human and flawed like everyone else. Possibly worse than many.

She looked at the quadcopter, its rotors already turning as Chris tugged her toward it. When she looked back at the sky, the drones had vanished. So had the sun, hidden once again behind its ubiquitous gray shroud.

She let Chris pull her toward the copter. As she started to climb aboard, he insisted on helping her into the copter, then insisted she move over to the next seat. She had to climb over a giant green duffle bag with squared edges, and she felt a flash of annoyance. He had always been somewhat controlling, but it had gotten much worse. Maybe the press attention and the adulation of the BetterLates had gone to his head.

She thought back to their early days together at Princeton, before she met Mondo. Those were their happiest days. But he was a different man now. He had already changed when they reconnected three years ago, even more when she'd seen him in Angola, but this was something else. She had sensed it immediately—would have even if he hadn't shot Diego and Matías. The hours they'd spent together since then had only confirmed it.

She told herself it was natural to have second thoughts at a moment like this. She had spent so long in anticipation, it was to be expected that the moment itself might be a letdown. But she wasn't having second thoughts about the *plan*. She was having second thoughts about Chris.

Part of it, she knew, was Mondo. She looked out through the open door to where they had been standing and talking, only minutes earlier. But he was gone.

She felt bad about leaving without a proper goodbye—again. She felt bad about leaving him in such a dicey situation—again. But mostly, she felt bad about leaving him. After just one day together again, she had glimpsed a future they might have had together, a past they might have shared.

Mondo had changed too, as surely as Chris had, but she liked the changes in him. He seemed more mature. Maybe a little weary, a little beaten down, but you'd have to be insane not to be, living in the world as it was. She had been certain, for a moment, that they weren't yet done with each other. But now it seemed they were.

As if he was reading her mind, Chris slid the door closed on his side of the copter, leaned forward to the pilot and said, "Let's get out of here."

The pilot—the same pilot who had flown them out of Venezuela—turned his head halfway around. "The bribes were more than I expected."

Chris smiled unpleasantly. "Sorry. We had a deal."

The pilot turned the rest of the way around. "Well the deal has changed."

Chris's smile remained in place, but his eyes burned as he and the pilot stared at each other. Finally, he said, "How much?"

"Ten grand," the pilot said, adding, with a smile, "in Small."

Chris seethed as he tugged open the zipper on the green bag, revealing cash, stacks and stacks of it, mostly fifties, but some twenties as well.

The pilot whistled. "Guess I should have asked for more."

Gloriana was stunned. "I thought you were broke."

Chris snorted. "You kidding? In the real world, this *is* broke. It's practically nothing." He fished out two bundles of fifties. "But soon it'll be worth much more."

He handed the two stacks to the pilot, who took them and said, "Okay then. We should be in Bermuda in… a little over three hours."

Gloriana's head snapped around at Chris. "Bermuda? We agreed we were going to stick around to help people, here and in Malaysia, everywhere, help them through this transition that *we* are setting in motion."

"I know, baby," he said, with an infuriatingly patronizing calm, as he tugged the zipper closed on the green bag. "But I've had to rethink some things here, while you were down in Venezuela. I had to change some plans." He turned to the pilot. "Let's go."

The pilot reached for the controls, but Gloriana snapped, "No!" and he pulled back his hand.

Chris said, "Go."

Gloriana immediately said, *"Don't,"* and he didn't. She turned to Chris again. "Tell me the plan."

"We don't have time for this. Close your door and let's go."

"What's the plan?"

He laughed in a performance of lighthearted exasperation, but his eyes smoldered. "We're going to hole up in Bermuda and wait out the worst of it. I've got a place that's secure and defensible and stocked for a year."

"A *year?*"

"It's going to be bad, at first."

"I know that, We talked about it."

He shook his head and forced that same smile. "I don't think you understand *how* bad it's going to be."

"That's why we *agreed* we needed to be out there helping. If we're going to do this thing, we also need to do whatever we can to minimize the suffering."

"And we will, once things have settled down. Now come on, close your door. We can talk about it when we get there." He turned to the pilot. "Go. Now."

"I'm staying," Gloriana said.

"No, you're not," Chris replied. "I forbid it." Then he pulled out a gun and pointed it at the pilot's face. "And I can find another pilot."

The pitch of the motors increased a step, and the copter began to rise.

Chris turned to Gloriana. "Now close your goddamn door!" He shouted over the motors. Then he reached past Gloriana to do it himself.

They were three feet off the ground.

Gloriana pushed his arm away, shouting, "*No!*"

Then he slapped her. Hard. Her eyes widened in shock even as they teared up. For an instant they stared at each other.

He'd never touched her like that before, but there had been moments throughout their relationship when his eyes got that look, when she had wondered if deep inside, he was the type of man that could.

She realized now that he was, that she'd always known it, but never had proof. Maybe he'd been different once, but she felt like for the first time, she was seeing who he truly was *now*.

Then it was hidden away again, behind a mask of regret. "Baby, I'm sorry..." he started to say. But it was too late.

They were six feet off the ground and the rotors were singing.

She turned away from him and jumped out through the open door.

She braced for impact, but instead of hitting the ground, her leg wrenched sideways, twisting as she dangled in the air, her head inches from the ground. Looking up, she saw the strap from the green bag wrapped around her foot.

The copter continued to rise as she hung upside down. She reached up and tried to untangle herself. Then the strap jerked and dropped her lower, as if the bag had shifted. Her hair was brushing the ground. From the corner of her eye, she saw an open-topped Humvee approaching, followed by a column of black UniC vehicles, lights flashing. She wondered if UniCon had figured out what was going on, if they had come here to try to stop them. No matter. It was too late for that as well.

She looked back up as Chris appeared in the hatchway, glaring down at her. He reached for her leg as the copter rose sharply. Then she was falling again, and the green bag was tumbling out of the copter too.

Chris frantically grabbed for the bag as the copter rose and banked away from her. She landed hard on her shoulder, and the bag landed heavily on top of her.

She pushed it off and saw Chris, ten feet off the ground now, twenty feet away, staring down at her and shouting commands at the pilot. From the corner of her eye, she saw a flash of light by the UniC vehicles. Chris must have seen it too, because he looked up, shock and horror splashed across his face. Then everything disappeared in an explosion of sound and light and heat.

Chapter Twenty-Eight

PIERCE GOT OUT of the Chevy and opened the back door, pulling out the large black bag Dugray had given him and settling it onto the front passenger seat. The rotors on Gloriana's copter started turning, but he was trying not to think about that, trying to focus only on the cargo plane with the big Billings Company logo on the tail fin being loaded with pallets of cash.

Four lanes of traffic and an eight-foot chain link fence stood between Pierce and the tarmac. He would need all the power he could get. He set the Chevy's motor to high/standby and waited as it powered up. The smell of ozone filled the air.

The BetterLate in the chair looked over at him, concerned. "Hey!" he called out. "You okay, mister?"

Pierce's finger hovered over the GO button, and when there was a break in the traffic, he hit it. The Chevy took off with the sudden, flesh-flattening acceleration that only a powerful electric motor can give you. He shot across the first two lanes of traffic, hit the median and went airborne.

The Chevy came down hard on top of the fence, flattening a large section of it. The tires screamed against twisted metal and concrete and asphalt, trying to get traction. One of the tires blew out, but the other three bit into whatever was under them and rocketed the Chevy out onto the tarmac, flinging broken fencing out behind it.

Pierce was headed straight across the tarmac, straight toward Billings' plane on the far side of the tarmac. To his left, Gloriana's copter was just lifting off the ground. To his right was a long diagonal row of low-slung hangars, extending halfway across the tarmac. Through the gap between two of them, he caught a glimpse of eight or ten UniC SUVs speeding toward the copter, on a path that would intersect Pierce's in the middle of the tarmac.

"Shit," Pierce whispered, as the UniCs disappeared again behind a row of buildings. A second later, through the next gap, he saw that the lead vehicle was an open-backed SUV with a mounted heavy machine gun, and standing behind it was Ryan Mansfield.

Pierce leaned on the accelerator and adjusted his angle, hoping to intercept them before they reached Gloriana's copter. He reached into the duffel and fished out one of the mini grenade launchers.

The copter lifted off the ground now, but instead of speeding away to safety, it hovered a few feet in the air.

"Go on, goddamn it. Get out of here," Pierce said through gritted teeth.

He emerged from behind the last hangar of the row, expecting to see the UniCs on a collision course with him, but he turned and saw that they had slowed to a stop. Mansfield was bracing himself, aiming some kind of rocket launcher at Gloriana's copter, still hovering close to the ground.

Pierce skidded to a halt, grabbed his mini grenade launcher, and jumped out. Leaning on the hood to steady his arms, he lined up the sight on Mansfield's Jeep. He slowly exhaled, but just as he pressed the button, the Chevy shook violently as something slammed into it, hard. Pierce's shot went wide and high, arcing into the air. He turned to see an armored Humvee bearing down on him. A pale figure with red-rimmed eyes sat behind the wheel, one ghostly arm aiming a super-large caliber hand cannon out the window.

It was Erno, alive, covered in cement and dust.

The grenade Pierce had fired exploded in the distance, just as a gout of flames shot out the back of Mansfield's launcher and a ball of smoke shot out the front. Pierce tried to track the missile, but before he could turn his head, the copter had exploded in flames, twenty feet off the ground.

A scream erupted from Pierce's throat—harsh and ragged and tasting of blood. Rotor blades knifed through the air as the wreckage of the copter fell to the earth and the fireball rolled up into the sky. Erno's Humvee slammed into the Chevy just as Pierce dove out of the way.

Pierce rolled to his feet, and saw the Humvee, still running, rolling slowly forward until it came to a stop against a piece of bright blue debris. Apart from the windshield, which was completely gone, the Humvee looked unscathed from the impact. But thirty feet away from it, Erno lay on the ground looking gratifyingly scathed, bloody raw patches making a striking contrast with the gray that covered the rest of him.

Dugray's duffel had split open, and several of the weapons inside it had spilled out onto the tarmac, including the other mini-grenade launcher. It lay on the tarmac between them, slightly closer to Erno.

They looked at each other, then it.

Erno started clawing his way toward the launcher, but Pierce got there first, stomping on the grip just before Erno could wrap his hand around it.

"They're *dead*. Because of *you*," Pierce said, his voice trembling with rage.

"You swore an oath, Pierce!" Erno spat out, bloody spittle flecking his lips and chin. "We all did. I don't care what happened to your shipment, to Rocha's shipment, any of them. It doesn't matter if it wasn't your fault. You swore a fucking *oath*."

Pierce stared at him. "You knew what was happening with the Large, and you still killed all those couriers?" All this time he'd been trying to prove his innocence, but the Guild already knew. They just didn't care.

"None of that matters. You swore an oath. If the Guild doesn't enforce it, people will lose faith in the Guild, and then where are we? The governors know that if the Guild is to survive, that oath has to count for something."

Pierce pictured Rocha, dead and mutilated, pictured it multiplied over and over again. All those couriers, dead. "If the Guild is going to survive, it can't blindly kill people who have done nothing wrong."

The flaming wreckage of Gloriana's helicopter shifted, and Pierce glanced over at it. In that momentary distraction, Erno snarled and yanked the grenade launcher free, rolling upright with it, ready to fire it at Pierce.

Pierce's muscle memory took over; almost without conscious thought, his boot knife was in his hand, then in the air, then in Erno's left eye. Erno's snarl relaxed, replaced by a placid half smile. As he slumped back, a spasm went through his body, and the mini-grenade launched, almost straight into the air.

Pierce turned and ran, scooping the duffel off the tarmac. He snuck a quick look around the wreckage of the Chevy, expecting to see the UniCs bearing down on him. Instead, they were milling about, two of them looking around with binoculars while Mansfield spoke into a big military walkie-talkie.

Pierce had a shot at him, the guy who killed Gloriana. But straight head of him, between two large airplane hangars, he saw Billings' plane. The trucks had finished loading and were backing away from it. The man who had killed his mother was preparing to escape with a billion dollars. And whatever Gloriana could have or would have done to make him pay for his crimes wasn't going to happen.

The grenade Erno had fired exploded harmlessly, high in the air, as Pierce threw the duffel into the Humvee, then jumped in after it. Pointing the vehicle at the gap between the hangars, at Billings' plane, he stomped on the accelerator and shot across the tarmac.

Glancing to his right, he saw a few of the UniCs pointing at him. Mansfield lowered his walkie talkie. Then they scrambled into their vehicles and came after him.

He heard the clatter of automatic weapons firing and a volley of bullets passed over his head.

Pierce reached into the duffel and fished out a hand grenade. He pulled the pin and tossed it over his shoulder. There was no time to aim it or throw it, and he just wanted to slow them down. He heard the explosion behind him and snuck a glance. One of the SUVs was heavily damaged and the remaining five were swerving around it, still firing at him.

As he plunged through the gap between the two airplane hangars, closing on Billings' plane, the shooting from the UniCs briefly stopped. A moment later, as his pursuers passed through the gap, it started up again, but Pierce realized none of the bullets were hitting the Humvee. The UniCs were now shooting at the plane.

Billings' men were now returning fire through the open hatch. Pierce couldn't tell if they were aiming at him or the UniCs, but bullets from both directions pinged off the Humvee as the fire intensified. Pierce angled off to the side, out of the crossfire. It occurred to him that maybe he should just get out of there, let the UniCs take Billings out. He could go find some place quiet to hunker down, process Gloriana's death and prepare for whatever she had wrought. Do what he could to help people make it through whatever was on the other side of it.

But as Billings' plane started moving, even with the hatch fully open, Pierce realized the UniCs weren't firing any heavy ordinance—no grenades, no fifty cal. They weren't trying to destroy Billings' plane. They were trying to capture it. And all the Small on board.

UniCon was so powerful that even if Gloriana's plan worked flawlessly and had the impact she intended, it could still come out of this in power. But if they got their hands on all that Small, it was practically assured that they would. And while he now knew the purpose of *Neptunomonas plastiphilos* had nothing to do with undermining faith in cash before the launching of U-Net, it could still have that effect—if UniCon remained intact.

He reached into the duffel, fishing around for any heavy ordnance of his own, but there was none. Probably scattered on the tarmac near Erno.

He knew it was probably better to let Billings keep the money than let UniCon get a hold of it. Except Billings was a monster and a murderer who had killed Pierce's mother.

The plane's engines roared and it started to pick up speed, the cargo hatch still open, scraping along the tarmac.

The lead UniC vehicle was closing on the plane, quickly enough that it could conceivably drive up the open hatch. Pierce angled closer and pulled a machine pistol out of Dugray's bag. He set it to fully automatic, leveled it out the window, and emptied the magazine in the direction of the UniCs. One of the UniC SUVs turned sharply and went into a roll. The other two slowed for a moment, losing ground on the plane as it continued to speed up. The runway was a quarter of a mile straight ahead as the hatch slowly began to close. The plane was picking up speed, but so were the UniCs, and so was Pierce.

The hatch was a few feet off the ground as Pierce pulled up alongside it. Inside, he could see the mountains of currency, pallets stacked on pallets, strapped together into three massive cubes. Matching the plane's speed, he set the Humvee's cruise control and stood on his seat. He was summoning the courage to jump up onto the hatch when the plane began to turn toward the runway, toward him. The edge of the hatch ground against the top of the Humvee's hood, crumpling it.

For an instant, the two vehicles were wedged together. The Humvee began to shimmy. Pierce dove for the hatch just as the Humvee slid out from under it. He rolled to his feet on the ramp as the Humvee curved sharply away, tipped up on two wheels, and tumbled into a roll.

Two of Billings' guards were crouched at the back of the plane, both strapped with firepower, firing bursts at the fast-approaching UniCs. They paused to look at Pierce, confused by his sudden appearance. The one closest turned his gun on Pierce, then took three rounds to the chest from the UniCs and fell on the spot.

Pierce grabbed the fallen guard's weapon and started laying down fire at the UniCs chasing them. The other guard stared at him for an instant, confused, then returned his focus to the UniCs as well.

The plane picked up speed, putting more distance between them and their pursuers.

The hatch was halfway closed by now. The remaining guard slung his weapon over his shoulder and plucked something off his vest. As he pulled a bulky ring off it and tossed it out the hatch, Pierce recognized it as a remote charge.

These guys were not fucking around.

The charge hit the tarmac and bounced several times. Just as the UniCs caught up with it, the guard pulled the tiny secondary pin out of the primary ring and the charge detonated, taking out three of the chase vehicles with an explosion so strong it shook the plane.

Only one SUV remained. Mansfield.

The remaining guard on the plane turned his weapon on Pierce and called out over the roar of the plane's engines, "Hands in the air, then tell me who the fuck you are."

Pierce put his hands up and shouted, "The enemy of your enemy."

The guard shook his head, then tilted it toward the mountain of money in the plane right next to them. "Not good enough," he said. "Not with all this." His nametag said WOOTEN. He pointed his gun at Pierce and said, "Drop the gun and get the fuck out of here."

A burst of bullets found the gap around cargo hatch, sparking off metal and raising tufts of paper from the wall of tightly wrapped currency behind them. Pierce dropped to the floor and looked up in time to see Wooten fall across the gap at the side of the hatch, bleeding from both sides of his neck. He was hanging halfway out as the door closed. He was surely dead, but Pierce was afraid the hatch was going to cut him in half. Then it stopped, and he grew even more worried as he realized it wasn't going to close at all.

Pierce was pinned back by automatic fire as the UniCs pulled up alongside the hatch. He could see the driver through the gap; next to him, Mansfield was aiming a machine gun.

Pierce pulled the handgun from Wooten's holster and fired through the gap. The driver swerved away, and Mansfield went tumbling.

Pierce found the override lever for the hatch and pushed it down, opening the hatch just enough to free Wooten's body. He felt bad as he pulled the body loose and unceremoniously dumped it onto the tarmac.

As he pushed the lever back up, the plane lurched, suddenly tilting upwards, and the floor dropped slightly under him. Through the last sliver of a gap, he saw the ground fall away. Then the hatch closed.

Chapter Twenty-Nine

PIERCE LOOKED AROUND him. Three mountains of cash sat in the middle of the cargo bay. A row of parachutes hung from the wall. He strapped one on as a plan took shape.

He looked out a tiny window. They'd started circling the airport, gaining altitude. Soon they'd be high enough that his parachute would open before he hit the ground. He thought about jumping right then; it was probably his best chance of surviving the day. But he looked at all that money. He had kept it out of UniCon's hands, but that wasn't enough.

For better or for worse, Gloriana had given the world a second chance, a reset. The last thing that world needed was to start its second chance with a mass murderer like Billings holding all the cards.

He didn't have much time. No way were they moving this much money with only two armed guards. Before long, the others would come check on these two.

He took the weapons belt off of Wooten's partner—

complete with three spare clips and another five remote charges. He strapped it on, careful not to impinge on the parachute. Pierce had done drills with remote charges in the army. Each grenade had a primary ring, and each primary ring had a secondary ring. The bulky primary rings were remote triggers. When you pulled them, it armed the grenade, and then when you pulled the secondary ring, that set the charge off. With five it was easy. He pulled each of the primary rings one by one and slipped them onto the fingers of his left hand.

He kept count as he slid the first three charges under the three pallet stacks. He peeled a piece of plastic off the fourth charge to expose the adhesive pad and stuck it on the hydraulics holding the cargo hatch closed. The fifth one he stuck to the side wall, where the wing attached to the fuselage. That was the one with the ring on his thumb.

As he finished placing the last charge, the door to the forward compartment opened and two more guards came through. They drew their weapons as they spotted him. Pierce dove for cover behind the closest pallet stack and heard a sound like sleet ticking off the bulkhead.

They were shooting darts, which made sense. The rear hatch was reinforced, but the sides were aluminum. You had to be careful about discharging weapons on a plane— unless, of course, you were wearing a parachute and indifferent to whether or not the plane remained airborne.

Pierce peeked back around the stack and saw the two guards coming toward him. He fired twice at them, and two small circles of light appeared behind them where the bullets punched through the bulkhead. The guards turned to look at it, then ran for cover, ducking around the other side of the first pallet stack, the opposite side from Pierce.

Pierce ran from the first stack to the far side of the second one. He pulled the pin from the ring on his little finger, and with a dim flash and a loud but muffled bang, the plane shuddered and the air suddenly filled with cash—some torn, some whole, some flaming. It was like the inside of a crazy capitalist snow globe. The guards were stunned as the pallet stack they'd been hiding behind suddenly disappeared, leaving them exposed beneath the shower of money.

They chased after Pierce as he ran from the second stack to the third, then pulled the pin from the ring on his ring finger. Once again, the plane shook as the second stack disappeared and the air was filled with cash.

Bills swirled around them, flickering as they passed through a dozen new shafts of light from new gaps that had appeared in the fuselage.

The door to the front compartment opened again, and this time Billings himself emerged, carrying a gun and wearing an actual pilot's cap. He stopped, a look of horror crashing over his face. Through the swirl of cash, he squinted at Pierce, and the horror was replaced with rage.

"*You?*"

As he raised his gun, the two guards said, "No!" diving toward him, but he squeezed off two shots before they could stop him. Two more holes appeared in the fuselage.

Pierce dove behind the third stack, but he knew he couldn't hide there long. They'd come after him on either side, then catch him in a crossfire of darts. The cargo door was just ten feet away.

"You've got no idea what you're doing," Billings called out. "This is much bigger than you."

"I know what you and Moreland set in motion," Pierce

shouted back. "And Gloriana." Saying her name out loud took the wind out of him. The sorrow threatened to diffuse his anger, but he couldn't let it. Now more than ever, he needed his anger.

"I could make you a rich man, Pierce," Billings shouted out. "Very rich."

"You murdered my mother!"

"Who?"

For that alone, Pierce felt an overwhelming urge to shoot him. He peered around the corner of the pallet. "Dorie Pierce. She lived in the Fairview."

Billings shook his head, like he was going to deny it. Then he almost started laughing. "Wait, you mean the head of the tenants' association?" He took a deep breath, his face serious; then he continued, his voice steady and earnest. "I didn't want to kill those people, Pierce. Didn't want to kill anyone. They *made* me do it. It was UniCon. We were all working for UniCon. You hate them and I get that. I hate them, too. You want to take them down? That's what I'm doing."

"You're taking them down so you can come out on top."

The gangster's facade cracked and he grinned. "Well, someone's got to."

"It's not going to be you."

Billings nodded to himself then said, "Okay. Look, asshole, I've tried to talk sense to you, but—"

Pierce leaned around the stack and fired at him.

Billings dove for cover. "You know, it was a shame about all those other people," he shouted. "But not your mom. I was glad about her. That bitch was a pain in my ass."

Pierce held up his index finger and pulled the pin, detonating the charge on the hydraulics.

A loud bang was quickly followed by the sound of wrenching metal and the deafening roar of rushing air as the rear hatch fell open. All the loose cash was swept up in a frantic vortex that swirled furiously inside the plane for an instant before corkscrewing out into the angry gray sky.

Pierce watched as hundreds of millions, maybe billions of dollars in small bills sailed past him. Even through the roar of the wind, he could hear Billings screaming in horror and fury, and some kind of primal money-lust.

Through the scraps of money still churning in the turbulence inside the plane, Billings came charging toward him around the last stack of pallets, a gun in his hand and murder in his eyes.

As Billings raised his gun, Pierce pushed off with his legs and fell through the open hatch. Plummeting to Earth, he looked up to see Billings in the cargo bay, shooting at him with a tinny *pop-pop-pop*.

Pierce smiled and raised his middle finger on his left hand, then pulled the pin from the ring on it.

A pale green cloud shot out the back of the plane—the cash from the third pallet stack, streaming past Billings. A half a second later, Pierce heard the dull, hollow thump of the explosion.

Pierce plummeted through the first cloud of money, reminding him how quickly he was falling, and to pull the cord on his parachute.

After the initial violent jolt, the rest of the fall was almost peaceful. Just him and all that money, settling slowly out of the air. The water surrounding the airport below him reflected the clouds above, distorting his sense of up and down. Rows of houses intermingled with the water, some high and dry, some collapsing into the wetlands.

To the south, he could see Manhattan, could even make out the bones of UniCon's new U-Net Tower rising where the Fairview once stood.

For some reason it made him think of his father instead of his mother, probably because he'd told Pierce what was being built on the site. Or maybe because he'd still be alive to see the turmoil to come. Pierce felt a moment of worry for Bradley, wondering how he would fare. Then he remembered Bradley's words: "It feels safer in here sometimes." Secure and protected, with meals and medical care, Bradley might find those words to be even truer in the times ahead.

It had been years since Pierce had skydived, but he remembered enough to steer toward a dry grassy expanse east of the quadport.

Billings' plane had straightened out of its circle and was now flying east, over the Bronx and toward Long Island Sound. Even with the back open, the plane seemed to be flying okay. Two specks fell from the back. Pierce squinted, but couldn't make out any details. He figured they were the guards. After a few seconds, their parachutes opened.

He didn't like to think of himself as a killer. But he had done a lot of killing just lately. Wartime was one thing, but Kransky and his men… Townsend's guards… Erno… That was all going to weigh on him for the rest of his life, he knew that.

What was coming next was different, though. This was deliberate.

As Pierce gently drifted back to Earth, he had to concede Billings' point. It was the way of the world that had killed Gloriana and Carla Ruiz-Vargas, had killed all those people in the Fairview, including his mother and

Dugray's. Pierce had known that from the beginning. And that world had been prosecuted and convicted. The sentence was being carried out at that very moment. That world was about to be over, soon replaced by a new one.

Pierce found himself oddly buoyed by the thought. He was under no illusions that things wouldn't be tough for a while, maybe brutally so, but he hated what the world had become. He was excited to see what would happen next.

But Billings was guilty, too. *Personally* guilty. He was a murderer many times over. He had confessed. He was guilty. His sentence needed to be carried out, too.

The plane was out over the water now, shrinking quickly. The remote charges had a long range, but he figured he must be close to exceeding it.

He closed his eyes and said a quick prayer for forgiveness from a God he didn't believe in. Then he opened them and pulled the pin from the ring on his thumb.

Nothing happened. Pierce couldn't have downed the plane over land, but he cursed himself for waiting too long. He told himself that with no money and no power, maybe Billings would suffer enough, or maybe the remnants of UniCon would get him. But he didn't believe it. Billings was a predator. He'd thrive in the chaos to come.

At least it was one less death on his conscience, he thought.

Then there was a flash in the sky and the plane came apart, followed a few seconds later by a tinny pop as the flaming wreckage slowly fell to the sea.

Pierce smiled.

Chapter Thirty

THE GROUND CAME up fast. Pierce flexed his knees when he landed, then ran out from under the parachute before letting himself collapse onto the grass.

The park was empty. A tang of smoke hung in the air. It wasn't good smoke, like firewood or barbecues or cannabis; more like burning plastic and rubber and houses and cars. It was the smell of chaos and destruction. But the park itself felt oddly peaceful. So did Pierce.

Some of the cash was already blowing around on the grass, but most of it was still in the air. Pierce lay on his back for a minute, watching it gently falling, like snow.

The moment took him back to his childhood, that feeling when a big snowstorm was coming: excitement, anticipation, and a hint of danger, when everything was quiet and everybody was hunkered down as those first few flakes began to fall.

A memory popped into his head, vivid and clear, of lying with his mom on the frozen ground behind their house, the big house—Bradley's house, in the end, but this was when they were all still living in it. Mom and Dad had just had an argument, Pierce's first inkling that all was not well between the two of them. He couldn't remember what the fight had been about, or if he had ever known, but though it was the first one that he had been fully aware of, it came with the realization that it was one of many, and that it was big. That things he had thought were permanent might not be.

Pierce had run outside to get away from it, and his mom had come out after him, to comfort him. And she did. She always did. She didn't say a word, because she didn't have to. She had lain down next to him, their heads touching, and together they had looked up at the sky.

Maybe she had checked the weather, or maybe she was just being her usual caring, patient self, but instead of coaxing him inside for cocoa and a hot bath, she stayed with him for a while like that, even though it was cold and the ground was hard, even though he had stopped crying. It was as if she knew what was going to happen next.

Maybe she saw it first, but she didn't say anything; she let him spot the first snowflake on his own.

He could remember bolting upright and pointing, gasping at the sight of it, how his mom had giggled, how they had both laughed out loud.

They had both lain back down and watched as one flake had become several, and very quickly a bazillion. They caught snowflakes on their tongues, felt them landing on their eyelashes and their hair, on their cheeks and their foreheads.

She must have been freezing, he realized, and he must have been, too; although that's not how he remembered it. But she didn't rush him, didn't hurry him inside. It's possible she didn't want to go inside—that's where his dad was, after all—but he was pretty sure that wasn't it.

She had reached out and taken his hand, squeezed it tight and held it, letting him know that whatever happened, she would always love him, would always be with him. And she always was, until the day she died.

And now, for better or for worse, he had killed the man responsible for her death.

Part of him was tormented by that fact: that coldly, deliberately, he had taken a human life. But for the first time in three years, he was free of the hatred and anger he had harbored for whoever had allowed such a thing to happen, *caused* such a thing to happen.

Maybe because of that, for the first time, he was able to truly mourn his loss.

He realized he was silently weeping. Tears were streaming down the sides of his face. He didn't know how long he had been crying, but his hair and his ears were wet, soaked with tears. But even as he realized it, the tears stopped. He felt hollow somehow, but in a good way, as if he were all cried out, as if his tears had purged a pain so deep and so constant he hadn't fully realized it was there.

Thunder rumbled in the distance, and he wondered briefly if it had something to do with the drones and the cloud-seeding, a portent of what was to come. Then a few droplets fell, and he knew it was just rain.

Rain and money.

He couldn't just lie there, but he didn't know what else to do. He savored the lightness that came with letting go of the past, letting go of all the things that had been weighing him down. Letting go of the Guild. But he also felt unmoored. Every constant of his life was gone, and he knew this was just the beginning. It would have been easier to embrace the future if he had the slightest inkling of what it would look like.

If *Neptunomonas* was for real, if it did what it was supposed to do, that would be the end of UniCon, and probably the Guild, too. And even if it was just in New York, Alaska, and Arizona, in the midst of trillions of dollars turning to dust, any case against him would fall apart like so much Large. With Erno gone and the Guild imploding, maybe he could just go home. It felt like a long time since he'd been there.

A few more raindrops fell, and he heard laughter. A bunch of kids emerged from the houses across the street, running around the far end of the park, grabbing cash off the ground, out of the air. More and more bills came down, but the vast majority of it seemed content to stay in the air, buffeted on the stiffening breeze.

More kids came out of the houses, grownups too, grabbing handfuls of money and stuffing it into their shirts and pants. They seemed happy.

Pierce knew it wouldn't last. Inevitably, fights would break out. There would never be enough money, no matter how much or how little there was of it. And everywhere else in the world, outside this little patch of North Jersey, there wouldn't be any money falling from the sky to help prepare them for the chaos to come.

But right here, right now, people were happy to have Frank Billings' money rain down on them. In that moment, Pierce smiled. Maybe he would just stay there for a while, right in that moment, right in that place.

He started to close his eyes again, but then a dented SUV appeared, driving slowly down one of the side streets abutting the park. It had a UniC insignia on the side, partially burned or scraped off. It coasted across the street, slowly bumped up onto the curb and rolled into the park.

Pierce closed his eyes and laughed. He didn't have it in him to fight anymore. If this was how it ended, killed by the Guild or UniCon, he was okay with that. Too tired to care, too sore to move. He'd felt for some time like this wasn't his world anymore. The next one probably wouldn't be either. Soon, he'd be two worlds removed from anything that made sense to him. He couldn't imagine taking on yet another a new world, and doing so alone. Maybe it was just as well that he got off now.

The wind picked up again, rustling the parachute around his head. Thunder rumbled closer. A fat droplet of rain landed on his forehead, warm and soft. He left it there, not even flinching as it quivered on his brow, deciding which way roll.

Then, surprisingly close, a quiet voice said, "Are you alive?"

He recognized it instantly, but he knew it wasn't real. A hallucination, maybe from exhaustion. Or maybe a psychotic break—if not now, when, right?

He wanted desperately to see her, but he didn't want to spoil the illusion, if that's what it was. He wondered vaguely about the quantum implications, if, until he opened his eyes, she was both real and hallucinatory. There and not there. Dead and alive.

But slowly he opened his eyes, and there she was, standing next to a UniC vehicle. Her shirt was torn. Her pants were bloody. One leg was slightly bent, like it was injured. Her cheek looked blackened with soot; then Pierce realized it was a burn, and a bad one. But she was alive.

For a long moment, they stared at each other. The world seemed to go still: no wind, no laughter, no cash fluttering in the air.

He still wasn't fully convinced she was real until she faltered, like her leg was about to give out on her.

He jumped to his feet and ran to her as the wind returned, pelting them with rain and soggy bills. Sound returned, too—laughter and shouting, the parachute rumpling, the thunder rumbling. Sirens in the distance.

Pierce drew close, but he couldn't quite reach her. He seemed stuck in slow motion, then rooted in place, then somehow moving away from her. It was like a bad dream, but it all seemed utterly real.

He took three steps backward before he realized the wind had caught his parachute, that's what was pulling him back. He braced his legs, determined not to give another inch while he found the clip and released it.

The parachute flew away from them as Pierce ran toward Gloriana. Then his arms were around her, holding her tight, taking her weight off her injured leg.

"I thought you were dead," he said, into her hair. It smelled of smoke, and just a hint of flowers.

"I almost was," she said, holding him with trembling arms. "I thought you were dead, too. When I saw the parachute, I hoped it was you. Hoped you were alive."

He held her tight, then pulled away from her. "Moreland?" he asked.

She shook her head and a tear rolled down her cheek, perilously close to her burn. "He was in the copter. I jumped out." She wiped away her tear, then buried her face against him. "He'd changed," she said into his shoulder. "We had a plan, you know? We were going to... help... however we could. Ease as much of the pain of this transition as we could. Do what we could to prevent UniCon from taking over again. But Chris decided on his own that we were going to spend a year in some tropical paradise until the worst of it blew over. I told him I was staying, and he said no. He *forbade* it. So I jumped out. Two seconds later and I would have died along with him."

She looked around at the bills swirling in the air, sticking to the surface of the water. Being collected by the people. "What about Billings?"

Pierce shook his head. "I killed him. For his crimes."

She pulled back, just an inch or so, studying his face. Then she held him even tighter. "Are you okay?"

"I think so," he said. "I will be."

"Good," she said. She looked up into the sky and waved her hand. "That's his? The money?"

Pierce nodded. "Every bit of it."

She smiled. "That's good."

Pierce looked around at the growing crowd, then down the adjoining streets. Money swirled in the air as far as he could see. The rooftops of the houses were speckled with damp bills.

At the far end of the park, two men standing knee deep in the pond started fighting. On the front steps of a nearby house, a little boy sat crying, alone.

A trio of police drones zipped past over the treetops, their red and blue lights illuminating the cash fluttering around them.

Pierce looked at the UniC vehicle Gloriana had driven up in. It wouldn't be long before others arrived. The indifference he'd felt about being apprehended by UniCon had evaporated the moment he'd realized Gloriana was alive.

"We should get out of here," he said. "They'll be coming after us."

She nodded and he helped her over to the car. She steered him toward the passenger door and handed him the keys. "You drive." She winced as he helped her get in.

As he got in on the driver's side, he pointed to the sky and said, "It occurs to me, maybe I should grab some of this. I'm pretty much broke." He cocked an eyebrow at her. "All my Large has mysteriously disappeared."

She let out a weary snort and hooked a thumb toward the back seat, which was taken up by a large, square-edged green duffel bag. A tear in the corner revealed the stacks of fifties and twenties inside. "It's okay. I've got some I can share."

"Jesus," Pierce said, looking at it. He'd been a courier so long, the sight of money generally had no effect on him. But somehow it was different now.

"A lot of people are going to need a lot of help in the coming months and years," she said. "It's more than I thought we'd have, but nowhere near enough."

He nodded and said, "Where to?"

She thought for a moment. "I have no place to go."

He started the motor. "You can stay with me."

The side of her mouth curled up, as if a glimmer of something bright had appeared out of the darkness. As the motor whined, she said, "Maybe. Maybe just for the night."

As the rain started coming down harder, he put the car in drive and drove. "Maybe, huh? So… maybe for longer?"

That smile seemed to tug harder at her mouth. She looked out the window and said, "We'll see how it goes."

Acknowledgments

THIS IS MY eleventh book and many of the people who I should thank have been thanked many times already. So, to all my writer friends and the booksellers, librarians, readers, and others who are always such a help but have been thanked numerous times before, I say, "Thanks again!"

There are, however, a couple of people whom I can never thank enough, so I am going to repeat myself a little anyway.

We have a joke about this book in my household, that it is my "most celebrated work," because of how many times I declared it finished and dragged my wife Elizabeth out for a toast, only to realize—usually with help from my agent Stacia Decker, beta readers, or Elizabeth herself—that no, it was not finished after all.

I actually once turned to Elizabeth as I pressed send and said, "I think this is the best thing I've ever written," only to hear back from Stacia, "Well, it's not the best thing you've ever written."

Ouch.

But she was right. And it is much, much better now because of it. (Although, is it now the best thing I've ever written? I have no idea.)

So, thank you, Elizabeth, for *everything*, but specifically for your help with this book and for being my partner in celebrating everything worth celebrating—and some things that, in retrospect, maybe weren't quite yet.

And thank you to Stacia, my agent and my friend, for so many things, including telling me when such revelry might have been premature, and for helping me turn this book into something more worthy of it.

There are also still a few people who haven't already been repeatedly thanked, so thank you to Nicole Weinroth and Sanjana Seelam and their team at WME for all their great work, keen insights, and support, and to my pal Ben Kalina, an incredibly talented documentarian, for fascinating conversations about geoengineering and for inviting me to play a tiny little part in his feature documentary on the subject, *Plan C for Civilization*.

It takes a long time to write a book that has been declared finished as many times as this one. I've had to put it aside numerous times to write other books and work on other projects. The central ideas began percolating more than a decade ago, but I began writing the first draft in 2015, at "Broke Hack Mountain," an informal writing retreat over a long weekend in the Catskills that could have devolved into debauchery but ended up (mostly) about writing. Thanks to organizers Rob Hart and Todd Robinson for including me, to my friend and fellow attendee Erik Arneson for turning the drive up and back into a mini writers room, and to the other attendees for their companionship and support.

This book is about many things. It is about climate change and the failure so far to take timely action in the face of existential threat. It is about wealth disparity and greed and the corporate/billionaire takeover of democracy. And it is about how those two factors are not unrelated.

Ultimately, it is also about bold action, and, perhaps, the *need* for bold action. So thank you to those who are fighting the good fight to combat these ills and calling out those who are exacerbating them.

Jon McGoran

About the Author

Jon McGoran is the author of ten previous novels for adults and young adults, including the YA science fiction thrillers *Spliced*, *Splintered*, and *Spiked*, the science thrillers *Drift*, *Deadout*, and *Dust Up*, numerous short stories and novellas, and licensed work for *The Blacklist*, *The X-Files*, and *Zombies vs. Robots*. A freelance writer, writing teacher, and developmental editor and coach, he lives outside Philadelphia with his wife Elizabeth, a librarian.

🦋 @jonmcgoran.bsky.social
📷 @jonmcgoran
🌐 www.jonmcgoran.com

FIND US ONLINE!

www.rebellionpublishing.com

 /solarisbooks

 /solarisbks

 /solarisbooks

SIGN UP TO OUR NEWSLETTER!

rebellionpublishing.com/newsletter

YOUR REVIEWS MATTER!

Enjoy this book? Got something to say?

Leave a review on Amazon, GoodReads or with your
favourite bookseller and let the world know!

THE TEN PERCENT THIEF

"SMART. VIVID.
ENGAGING."
THE GUARDIAN

LAVANYA
LAKSHMINARAYAN

⟲ SOLARISBOOKS.COM

BANG BANG
BODHISATTVA

AUBREY WOOD

"High octane cyberpunk — entirely brilliant!"
Lavanya Lakshminarayan, author of *The Ten Percent Thief*

SOLARISBOOKS.COM